CW01082007

A RESISTANCE of WITCHES

www.penguin.co.uk

A RESISTANCE OF WITCHES

MORGAN RYAN

bantam

TRANSWORLD PUBLISHERS

Penguin Random House, One Embassy Gardens,
8 Viaduct Gardens, London SW11 7BW
www.penguin.co.uk

Transworld is part of the Penguin Random House group of companies
whose addresses can be found at global.penguinrandomhouse.com

First published in Great Britain in 2025 by Bantam
an imprint of Transworld Publishers

A CIP catalogue record for this book
is available from the British Library.

ISBNs
9780857506139 hb
9780857506146 tpb

Designed by Meighan Cavanaugh and Marianne Issa El-Khoury

Printed and bound in Great Britain by Clays Ltd, Elcograf S.p.A.

The authorized representative in the EEA is Penguin Random House Ireland,
Morrison Chambers, 32 Nassau Street, Dublin D02 YH68.

For Matt—

who held the door open long enough

for me to walk through

THE
HIGH
PRIESTESS

One

Years later, when Lydia recalled that day at Downing Street, she would often find herself thinking about *the door.*

It was an ordinary door in almost every respect, if unusually beautiful—glossy black, with a sheen so high she could nearly see her reflection. Gleaming brass mail slot. Iron knocker. The number ten, painted with the zero at a slightly whimsical tilt. And yet, to Lydia, there was something enchanted about it as well. In hindsight, she would think that perhaps it was because in all the stories, passing through a magical door was a rite of passage—the black-and-white partition where one's old life ends, and a newer, stranger one begins.

It was a chilly day in London, the coldest they'd had since March, and an icy mist fell across the paving stones like lace. Lydia would forever remember the way her jacket itched at the back of her neck, how her stomach twisted into knots as she stole a glance at the woman beside her: Isadora Goode, her mentor of just two weeks. She watched in fascination as the frozen raindrops twisted away from Isadora's form just before impact, as if each one had considered the cost of the collision and then thought better of it.

Isadora reached out and rapped the knocker, hard.

One. Two. Three.

The face Isadora wore that day was thirty-four. Thirty-four, she had informed her young charge, was exactly old enough to be taken seriously, but still young enough to be interesting. Lydia was sixteen and two weeks and wore her face exactly as it was. By graduation she would master the art of glamouring her features, making herself appear pink cheeked and button nosed, a sweet rose of a girl like so many of her classmates, instead of skinny, pale, and hawkish. She would wear her glamour daily, the way some women wear lipstick. Soon. Very soon. But not yet.

A butler opened the glossy black door and peered at the two women.

"Miss Isadora Goode and Miss Lydia Polk, to see the prime minister," Isadora said briskly.

The butler scowled. "I'm afraid the ladies do not have an appointment."

Lydia watched as Isadora pulled a mother-of-pearl case from the pocket of her peacock-blue overcoat and, from the case, a card. It was inky black and bore no name, just a single inscrutable symbol, embossed in gold.

"I believe you must be mistaken," she said.

The butler blinked at the card, then back up at the two women in the doorway. He appeared momentarily confused, then seemed to remember himself.

"Yes, of course. The prime minister has been expecting you." He looked surprised as the words fell out of his mouth, as if they'd been spoken by someone else.

When she thought back on that day, Lydia recalled that there had been a change in the air as she passed over that threshold—a prickling of the skin, a sensation of falling, like Alice down the rabbit hole. Funny, as the place didn't look like anything very special to her. She'd expected glittering crystal chandeliers and tall, light-filled rooms, something like the great hall of the academy, only grander. Instead, it was rather drab and smelled of cigars. The windows had been fitted with blast-proof shutters that blocked out the light, and there was an abandoned quality about the place. Above her head, the electric candlesticks in the light fixture gave off a faint hum.

"Miss Polk, do stop goggling." Isadora frowned as the butler disappeared with their coats.

Lydia quickly turned her attention to her shoes. They were cobalt-blue suede, and already beginning to bite into her ankles.

"Isadora Goode!" Lydia looked up again to see a rotund man approaching them at a swift pace. Isadora's face broke into a perfectly arranged expression of joy.

"Winston!" Isadora embraced the older man, kissing him once on each cheek.

"My God, how long has it been?"

"Too long." Isadora smiled warmly.

He looked extremely old to Lydia, older than he had appeared in the black-and-white newspaper photographs she'd seen of him before that day. He was jowly, with thinning hair, and wore excellent clothes that somehow managed to look rumpled on his round frame. Still, his eyes were a shocking shade of blue, and there was a sharpness there that Lydia liked.

The prime minister's brow furrowed as he took in Isadora's face. "Why, it must be more than thirty years. But you look . . . why, you're . . ."

"Winston, you embarrass me." Isadora laughed softly. Lydia didn't think Isadora looked embarrassed at all.

"Please allow me to introduce my apprentice, Miss Lydia Polk. Lydia Polk, Mr. Winston Churchill."

Lydia curtsied. "Prime Minister."

"Charmed, Miss Polk." Churchill leaned over and took Lydia's hand, bringing it to his lips. "Now. What brings two such lovely creatures to call on a tired old man?"

"I'm afraid this isn't a social visit," Isadora murmured, and Churchill nodded gravely. "May we speak privately?"

"Of course." Churchill gestured for Isadora to come with him. Lydia began to follow, until Isadora stopped her with a sharp look.

"Lydia, stay here."

With that, Isadora and the prime minister disappeared into another room, leaving Lydia behind.

She stood alone, feeling awkward and insignificant without Isadora by her side. The walls were bare, with only empty nails and ghostly outlines to suggest the art that had been hastily taken down and carted away in the wake of the Blitz. Rain pattered on the shutters, too loud in the cavernous silence. After a moment of fidgeting, Lydia sighed and seated herself in a hard, high-backed chair against the wall. She thought she heard the tinkle of Isadora's familiar laughter, but she couldn't make out any words.

Why bring me along only to have me wait outside? she wondered irritably.

Then an idea occurred to her. She would be in terrible trouble if she were caught, but projection *was* her strongest subject. She felt sure she could manage without being detected.

Lydia chose a spot on the wall upon which to fix her gaze and allowed her eyes to relax. Her breathing slowed. If the butler had walked by, he might have thought she was extremely deep in thought, or perhaps a little odd, but he did not appear. She waited until her body began to feel heavy, almost as if it were sinking into the floor, and then, very quickly, she stood.

When she turned around, she saw herself sitting in her chair with a far-off look on her face. She hated seeing herself like that, even more than she hated looking at herself in the mirror. In the mirror she could arrange her face in a way that would minimize its flaws, turn up the corners of her lips to make herself look softer, although not necessarily prettier. Now that she'd stepped outside of herself, her face had gone slack, mouth turned down, eyes fixed on nothing. She resisted the impulse to reach out and fuss with her hair.

Isadora's laughter rang out again. Leaving her body where it sat, Lydia followed the sound, walking unseen past room after empty room, noticing the deep marks left in the plush carpets where desks and chairs had once been, until she heard Isadora's voice again, coming from just behind a set of heavy wooden doors. She took a breath and stepped through, bracing herself against the uncomfortable way the matter tugged at her as she slipped through to the other side.

Unlike the rest of the house, this room was furnished, with shelves of books lining the walls, and an enormous mahogany table running the length of the room. Churchill and Isadora were seated at one end of the table, their bodies angled toward one another. Churchill had already begun working on a fat cigar, while Isadora pulled a black cigarette from a sleek, monogrammed case. Churchill offered Isadora a light, which she accepted with a coy smile and tilt of her head.

"How is Clementine?" Isadora asked.

"She's managing. You know Clemmie. Unflappable as always."

Isadora exhaled a plume of lavender smoke. "And you? How are you?"

"Well, the damned Huns haven't managed to kill me yet, although they do keep trying." Churchill coughed and gestured with his cigar toward the shuttered windows. "It's only dumb luck the Luftwaffe haven't blown Downing Street to kindling, although they did get close. Last month they blew up my kitchen. Very nearly killed my poor cook, as well."

It felt treasonous, spying on Isadora, to say nothing of the prime minister. Lydia found herself slowly backing into the gloomy corner by the door—although she was certain she could not be seen—as Isadora offered some polite, sympathetic comment regarding the prime minister's cook.

"*Isadora.*" The way Churchill said the name was so familiar, Lydia would have blushed had she been inside her body. "It is wonderful to see you after all these years, but neither of us has ever been very good at idle chitchat. Why are you here?"

Isadora held his gaze and drew on her cigarette, taking her time.

"The war," she said. "You're losing."

The prime minister pursed his lips, then nodded.

"I'd like to offer my help."

Churchill raised an eyebrow. "Like in Pretoria?"

Isadora smiled. "Pretoria was personal. This would be something more . . . official."

"Isadora, forgive me, but I'm old and grumpy and, as you yourself pointed out, quite busy at the moment losing a war. So, I'd appreciate it if you'd speak plainly."

Isadora lifted a snifter of brandy from the table and sipped it slowly before speaking. "I'm offering you the aid of the academy."

Something dropped inside Lydia's chest, as if she'd tripped coming down the stairs.

Churchill's cigar sat forgotten in his hand, ash gathering on the tip. "You mean . . ."

"The witches of Britain are at your service."

Churchill sat very still, regarding Isadora through a plume of smoke. Lydia held her breath.

"Why?" he said finally.

Isadora raised her eyebrows.

"The witches of Britain have never offered their assistance before.

Not during plague, or war. I daresay you've had good reason not to. Why, before this moment, I only had the vaguest notion that your academy even existed. If it weren't for the things I've seen with my own eyes, the things I've seen *you do* . . . well, I would think you were quite mad."

Isadora waited patiently.

"Britain has been no friend to witches." Churchill tapped the ash from his cigar. "Why help us now?"

"Because without us you will lose, and then we are all doomed."

Churchill regarded her in thoughtful silence before speaking. "You've seen it?"

"Not me, I have no talent for spying the future. But our Seers' visions have been clear: Hitler's army will never stop, not until they've overrun all of Europe."

"If the Americans—"

"It won't be enough. The Americans will only delay the inevitable."

Lydia was growing tired. She could feel her body pulling her back like a fish on a hook, but she couldn't leave. Not now. Isadora was the grand mistress of the Royal Academy of Witches—the most powerful witch in Britain, sworn to safeguard the secrecy of the academy with her life. Lydia couldn't conceive of what horrific vision of the future could have caused Isadora to break that oath, and that failure of imagination frightened her more than anything her sixteen-year-old mind could have conjured up.

Churchill appeared to have aged in the last few moments, as if cursed with the terrible knowledge of things to come. "If you join us, will we win?"

Just before Lydia was flung back into her exhausted body, she heard Isadora's reply.

"If we join you, you will have a chance."

. . .

LYDIA MAINTAINED A CAREFUL SILENCE as Isadora and Churchill said their goodbyes, then followed her mistress to the waiting car. She noticed it again, the subtle change in the weight of the air as she passed back through that shining black door—not a magical feeling, but not exactly mundane either. Lydia had the disconcerting sense that she was returning to the ordinary world, only to find that there was no such thing as ordinary anymore.

Once they had settled into the back of the grand mistress's chauffeured car, Isadora allowed her glamour to fade. She was sixty years old—handsome and well kept, but sixty just the same. Lydia had never seen her true face before that moment, and something about the sight of it, with all its lines and imperfections, drove home the gravity of what had just occurred.

"Well?" Isadora broke the silence. "What did you think?"

Lydia looked up sharply. "The prime minister seems very nice." She paused. "I was glad to be able to see Downing Street for myself."

Isadora held Lydia in her gaze.

"Miss Polk, if I didn't want you to observe my conversation with the prime minister, you would not have been able to observe it."

Lydia felt the blood drain from her face. "Grand Mistress—"

"Your skill as a projectionist is impressive. Most girls your age can't remain hidden for nearly so long. They always end up showing their faces at the most inopportune moments." Lydia stared, unsure how to respond. "The prime minister would never have been so candid in the presence of a stranger, particularly one so young. Still, I hoped observing might be instructive for you." She arched one slim brow. "Tell me what you thought."

Lydia swallowed. "Swearing the academy to the war effort, revealing our existence . . ."

"To the prime minister alone."

Lydia nodded. "It's never been done. We've always remained separate. Hidden." She had a sudden, jarring thought. "The high council approved this?"

Isadora studied her. "The high council was not asked for their approval."

Lydia was stunned. She knew almost nothing of the twelve witches of the high council, although she would soon learn. Some of them were her teachers, ordinary enough in the light of day, but together, under cover of darkness, they became something else entirely. She imagined them as otherworldly, like the Fates, or the Norns. Frightening, powerful women, not to be trifled with—and each with their own alliances and agendas. A decision of this magnitude would have required their unanimous approval. To proceed without it was unimaginable, even for one as formidable as the grand mistress.

Isadora chuckled softly at Lydia's expression. "Have I shocked you?"

Lydia quickly fixed her face. "No, Grand Mistress."

"The council still believes that secrecy and isolation will protect us from Hitler's war. They're wrong. I thought it best in this instance to ask forgiveness, rather than permission."

Lydia tried to imagine begging forgiveness from the witches of the high council and shuddered. "It must be of utmost importance that we help, then," she said carefully.

"Do *you* think we should help?" Isadora's face revealed nothing.

Lydia looked out the window at the violence wreaked on the streets of London by the Blitz. Piles of brick and stone lay scattered where buildings had stood just days before, and massive craters gaped like wounds where bombs had fallen in the night. Sandbags sat in heaps in front of shops and banks, and everywhere men and women glanced anxiously at the sky, searching the clouds for German bombers.

For the rest of her life, Lydia would remember the Blitz. She would vividly recall the bone-rattling explosions and the screams of air raid sirens, dozens of witches chanting long into the night to protect the academy from destruction. How it had felt, lying awake and terrified all through the night, whispering the secret words to herself, adding her small scrap of power to the current of magic coming from the elder witches in the hall below. And each morning, she would wake and find the academy still standing. She should have been relieved, but deep down, she was racked with a terrible guilt, knowing that thousands were dead while she lived. Innocent people, without any magic to protect themselves, lying beneath the rubble.

"Yes," she said. "We should help."

Isadora nodded.

"Do you know why you were chosen to be my apprentice?"

Lydia had often wondered. There were other, more obvious choices. Girls with more natural talent, more charm, better families.

"Mistress Jacqueline says it's because we must be very much alike."

Isadora snorted. "Oh, my dear girl, we are nothing alike." Lydia's face burned, but if Isadora noticed Lydia's dismay, she showed no sign of it. "I was always very skilled at charms. Manipulations, influencing the minds of men. I mastered glamours two years ahead of the rest of my class."

Lydia felt a fresh wave of humiliation wash over her.

"Politics and influence, that was my talent, right from the beginning. Bringing others along to my side of things. That was why I was selected. Because that was what would be required."

Lydia's mortification slowly gave way to curiosity. "Required for what?"

Isadora smiled but did not answer. She took another black cigarette from her case and lit it, filling the car with an aroma that reminded Lydia more of incense than tobacco smoke. "You have no talent for diplomacy. Your teachers tell me you are hardheaded, and honest to a fault. You bow to no one when you know you're right, not even when doing so would save you pain and trouble. And when you have decided upon a thing, you will see it through to the end, even if it costs you dearly."

Lydia could scarcely feel insulted. She'd been summed up too accurately to deny a word of it.

"Why, then?" she asked. "Why choose a graceless, obstinate, irritatingly principled girl to be your apprentice?"

Isadora looked at her a little sadly.

Lydia would remember that look. Years later, she would recall every detail, every line and curve, and she would wonder if perhaps Isadora had known every terrible thing that would come to pass, right from the beginning.

"Because that is what will be required."

THE
MOON

Two

LONDON, OCTOBER 1943

ydia sat at her mother's kitchen table and reminded herself, not for the first time, that she was a grown woman now.

She told herself that she was the right hand of the grand mistress, and had been for nearly three years. That she was a graduate of the academy, nineteen years old and in the full bloom of her power. That she had the respect of her peers and of her students and of the grand mistress herself.

And yet somehow, sitting in her mother's kitchen, Lydia may as well have been eleven years old.

"What do they have you teaching now at the academy?" her mother asked.

"Projection. Mistress Sybil has decided to dedicate herself fully to council matters, and they've asked me to take on her classes."

"Oh. That's nice." Both women sipped their tea.

Lydia glanced around the cluttered flat, taking in the hodgepodge of amber bottles and canning jars, each one holding something more disagreeable than the last. Fat bundles of herbs hung from the ceiling—calendula, feverfew, primrose—all giving off the same musty, herbal smell that had always given Lydia a headache, even when she was a child. On the cookstove, some murky concoction simmered away, stinking like hot, wet laundry.

Lydia's mother, Evelyn, had never attended the academy, nor was she interested in the political or magical goings-on inside its walls. She was an herbalist, with a talent for soothsaying she had inherited from her own mother, who had inherited it from her mother before her. She made a modest living selling tea and telling fortunes and had always assumed her daughter would do the same, until the day Lydia, then eleven, announced that she'd applied for entrance to the academy, unbeknownst to anyone at all, and had been accepted.

"Do they teach herbs at the academy?" Evelyn asked.

Lydia sipped her tea. "They teach Advanced Botanical Philosophy as an elective."

Evelyn frowned. "Would you say the class is more botany or . . . *philosophy?*"

"I wouldn't know. I didn't take it."

Evelyn pressed her lips together like she had something to say but was determined to keep it to herself. She often looked like that, as if she were biting her tongue, trying to hold in something that desperately wanted to come out. *Minding my mouth,* Lydia once heard her say. As if that made her meaning any less obvious.

They made a strange pair, sitting across from one another at the rickety kitchen table. Evelyn Polk was forty-four and barefaced, with no evident interest in fashion or appearances. Her hair, once dark, had now gone woolly gray and hung in a single plait down her back. Lydia, on the other hand, wore her glossy black hair swept up and rolled in the fashion popular among the other young women of the academy. Her dress was a deep indigo, and on her lapel, she wore a silver rose entwined with thorns—the emblem of the academy. The brooch had been a gift from Isadora upon Lydia's graduation.

She finished her tea. Evelyn reached for her cup, but Lydia placed her hand firmly over the top and kept it there. Evelyn made an exasperated sound.

"*Mother.*"

"What, I'm not allowed to read your tea leaves anymore?"

Lydia left her hand over her cup and said nothing.

"Why? Because it's not *high magic*? No classes on reading tea leaves at the academy I suppose?"

"No, it's just none of your business."

Evelyn looked bruised, and Lydia immediately regretted hurting her feelings. She'd always resented that nothing was a secret from her mother. Every private longing and event of Lydia's childhood had been spied by Evelyn in the bottom of her teacup, to the point that as an adult, Lydia had developed a strong preference for coffee.

Evelyn began to clear the dishes, leaving Lydia's teacup behind.

"Mother," she said again.

Evelyn puttered at the sink, keeping her back turned. "I understand you've been busy at the academy, Lydia. I understand you're a young woman now, and you want your privacy. And I know you're supposed to present yourself a certain way, being the right hand of the *grand mistress.*" The dishes clattered loudly in the bottom of the sink. "But, Lydia Polk, you are still my child, and when you come into my house, I would appreciate it if you wore the face I gave you."

Lydia was surprised by her mother's sudden intensity. She considered standing her ground, then thought better of it, and allowed the subtle glamour to fade.

"I thought it was quite tasteful."

"There's nothing wrong with the face you've got." Evelyn came closer to get a better look at her daughter. "You've got my mother's cheekbones, I think."

"As well as her nose," said Lydia.

"It's a lovely nose!" Evelyn gave it a tap with her index finger. "I'll never understand why you hate it so." She turned back to the dishes in the sink, taking more care now that the tension had dissipated. "I have an idea. Why don't you stay for supper? I have a little gin if you're tired of tea. We could stay up, get tipsy, and read each other's cards. What do you say?"

"I can't. I have academy business this evening." Lydia watched Evelyn's face fall again.

"So late?"

"I'm afraid so."

"What type of business?"

"Mother, you know I can't—"

"Is it to do with Project Diana?"

Lydia felt herself go very still.

Damn her, she thought. She never could keep anything secret from Evelyn.

"I don't know what you mean." But the lie was somehow worse than saying nothing at all. It fell flat on the floor between them, clumsy and obvious. Lydia retrieved her handbag from the kitchen chair and wrapped her mother in a stiff embrace. "I've got to go. I'll see you next week. All right?"

"Next week. Right." Evelyn looked deflated.

Lydia kissed her on the cheek. "Goodbye, Mother."

She made for the door and had scarcely turned her back before the glamour appeared once again, a softer version of her own face, with full pink cheeks and a perfect, upturned nose.

"Lydia—"

But the door closed, and Lydia was gone.

LYDIA FELT AN UNEASY GUILT settle on her as the taxi carried her away from her mother's flat in Hackney. Her relationship with Evelyn had always been fraught, even when she was a child. Lydia had felt like a changeling in her mother's house—a fastidious, particular child, raised among the cheerful chaos of Evelyn's life. Lately the chasm between them had become wider still as Lydia's role in the war effort had grown, and secrets had begun to pile up between them. Lydia reminded herself that she kept things from Evelyn for her own protection. Still, lying had never been easy for her, least of all when it came to her mother, who had a tiresome habit of knowing everything all the time, whether you wanted her to or not.

And now Evelyn knew about Project Diana.

No, Lydia thought, she knew the name, nothing more. There was no telling where Evelyn had come up with it—likely from some dream she'd had, or from dabbling in a bit of bibliomancy, as she had a habit of doing. But there was nothing at all to suggest that she knew anything more than that. Evelyn wasn't omniscient, after all. Just nosy.

As she paid the driver and stepped from the taxi, Lydia looked out across the mass of brown-and-gray-clad commuters and spotted a flash of red hair atop a brilliant, kelly-green overcoat—it was Kitty Fraser, navigating the current of bodies at a brisk pace, a stack of parcels under her arm. Lydia waved, and Kitty grinned and waved back, nearly dropping her cargo.

"What did you buy?" Lydia called as she quickly crossed the busy street.

"Oh, a few things I've been needing, and then a lot of things I didn't need at all." Kitty spun on her heels, momentarily distracted by a handsome fellow in uniform. "How's your mum?" she asked, hooking her free arm through Lydia's as they walked together toward the academy.

Lydia sighed. "Evelyn is . . . *Evelyn*."

Kitty was a Scottish girl of twenty and Lydia's best friend for the last eight years. She was a full head shorter than Lydia, and sportily built, with a mass of flaming red curls that refused to be tamed and a smile that could get her out of almost any kind of trouble. She and Lydia had met their very first day at the academy, and they'd been inseparable ever since.

"I don't know why you're so tough on your ma. I think she's brilliant. She's like the witches in the old stories."

"You didn't grow up with her. She's never understood why I joined the academy. She still wishes I would move back home and become a fortune teller, like her and Gran." Lydia turned to say something else but quickly recoiled, finding that suddenly it wasn't Kitty by her side at all, but Evelyn.

"Oh please, love, don't be so hard on your old mum. Why, I only want you to come back home and make charms and potions with me forever and ever. Maybe we'll find you a nice husband and you can make lots and lots of wee witch babies!"

"*Great Mother*, that is creepy, Kitty!" Lydia choked, but she couldn't keep herself from doubling over with laughter. "You know you shouldn't change out in the open like that."

Quick as a blink, Kitty was Kitty again. She rolled her eyes. "People only see what they expect to see." She grinned, and where just a moment ago Kitty had stood, now there was Isadora Goode, in her full glory. "Miss Polk, do stop goggling," Kitty intoned, in a perfect imitation of the grand mistress's voice.

Lydia fell into another fit of laughter as she pulled open the door of a little flower shop with a green awning that bore the name Shipton Flowers. The store was small and unassuming, and had existed in this exact location for longer than anyone could remember. The smell alone—freshly cut stems, dust, the sickly sweet perfume of moldering rose petals—filled Lydia with a sense of familiar nostalgia every time she crossed the threshold. Inside was cool and dark, with tidy rows of tin buckets bursting with fragrant white lilies, enormous yellow sunflowers, and pillowy garden roses in shades of pink, yellow, and violet. Spools of brightly colored ribbon hung along one wall, while jumbled rows of blue and green glass vases shone like jewels on the other.

The shopkeeper looked up as they entered.

"Miss Polk." She gave Kitty a wry look through her spectacles. *"Miss Fraser."*

Kitty dropped her glamour and offered a playful curtsy. "Judith. The hydrangeas look lovely today."

"Thank you, Miss Fraser."

They walked to the back of the shop, where the sweet smell of flowers gave way to the musty odor of trampled leaves and standing water, through the cluttered workroom, and past buckets, mops, and brooms to stand before a chipped green door. The door looked in every way like a storage closet, save for the faded white rose painted on its center, surrounded by thorns—forever locked, for all but a select few.

Lydia laid her left hand on the rose, and the door swung open easily.

Beyond the green door, the full grandeur of the academy sprawled before them. Gleaming white marble floors threaded with gold stretched far beyond the boundaries of the squat, brown brick building they had entered just moments ago. Elder witches dressed in modern, jewel-toned fashions went about their business, while academy students in their cobalt-blue uniforms traveled in gaggles of threes and fours, gossiping and laughing. Two matching spiral staircases flanked the great hall, intricately carved from gleaming ebony wood like the wings of an enormous black bird, soaring up toward a high domed ceiling, which glowed with stained glass depictions of beasts, flowers, stars and moons, and scenes of beautiful women caught performing heroic acts and feats of magic. It had taken Lydia most of her first year at the academy to determine that it was in fact the shabby exterior of the building that wore the glamour, rather than the opulent interior.

Kitty bid Lydia a quick goodbye and bounded up the spiral stairs with her parcels, nearly colliding with a trio of young teachers as she went. Lydia watched her go, then continued making her way across the great hall until she reached another door, this one jet black and bearing a raised carving of a raven. She laid her hand on the carving, and the door opened.

The grand mistress's personal study was a circular room lined with books stacked several stories high. Wrought iron catwalks lined the perimeter like scaffolding, and Persian carpets in shades of burgundy and gold covered the floors. A single, enormous arched window flooded the room with a hazy glow, giving the study a dreamy, enchanted feeling. In the center of the room, two lush green velvet sofas faced one another, and between them, an ornately carved table held a statue of the goddess Diana—the huntress—bow in hand, a small deer by her side.

Isadora was standing at the window, wreathed in a halo of rosy light. She turned when Lydia entered, and crossed the room to greet her with a kiss on each cheek. "How is your mother?" she asked.

"She's well, Grand Mistress, thank you for asking." Lydia always felt uncomfortable whenever Isadora asked after her mother. Isadora seemed to have no strong feelings about the woman either way, yet Evelyn Polk harbored a profound resentment toward Isadora Goode, which came out anytime her name was spoken.

They sat, and Lydia felt herself being swallowed up by the plush green sofa. Isadora lit a black cigarette, and a rich, floral perfume filled the air.

"I wanted to speak with you before this evening's ritual, to ensure you are adequately prepared," Isadora said. "Our success is essential to the war effort. I will require your complete focus."

Lydia hesitated. She'd been a part of Project Diana since she was still just a student, using her skill as a projectionist to track magical objects before they could fall into Nazi hands. Hitler and his army of sycophants had shown a troubling interest in the occult for some time now, twisting whatever lore best suited their needs, gathering up whatever arcane objects caught their fancy and stashing them in mines and castles all over Europe. Most were harmless, shiny bric-a-brac with no real magic. Every once in a while, however, Hitler's treasure hunters would stumble upon something with real power. This was where Project Diana would step in. *Hunting*, Isadora called it. Lydia's projection would venture out in search of the artifact, gathering clues from the object's surroundings to determine where it might be hidden. Then it was a simple matter of sending an academy Traveler to snatch up whatever tome or relic the Nazis were targeting and hiding it away, safe and sound within the walls of the academy. Lydia usually liked to know as much as she could about the artifacts she tracked, but everything about that evening's ritual had been kept a closely guarded secret. Strange, as Isadora usually kept her in the closest confidence.

"I'm afraid I haven't yet been briefed, Grand Mistress," Lydia said carefully.

Isadora exhaled a plume of smoke, considering her apprentice. "It is essential that you do not discuss what I'm about to tell you with anyone. Do you understand?"

Lydia nodded, but Isadora's tone made her uneasy.

"You'll be locating a grimoire. People have called it by different names over the centuries, but the one that seems to have stuck is *Grimorium Bellum*. Roughly translated, *The Book of War*. The book's exact contents have long been a closely guarded secret, one that I'm afraid has become lost over time, although theories persist—spells to rain down fire, shudder the earth. Spells to bring about famine, plague, madness. Some even say it can call forth an army of spectral assassins, capable of razing entire civilizations to the ground." She examined the glowing end of her cigarette, watching the smoke rise in a single, twisting column. "Rumor and speculation, all. The only thing we do know for certain is that wherever the book goes, death inevitably follows."

Isadora stopped and held Lydia in her gaze for what felt like a very long time. "I'm sure you can imagine what the Nazis would do if they were to find such a weapon." It began to rain, droplets splashing against the windowpane.

Yes. Lydia could imagine. She'd seen the newsreels and heard the madman speak. He'd already invaded Poland, Denmark, Norway, and France, only to name a few. It seemed he wouldn't rest until he held the whole of the world in his fist. His Luftwaffe had already killed thousands of innocent Britons in the Blitz, leaving all of England battered, scarred, and traumatized. And then there were the camps—Jews, Roma, homosexuals, men, women, children, all swept out of the cities and the ghettos, carted away like cattle as part of the Nazis' monstrous mass extermination effort. She'd heard it from the Seers at the academy, who wandered listless and weeping after the things they'd witnessed in their visions. Millicent Corey lived just down the hall from her in the teachers' residences. She'd woken screaming one night and didn't stop for hours, no matter how they'd tried to soothe her, until Lydia had finally gone to the infirmary to get her something to help her sleep.

"Yes, Grand Mistress. I can imagine." Lydia's voice did not betray the flush of horror she felt, remembering the things Millicent described.

Isadora leaned forward, and Lydia thought she saw Isadora's black cigarette tremble slightly between her fingertips.

"Then I don't need to tell you how important it is that the Nazis do not succeed in finding that book."

Very far away, Lydia heard what might have been thunder, or the roar of an airplane engine. Isadora's stoic demeanor returned, and when she spoke again, it was with her usual businesslike tone.

"Our intelligence tells us that the Nazis have been recruiting. Young women, specifically. Many of them orphaned, or otherwise vulnerable. All of them from magical families."

Lydia felt her blood turn icy. "You think they're forming a coven?"

Isadora exhaled, perfuming the air with smoke. "I do. However, many on the council disagree with my assessment." Isadora paused for a moment. "The truth is, the council has lost its appetite for the war effort. They never had much of one to begin with, but I managed to force their hand on the matter three years ago. Now, well . . ." She trailed off, her gaze fixed on something far away. "I think many of them find it easier to pretend the threat does not exist than to admit that it does and then have to face it."

Lydia watched Isadora's face, afraid to speak or even breathe. After a moment, Isadora looked at Lydia, her gaze steely once more. "Dark magic like what's found in the *Grimorium Bellum* is extremely taxing to perform. Magic like that requires a full coven, and an auspicious time. The winter solstice is in ten weeks. Whatever the Nazis are planning, I expect they will attempt it then. Our spies believe the Nazis are close to finding the book. I'm asking you to find it first."

Lydia felt something hardening inside her, crystallizing into a single-minded determination. "How will I track it?"

Isadora put out her first cigarette and lit a second.

"The book was in the antiquities collection at the Louvre, before the Nazis invaded Paris three years ago. Just before the invasion, the most valuable pieces were packed up and taken to Château de Chambord for safekeeping. Many of the pieces have been moved several times since then, scattered across the French countryside in the hopes of keeping them out of Nazi hands. We have reliable intelligence that the

Grimorium Bellum was sent to Château de Laurier in Dordogne. One of our agents was deployed last week to retrieve it, but she was intercepted and forced to flee. By the time she returned, the book had already been moved."

"Intercepted by whom? The Nazis?"

"The *curator*," Isadora said, with obvious irritation. "However, our agent had the book in her hands before she was stopped, and was able to get away with a small piece of one of the pages. The agent will be joining us in the ritual, and you will have her energy to work from, as well as the piece she tore from the book."

Lydia nodded. It would be enough. More than enough. "Who is the agent?"

Isadora stabbed out her cigarette, and sighed.

Three

I cannot believe you didn't tell me!" Lydia stood in the open doorway of Kitty's cluttered bedroom, inside their shared suite on the teachers' floor of the academy. Kitty lay sprawled on her stomach across her unmade bed, swinging her feet behind her. She looked up from her book with a mix of feigned innocence and gleeful pride.

"Och, I'm so sorry! I wanted to tell you everything, but Isadora was so serious about the whole thing, I was sure she'd hex my whole family if I told."

"I forgive you, you silly thing." Lydia tossed herself onto the bed next to Kitty and kicked off her shoes with a sigh. "But only if you tell me everything, I'm dying to know."

"It was boring, really. Mostly I was just hanging around some drafty castle, pretending to be a pudgy old Frenchman until I could get the book. It was honestly the dullest mission I'd ever done, right up until I got punched in the face."

"Punched?" Lydia was aghast. "Who punched you?"

Kitty grinned. "Henri Boudreaux."

"*Who?*"

"One of the curators. Well, the curator's assistant, I think. Big fella with a nasty right hook. Handsome, too, but we didn't exactly have time to get acquainted, what with me being a fat old Frenchman at the time."

The realization was dawning on Lydia now. "Last week you went home for a few days and came back with that horrible fat lip. You told me you'd been out walking and fell on your gob."

"I know, but I didn't! I was in Dordogne, getting punched in the face!" Kitty was obviously delighted with herself.

Lydia wrapped her arms around her friend. "Kitty, I love you, but you are absolutely mad."

"I'm just glad I can finally tell you! So there I am, being old, and dull, and *French*, and praying to the Mother that I can get my hands on this bloody book before the fella I'm impersonating comes back from the café where my Traveler, that absolute *prig*, Fiona McGann—"

"Fiona McGann is no prig! Why, she abducted that Nazi scientist last month with nothing but a nail file and a simple muddling charm. Really, Kitty, if I didn't know better, I would say you're jealous—"

"*Jealous?* Why would *I* be jealous?"

"Because Fiona's nearly as good a Glamourer as you are, and we both know you couldn't travel into the next room if I paid you."

Kitty gave her a filthy look. "I happen to be a *specialist*. Can I finish?" She waited until Lydia gave her an exasperated nod. "Right, so horrible, uptight Fiona McGann is batting her lashes and getting the real French-man pissed in some café. Meanwhile, I find where they're keeping the book, and pop open the crate, when who comes along but Henri bloody Boudreaux!"

"And he just punched you? With no provocation?"

"Well, no. First, I tried to talk my way out of it, and then I tried running, and then we tussled for a little bit, and *then* he punched me."

"*Oh, Kitty.*"

"But when he punched me, I dropped my glamour. So, there we are, he's just seen a fat old Frenchman turn into a beautiful fiery-haired maiden, and he's punched her right in the mouth! He was off me in a second, but he'd also grabbed the book. Anyway, I had to get out of there, so I took off running. I broke in and tried again the next night, but by then it was too late. The book was gone. So here we are."

"Kitty, he saw you?" Lydia sat up on the bed. "The curator saw you drop your glamour?"

"Relax. Nobody will believe him. I'd be surprised if he still believes it himself."

Lydia couldn't imagine how the man could ever forget such a thing, but held her tongue. "That piece of the book you stole. Where is it?"

"Isadora has it. Said it needed to be kept under lock and key until the full moon, when we could trace it, just for safekeeping."

Kitty was getting bored now that the topic had shifted away from her grand adventures in France. She sat up and began fussing with Lydia's hair, pulling out the pins and rearranging the curls.

"What do you need me there for, anyway? I thought you Projectionists could find anything, anywhere, just by putting your mind to it."

Lydia laughed; Kitty had never had the patience for advanced projection. "It doesn't work like that. If I've touched something, like, say, this hairpin, then I can project to it anytime I like. I could even project to *you*, if I had to. But I've never touched the *Grimorium Bellum*. I wouldn't know where to start."

"You've never touched the *Grimorium Bellum*, but I have. Is that right?" Kitty fluffed Lydia's hair, making it go wild.

"Exactly. The *Grimorium Bellum* left a mark on you the second you touched it, and that's what I'll use to track it. There are other ways too. Using a piece of the thing, like that scrap of paper you nicked. Or if I go to the place where an object once was, sometimes I can follow the trail from there."

"So you don't need me after all." Kitty sprawled across the bed with her feet in Lydia's lap. "*Thank the Mother*. I can't stand these fussy late-night rituals, and black really isn't my color."

Lydia gave Kitty's leg a swat. "I do, too, need you."

"Och, *why?*"

"For insurance, mostly. Using a piece of the thing can be difficult if it's too small or too damaged. If that happens, I'll have you to draw from instead."

Kitty groaned. "Fine. But I'm wearing your pearl earrings to the ceremony."

"Go ahead. They're fake."

Kitty gave Lydia's shoulder a playful nudge. "What will it be like, anyway? Will you go into a trance and speak in tongues?"

"*No.*"

"Will the whole council be there?" A hint of nerves crept into Kitty's voice, although she did her best to hide it.

"Yes. Like I said, if I've touched a thing, I can project to it anytime I want. But tonight, I'll have to send my projection who knows where, and with nothing to guide me but a scrap of paper and your silly self. That's tricky business, even for me. Something like that can only be done under a full moon at midnight, and it's near impossible without a full coven. The council will act as a sort of amplifier, to make the book easier for me to trace."

"Lord, will it be a lot of horrible chanting?"

"Only for the first few minutes. After that it's mostly silent."

"So I shouldn't try to make you laugh," Kitty said with a wicked grin.

"Definitely not."

Kitty tossed herself across Lydia's lap. "But I'm so good at it!" Quick as a blink she transformed her face into that of Mistress Helena, who had taught them both healing arts when they were still just girls. Helena had always been a ridiculous figure to Kitty and Lydia, simultaneously self-important and exceedingly sensitive. Kitty loved to imitate her whenever Lydia was taking herself far too seriously. Lydia squawked with laughter, pushing Kitty away, and Kitty tumbled to the floor shrieking, wearing her own face once again.

"I have to get ready!" Lydia wiped tears of laughter from her eyes.

"Will she be there?" Kitty lay sprawled across the floor. "Please say yes!"

"I'm getting dressed." Lydia walked across the hall to her own tidy room, leaving Kitty where she lay.

"Should I go like *this?*" Lydia turned back, and Kitty was Helena once again, grinning up from the floor in Kitty's bright green dress.

"Get dressed, Kitty!" Lydia shouted, still laughing, and slammed the door.

KITTY ANNOUNCED she was going to dinner, and was still gone when Lydia emerged from her room, freshly made up and dressed in a slim black velvet gown with a matching clutch. She thought about joining Kitty in the dining room, but then thought better of it. Lydia rarely ate before a tracking spell, as she was almost always too anxious, and the spellwork often left her feeling queasy. Kitty, on the other hand, could seemingly eat any time of the night or day, and often did, claiming that all her constant shape-shifting required extra fuel.

When Lydia arrived in the ceremonial chamber, the high council was already there, gathered like black crows in groups of twos and threes in the dimly lit chamber. The sight of them put a sudden twist of uneasiness in Lydia's stomach. Mistress Jacqueline was grumbling in a low whisper to Mistresses Helena and Pearl, all three looking annoyed to be there at such a late hour.

"*. . . don't even see why it's necessary. It's no business of ours if . . .*"

"*. . . what has Britain ever done for us? Why should we continue to risk witch lives for . . .*"

"*. . . power hungry, that's what it is. She never should have been allowed to involve the academy in . . .*"

Just then, Mistress Jacqueline caught Lydia's eye and fell suddenly silent. She offered a syrupy smile and quickly turned away.

Moonlight cascaded down from the round skylight above the altar, the soft silver glow mingling with golden pinpoints of scattered candlelight. Isadora stood alone in the center of the room, cutting a severe figure in her black satin evening gown. She nodded to Lydia when she arrived, but did not move to greet her.

Lydia scanned the room, passing over the gaggles of whispering gossips and the false, sickly sweet smiles, until she found a friendly face at last—Mistress Sybil, who appeared to be caught in a rather one-sided conversation with Mistress Alba. Lydia watched with amusement as Sybil made her apologies and crossed the room to greet her with a kiss on the cheek.

Sybil Winter and Isadora Goode had come up through the academy together as girls, and while Isadora had few close friends, Lydia had always observed a respectful camaraderie between the two women. Sybil had taught projection at the academy until her recent retirement and had always shown a special interest in Lydia, whose talent for the subject had been evident from her very first lesson. Lydia, meanwhile, had always taken comfort in Sybil's motherly attention and companionship. Being Isadora's apprentice was rewarding in its own way, of course, but Isadora could be prickly and demanding. Sybil, on the other hand, had always coaxed Lydia's talents to the fore with warmth and good humor. Sybil wore no glamour today, or any other day, and although her face was creased, her blue eyes still held a spark of youth, and her hair had stayed mostly golden, threaded with silver.

"Where is Miss Fraser?" Sybil whispered.

"She's coming."

Sybil clucked softly. "She really cannot be late. Not for this."

There it was again, the same murmur of apprehension she'd heard from Isadora earlier that same day. Lydia found herself overcome by a sudden wave of uneasiness, as if it were contagious.

"If she's late, I can manage without her. But she'll be here."

"I'm sure you can." Sybil gave Lydia's hand a squeeze. "Still, if she doesn't arrive in time, I'm certain Isadora will make her sorry." She cast the grand mistress a wary glance. "Let's both hope she gets here soon."

Lydia looked at Isadora, who was watching her, waiting. Her heart fluttered slightly. It was nearly time. She stepped forward, but Sybil pulled her back.

"Wait." She reached out and smoothed one of Lydia's dark curls with her fingertips. "There. Perfect."

KITTY DID ARRIVE IN TIME, but barely. The council had already begun to arrange themselves in a circle, shifting nervously where they stood. Lydia ran over and embraced her as she walked through the door.

"Isadora looks like she's been sucking lemons," she whispered. "What on earth took you so long?"

"I'm sorry." Kitty's gaze barely landed on Lydia's, skimming instead across the room full of black-clad council members. Lydia thought her friend must have been quite nervous after all. Kitty was such a funny thing, perfectly happy to waltz into a German army base or a top secret cabal with nothing but a borrowed face and a lot of gusto, but the pomp and circumstance of traditional spellwork had always made her itchy.

Lydia draped her arm through Kitty's as she guided her toward the black stone altar. "Don't worry, you don't need to do anything special.

I'll do all the work. All right?" It felt strangely calming, playing at being so cool and confident. For a second it almost felt true.

Kitty smiled weakly. "All right."

Isadora approached, accompanied by the soft rustling of satin.

"Miss Fraser," Isadora said.

"Grand Mistress."

There was a moment of silence as Isadora regarded her, eyebrows raised in silent recrimination for her tardiness. Then Isadora turned to address the council.

"Hail, sisters," Isadora began.

"Hail, Grand Mistress," the council called back in unison.

Isadora allowed the silence to settle back over the room before she continued. Candlelight flickered across the gathered faces.

"We gather tonight in support of our sister Lydia as she seeks the *Grimorium Bellum*. May the full moon light her way on her journey. May our voices guide her to her prize. May the Great Mother bless our cause. Blessed be."

"Blessed be," said the council.

Lydia stole a glance at Kitty, hoping to see a glimmer of that familiar mischief, but Kitty was staring intently at the silver bowl on the altar before them.

Isadora returned to the altar and produced a small silver box from the pocket of her gown. The box flipped open, revealing a brittle scrap of stained brown vellum no larger than Lydia's fingertip. Ever so carefully, Isadora placed the piece of paper into the bottom of the silver bowl. Lydia might have imagined it, but she thought for a moment the candles glowed brighter in the bowl's reflection. Isadora took Lydia's hand, and she in turn reached for Kitty.

Isadora looked around the room, finally resting her gaze on Lydia. "Let us begin."

The grand mistress was the first to recite the incantation, her voice filling the chamber like a bell. After a moment the others joined, and now a dozen voices were rising together to call out the words of power that would propel Lydia toward the *Grimorium Bellum*.

In past ceremonies the council's chanting had honed Lydia's senses, easily sending her consciousness away from her on the tide of their voices, but tonight she felt stymied. The piece of the *Grimorium Bellum* Kitty had retrieved was barely more than dust, and its connection to the book was weak and threadbare. Lydia could just barely feel the low pulse of magic emanating from the bowl on the altar, reaching out for its missing piece like a phantom limb, but the signal was dull, like trying to listen to a radio through a heavy wooden door. Given enough time, perhaps she could have made sense of it, but the council was watching with impatience. She could feel their eyes like insects crawling on her skin, hungry and expectant.

No matter, she thought. *There are other ways.*

She turned her attention away from the scrap of paper on the altar and reached for Kitty with her mind. Tracking through another person had a way of opening up a sort of channel, like a long hallway between their minds, where memories could flow, if only for a second. She'd never tracked through Kitty before, but she thought she knew what she might find inside her best friend's mind—bracing hikes in green rolling hills; half a dozen squawking, red-haired siblings; the taste of biscuits and black tea on her tongue, so sweet it made her teeth ache. Scenes from an idyllic Highland childhood.

But as Lydia reached for her friend with her mind, she found no flash of Highland green, no comforting fire. Instead, a burst of memories blazed through her, so bright and sharp it was almost blinding— *Hunger like a wound. A woman's voice, ranting and raving. Freezing water all around her, lungs burning, terror so profound it blotted out everything else.* Kitty's hand felt cold in hers. *Odd,* Lydia thought. Kitty's hands were always warm.

She opened her eyes.

Kitty was watching her, and now, finally, there was the smile Lydia had been waiting for all evening, but it was wrong somehow. Joyless. Kitty released her hand, and from inside her dress she pulled a bone-handled dagger. Lydia opened her mouth to speak, but before she could form the words, Kitty lashed out, fast and sure, and slashed Isadora's throat.

Four

I sadora's eyes went wide as she slid to the floor, blood spilling from her neck in a torrent. As she did, Kitty's visage seemed to fall away like water, replaced with the face of someone Lydia had never seen before—an icy blond with blue eyes and a smile like a wolf. Lydia screamed, and her scream seemed to awaken the council, who until now had been watching in silent shock. The chamber erupted in pandemonium, several council members running for the door, the rest screaming, frozen in fear.

The blond woman knelt by Isadora's side and lifted her dagger, meaning to finish her work, but Lydia had returned to her senses. She screamed again, a jagged, rage-filled sound, and as she did, she left her body, her projection driving into the woman like a cannon, knocking her to the ground.

The blond woman hit her head on the stone floor with a crack, but she didn't stay down for long. She scrambled to her feet, searching for her dagger as Lydia returned to her body. Lydia had the strength for only one projection attack, but she pursued the woman regardless, forgetting fear or sense, thinking only one thing. *Stop her.*

She turned to the clutch of elder witches, cowering in the far corner of the ceremonial chamber, and felt a flush of disgust. *They've never had to fight*, Lydia realized with sudden, sickening clarity. Battle magic was a standard part of the school's curriculum, but with the academy's policy of total isolation, the exercise had always been purely theoretical. Only the academy's most recent graduates had been prepared for real war.

"Witches," she shouted, "defend your mistress!"

Sybil was the first to regain her head. She stepped forward and repeated Lydia's earlier attack, sending her projection out from her body with vicious speed, but the blond witch uttered a word and sidestepped, and Sybil's attack flashed by harmlessly and crashed into the far wall, shattering the black stone beneath the force of her impact. Mistress Alice followed, calling out a spell to muddle the senses, but her voice lacked the necessary conviction, and the words fell flat. The blond witch laughed, and Lydia felt a hard, sharp-edged rage, like a stone beneath her breastbone.

"*Astyffn ban*," she spat.

The blond witch froze where she stood for just a moment, caught in the web of Lydia's words, before a terrible tremor ran through her and she was free of the spell once again.

Spells be damned, Lydia thought, and ran at the woman, intending to throw her to the ground with her own two hands, but the woman drew herself up to her full height and hissed a word in a tongue Lydia had never heard before. The four elder witches closest to her slumped to the floor. A second later Lydia felt herself sinking helplessly to the ground, her arms and legs useless. She tried in vain to speak a word of power that would counter the spell, but found her tongue too heavy to use. The blond witch grinned, and something about that grin made Lydia remember to be afraid. It made her think of creatures that hunt their prey in the night. It made her think of death.

The witch walked past Lydia toward the altar, stepping over Isadora's prone body as she went. Lydia watched, powerless, but noted with a rush of hope that Isadora's chest still rose and fell. The woman reached into the silver bowl and carefully placed the scrap of paper into a tiny case, which she then tucked inside her dress. Lydia tried to speak, but only a low moan came out. The witch looked at her with amusement and bent to retrieve her dagger before crouching by Lydia's side. She examined her blade, turning it over in her hands, taking her time. Lydia's gaze fell on the dagger, the blade still slick with Isadora's blood. The bone handle bore a symbol she recognized from her studies—a rune. Othala, it was called. It meant "homeland."

The witch took Lydia by the chin, tilting her head to expose the soft flesh of her throat. Lydia's breath quickened, bracing for what was to come next. More than anything she wanted to close her eyes, but she forced herself not to look away. She could feel her magic pulsing just under her skin, rushing from sheer terror, but with no means of release. Through the pounding of blood in her ears, she thought she heard a voice calling her name—Sybil's voice.

"Get away from her!" Sybil shouted.

The blond witch looked up and frowned.

Sybil did not ask a second time. "*Wyrian-lif, wyrian-ban!*" she called. "*Wyrian-lif, wyrian-ban! Wyrian-lif, wyrian-ban! Wyrian-lif, wyrian-ban!*"

Lydia felt Sybil's protection spell weaving itself into being all around her, prickling her skin. The blond witch seemed to feel it, too, and dragged her blade across the invisible barrier, rippling the air. Outside the chamber door, a commotion was building; Lydia could hear cries in the hallway and the drumming of running feet. The witch seemed to consider her options. She turned her back on Sybil and leaned closer to Lydia's face. Strands of silver hair fell into Sybil's warding and lifted into the air as if they were carried by electric currents. The witch smiled again.

"Heil Hitler," she said. And disappeared.

All at once, Lydia could move again. She scrambled across the floor toward where Isadora lay. Blood poured from the gaping wound in her neck, soaking the front of her dress and pooling on the floor around them. Isadora was conscious, but her face was a sickening shade of white, her eyes darting around the room like a frightened animal. The ceremonial chamber smelled strongly of ozone, the unmistakable calling card left behind by every Traveler.

"Isadora, look at me." Lydia placed her hands to the wound on Isadora's throat and spoke the words of power she had learned so long ago in Mistress Helena's classroom. "*Siowan-ban, hela-ban, siowan-lif, hela-lif!*"

Lydia had never had any special talent for healing, but she was determined to try just the same. Under her shaking fingertips, Isadora's throat knit itself together but came apart like tissue paper seconds later, again and again, as Lydia frantically chanted.

"Helena, I need you!" In the far corner of the chamber, Helena wept and fretted the edges of her robe between her fingers.

"Helena, please!"

The wound was too deep, and as fast as the skin would heal itself, it would open again a moment later. Lydia began to cry, but still, she spoke the words, even as Isadora's eyes went still, even as Lydia's own sobbing made the syllables unintelligible and the wound stopped closing under her hands. She said the words, gasping for air, until someone came and placed a hand on her shoulder.

"Don't touch me!" Lydia hissed, and the hand retreated. She sat there, cradling Isadora in her arms as her tears fell and mixed with the blood that covered them both. Finally, she looked up. Half a dozen council members remained, watching Lydia with frozen masks of horror. The ones who had run away were slowly returning, gathering in the doorway and staring with wide eyes and open mouths. All looked at Lydia, and she stared back, barely comprehending, holding Isadora's body in her arms.

"Where did she go?" someone asked.

Mistress Jacqueline sniffed, taking in the rainstorm smell that still clung to the air. "If she's a Traveler, she could be anywhere."

"Not just a Traveler, but a Glamourer as well. Why, she made herself look just like Kitty Fraser."

The words seemed to slither into Lydia's mind, churning something to the surface.

"Kitty." She looked up at Sybil, whose eyes widened with sudden, terrible comprehension. "Where is Kitty?"

Lydia sprinted from the chamber. She ran through the great hall, with its kaleidoscopic dome, feeling the glassy eyes of ancient witches and magical beasts leering down at her. Up the spiraling staircase she ran, through corridors and hallways, until, panting, she reached her own suite. The door was ajar.

"Kitty!" She crashed into the room. Then she saw her.

Kitty lay in the entrance to her own bedroom, on her back, in the same green dress she had been wearing earlier that day. Her arms and legs were splayed at an awkward angle, her eyes fixed on nothing. A dark stain spread from the center of her chest.

Lydia was on the floor. She couldn't understand what she was seeing—the impossible amount of blood, the cold curl of Kitty's lifeless fingers. She heard screaming, and it took several long, horrible moments before she realized that it was coming from her. Someone came in behind her and tried to gently guide Lydia from the room, but she wouldn't be moved. "Kitty," she wept. "Kitty, Kitty, oh no, oh, Kitty, Kitty, Kitty . . ."

She lay down on the floor next to her friend, and held her, and howled.

. . .

LYDIA SAT IN the ceremonial chamber, staring at the blood under her nails as the council spoke in hushed tones around her. Someone had managed to get her to her feet and wipe most of the blood from her hands, but streaks of it remained on her neck and chest, and her dress was stiff with it. The rainstorm smell had dissipated, replaced by the tang of copper.

"Arrangements must be made," Lydia heard someone say. ". . . announce it to the academy. It must be handled delicately."

Lydia's gaze fell on the place where Isadora had died. The body had been taken away, but the blood remained.

". . . how much to say about what happened?" someone whispered.

"Why say anything at all?"

Murmurs of agreement filled the room.

Lydia wanted a hot bath and a long, hard cry. She couldn't understand why she had been brought back to the ceremonial chamber. Her own room was no longer an option, of course, but there were other places she could go. Even her mother's flat would do, under the circumstances.

One fat, silent tear fell from Lydia's face onto her shaking hands as all around her, council members spoke among themselves about what to do next—protection circles, funeral rites, the proper way to cleanse the ceremonial chamber after the violence of the past few hours.

"We need to find the book," Lydia said. The chatter in the room carried on uninterrupted.

"What?" Sybil paused in her conversation with Mistress Josephine. "What did you say, darling?"

"The *Grimorium Bellum*. We must find it before the Nazis do."

"One thing at a time, my dear," said Mistress Josephine. "I'm sure the Nazis are nowhere close to finding the *Grimorium Bellum*."

Lydia felt her agitation rising. "Of course they are. She took the piece of the book from the altar. At the next full moon, they can use it to track—"

"Are you sure it wasn't lost in the commotion?"

"I'm certain. I saw her—"

"Don't be ridiculous," Mistress Jacqueline chimed in. "Even if the Nazis did find the *Grimorium Bellum,* it would require a full coven of witches to wield it. The Nazis have no such coven."

"How can you possibly say that?" Lydia's voice broke, and she despised herself for it. Around her, conversation began to fall silent. "If they have one witch, why is it so impossible to believe they have twelve? Why would they go to the trouble otherwise?"

"It's been a difficult night. Let's discuss this in the morning," Sybil said reasonably.

"Agreed," said Mistress Jacqueline.

"There is one other piece of pressing business before we retire." Mistress Alba stood, polishing her spectacles. The room fell silent. "That is, the selection of the new grand mistress."

Lydia looked up sharply. "What? Tonight?"

"Of course. The academy cannot be without a grand mistress. A successor must be chosen."

Lydia could not hide her contempt. Isadora had bled to death hardly an hour before, and now here they were, discussing her replacement. She stood. "I'll leave you to it, then."

Sybil caught her by the arm. "Oh no, Lydia, you must stay as well. After all, as Isadora's apprentice, you are the obvious choice to succeed her." Sybil turned and addressed the room. "I nominate Lydia Polk for grand mistress of the Royal Academy of Witches."

Lydia stared at Sybil in disbelief. *She can't possibly be serious,* she thought.

Mistress Phillipa stood. "Seconded."

"With all due respect," Mistress Jacqueline said, "I believe the academy requires a seasoned leader to steer her through these trying times. Miss Polk is young and untested."

Sybil smiled mildly. "Isadora was nearly the same age when she became grand mistress."

"And look where that got us," grumbled a voice in the back of the room.

"What was that?" The words struck Lydia like a hammer, shaking her from her stupor. "Speak. Answer for yourself."

Mistress Vivian stood and met Lydia's gaze. Vivian was the eldest witch on the council, an imposing, broad-shouldered woman, even in her old age. Lydia had always known her to be dour and humorless, and no friend of Isadora's. Still, she had never dreamed that Vivian could be so tactless, so unfeeling as to speak ill of Isadora while her blood still cooled on the chamber floor.

"I said what I meant. It was Isadora who insisted that the academy join the war effort. Isadora who broke a tradition of centuries of secrecy by revealing us to that pompous windbag, Churchill. Isadora wanted to join the war, and war was what she got. And for what? Britain is no closer to victory, the academy has been infiltrated, and Isadora is dead. I'm only glad it was her and not one of us."

Lydia's rage overwhelmed all sense or restraint. "Evil, poisonous, vicious-minded *hag*," she seethed. "Your grand mistress lies dead, and you dare to speak ill of her? I should bind your tongue before you speak her name again."

Now it was Helena who spoke. "Lydia, darling, all Vivian meant was that—"

"Not a word from you, you useless cow." Helena's mouth fell open in a silent gasp. "Isadora lay bleeding to death in front of you, and you did nothing. I begged you to help her, and you let her die."

The council was stunned to silence. Lydia stood before them, fury making her pulse race, blood rushing in her ears. She had never spoken so to anyone, let alone a witch of the high council. Any one of them could have silenced her forever with a word, but Lydia was beyond caring.

"Have any of you even stopped to wonder how this witch got *inside?* How she could have possibly bypassed the warding?" The council only looked at her, dumbstruck and silent. "The academy is *vulnerable!*" Lydia stared, disbelieving, at their blank faces. "Great Mother! The most feared witches in all of Britain. An enemy witch desecrates your home and murders your mistress before your very eyes, and none of you lifts a finger. Weeping, cowardly hens, the lot of you. You don't deserve your gifts. I am ashamed to be among you."

Lydia waited to be turned to stone. Moments passed, and the silence seemed to extend forever, heavy and bottomless. Slowly, she realized that she would not be struck down. Not tonight, at least. *Perhaps they've forgotten how,* she thought bitterly. She turned her back on the council, unwilling to look at their astonished faces for one second longer, and slowly walked toward the chamber door, her footsteps echoing in the silence.

Sybil stepped forward. "Lydia—"

Lydia did not look back as the door swung closed behind her.

SHE BURST ONTO THE STREET, gulping night air as if she had been held underwater. London stretched out before her, streetlights extinguished, draped in darkness.

Soldiers stood on street corners, smoking and talking to one another. *Americans,* she thought dully. They watched her as she passed, and Lydia realized that she was still covered in blood. She considered a glamour but couldn't muster the energy. One American approached her, calling her *sweetheart,* but recoiled when she looked into his eyes. After that, no one came near.

Slowly, she returned to herself. She was cold and disoriented, and her feet were beginning to blister. The air was damp, making the hairs rise on her flesh.

She looked up. Row after row of darkened windows looked down on her like glassy eyes, black curtains drawn tight. Across the way stood a park, its trees stripped half-bare. She was in Grosvenor Square, where Isadora had her secret flat. Lydia had been a regular visitor, had even been given her own key. She rummaged blindly through her handbag until her fingers closed around the familiar shape.

The silence inside the flat was thick as fog, as if the place already knew it was home to a dead woman. Lydia left her shoes by the front door and made her way on tender feet through the darkened foyer. Isadora had loved this flat, had carefully curated every detail. The walls were papered in deep, rich florals in shades of purple and gold, and paintings hung on every wall—portraits, landscapes, vibrant modern works, pieces Isadora had lovingly selected and brought back with her from Berlin and Paris before the war. The drapes were gold and violet brocade, and were pulled back to reveal the full moon, impossibly huge and shining like a coin in the night sky.

Lydia made her way to the bathroom in the dark, leaving the sconces unlit as she crouched on the marble tile and filled the copper standing tub all the way to the top, as hot as it would go. She left her bloody dress on the floor and sat in the water, letting it scald her. She sat until the water turned cold and a sliver of pewter-colored sunlight crept over the horizon. Then she wrapped herself in a towel and crawled into the guest room bed.

She stayed there for hours, dreaming fitfully, until she was startled awake, hungry, wet haired, and heart racing, to a harsh afternoon light coming through the window, and the sound of someone at the front door.

Five

I didn't think anyone knew about this place."

Sybil set down a pot of tea for herself, and a cup of coffee for Lydia, already prepared with milk and two sugars. "Oh, darling. You'll find that each of us has our own little hideaways. Why, I have a lovely cottage in Surrey with a garden full of roses, and a gardener who looks like Errol Flynn." Sybil smiled a sly, private smile. "This place wasn't much of a secret."

Lydia took a sip of her coffee. A hollow, unsteady feeling still clung to her like wet clothes, and she found herself unable to stomach small talk, even with Sybil.

"I assume you've come to tell me I've been dismissed from the academy." She set down her cup to keep it from shaking in her hand.

"Don't be ridiculous. If that mouth of yours was enough to get you tossed out, you wouldn't have made it past your first year. Besides . . ." Sybil grew more somber. "Your delivery may have been a bit dramatic, but . . . I do believe your message was spot on." Lydia watched as Sybil's eyes filled with tears. "We all let her down, didn't we?"

Lydia had to take a breath to keep her own composure. "We did the best we could." It was a lie, of course. A kindness. Sybil shook her head.

"*You* did the best you could. You were the only one of us worth her training last night. You were courageous and clearheaded. A credit to the academy."

Lydia felt the shame rise in her throat, hot and wet and hateful. "I failed her." A sob burst through her chest, and she hung her head, unable to look Sybil in the eye. Sybil offered a lace-edged handkerchief, which Lydia took without looking up.

"No, my darling. You made her proud. You made *me* proud. Why do you think I nominated you for grand mistress?"

"Honestly, Sybil, I can't imagine. How could you possibly think I would be the right choice?" Lydia looked up, dabbing away her tears.

"I don't know why you're so surprised. You must have known you would be the obvious candidate to succeed Isadora when she passed."

Lydia had assumed so, although they had never discussed it directly. She'd even thought she wanted it. Now the prospect only filled her with dread. "I thought there would be more time. I can't be grand mistress, not now. Not yet."

Sybil smiled kindly. "Who else would you have lead us, hmm? Vivian? Helena?"

At this Lydia let out a snort.

"'Cowardly hens,' that's what you called us, and right you were. None of us are fit to lead. None but you."

"You could do it."

Sybil shook her head. "I'm as bad as the rest. And I will live with that shame for the rest of my life. The best I can do now is try to make things right."

Lydia looked at Sybil. "How?"

"I convinced the council to postpone the selection ceremony. As of this moment, the academy is still without a grand mistress. Vivian will serve as the interim head of the high council until a successor is chosen."

Lydia let out a disgusted huff. "That hateful—"

Sybil made a quick tsking sound, silencing Lydia before she could say any more. She reached out and squeezed Lydia's hand. "The selection ceremony for the new grand mistress will take place on Samhain. That gives you two weeks to form alliances on the council—"

"Sybil—"

"Isadora believed in you. She knew her time was running out, and she knew you would be the one to lead when she was gone."

Lydia thought about that day three years ago. Isadora's face had looked so tired and so regal as they'd pulled away from 10 Downing Street. She remembered what Isadora had said, about *what would be required*. Had Isadora known, even then, that she would never see the end of the war?

"I'm not ready," Lydia whispered.

"No one is ever ready. But last night you proved yourself as ready as any witch in that room. More, in fact. I'll support you. We all will."

"No. I'm *not ready*. Isadora's been dead less than a day, and Kitty—" The sound of Kitty's name seized in Lydia's throat in a sudden, painful spasm. Sybil's hand tightened around hers. *Oh, Kitty, Kitty, Kitty.* "Has anyone told her parents?"

"I did. First thing this morning." Sybil looked as if she were still haunted by the memory of the conversation. Lydia wondered whether Kitty's mother had screamed when she heard her daughter was dead, if her father had wept. She felt as if she could hear the sound of it inside her skull. Awful, throat-closing grief washed over her like waves, pushing her under so she couldn't breathe.

"Does it ever stop?" Lydia gasped.

"No." Sibyl looked down at her hands. "It comes and goes. Eventually it will begin to feel less unbearable. Maybe it will come over you only once a day, and then once a week. One day you'll even think you're free of it, but then you'll see some . . ." She sighed, gesturing toward nothing in particular. "Some face that looks like hers, or you'll smell her perfume, and then . . ." Sybil's eyes shimmered slightly. "I couldn't bear the smell of rosemary for a year after my grandmother died. One moment I'd be fine, and then . . ." She took a shaking breath and smiled weakly.

"I feel like I'm going mad." Lydia felt the loss like a hot poker in her throat.

"You're grieving," Sybil said gently. "Give yourself time." She paused for a moment, thinking. "I've decided I'm coming out of retirement. I'm taking over your classes."

"What?"

"Only for a little while. You are an excellent teacher, Lydia. As good as me. Better. But you need time to heal. And to think about what comes next for you."

"No, I can do it." Lydia pressed her eyes with the palms of her hands. "I can carry on teaching, really. I just—"

"It's already decided. I taught those girls for forty years. I think I can manage a little while longer."

Lydia wanted to argue, but there was no point. Sybil had made up her mind.

"Thank you, Sybil."

"You can thank me by using this time to rest. And, Lydia—"

But Lydia already knew. *Grand mistress.* Terror surged up inside her at the thought of it. "Please don't ask me to do this, Sybil. *Please.*"

"I'm sorry. But I have to."

The terror ebbed away, leaving only a terrible sadness. "I know." She looked down at Sybil's lace handkerchief, crumpled into a knot in her fist. "Could you please not ask me today?"

There was a moment's hesitation. Sybil rose from her seat and came around to kneel next to her. She held her tightly, like a child.

"All right," she said. "Not today."

LATER, AFTER SYBIL LEFT, and the light streaming through the windows had turned a deep, sunken purple, Lydia went and stood in front of the red door at the end of the hall. This was the place where Isadora had once conducted her own private spellwork, the only room where even Lydia had never set foot. Any protective charms Isadora had placed on this room had been broken the moment she died, but Lydia still felt like she was violating something sacred as she stepped over the threshold. The walls and floor were painted a flat black, and a simple cherry-wood altar sat in the middle of a white chalk circle on the floor. Lydia went to the glass-fronted cabinet standing against the opposite wall, which held all manner of provisions for spellwork—pungent oils; sweet-smelling beeswax candles; rough chunks of smoky quartz, amethyst, moldavite, and jasper; black scrying mirrors; hammered pewter bowls. Lydia noticed the silver bell she had given Isadora as a gift on her last birthday, and was seized by a fresh wave of grief.

A pile of fine ash lay on the center shelf, where Isadora had once kept her personal grimoire. It had been encyclopedic, a great tome bound in soft black suede, each page densely packed with Isadora's own eccentric, looping script. The grimoire had been bound to her, as was tradition—a sort of magical failsafe to ensure total privacy, even in death. No witch could read or even touch another witch's grimoire, and the book would be turned to ash upon the witch's death. Seeing the pile of fine gray dust where Isadora's life's work had once sat drove the horrible truth home for Lydia all over again.

Isadora was gone. She was never coming back.

Lydia stepped from the chamber, closing the red door gently behind her, and stood before the sitting room window. The moon had begun her rise over the city. Already she was waning slightly, making her slow journey into darkness, and back again toward the light. Toward the next full moon, and with it, the moment the Nazis would be able to perform the tracking spell and find the *Grimorium Bellum*.

Lydia watched as lights winked out in homes across the city, preparing for the nightly blackout, and thought about the dead. Not only Kitty and Isadora but a hundred thousand others whose names she would never know. Countless Londoners, buried under the rubble. Entire families, mothers and fathers and children, dying in squalor, shoveled into mass graves. Soldiers and civilians, snuffed out, like so many lanterns. She couldn't bring them back. Not a single one of them, no matter how hard she tried.

But there was one thing she could do. One thing that truly mattered. Because out there, somewhere, the *Grimorium Bellum* lay hidden.

Waiting for the next full moon.

Waiting to be found.

Six

It was a cold, bleak morning, and Lydia was sleeping on the floor.
She'd been scouring Isadora's private library for days, searching for anything about the *Grimorium Bellum*—what it was capable of, where it came from, how she could find it. Sometimes she was sure she heard the sound of ticking, like that of some monstrous clock, counting down the seconds until the next full moon, to the moment when she would be able to track the book again. She dared not think about what would happen if the Nazis found it first. Lingering on it too long made her despondent, and so she pushed her feelings aside and carried on.

She'd started with Isadora's *Encyclopedia of Magical Objects*, which made a single, fleeting reference to the *Grimorium Bellum* in only the vaguest possible terms. Lydia had tossed the useless thing into the corner in a fit of rage, and there it had stayed ever since, pages splayed and spine broken. There were other possible leads—murky references woven into texts like tangled threads. One story spoke of a living book that whispered lies into the ear of its unwitting host, until eventually the poor soul went mad. Another told the legend of the Witch of Bath, who carried a grimoire written in a dead language only she could read, and who committed atrocities before eventually being burned alive by her own coven. Before her execution, the repentant witch claimed it was the book itself that made her carry out these abominations. The witch was burned just the same, and the book was lost.

Then there was the witch who had murdered Kitty and Isadora. Lydia had become obsessed with her too. She read ferociously, learning anything she could about German witches—books on runes, Germanic lore, one book titled *Magical Traditions of the Black Forest*, with pages so brittle they crackled like dry leaves under her touch. There were ancient texts that described shadowy Germanic covens of myth—*The Daughters of Freyja. The Cult of the Valkyries.* All those groups were long dead and gone, with no ties to any modern coven that Lydia could find, and she was forced to give up, falling asleep in a fog of despair and frustration.

That morning Lydia woke gasping, a copy of *Warp & Weft: Advanced Warding for Magical Spaces* clutched to her breast like a shield. Her mouth tasted sour, and she was shivering in her thin silk dressing gown and bare feet.

There was a horrible buzzing sound in the air. *The doorbell.* Lydia winced. She was certain it was Sybil. Samhain was coming, after all, and with it, the selection ceremony for the new grand mistress of the academy. Sybil would be wanting her answer.

Lydia stood on wobbly legs, cursing her aching body as she roused herself from the floor.

"Coming."

She didn't bother making herself decent before answering the door. Sybil would understand.

It wasn't until she had opened the door to reveal Mistress Vivian standing before her that Lydia realized her error. She quickly arranged her glamour, but could do nothing about the fact that she was still in her dressing gown. She pulled the neck closed tight against her chest and stood as tall as she could manage.

"Miss Polk." Vivian's eyes flicked down, then up again.

"Vivian," Lydia said, abandoning the honorific *mistress*. Vivian's mouth puckered at the slight. Lydia let her stand there in the doorway until the cold and the weight of Vivian's gaze became more than she could bear. Only then did she step away from the door. "Won't you come in?"

Mistress Vivian looked altogether out of place inside Isadora's richly decorated flat. Lydia noticed how the color seemed to drain away around her, as if only the room was real and Vivian was some flickering image, captured on film in shades of gray. Lydia realized that this was the first time they had ever been alone together.

Lydia allowed a beat to pass. "It seems everyone knew about this place. Not so secret after all, I suppose."

"I'm a Seer, Miss Polk." Vivian stood in front of one of Isadora's framed portraits—a vibrant, dreamy nude, wreathed in gold. She curled her lip. "There are no secrets from me inside the academy."

"Except one." Lydia spoke the words before she could stop herself.

Vivian turned on her. "I beg your pardon?"

Lydia raised her chin. "How did an enemy witch get inside the academy?"

Vivian's eyes narrowed. "Miss Polk, I don't think I care for your tone—"

Lydia cut her off. "I see only two options. Either this enemy witch, and by extension, her *coven*, is in possession of some great, unforeseen power, strong enough to bypass dozens of layers of our own warding magic—"

"Miss Polk—"

"*Or,*" Lydia continued, "the witches of the high council were power-less to protect against an enemy attack inside our own walls, which would make you lot no better than a bunch of half-rate parlor magi-cians. Frankly, I can't quite decide which option is more unsettling."

Vivian stared, stunned to silence. It felt good, offending her, after the way she'd spoken that night in the ceremonial chamber. The way Viv-ian had disparaged the grand mistress before the Great Mother herself not an hour after her death and felt not an ounce of shame.

Vivian screwed up her mouth before speaking. "You always have had a bloody cheek."

"So I'm told."

Vivian huffed. "I didn't come to quarrel. I'm here to offer you an olive branch, if you will cease your insolence long enough for me to do so."

Lydia waited.

"Sybil tells me you are considering accepting her nomination for grand mistress."

"It would be my right, as Isadora's apprentice."

"The position of grand mistress is no one's *right,*" Vivian snapped. "It is a grave responsibility, too heavy for most elder witches to carry, and you are a moody, ill-bred child."

"Is this your olive branch?"

Vivian glared. "Do you plan on accepting the nomination?"

Lydia considered lying, if only to see the look on Vivian's face. In-stead, she opted for the truth.

"I haven't decided. Do you plan to challenge me if I say yes?"

Vivian cast her cloudy gaze over Isadora's paintings and baubles, her collection of books, which now lay strewn across the floor. She studied Lydia, barefoot and half-mad with loss, standing in the middle of Isa-dora's parlor.

"I never liked Isadora. She was . . . *showy*. Arrogant. She saw tradition as something to be challenged, rather than respected. *You*, I trust even less. You've been under her influence for too long. You are rash. Obstinate. And you lack judgment."

Lydia considered a thousand bitter words to fling at Vivian but held her tongue.

"I am eighty-seven years old. Too old, if you ask me. I have no interest in glory, and I have no desire to be grand mistress. What for? I'll be dead soon enough." Vivian paused, as if waiting to see if Lydia would offer any clever remarks. When she didn't, Vivian went on. "You have a reasonable claim to Isadora's seat, I'll give you that. But if I were to challenge you, you would undoubtedly lose."

Lydia knew it was true. Vivian had been on the high council for sixty years, with strong alliances inside the academy. And while no one could accuse Vivian of having charm, she did possess a certain gravitas that made others sit up and take note when she spoke. A challenge from Vivian would mean Lydia's inevitable loss.

"Why challenge me at all if you don't want it?"

"Because I want what's best for the academy. If you were to become grand mistress, I have no doubt you would carry on in Isadora's footsteps—sending witches gallivanting across Europe on these ridiculous treasure hunts. Playing at being soldiers and assassins. And for what? A country that would just as soon see us all hanged." She scowled. "I can't allow it."

"You talk as if we were still in the Middle Ages. The world has changed, Vivian."

"Has it?" Vivian's tone was mocking. "Show me a world that does not hate a powerful woman, and I'll show you a world without men." She held Lydia in her gaze. "This institution was founded for *us*, Miss Polk. Entire generations of witches were orphaned during the trials—"

"I remember your history lessons, Vivian, there's no need—"

"Their mothers and grandmothers hanged or drowned. Their daughters left untrained. The academy was founded in the midst of that tragedy, Miss Polk, to ensure that our knowledge could never be lost. To ensure that our own would be protected. Not so we could fight and die on behalf of a country that has always despised us." She pursed her lips. "Why should witches care about Britain's war, when Britain has never cared for us?"

Lydia felt her anger rising. "Because it's the right thing to do."

"The pontifications of a child," Vivian sneered. "You'd think losing your friend and your grand mistress in a single night would have taught you better, but—"

"*Shut your mouth.*" Lydia was shocked by Vivian's cruelty. She felt as if she'd been slashed open with a knife, and all of her fury and grief and loneliness were spilling onto the floor.

Vivian offered a pitying glance. "There is only one way you will ever succeed in becoming grand mistress of the academy, and that is with my support. Sybil has been campaigning on your behalf, and currently you have five members of the high council on your side. Three others are undecided. The rest firmly oppose your nomination. One can hardly blame them after that ugly spectacle you created. But . . ." Vivian smiled. "One word from me, and you will have the full support of the entire council."

"And why would you do that?" But even as Lydia spoke the words, she already knew the answer.

"Because you are going to withdraw the academy from the war effort. You will shut down Project Diana, and we will return to a proud tradition of secrecy that has lasted for five hundred years. You will do this, and you will keep *me* as your closest adviser. I will shape you into a witch worthy of your title, and you will reign as grand mistress for the rest of your days, with the full backing of the high council."

"And if I refuse?" But then, of course, she knew that, too.

"Then I will take it from you. I will challenge your nomination, and I will become grand mistress. I will withdraw the academy from the war effort, just as I have instructed you to do. And then, I will cast you out of the academy as punishment for your insolence, and you can spend the rest of your days just like your mother, reading fortunes and selling tea in that dirty little flat in Hackney."

Lydia was reeling with rage but could not think of a single thing to say.

"It will bring me no joy to do this. I'd much prefer to spend my remaining years in relative peace and quiet. But I will do as my duty demands. I will do what is best for the academy. The choice is yours."

It took Lydia a long moment to find her voice. "What about the *Grimorium Bellum?*"

"What about it?"

She did her best to remain calm. Rational. "You're a Seer, Vivian. You must know the Nazis have formed their own coven. *You know* that if they find that book, the war will be lost."

Vivian scowled. "I know no such thing."

Lydia carried on without pausing. "Hitler doesn't just want Poland or France, or even Britain. He wants the *whole world*, and with the *Grimorium Bellum*, he can have it. How can you not see that we have to stop him?"

Vivian didn't respond right away. When she did, she spoke slowly, as if addressing a particularly dim student. "Miss Polk, may I offer you your first lesson on leadership?" She did not wait for an answer. "True leadership is knowing the difference between the things that concern you, and the things that don't. You would do very well to remember that."

Lydia did not think she could be shocked by Vivian's coldness any longer. Now she realized she'd been wrong.

"I want you *out*," she hissed.

Vivian smirked. "As you wish." She made her way laboriously to the door, and Lydia found herself wondering if it was age or spite that made the woman move so slowly. When she had nearly reached it, Lydia spoke again.

"Vivian."

She turned.

"Great Seer that you are, I have to wonder. How is it that you never saw this assassin in any of your visions?"

Vivian's smug face collapsed, leaving only a deep frown in its place.

Lydia held her head high. "I look forward to seeing you at Samhain."

Seven

The evening of the selection ceremony, Lydia washed and dressed, and arranged her glamour to mask the dark circles under her eyes. The gown she chose was the most subdued in her collection—a high-necked sheath of black silk, with a long row of onyx buttons down the back. As she looked at herself in the mirror, it occurred to her that even in her full glamour, she didn't look quite the same as she had just two weeks prior. It was as if someone had drained just a little bit of the color from her face, and no amount of clever magic would ever bring it back.

Lydia and Sybil had been hard at work campaigning, enduring simpering smiles and infuriatingly banal conversation over lukewarm cups of tea, and though Lydia had her supporters, the council remained divided. Mistresses Alba and Josephine were still undecided, while Helena and Jacqueline were staunchly in Vivian's camp and showed no signs of wavering.

"They'll all come around eventually," Sybil had assured her. "Once we secure Alba and Josephine, they'll see that there's no use in prolonging the inevitable."

It had been two weeks since the attack. Two weeks since that precious scrap of paper had fallen into the hands of the Nazis. It made Lydia want to scream. Her only comfort was in knowing that no lone witch, no matter how skilled, could project to the book's location with nothing but a scrap of tattered paper to guide her. A feat like that would require the help of a coven under a full moon, and that was nearly a fortnight away. It wasn't too late.

Soon, she told herself. Soon she would be grand mistress, with the resources of the academy at her command. She would have a dozen witches searching for the *Grimorium Bellum* by morning.

And if you lose? a small voice asked. Lydia did not have an answer for that.

The sun had set, but the selection ceremony was still hours away. Lydia thought she would go mad from pacing Isadora's flat. Books lay in haphazard stacks across the floor where she'd left them, forming a rough circle, like a fairy ring. She sat in the center, feeling like a child in a fort—hidden and safe. She reached for the nearest book, the one she'd tossed aside the day Vivian had come to call.

Warp & Weft: Advanced Warding for Magical Spaces.

How had the assassin managed to get through the academy's warding? The question had burrowed into her mind like a worm the night Isadora and Kitty were murdered, and she could not seem to dig it back out, no matter how hard she tried. The wall of protection magic surrounding the academy should have been impenetrable, even for the most skilled Traveler. Was it possible that dozens of layers of centuries-old protection magic could be so easily bypassed? Could the high council really be so inept?

Lydia had tried making veiled allusions to the question during those interminably long teas with the high council but had been stonewalled at every turn. She had assumed it was simple pride that made the council so cagey. No one liked to be confronted with their own inadequacies, least of all the most powerful witches in Britain. Now, she looked down at the book in her hand, as another, even more unthinkable possibility began to root itself like a weed inside her mind.

Had someone *allowed* an enemy witch inside the academy?

She stared around her at Isadora's flat—her books and art and carefully curated baubles, the air as still as a held breath—and felt as if somehow, Isadora were there in the room with her. Watching her silently, the way she so often had, waiting to see if Lydia would come to the correct conclusion all by herself.

"Sod it," she said.

There was only one way she would ever have any peace, and that was to see for herself. The ceremony was still two hours away. She had plenty of time.

She tucked the book under her arm and dashed out into the night.

IT WAS PITCH DARK when Lydia arrived at the academy. The moon had hidden herself away, the night draped across her face like a mourning veil. The streetlights had been extinguished to protect from German bombers, and so Lydia found her way to the back of the academy by memory, running her hand along the brick facade in the dark. She could feel the warding there, like a net of electricity buzzing along her fingertips.

She opened her copy of *Warp & Weft*, and from her pocketbook produced a cigarette lighter. She held the flame close to the page, straining her eyes to read the words.

"*Wryón iwanan, wryón scylda, scylda lyte, scylda lyte.*" She shut the book and moved closer, holding out her hand in the darkness until she was touching the warding itself. "*Wryón iwanan, wryón scylda, scylda lyte, scylda lyte.*" She could feel the spell collecting in her fingers and moving outward like blood rushing to an appendage. The spell left her body, and as it did, it illuminated the warding like a silver web, moving ever outward from her hand. The spell extended on and on, expanding across the building's surface, until the entire edifice glowed like a will-o'-the-wisp, the wall of spellwork glittering like spectral cobwebs in the darkness.

"Just like a fairy castle," she whispered.

She walked the perimeter of the warding, taking note of the depth within it—gossamer-thin layer upon layer of magic. A witch's magic could never outlive the witch who cast it; the warding was the only known exception. It was the work of hundreds of witches, most of whom had died long before Lydia was born—but not all. In this warding, delicate threads of magic from witches both living and dead existed side by side, braided together in a single wall of spellwork that served not only to protect the academy itself but to maintain the magic of those witches long gone. So long as even one witch lived who had cast her power into the warding, the magic preserved within would exist forever. It was a work of magical cooperation that spanned centuries. And it was beautiful.

Lydia walked the length of the warding, searching as she went for anything out of the ordinary. She came to a place where the spellwork extended past the walls of the shop and into the lot behind, revealing the footprint of the academy hidden beneath the glamour. She knew from the map inside her mind that there was a library here, tucked and folded inside the academy's glamour like a magician's silk. She followed the warding, imagining the jumble of ancient books and folios just on the other side of the shimmering boundary. She took one step, then another, and then stopped.

There, cut into the centuries-old warding, was a doorway, not much taller than Lydia herself. She stepped closer, noticing how the mangled warding seemed to sway in the breeze, as if it had been shredded by a knife. There was something violent about the image, and Lydia shuddered to see it. She peered closer, and there, sliced like a tattoo into the top of the doorway was a symbol. A rune.

Othala. Homeland.

Eight

ybil stood before the tattered portal, holding tightly to Lydia's arm.

"Great Mother." Her hand reached out toward the glowing rune, then stopped. She drew a protection sign in the air in a quick, automatic gesture.

Lydia watched, waiting in desperation for Sybil to tell her what to do. "It's the same rune," she said. "The same one that was on her knife."

Sybil turned to Lydia then, like someone just waking from a dream. Lydia didn't think she had ever seen Sybil look so shaken.

"Right." She wrung her hands and looked around, as if someone might still be lurking somewhere out there in the shadows. "Inside. Quickly. Before someone sees."

SYBIL PUTTERED ABOUT HER OFFICE, adding wood to the fire, fixing tea, rifling through books and papers as she muttered under her breath. Lydia had always felt at home in Sybil's private study. Something about the clutter of threadbare furniture in shades of purple and mauve, the jumbled array of old books and mismatched teacups abandoned on every surface, had always felt comforting to her. Now, it only felt cramped and airless.

Lydia heard footsteps in the hallway. The high council was arriving. The ceremony was less than an hour away.

"Sybil . . ." Sybil carried on with her fussing. "*Sybil.*"

Finally, Sybil looked up at her.

"How could this happen?"

Sybil eased herself into an overstuffed chair. "I'm not sure."

"Who could have cut that door in the warding? Could someone from the outside have—"

Sybil shook her head. "No. That would be impossible. No part of the warding can be dismantled by anyone who wasn't a part of its making. That's its entire purpose, to protect from outsiders."

"But that means . . ." Lydia saw no other possibility. She felt a tremor run through her as she finally gave voice to the unthinkable. "That means someone inside the academy *allowed* that woman in."

Sybil stared into the fire, momentarily lost in thought. She exhaled and looked at Lydia. "Have you told anyone else what you found?"

"No. Only you."

She nodded, fidgeting anxiously with one of her rings. "We need to alert the council. The selection ceremony will have to be postponed until—"

"No," Lydia said. "We can't allow anyone else to find out. Not until we know who is responsible."

Sybil stared at her. "Good heavens, Lydia. You can't possibly think that someone on the council could have . . ." She trailed off, the thought too terrible to contemplate.

Lydia felt a growing unease creeping over her. Speculating felt like heresy, and voicing her suspicions somehow even worse. And yet . . .

"When Vivian came to see me, she told me she would support my nomination for grand mistress, but only if I withdrew the academy from the war effort. She told me if I refused, she would challenge my nomination and do it herself. Is it possible Vivian could have—"

"Vivian has been a member of the council for as long as I've been alive. I can't imagine she could ever do such a thing." Even as Sybil said the words, Lydia didn't think she looked very sure.

"Not even if she thought she was protecting the academy? By returning us to the way things were before?"

Sybil looked deeply troubled and did not answer.

"Something else has been bothering me. How could Vivian, of all people, not have known that Isadora was going to be murdered? How could she not know there was a traitor inside the academy, unless . . ."

Sybil shook her head. "Visions aren't always like that, my darling. Seers aren't all-knowing, and Vivian . . ." She paused, uncertain how to continue. "Vivian is *old*. Her power isn't the same as it once was. She would never admit it, not to herself, or anyone else for that matter, but her visions have been fading for some time now."

The fire popped and crackled. They sat in silence for a long moment.

"Someone let that madwoman into the academy," Lydia said quietly. "Not just to kill Isadora. I saw her, Sybil. She came for that piece of the *Grimorium Bellum*. Why do that if they don't plan to use it?" Sybil looked thoughtful but did not reply. "This wasn't one rogue witch. This was an organized effort, with help from inside our own academy. We have to stop them."

"I know. But, Lydia, the council will never let you go after it."

"Nonsense. Half the council supports my claim for grand mistress. If we can sway Alba and Josephine—"

"It won't matter."

Lydia stopped. "What?"

"There was a vote, earlier today. Limiting the grand mistress's wartime powers. No further action can be taken on behalf of the war effort without the unanimous agreement of the high council." Sybil looked down, twisting one of her rings. "I tried very hard to stop it."

Lydia sat in silence as Sybil's words sank in.

"Who requested the vote?"

Somewhere, a clock was ticking. Sybil held her gaze. "Vivian."

Black despair reached up and caught Lydia by the throat.

"Then there's no point. Whether it's me or Vivian, it's all the same now. She's won."

"No," Sybil said firmly. "No, it is not all the same. Isadora did not choose you out of a hundred other girls for no reason. She chose you because she knew that you are what the academy needs. Vivian will drag us back in time, but *you* . . ." She trailed off, then looked intently into Lydia's eyes. "What if you're right? What if it's Vivian? And then she becomes grand mistress?" Sybil pressed her fingers to her lips, unable to finish the thought. "It has to be you, Lydia. It can't be anyone else."

LYDIA STOOD BEFORE the shining black doors of the ceremonial chamber, her heart thrumming like an engine. Carved roses in every stage of bloom erupted through the wood, surrounded on all sides by razor-sharp thorns, gleaming like the talons of some terrifying creature. She heard muffled voices and smelled burning incense.

It was nearly midnight.

"Merry Samhain, Miss Polk." Lydia turned. Vivian was standing beside her.

Sybil had cautioned her about this moment. *Don't antagonize. Don't rise to her bait.* Still, now that they were face-to-face, Lydia felt a surge of fury rise up in her.

"I should congratulate you," Vivian said. "My sources tell me that before the night is out, you will be our new grand mistress."

Vivian's condescension was too much for Lydia to stomach. "Not that it will make any difference at all. You saw to that."

Vivian cocked her head, a faint smile on her lips. "No lone witch should wield so much power. I'm simply ushering in a new age of democracy on the high council. I thought you would approve."

Lydia felt her anger rising like a fever. She focused all her senses on that black door and kept her gaze straight ahead, counting roses and thorns, but it wouldn't do.

"I know what you did," she whispered.

"Oh?" Vivian chuckled. "And what is that?"

Lydia looked at her. "The door in the warding. I saw it. I know it was you."

Vivian frowned. "Treason against one's own coven is a crime of the highest order, Miss Polk. Accusations like yours have ugly consequences. I would advise you to choose your next words very carefully."

The corridor seemed to yawn like a cavernous mouth around her. Lydia felt as if she were perched on a high, narrow ledge, and that at any moment she would lose her balance and go toppling into the ether.

"When I am grand mistress," Lydia rasped, "I will dedicate every resource at my disposal to finding out who was behind the plot to murder Isadora. And if I find that you are responsible, please believe there will be nowhere on this earth you will be able to hide from me."

Vivian looked into Lydia's eyes. Her face softened. "When you are selected as grand mistress, you will be nothing more than a figurehead, with no more power than you have in this very moment."

Then Vivian stepped forward and entered the ceremonial chamber.

Lydia stood alone before those shining black doors, heart reeling, listening to Sybil's sensible words inside her head. Willing herself to put aside her stubbornness just this once and do the reasonable thing.

But somewhere, out there in the darkness, the *Grimorium Bellum* waited like a sleeping monster. She closed her eyes and thought she could almost hear its wet, rasping breath. It was beckoning to her. Waiting for her across the channel.

The moon would be full again in two weeks. There was still time.

She turned and ran.

Nine

Rebecca watched the beach from her hiding place, crouched between the trees overlooking the shore. Sunrise was still hours away, but silvery-gray light had begun to seep into the black, announcing that morning was coming. Overhead, birds began to wake, calling softly to each other.

When Rebecca was a girl, her mother used to tell her that birds sang to each other in the morning as a way of making sure everyone had made it safely through the night. Ma petite colombe, her mother would call her—"my little dove." As a child, Rebecca would lie awake in the early morning hours, listening to the birds calling to one another, and would feel a sense of hope and wonder cracking open like an egg inside her chest. Now, as she sat in the half dark with the soft murmur of birdsong all around her, she felt a familiar pain—grief and guilt sliding under her breastbone like a knife.

Somewhere off in the trees, a birdcall, different from the others. Rebecca scanned the surf. It was difficult to see in the dark, but yes, there, just offshore, a small fishing boat. Rebecca emerged from her place in the trees. Four men materialized on the beach from the mist, dragging two small skiffs between them, and began to row out to meet the boat. Rebecca kept watch as the skiffs were loaded up and returned bearing several wooden crates, along with two extra people—a man and a woman.

The man, Rebecca knew. He called himself David Harlowe, although she was never sure whether that was his real name. He was an Englishman, though he spoke perfect, unaccented French. He'd been introduced to Rebecca as a member of the Special Operations Executive— English spies charged with giving aid to the Resistance, providing training and supplies. Rebecca had heard David refer to the SOE as "the Ministry of Ungentlemanly Warfare," and he'd laughed when he said it, as if he'd made a very clever joke.

The woman was new. Rebecca took her in as the boats approached the shore. She was dressed in the French fashion in a full skirt and burgundy coat, but mist clung to her hair and clothes, making her look sick and bedraggled. Dark circles stood out under her eyes, and her lips were pale. Rebecca suspected that her time at sea had not agreed with her.

"Welcome back, David." Rebecca admired David's skill with French but always took advantage of any opportunity to practice English with a native speaker.

"Good to be back." David stepped from the boat. "I see the Huns haven't managed to capture you yet."

Rebecca peered out across the water at the rickety fishing boat. "I thought you boys normally like to jump out of airplanes when you come to France."

"Nothing I like better. But I don't think my companion would have cared for it as much."

Rebecca glanced toward the woman. "Who is she?"

"To anyone who asks, she's Chloe Moreau: Parents are from Quebec, hence the accent, educated in Paris. Wife of a French wine merchant, traveling with her cousin to Dordogne."

"Sightseeing, is she?"

"Something like that."

"Enjoy your vacation."

David grinned. "Oh, you misunderstand. *I'm* not going to Dordogne. You are."

Rebecca stared at his smug face until she realized that he was serious.

"The hell I am. Do I look like a taxi driver to you?"

"It'll only be a few hours out of your way."

She planted her feet hard on the rocky beach. "Take her yourself."

"I have business up the coast." Rebecca knew better than to ask what sort of business.

"Let her take the train."

"I can't put her on a train by herself, she's a civilian."

Rebecca felt a jolt of alarm run through her. "What the hell do you mean, she's a *civilian*? Who is she?"

David did not answer.

"*David.*"

"They don't tell me everything, believe it or not." The self-satisfied tone evaporated, replaced with something more honest. "I checked with my man at Baker Street, and he tells me no one had heard of her before two weeks ago. Rumor is the order to get her into France came from Winston Churchill himself. That's all I know."

Rebecca turned and looked to her coconspirators, who had nearly finished loading their trucks. "I have business myself, you know."

"Your business will still be there after you drop her off in Dordogne."

"I don't have the petrol. Where am I going to get the fuel for the trip? From you?"

"As a matter of fact, yes. Your friends are unloading it as we speak. I think you'll find it's quite a bit more than the trip requires. Consider it a gift."

Rebecca considered it a bribe, and not one she could afford to turn down.

"Think of all the mischief you could make." Even in the dark, she could hear the smile in his voice.

Rebecca watched the woman from a distance. "How is her French?"

"Fluent."

She looked up over the scrubby hill. A strip of rosy light was beginning to creep over the horizon. She huffed and turned to the woman.

"Welcome to France, Chloe Moreau."

The woman did not respond.

David cleared his throat. "Lydia."

The woman called Lydia looked up. "Oh. Yes. Thank you."

Rebecca looked at David. "If they execute me, I'll haunt you."

He grinned. "I'm sincerely looking forward to it."

CLEAN MORNING LIGHT washed over the landscape as Rebecca drove toward Dordogne in her trusty Citroën. She'd changed out of her soggy trousers and into a nondescript skirt and blouse. The sea air had caused her hair to frizz, and she arranged it the best she could in her tiny compact mirror, making herself look as meek and ordinary as possible. Lydia seemed to have recovered from her journey, but still appeared anxious, fiddling with her new French clothes as she stared out the window.

"You need to relax," Rebecca said.

Lydia looked startled.

"If you look like you're nervous, people will wonder why. Do you know your cover?"

Lydia cleared her throat. "Chloe Moreau. Born in Quebec. Came to

Paris before the war to attend school. Married to Philippe Moreau, a wine merchant from Bordeaux, for two years, no children. On my way to Dordogne to see the castles, with my cousin, Rebecca Gagne."

Rebecca kept her eyes on the road. "Good. Now say it again, but try not to sound like you're giving an oral exam."

Lydia opened her mouth, but nothing came out.

"Let me make something clear," Rebecca said. "I've done things since the occupation that are punishable by death. I'm not talking about distributing pamphlets, although they'll kill you for that too. I've been fighting these bastards tooth and nail for three years, and I've never been caught. And do you know why? Because I'm careful, and I'm smart, and I'm an excellent liar. You? I don't think you're a good liar, which means you're going to get caught. And if you get caught, I get caught. And I have not survived this long only to die in front of a Nazi firing squad because some English tourist wants to play at being a spy."

Rebecca drove with her knuckles white against the wheel, anger simmering just under her skin. Harlowe had put them all in danger by saddling her with this ridiculously unprepared Englishwoman, and for what? What could possibly be so important in Dordogne that it could justify the risk?

Lydia's gaze fell to her lap, and Rebecca heard her take a shaky breath. She was just beginning to feel the slightest pang of guilt for her harshness when Lydia spoke again.

"Do you really want to know what I'm doing here?" she asked quietly. "I'm here because Philippe and I had a fight." Rebecca glanced at her. "I suppose I'm the one who started it. I thought we were going to try for a baby. He promised we would, but now he hasn't touched me in months." Lydia's lips trembled, a red flush creeping into her cheeks. Her eyes were rimmed with tears. "I finally got up the nerve to talk to him about it, and . . ." She shook her head. "He doesn't want a baby. He said he did, but now he doesn't. I think there are other women." Lydia removed a handkerchief from her handbag. "He doesn't love me. And I'm just . . . I'm so ashamed. I needed to get away, but what to tell everyone? What to tell my *parents?* So I told them all I was going to Dordogne to see the châteaux. But actually, I'm running away from my marriage. Oh, Rebecca. You won't tell anyone, will you?"

Rebecca stared at Lydia, and Lydia smirked, dabbing away the tears.

"Bien joué. That was very good. A little melodramatic, but still."

"Thank you. I thought perhaps if I cried, it might make anyone who talks to us—"

"Want to stop talking to us as quickly as possible. Yes. Perfect. Can you do it in French?"

"But of course." Lydia launched into her story again, in French, and this time with fewer tears. Rebecca listened carefully, then pulled the car to the side of the road and turned off the engine. Lydia looked around, confused.

"Get in the boot," Rebecca said.

Lydia stared. "I beg your pardon?"

"The luggage compartment. I believe you British call it 'the boot.' You need to get in it."

"Why?"

"Because your French is shit."

"It is not! I was top of my class. I speak French like a native."

"You speak French like you learned it in an English boarding school. The town up ahead is crawling with milice, and we will be stopped."

"Milice?"

"French militia. Nazi-collaborating scum. Looking for spies and Resistance fighters, and with that accent, even an imbecile will know that you are an Englishwoman."

"I'm not getting in the bloody boot," Lydia said.

"Then you can walk to Dordogne."

Rebecca waited as Lydia considered her options and then got out, slamming the door behind her. For a moment, Rebecca was sure she would storm off, but she only stood by the back of the car, arms crossed, waiting. Rebecca got out and opened the boot.

"The moment we're clear of them, you let me out," Lydia said.

"Fine."

Rebecca watched as Lydia arranged herself. She curled up on her side, then seemed to think of something.

"What if they look—"

Rebecca slammed the hatch and returned to the driver's seat. She took a deep breath, gripping the wheel to steady her hands.

"If they look inside the boot," she said, "then we are both dead."

Ten

It had turned into a beautiful morning by the time they reached the town. The air was cool and crisp, and the sky had gone a vibrant, cloudless blue. Up on the hilltop, an old stone church looked down over the town, surrounded by bare trees.

Rebecca inhaled, taking in the sharp smell of burning leaves. There was something comforting about that smell. It reminded her of her childhood, when her father would pack the whole family up every autumn and take the train from Paris to the Alsace, where he'd grown up, for a week of grueling hikes and history lectures. Before her father had been forced to resign from his teaching position at the Lycée Henri-IV. Before the whole world had gone mad.

She kept both hands firmly on the wheel as she approached the center of town. Off to her left, she could see a gathering of uniformed milice, with their blue jackets and berets, congregating outside a school. Against the schoolhouse wall, a dozen townspeople stood in a line as uniformed men rifled through their papers. Rebecca watched as one blue-clad milicien slapped an elderly man in the mouth, then shoved him to the ground and laughed.

Cruel, angry, impotent boys, Rebecca thought. She recalled the story of a village where a group of Resistance fighters had sabotaged the local power grid, wreaking havoc for the nearby garrison. The milice were never able to round up the saboteurs, so instead they went to the nearby town and filled the church with as many people as they could fit— women, children, the old and infirm. They asked them some questions, but no one knew anything about the saboteurs, so the milice took the people out back a dozen at a time and gunned them down, leaving their bodies where they fell. They left the corpses to rot in the sun, as a warning to those who would dare conspire with the Resistance. Even now, the thought of it filled her with a helpless rage.

Two miliciens stepped into the street in front of Rebecca and waved for her to stop the car. David had once told her she had a suspicious face, and so she forced herself to smile as they approached the window.

The taller of the two men had a mean, stupid face, like he'd been molded from putty by a slow-witted child. The shorter man was skinny, slouched and chinless, and seemed to wear a permanent smirk, as if he were always thinking of a particularly filthy joke. Rebecca wondered what it would feel like to drive her knuckles into his pronounced Adam's apple.

"Bonjour, mademoiselle," the smaller man said. "Where are you heading this morning?"

"Dordogne," she said lightly. "I'm spending a few days with my cousin there."

The shorter of the two men squinted into the distance as if he had not heard her. Behind him, the larger man loomed, looking slow but menacing.

"We've had some reports of Resistance activity in the area. Heard they're transporting guns from the coast. You wouldn't know anything about that, would you, ma mignonne?"

Rebecca arranged her face in a mask of shock and outrage. "My God, no, I had no idea."

Behind the men, another milicien hovered over a young girl as she shrank against the stone wall.

The larger man's eyes settled on the hood of the automobile, and he pursed his lips in approval. "I like your car."

"Thank you."

The smaller man snickered. "Maybe we should requisition it, if you like it so much."

Rebecca felt her throat constrict. "I'm afraid my boyfriend wouldn't like that. The car belongs to him."

"Oh? And who is your boyfriend?"

"His name is Hans. Captain Hans Müller."

The man's smile evaporated. *Pathetic*, Rebecca thought. These boys wanted so badly to play at being Nazis, but the idea of a Frenchwoman warming a German bed still filled them with disgust.

"Papers, please."

"Of course." Rebecca retrieved her identification, careful not to reveal the Browning semiautomatic pistol in her purse as she did. The papers had been crafted for her at great expense and bore her image—brown hair cut to her shoulders, downturned lips, permanent circles under the eyes, just like her mother—as well as a name that was almost hers, but not quite.

"You're twenty-two? You look older."

"Times are hard." Rebecca offered an apologetic smile. The man didn't smile back.

"I'll need to open the luggage compartment."

Rebecca's guts turned to ice. "Is something wrong?"

"Probably not. But we have to check. Wouldn't want to be fooled by a pretty face."

"You think I have a pretty face?" *Please, please, oh please.*

The man made a gesture, as if to say, *Eh, I've seen better,* then held out his hand. "The key?"

She thought fast. There were half a dozen miliciens here, all armed. She could speed off, but she would almost certainly be gunned down. If she handed over her keys, she would have precious seconds to get the pistol from her purse while they opened the luggage compartment. She would have no way to escape, but she was a good shot. She was sure she could kill at least two of them before they cut her down. Who knows? She might even live. *Two dead traitors are better than none.*

Rebecca smiled. "Of course." She handed over the keys.

The two men walked to the back of the car. Rebecca reached inside her purse. Next to her lipstick and her pistol was a burgundy leather glasses case, and inside, a pair of round, wire-rimmed spectacles, with both lenses crushed. She pressed her hand to the case, and felt the familiar, comforting texture under her fingertips.

"May my memory be a blessing," she whispered. "To someone." She realized that there might not be anyone left who knew her real name.

Rebecca shifted her hand to the pistol as she watched the two men in her mirror. She would aim for the heart. Shoot the two by the car, then start on the others, if they didn't kill her right away. She listened for a shout of surprise, of anger, but it never came. *Perhaps they knew all along.* One hand on the door, the other on the gun, she was about to step out of the car, when the hatch closed again. The men returned to the driver's side window. The little man handed Rebecca her papers and her keys.

"Enjoy Dordogne."

Rebecca's hand was still inside her purse. She took it out and placed it back on the wheel.

"Merci."

She drove and watched the two men grow smaller in her mirror, while her heart leapt inside her like an animal trying to claw its way out.

REBECCA KEPT HER EYES on the rearview mirror, waiting to see if she was being followed. Thirty minutes went by while she sweat through her blouse, one hand on the gun in her purse. Her mind raced. It was impossible the two men hadn't seen the woman in her luggage compartment. Which left only one possibility—they had seen her, and they had let them go anyway. Why?

When she was sure they were alone, she pulled to the side of the road and circled quickly to the back of the car, pistol in hand. She unlocked it and threw the hatch open. Lydia was there, curled on her side, disheveled and squinting at the sudden burst of light. Rebecca shoved the pistol in her face.

"Get out."

Lydia's eyes went wide. "What are you doing?"

"Get out of the car. Now."

Lydia scrambled to sit up in the cramped compartment. Once she was upright, Rebecca grabbed her, throwing her to her knees in the middle of the empty country road.

"Why did they let us go?"

Lydia's hands were raised and bleeding from where they had broken her fall. "I don't know."

"*Bullshit.*"

"I don't! I have no idea!"

"Who do you work for?"

"I don't work for anyone. I'm not a spy, you know that."

"Exactly. You're not SOE, not French Resistance. Even David doesn't know who you really are. Do you want to know what I think?" She didn't wait for a reply. "I think you're setting me up."

"No, Rebecca, I swear—"

"*Shut up!* Are you an informant? Is that why they let you go?"

"No."

Rebecca looked around. No cars coming in either direction. The Englishwoman knelt in the gravel at her feet. She felt a familiar sensation inside herself—something calcifying around her heart, making her feel hard and numb as she prepared herself to do a terrible thing.

"Tell me something true in the next three seconds, or I will put a bullet in your head."

"Rebecca—"

"Three."

"Rebecca, listen to me—"

"Two."

Lydia disappeared. One second, she was cowering at Rebecca's feet, and the next, there was nothing but empty road, and blue sky, and golden fields stretching for miles in every direction. Rebecca stumbled back. She could hear gravel moving around her, footsteps that weren't her own, but she couldn't see anyone there.

"Merde. Merde, merde, merde."

Then Lydia was back. Off to her left, facing her, not trying to run. Rebecca turned and aimed her pistol.

"*Astyffn ban,*" Lydia said.

Rebecca froze. She could still breathe, a small comfort as she listened to the frantic panting of her own breath, but try as she might, she couldn't move. She focused all her energy on the trigger, but even that tiny movement felt as impossible as flying. A wave of terror washed over her as Lydia approached, slowly and calmly, and took the gun from her hand.

"I'm not your enemy, Rebecca." Lydia held the gun by her side. She walked to the driver's side door, opened it, and placed the gun back inside Rebecca's purse. Then she returned and stood before Rebecca's frozen body.

"I'm going to release you. And then we can talk."

Rebecca stared at Lydia, trying to convey something with her eyes—submission. Lydia seemed to understand.

Rebecca fell to the ground, the sudden release leaving her limp, like a marionette with her strings cut. She scrambled backward, gravel scattering around her, as Lydia stood placid and motionless.

"What the fuck was that?"

Lydia looked around. Off in the distance, a car was approaching.

"We should get off the road," she said.

REBECCA GUIDED THE CAR onto a little-used dirt path, then turned off the engine and stared straight ahead. Lydia sat beside her, murmuring strange words under her breath, running her fingertips across her injured palms. Rebecca looked down and saw the wounds close under her touch.

She had always loathed scary stories. Ghosts, witches, even fairy tales meant for children. Anything that gave off even a whiff of the supernatural had always filled her with a visceral dread. Rebecca preferred her world to be orderly. She glanced down at Lydia's now unblemished hands, then quickly looked away.

Lydia was quiet, waiting for her to speak.

"What did you do to me?" Rebecca rasped.

"It's a simple defensive spell. A temporary paralytic. I've had it done to me in class, I know it's not pleasant. I'm sorry I had to do that."

Rebecca swallowed. "You disappeared."

"Yes."

"How?"

"It's called a glamour. Normally it's used for changing one's appearance, but a very skilled Glamourer can use it to disappear entirely."

"And you're a very skilled Glamourer?"

Lydia shook her head. She smiled, but there was something broken behind it. "No. My friend Kitty. She was the best Glamourer I ever knew. She taught me that trick, but I'm not very good. I can only hold it for a few seconds."

"That's why the milice let us go? They opened the boot, and you . . . what, you became invisible?" Rebecca looked at Lydia. There was dirt on her blouse and on her face, and her hair was coming undone. "You're trying to tell me you're what . . . a sorcière? A witch?"

Lydia grimaced. "I'd rather not have told you at all."

Rebecca was sure she was going mad. She felt idiotic, but she could not deny what she'd seen. What she'd *felt*. She shuddered, remembering the total loss of control.

"What's in Dordogne?"

"You won't believe me."

She removed her hands from the wheel. "You're not going anywhere in my car until you tell me."

Lydia made her wait. Then she sighed. "A book of spells. The Nazis want it. I need to find it first. If I can get to the last place it was kept, I'll be able to use the magic left behind to track it down."

"And the book was being kept at this château? Château de Laurier?"

"Yes."

Rebecca was quiet for a moment. "Why do the Nazis want it?"

"It's hard to say. What it does exactly is a bit of a mystery. What I do know is that the book contains ancient magic, *wartime* magic . . . and that wherever it goes, death and ruin inevitably follow. If the Nazis find it, they'll be in possession of a well of unimaginable arcane power—"

"You're telling me they don't intend to lock this book away behind glass somewhere. You're telling me they're planning to use it."

Lydia nodded. "They would need a coven to wield it. Magic that powerful would burn through a lone witch like kindling. I've met one of their witches already, I'm afraid, and I believe there must be more. . . ." She swallowed. Rebecca thought she looked pale. "I believe they have something planned for the winter solstice. That's in six weeks."

They sat in silence for a moment.

"Your friend," Rebecca said slowly. "The one who taught you to disappear. You talked about her in the past tense. She's dead, isn't she?"

Something complicated happened behind Lydia's eyes. "Yes."

"I'm sorry. Who did it?"

"I don't know her name. She broke into the academy, slipped past our warding, and murdered the grand mistress, and Kitty. She carried a knife with a rune on the handle. *Othala*. It means 'homeland.'" A pause. "I'm going to kill her." She sounded like she had just realized it herself, and it surprised her.

"Good." This, at least, Rebecca could understand.

Lydia looked at her. "Are you all right? I imagine this must all be quite a shock."

Rebecca wasn't sure what *all right* even meant anymore. All she knew was that more than anything, she wanted this Englishwoman out of her car. She wanted to drive off, leave her standing on the side of the road with the weeds and the cows. But she remembered what David had said: the order to get Lydia into France had come from Churchill himself. For whatever reason, Churchill believed the English witch was essential to defeating the Nazis.

And that was all that mattered.

"We should get you to Dordogne."

They drove in silence, hilly farmland rolling by their windows. After several long, quiet moments, Rebecca heard Lydia murmur something softly to herself.

"What was that?"

Lydia looked at her. "You said you'd been at this for *three years?*" Her eyes were probing. Trying to guess her age, Rebecca was fairly certain. "How on earth did you get involved in all this?"

She almost didn't answer. She'd learned to be suspicious of strangers, of people who asked questions, of everyone, really. But the drive was long, and Lydia's secrets were somehow even stranger and more dangerous than her own.

"The first year it was little things," she said. "Vandalizing posters. Slashing tires. Stealing road signs so the Nazis wouldn't know where they were going, things like that."

Lydia laughed. "You stole road signs?"

Rebecca shrugged. "It's surprisingly effective. After that I joined a group that was doing more . . . active resistance." She glanced at Lydia and saw that she understood. "I moved from place to place, went where I could do the most good. I wanted to *punish* them. To make the bastards regret ever coming here in the first place."

"And now you're a regular Joan of Arc—outwitting the milice, smuggling guns and Englishwomen from the coast. That's quite the step up from sign theft and petty vandalism." There was a silent question in her tone: *What happened to you? What did they take from you, that would make you willing to risk so much?*

Rebecca glanced at the glasses case in her purse. The answer felt heavy on her tongue. She hesitated, then swallowed the words like a dry pill.

"What will you do, once you find your book?" she asked, cutting Lydia off before she could ask anything more.

Lydia looked strangely uncertain. "Take it to the academy, I suppose."

"Will you try to use it yourself?"

Lydia looked as if she had never considered the possibility. "Of course not."

"Why not?"

"It's dark magic. Evil. We don't do that sort of thing." Lydia didn't look entirely convinced by her own argument.

"It would save lives."

"It would *end* lives, that's what it does."

Rebecca was quiet for a long time. "They would do it to us."

"We're not like them."

"Maybe we should be."

Lydia turned, surprised. "You don't mean that."

"I do, actually."

Lydia stared. "I don't think you know what you're suggesting."

Rebecca was suddenly furious with this stupid, naive Englishwoman, lecturing her on morality with such confidence. "You know what I think? I think you've only heard about war on the BBC. You've never seen it up close. You have no idea what it's really like here."

"That's not true—"

"No? Have you had to watch little children starve to death? Have you watched innocent men and women shot like dogs in the street? Have you seen your entire family carted away like animals? These aren't men we're fighting, they're *monsters*. They don't care for our humanity, so why should you care for theirs?"

"We can't become like them."

"How many will die if you don't? You could stop this war, but you won't, because you have nothing at stake, and because you're a coward. You'll go back to London, and you'll read your newspaper, and shake your head, and when you get tired, you'll put it away, and you'll think about something else. And we will still be dying." Rebecca's throat burned, but she would not cry.

"We're dying, too, you know," Lydia said, but all the conviction had run out of her voice.

Rebecca looked away. "Not like this."

It was late afternoon by the time they reached Château de Laurier. The sun had begun to slip in the sky, and the air had taken on a new chill. Rebecca was tired and hungry, and eager to be rid of the uncanny Englishwoman once and for all.

"I appreciate your help," Lydia said as the car came to a halt. Château de Laurier loomed before them. Time had peeled away the castle's beauty, and water and moss stained the stones. The building cast a sad pall over the landscape, a dark smudge on the hillside.

Lydia stepped out of the car and pulled her bag from the boot, peering up as she stood in the shadow of the crumbling château.

"I hope you find what you are looking for." Rebecca hadn't known she was going to say it, but the words came out anyway. "Think about what I said."

Lydia nodded. "Be safe."

Rebecca drove away and did not look back, leaving Lydia standing alone on the windswept hill.

Eleven

ydia watched the black Citroën disappear into the distance.

The temperature had dropped in the last few hours, and a biting wind tore through her coat. Night would be here soon. She looked up at the battered face of Château de Laurier. None of her magic lent itself to getting inside, and for the first time, she wished that she could have been born a Glamourer or a Traveler instead of a Projectionist. Kitty would have made short work of a problem like this one. No, she would need to devise a more practical method of gaining entry to the château in order to complete the tracking spell and find the book.

Lydia looked up, expecting to see the silver moon hanging above her like a guillotine, but there were only murky clouds. The full moon was just one day away. One day until she could reattempt the tracking spell and find the *Grimorium Bellum*.

As her thoughts began to quicken, she became alert to a sensation just on the periphery of her consciousness—a creeping feeling, like seeing movement just out of the corner of your eye. Lydia gave the feeling her full attention. After a moment, she smiled.

"Hello, Sybil."

Sybil appeared a moment later, her image swimming like a drop of ink in a glass of water. "I should have known I couldn't spy on you for long. You've always had a talent for spotting a hidden projection."

"I had an excellent teacher. I'm only surprised I didn't hear from you sooner."

Sybil looked chagrined. "I popped in on you once or twice, after you didn't appear for the selection ceremony. I was worried. Terrified, actually. Imagine my surprise when I found you getting a primer in spy craft from the SOE. After that I thought it best to give you some space. In case . . ."

In case Sybil was being watched. Lydia cringed to think how worried she must have been.

"I'm sorry, Sybil."

Sybil's image wavered ever so slightly. Her face was lit by yellow lamplight, making her look out of place in the fading dusk. Behind her, Lydia could see the watery outline of an enormous window, surrounded by books.

"You're in Isadora's study."

Sybil's smile faltered. "Actually, it's my study now." She looked slightly embarrassed, and all at once Lydia understood.

"Oh, Sybil, you angel!" Lydia had taken for granted that Vivian had been selected as grand mistress in her stead. She hadn't even considered that the council might elect another. "Congratulations. I can think of no one more deserving. How did you manage it?"

"Through a great deal of fawning and bootlicking, I'm afraid. But desperate times call for desperate measures. I couldn't simply stand by and let Vivian have it. Not after what she's . . ." She stopped, still unable to give voice to what they both suspected. She cleared her throat. "You should know I plan on abdicating when you return. I never did have the stomach for politics." She looked around, her face becoming serious. "Darling, please tell me you're not where I think you are."

"Where do you think I am?"

"Don't be cheeky. You're in France, aren't you? You're going after the *Grimorium Bellum.*"

Lydia didn't answer.

"Are you safe?"

"A few close shaves, but so far I'm all right."

Sybil sighed. "I don't suppose there's any way I can convince you to come home?"

Lydia looked around her. Bare trees swayed in the wind, and the sky had gone as purple as a bruise. *Tomorrow. This can all be over tomorrow.*

"No. I need to finish this. If there's even a chance I can prevent more carnage, then—" She stopped as the familiar serpent of grief coiled itself around her lungs.

"It won't bring them back." Sybil looked sad, and for the first time Lydia noticed how tired she looked, the puffiness under her eyes, the lines around her mouth.

"I know."

Sybil huffed. "Damn your stubbornness. I won't force you. But I can't help you either. Vivian and the council have left me rather toothless, I'm afraid. The best I can do is offer you a way home. Say the word, and I'll have a Traveler there for you within the hour. Unless you'd prefer to hike the Pyrenees?"

"A Traveler would be much appreciated. Thank you."

Sybil's tone softened. "Please be safe."

"I will. I promise."

And as quickly as she had appeared, Sybil was gone, leaving Lydia under the swiftly darkening sky. For the first time, Lydia felt the true magnitude of what she was undertaking. She was alone, in occupied territory, without the support or protection of the academy.

She looked up at the château and held herself tightly against the cold. She had made her decision. She would need to find a way to see it through.

"Excusez-moi?" a voice came from behind her, making her jump. "Puis-je vous aider, mademoiselle?"

Lydia turned to see a man a little older than herself standing several meters off, regarding her cautiously. He was tall, well over six feet, lean but broad through the shoulders, with dark brown skin and closely cropped black hair. He was dressed for hiking, and carried a walking stick in his hand.

"Bonsoir, monsieur. Je suis désolée d'imposer—"

"You're English." He eyed her suspiciously. Lydia silently cursed every instructor who had ever praised her accent.

"And you're American," she replied. His voice was deep and soft, with just a hint of some regional inflection she couldn't quite place.

The man looked around warily, as if he expected the Gestapo to jump out of the bushes at any moment.

Lydia set down her bag. "I came alone, Mister . . ."

"Boudreaux. Henry Boudreaux."

So, this was the curator, the one Kitty had mentioned. And not a French *Henri*, as Lydia had thought, but an American *Henry*.

She had an idea. A bad one, possibly, but with the temperature dropping and the sun going down, it would have to do. She extended her hand. "Lydia Polk. From the British Museum in London. Mr. Boudreaux, I'd like to talk to you about your art."

. . .

IT WAS NEARLY AS COLD inside the château as it was outside, with a chill that seemed to radiate from the stone walls themselves. The kitchen had been wired for electricity, but otherwise appeared exactly as it might have in the fifteen hundreds. Centuries of soot blackened the walls and ceiling above the hearth, giving the room a dingy feel. The furniture was a hodgepodge of old and new, and not enough of it to properly fill the space. There was something profoundly sad about the place.

Henry lit a fire. "I would offer you a cup of tea, but we're fresh out." Lydia could sense his wariness, and noticed how he kept his distance from her, even after he'd invited her inside.

"Quite all right. I've actually always preferred coffee."

"Are you sure you're a Brit?" It sounded like it was meant as a joke, but he didn't smile.

"Last I checked."

The fire crackled as he watched her. The air in the room was heavy with the smell of damp and wood smoke.

"I understand you were with the Louvre, before the evacuation," Lydia said. "You must be very good at what you do. The French can be rather superior, I shouldn't think they typically hire—"

"Colored men?"

Lydia felt a flush of embarrassment. "I was going to say Americans, actually."

Henry gave her a long look. "My aunt's a singer. She came over and made a name for herself in Paris after the Great War. Easier for a Black woman to be a respected artist in Paris than stateside these days. I came to live with her while I finished school, then applied to the École du Louvre. I was apprenticing under one of the curators when the Nazis invaded, and the museum was evacuated. He told me I should go home. I refused."

"And you've been here ever since?"

Henry didn't answer. *He doesn't trust me*, Lydia thought. She suspected he hadn't had much reason to trust anyone in a very long time.

"Forgive me, but how does Lydia Polk from the British Museum make her way, alone, into the middle of Nazi-occupied France?"

Lydia opted for something close to the truth. "I crossed the channel on a fishing boat late last night. And I'm not alone, strictly speaking. The museum has partnered with the Special Operations Executive to locate and extract world treasures from the country so they don't end up on the wall of Hitler's mansion or, worse, destroyed. My SOE counterpart is setting up operations nearby."

"And you?"

"Doing inventory." Lydia smiled her warmest, most disarming smile. "I'm to make a list of which pieces are here, then report back. Arrangements will be made for the safe transport of the art out of the country until after the war, at which point they will be returned to the Louvre."

"And where exactly will you be taking them?"

"I'm afraid they don't tell me those sorts of things. Not London, for obvious reasons. Somewhere safe."

Henry crossed his arms. "Miss Polk—"

"Lydia, please."

"Miss Polk. With all due respect, I don't know you. I don't know who you work for. Who's to say that once I hand over these pieces, you won't take them straight to Berlin? Or burn them in a bonfire if they aren't to Hitler's taste?"

Lydia stood a little taller. "With all due respect to *you*, Mr. Boudreaux, how do you think we knew where to find you? Your presence has not gone unnoticed in the village. The Germans will discover you soon enough if they haven't already. If I leave here empty-handed, rest assured, your next visit will undoubtedly be from the SS. And I promise you, they will not ask permission before taking what they want."

Lydia waited as Henry considered her. She imagined that moon again, hanging above her head like a blade, ready to fall.

"Please," she said. "Let me help."

THE STONE STEPS UNDER LYDIA'S feet were perfectly smooth and dipped in the center where four hundred years of footsteps had worn them away. Henry led the way until they reached the topmost floor of the château.

"Where is he now?" Lydia asked. "The curator you came here with?"

"René had personal business to attend to. He should be back in a day or two."

They came to a long, dark room, cold and bare of any furniture save for a handful of scarred tables and chests of drawers. Along the walls, wooden crates of all shapes and sizes leaned against one another. Some were marked with colored circles—red, yellow, green—while others lay hidden under sheets. Henry carried a small oil lamp, which he lifted high, making eerie shapes along the walls.

"Are these all . . ." Lydia trailed off.

"The greatest treasures of the art world. Some of them, at least." Lydia stood for a moment in silence. Henry cleared his throat. "You're an art historian?"

"Yes." She could feel something pulling her into the next room. A low, energetic pulse. *That must be where they kept the book,* she thought with a sudden, exhilarated rush.

"Here, let me show you something." Henry took a crowbar from the floor and used it to crack open a flat crate, letting handfuls of packing straw fall to the floor as he did. Inside was a painting of a seated woman, attended by another woman, who knelt at her feet. The subject was nude and round bellied, with skin the color of milk. She reminded

Lydia of the fertility goddesses she had seen depicted on the walls of the academy.

"She's beautiful." Lydia stepped closer to see more clearly in the flickering lamplight.

"*Bathsheba at Her Bath*. Botticelli."

She could feel his eyes on her, assessing. She tried her best to sound authoritative. "Yes, I know." In the next room, the magical hum continued, demanding her attention. "Is there more in here?"

"Mm-hmm. Follow me."

The next room was much like the last, but smaller and darker. There were more crates, along with some scattered figures draped in sheets, giving Lydia the unnerving sensation that they weren't quite alone. She could feel the diluted power of the *Grimorium Bellum*—smudgy handprints left behind by old, powerful magic. But there was something else, as well. Some newer, fresher magic, laid like a blanket over the old, mixing the signals. The mingling of the two created a dissonant hum that felt like a migraine, and Lydia grimaced, trying to make sense of it.

"Where did you say you went to school?" Henry was standing in the doorway, watching her.

"What?" Lydia couldn't concentrate. The messy, dueling magic seemed to vibrate together, creating a static charge in the air. "What is that smell? Incense?"

"Cedar."

A slow, mounting dread bubbled up inside her. "You burned cedar? Why?"

"Miss Polk." His voice had changed.

"*What?*" She forced herself to block out the tangled hum of magic all around them and looked at Henry.

"You don't work for the British Museum." He leveled his gaze at her. "And you don't know a thing about art."

Lydia blinked. "How dare you. Of course I—"

"That was a Rembrandt back there. Not a Botticelli. A first-year art student would know the difference, but not you. Why is that?" He was blocking her exit.

"I . . . I don't . . ."

"Did you come here for the book?"

Lydia looked around. She smelled the cedar smoke, saw the salt piled in the corners of the room and along the windowsill.

She felt something like panic, rising hot and dangerous in her throat. "What did you do?"

"I sent it away. I hid it."

"I know that. I know you sent it away, but what did you do after that? What did you do to this room?"

Henry tilted his head. "Something my mother taught me back in New Orleans, something she would do when a place had a bad feeling around it. I'm a little out of practice these days, but . . ."

Lydia felt as if she might scream. She opened her mouth, but only a frantic whisper escaped. *"You cleansed the room."*

Now she understood. The magic of the book was too powerful to be wiped away completely, but whatever cleansing ritual Henry had done had been enough to dilute its presence. All that was left was a jumbled signal, like a radio caught between two stations. Lydia would never be able to trace it now.

"Where is the book?" she demanded.

"Whatever you want with it, it's too late. You'll never find it."

Lydia was seething. "Do you understand what you've done? They'll find it now."

"Who?"

"The Nazis, you idiot!" She was shouting, but she didn't care. "You don't have any idea what it really is, do you? You had it in your hands, and you threw it away!"

"I know enough." Henry's voice rose to match hers. "I know that a month ago someone tried to steal it. Someone who looked like René, but *wasn't*. I know how I felt when I held it, like it was whispering to me inside my head."

"Well, congratulations. By tomorrow the Third Reich will have all they need to bring about the end of the world, and you will have helped them do it."

He stood in the doorway, still blocking her path with his body.

Anger and caution battled inside her, but in the end, anger won out. One moment Lydia was inside her body; the next she had projected outside herself and was standing like a specter just behind Henry's left shoulder, making no effort at all to cloak her projection, her strange doppelgänger clearly visible in the dim lamplight.

"Move," she said quietly, "or I will make you."

She waited for him to turn and register her face before returning to her body, and for the first time she thought she saw something that might have been fear in his eyes.

He knows what I am now, she thought. *Good.*

He hesitated for just a moment, then stepped to the side. Lydia walked past him, down the stairs, through the kitchen, and out into the night. She was breathless with rage and unable to stomach the sight of the damned, meddling curator for one second longer. She was already outside when she realized she'd left her coat and bag behind.

To hell with it, she thought. *Soon it won't matter.*

She heard Henry behind her, calling her name. She kept walking across the frozen hillside toward the hazy outline of the village below.

"Miss Polk!"

She turned. Henry stood on the hill, dim firelight pouring from the open door onto the grass. The wind howled, whipping her hair and pulling at her clothes. They faced each other.

"How do I know you're not one of them?" He shouted to be heard over the wind.

Lydia stared at him. "You don't. But I'm not."

He looked as if he'd known that was what she was going to say. She watched as he rubbed one hand over his jaw, muttering to himself.

She stepped closer to hear him over the howling wind. "Excuse me?"

Henry looked at her, and now he didn't look afraid at all. Angry and frustrated, perhaps. But not afraid.

"I said, I can't let you leave."

Twelve

hat do you mean, *you can't let me leave?*"

Henry took a step closer, his hands raised in a placating gesture. Lydia stepped back.

"Listen, if you're a German spy, I can't just let you walk away. If I do that, I'm as good as dead, and nothing I did here will make a bit of difference."

"I'm not a German spy."

"That may be. But I also can't let an Englishwoman wander around the French countryside in the middle of the night. It's not safe. I wouldn't feel right about it."

Lydia considered him, standing there with the wind pulling at his shirtsleeves. He certainly couldn't stop her—she could have overpowered him with a word, although he didn't seem to realize it. She looked around. Night was fully upon them now, and the air was bitterly cold. She had no plan, no allies, and nowhere to take shelter for the night.

She huffed. "What are you suggesting?"

Overhead, the moon peeked her face from behind a drifting cloud. Not quite full. Waiting.

"Come inside," he said.

HENRY LED HER to a small room with a lumpy bed and a high, narrow window, covered over with ironwork.

"Have you eaten?"

It struck Lydia as an incredibly odd question. Moments ago, he'd informed her that she would essentially be his captive, and now he was asking if she'd had any supper. She shook her head.

"There's a little soup left. I'll bring you some." He didn't look at her when he spoke. Lydia wondered if he was still rattled by her trick from earlier. She hoped he was.

"Thank you."

Henry gripped an iron key in his hand. "This is just a precaution, you understand. Just for tonight."

"Locking me in so I don't go running off to my German handler?"

Henry hesitated. He was examining the key with a sudden intense focus. Lydia could guess what was on his mind.

"Are you wondering if that will hold me?"

Henry looked at her and didn't answer.

He still hadn't asked how she'd managed the trick with her projection. *Strange.* Most people would have run screaming or demanded to know how it had been done. But not him.

"You needn't worry," she said. "It's a bit chilly out there for my liking. I have no intention of going anywhere."

To her surprise, Henry nearly laughed but sobered fast. "I'll bring you that soup and some extra blankets." He turned to go, then stopped. "Oh, um . . ." He glanced at her, then away again. "You don't need to worry about me. I understand that's not much comfort under the circumstances, but . . ." He gestured toward a wooden chair tucked away in the corner. "You can stick that under the door handle tonight. If it makes you feel safer. I'm not going to . . ." He stopped, flustered, then tried again. "You don't know me. So I understand if you're anxious. But you don't need to be." He looked like he wanted to disappear.

"I understand. Thank you."

THAT NIGHT Lydia went exploring.

It was true, she could have opened the lock with a word, but projecting was safer, not to mention quieter. She could cloak her projection and wander the château in perfect secrecy, without ever alerting the high-strung curator.

First, she returned to that dark little room where the *Grimorium Bellum* had so recently been kept. She stayed for a long time, trying to make sense of the dissonance in the room—two distinct tones, each making the other's magic unintelligible. She listened, desperately trying to unsnarl the signals, but it was no use. The more she tried, the more tangled they became, and she was forced to give up, panic-stricken and cursing everything—the late hour, that relentless moon, and herself, most of all.

She found herself tuning her ear to that newer magic—Henry's cleansing spell. He was no expert, that much was clear. The magic itself was sophisticated—old, deep magic from a tradition altogether unfamiliar to Lydia. But Henry's execution was clumsy. It was as if he'd been darting glances over his shoulder as the spell came together. An unpracticed caster, Lydia decided. And a fearful one.

She glided on, exploring room after room. There was an extensive library, a music room, several chambers that appeared to have been used only for storage for quite some time. At length she came to a lovingly furnished little bedroom with a cluttered writing desk and a bed piled high with blankets. The desk was covered with journals and papers with scribbled notes in the margins, all in French. There was a half-finished bottle of wine collecting dust on the side table. The glass beside it showed rings where the wine had evaporated over time. Not Henry's room, Lydia decided. This room must have belonged to the other curator. René.

The next chamber was empty, and the one after that. Most doors were locked, but that made no difference to Lydia, who moved through each one like a ghost. She'd begun to feel quite comfortable floating through the musty old château, passing through locked door after locked door with ease.

Until she came face-to-face with Henry Boudreaux, shirtsleeves rolled up and collar unbuttoned, perched on the edge of his bed.

Lydia nearly yelped out loud. She couldn't be seen or heard, that much she knew. Not unless she intended to be. Still, she was unnerved to find herself in such close quarters with the curator, not to mention a little guilty—no one liked to be spied on in their own bedroom. She was just about to go, when she heard him speak.

"Please get out."

He was looking down at his feet, hands folded and head bowed, as if she'd barged in on him in prayer. For a moment she wondered if she'd imagined he'd spoken at all. She was perfectly invisible, she was certain of it, even though at that moment she felt more exposed than she'd ever thought possible. She knew she should leave, and fast, but something, a deep curiosity, made her stay.

"*Please*." There was a soft hitch in his voice. "I can't do this right now. I know you think I can do something for you. And I'm sorry. I really am. But I'm tired, and I just . . . *can't*. So, please, just—" Henry looked up and around the room, searching. "*Please*."

She felt a sudden, intense flush of guilt. This, whatever *this* was, was personal and intimate, and absolutely none of her business. The desperate, pleading tone in his voice could only have been intended for some demon known only to Henry, and certainly not for Lydia herself. She turned, ready to go, when suddenly Henry looked up, and his eyes locked onto her.

"Hello?"

Lydia felt a cold, sinking feeling wash over her. She froze where she stood, waiting for him to look away, but he never did.

"Hello?" he said again, quieter this time.

He wasn't really looking at her. He was looking intently at the space she occupied, but his eyes never met hers. She tried to calm herself, to remember that even Sybil often had trouble detecting her projections, but then Henry stood, coming closer until he was right in front of her. His eyes floated across her face, searching, but never truly seeing. She could see his pulse in his neck, ticking fast. Then his eyes focused.

"*Who are you?*" He spoke so softly that Lydia only knew what he'd said by watching the movement of his lips. She panicked, and a second later was flung back into her body, sitting rigid in her own room on the other side of the château.

She sat, catching her breath for a long time. He'd seen her—no, that wasn't right. He'd *felt her* there in the room with him, something most trained witches could never do. Henry had stood inches from her projection, and on some level, Lydia was certain of it, he had known she was there.

"Who are *you?*" she whispered.

THE NEXT MORNING, Henry came to retrieve her. He stood outside the cracked door with his face turned away.

"There's breakfast downstairs," he said stiffly.

"I'm decent, Mr. Boudreaux, if that's what you're worried about." Henry glanced at her, then away again.

"I'll meet you in the kitchen."

. . . .

THEY SAT ACROSS from each other at the long kitchen table. The fire in the hearth burned merrily, but there was a damp chill that felt endemic to the place. Lydia rubbed her hands together to keep them warm.

"Have you decided yet whether I'm a Nazi spy?"

Henry set down his cup. "I don't think you're a Nazi spy."

"That's something, at least. Why is that, if I may ask?"

"Because your English is perfect and your French is awful. Plus, you're a lousy liar. Doesn't seem like you'd make much of a spy. I'm still trying to decide what you *are* exactly, but . . ."

"What I *am*?" Lydia raised an eyebrow.

She kept waiting for him to come out with it, but he never did. Eventually she took pity on him.

"You're wondering how I left my body yesterday, when you were blocking my path. How I could be standing in front of you one moment and behind you the next."

She almost said, *You're wondering if that was me in your bedroom last night*, but didn't. Henry looked at her and said nothing.

"Come now, Mr. Boudreaux. From what I understand, I'm not even the first of my kind that you've met." Henry flinched. "She was a friend of mine, by the way. Kitty. Your shape-shifter."

"Is that her name?" Henry looked like the memory unsettled him. "That was just about the craziest thing I've ever seen. One second, I think I'm looking at René, a man I've lived with for three years. A man who's like a father to me. The next second, he . . . well he's not even a he anymore, he's . . . *Kitty?* Just about the strongest damn woman I've ever met in my life, by the way, who kicks and bites and screams like a banshee, then disappears before my very eyes."

Lydia smiled, picturing it.

"I think I socked her pretty hard. She okay?"

The pain was instantaneous, like an electric shock. Lydia took a moment to catch her breath. "No. She's not. But through no fault of yours."

Henry looked surprised. "What happened?"

"A Nazi witch murdered her."

Henry seemed at a loss. He inspected a groove in the table, worrying it with his finger. "A witch."

"Yes."

"So, then Kitty . . ."

"Was a witch. Yes."

Henry looked at Lydia. "And . . . *you?*"

She smiled. Henry stood and refilled his cup with shaking hands.

"Henry, I know this is difficult, but I need to know. Where is the book now?"

"I don't know."

"Henry—"

"No, I honestly don't know. When René took it away, I told him I didn't want to know where he was going. I figured your friend Kitty probably wasn't the only person looking for it. If someone else came around, I wanted to be sure they wouldn't be able to find out where he'd taken it."

Damn. "Where is René now?"

Henry exhaled. "I don't know. He said he would write after he'd hidden the book to let me know he was okay. That was over a month ago. I haven't heard anything since."

He was in pain. The love for his mentor sharpening into a weapon, pointed at his own heart. Lydia understood. "I'm sorry."

He nodded, but didn't look at her.

"Henry, yesterday you said that it felt like the book was whispering to you. What did you mean by that?"

Henry stared into the fire. Lydia waited. He said something under his breath, so softly she couldn't make it out.

"Henry?"

"It wanted me to read it. Out loud." He looked at her. "I don't know how I know that. I just do."

Lydia felt a chill run through her. "But you didn't."

"I couldn't. I didn't know how. But that didn't make it stop. Every time I touched it, it was like voices in my head, this constant chattering. I thought I was losing my mind."

"What about René? Did he hear it too?"

Henry shook his head.

"Fascinating." Lydia watched Henry with new interest. "Your mother. I think she must be a witch."

Henry looked up at her so sharply that Lydia felt her breath catch. "What makes you say that?"

She forced herself to smile, even though his reaction had caught her off guard. "I meant no offense. Not all who practice the old ways call themselves witches. But I believe she must have some magic in her. That's why the book spoke to you. You have her blood."

"So, I'm a witch now too?"

Lydia considered it. Magic in men was rare, but not unheard of. What was it her gran used to say? *Men have power the moment they enter the world. Women have to make their own.* Only that wasn't quite true, was it? Only certain men were born with the sort of power her gran had been referring to. And Henry was most certainly not one of them.

"I don't know. Do most ordinary men know how to cast a cleansing spell like the one upstairs?"

He stood with his hands in his pockets and didn't answer.

"Henry, I realize you have no reason to trust me. But if the Nazis get to that book before I do, it could mean the end of everything. I have to find it."

Henry regarded her for a moment, then looked away. "I don't know how to help you. I don't even know if I *should* help you, but it doesn't matter. The book is gone."

"There are ways to track it down. I could have traced it from the room upstairs, but that cleansing spell you cast has made that impossible. That leaves me with one other option."

"Which is?"

"*You* touched the book. An object that powerful leaves behind a mark. It will be faint, but it could be enough."

Henry stiffened. "No."

"Henry . . ."

"*No.* Maybe you're telling me the truth, and maybe you're on the right side of all this, but I can't take that chance."

"Henry, please just—"

"What would you even do with it once you found it?" His eyes bored into hers, accusing her. "This thing must be pretty powerful for you to go to all this trouble. You're afraid of what the Nazis will do once they get their hands on it, but what about you? What will *you* do?"

"I would never—"

"*I don't know you.* You want my help, but all you've given me since the moment we met is lies and magic tricks. Why would I trust you?"

His intensity was startling, and Lydia felt herself go still as a rabbit under his gaze. After a moment he seemed to deflate. "I'm sorry," he said quietly. "I just . . . I can't help you."

They sat in silence as the fire burned down, and the chill that had been creeping at the edges of the room seemed to unfurl. After a long time, Henry stood and began clearing the plates and cups from the table. Lydia watched him, and just as he was about to finish, she spoke.

"What about your friend?"

He cocked his head. A warning. "What about him?"

"He's been missing how long now?"

Henry exhaled slowly. "Almost five weeks."

"I can find him, you know. If he's still with the book, that is. Even if he's not, it would be a start."

Moments passed, and she watched as his features seemed to sag. He shook his head.

"That's not right," he said softly.

Lydia felt a shudder of something like shame go through her. "What?"

He looked away from her. "You're ransoming my friend so I'll help you." He shook his head again. "I'll do it. But it's not right." Henry turned to go.

"Wait." Lydia's cheeks were hot, and there was a sick, churning feeling inside her stomach, but she carried on. "There's something else."

Henry looked at her. She hated that look, the resigned contempt in it.

"Tracing an object through another person. It's hard. Messy. I've done it before, but I was with a full coven. I'm not strong enough to do it alone."

Henry rubbed his hand along the back of his neck. "I'm not sure how to help you there. I don't think there are any covens around here I can just call up."

"No, I didn't think so." She swallowed to steady her voice. "I might be able to do it alone, if we were in a place of power."

"A what?"

"A place of power, like a stone circle, or a spring, perhaps a burial mound. England is covered with them. I suppose France is, too, but I don't know the land here. Not just any spring will do, you understand. There's a feeling, it's . . ." She faltered, unsure how to explain what it felt like to stand in such a place to someone who had never experienced it.

He regarded her for a moment in silence, and Lydia saw something settle over him—a decision being made. The wariness was still there in his eyes. She couldn't blame him. Still, she held her breath and hoped.

Thirteen

They set out that night with the full moon hanging above them, silent and watchful. Henry led the way through the thick woods, the light from the electric torch bouncing in the darkness. The forest stretched out before them, the moon bathing the trees in silver. Lydia felt a lump of anxiety forming in the pit of her stomach. If she failed tonight, all her efforts would have been for nothing.

"What if we get lost?" she whispered.

"We won't. I've been hiking these trails for three years. I could find my way blindfolded."

They walked in silence, occasionally pausing when a sound from the darkness made them stop in their tracks, listening and waiting.

"Are you worried about animals?" she asked.

"Only the kind that walk on two legs and speak German."

Lydia was reminded of hiking through the Scottish Highlands on a trip to visit Kitty's family several years before. They had walked until they were both red-faced and sore, and sat, looking out over the rolling hills of moss and thistle, drinking the scotch they'd nicked from Kitty's father. Just thinking about it made the grief rise in Lydia's throat.

Henry broke the silence. "Can I ask you a question?"

She coughed to hide the tremor in her voice. "Of course."

"Why don't you just kill Hitler?"

"Using magic, you mean?"

"Yeah. Careful here." He scrambled down a steep and rocky hill. To Lydia's surprise, he turned and held out his hand for her as she followed, steadying her, but he pulled away again the moment she was on solid ground.

"We tried. Several times, actually. It's not as simple as chanting a few words from across the channel, you know. To kill, you need to be close, and it's taxing on the witch, too taxing for most of us to even attempt it."

"And?"

Lydia shuddered. She hadn't known any of the girls well, but their names had haunted the halls of the academy for months after their deaths. *Genevieve Wood. Sarah Marlowe. Gillian March. Juniper Flynn.*

"None of them ever came back. After the last time, the council wouldn't approve any more attempts, and the mission was abandoned. Their poor families. None of them ever found out what really happened."

"What did happen?"

Lydia's mind turned involuntarily to the shredded doorway in the warding of the academy. "I used to think they were just unlucky. Now I wonder if he isn't protected by some magic. Or else . . ."

Or else someone warned Hitler about the assassination attempt. The thought came to her unbidden, quick and ugly. She imagined Vivian, how smug she'd looked that Samhain night. Vivian, the great Seer, standing by as Isadora's throat was cut before her very eyes.

"Or else?" Henry watched her, waiting.

Lydia shook her head. "I don't know."

They walked for over an hour, as shrubs and trees gave way to limestone cliffs. Henry walked ahead of her, his broad frame aglow with soft silver light filtering down through the trees, and Lydia found herself thinking that he was surprisingly graceful for a man of his size.

She looked up at the moon overhead. Her stomach turned inside her as she wondered again if Henry could be right about this cave. There would be no other chances.

They scrambled over rocks and between trees until they came to what appeared to be little more than a hole in the ground. Lydia's heart sank as Henry ducked inside, then held out a hand to her. She approached the mouth of the cave and peered inside.

"Henry, I don't think—"

"Please. Just look."

Lydia huffed and took his hand. The darkness inside the passage was so total that the light from the torch seemed to be swallowed up by it, the narrow tunnel threatening to collapse in on them at any moment. Lydia breathed deeply, trying to overcome the smothering claustrophobia.

The atmosphere changed as they reached the end of the passage and emerged into a large chamber. The air was cool and still, and so silent it was as if someone had enveloped them in cotton batting. Lydia's eyes struggled in vain against the wall of total darkness. She took one uncertain step, then lost her footing as the ground dipped under her feet. Before she even realized she'd cried out, Henry was there, one hand around her waist, the other on her shoulder, catching her midair, almost as if they'd been dancing.

"Careful." Lydia felt Henry's breath on her ear as he set her back on her feet, making her skin prickle. His body felt surprisingly solid under her hands, and she backed away, flustered. She suddenly remembered that Kitty had called him handsome, and she had to admit that he was, in a quiet, unassuming sort of way. Funny, in the daylight she'd thought of him as rather bookish.

Lydia stilled her heart and listened. She felt the thrum of something alive, there in the cave with them. It tasted like copper and made the blood rush in her throat. Ancient magic, she realized with a wave of astonishment. So old and wild she almost didn't recognize it for what it was.

There was a spark in the darkness, followed by a swell of light. Henry knelt over an old kerosene lamp that had been left sitting in the middle of the chamber floor, and Lydia breathed a sigh of relief as the contours of the cave revealed themselves. Henry brushed himself off and stood, holding the lamp high over his head.

Lydia looked up and gasped.

Massive creatures adorned the ceiling of the cave, painted by some unknown hand in shades of black and ocher. Bulls and horses appeared to stampede across the stone in undulating waves. Great horned oxen several meters long towered over herds of tiny, delicate red deer. Lydia turned and turned, trying to take them all in at once, marveling at the beauty and the scale of the creatures before her.

"What is this place?"

"A couple of local kids found it a few years ago." Henry stared up at the painted ceiling in appreciation and wonder. "Their dog went down a fox hole, and when they went after him, this is what they found. Started charging their friends admission to see it."

"It's incredible." The magic in the cave seemed to bump up against her, making the hairs on her arms stand on end. It felt like being in a confined space with a wild animal, powerful and beautiful, and dangerous. "Who made them?"

"I don't know. It seems like it might have been many people, over thousands of years."

"They were all drawn to this place."

"Yes."

Lydia turned to see Henry's face as he gazed at the paintings. In his eyes, she thought she saw something like religious devotion.

"There's more, if you'd like to see it."

Lydia did want to, desperately. She would have liked to spend hours exploring every corner of the cave, discovering every shape and figure and committing them to memory. But she shook her head.

"Not tonight."

Henry looked at his watch and nodded. "How do we start?"

Lydia walked to the center of the cave and knelt on the cold stone. After a moment she beckoned for Henry to join her. All around them, horses and bulls were cast into shadows. Lydia thought they seemed to move in the darkness.

"Time?" she asked.

"Nearly midnight."

"Good."

Henry looked around. "Will it, uh . . . hurt?"

"Not at all. I'm simply using the energy left behind on you from the book to project my consciousness to where it's being kept now."

"Right. Sounds simple."

"It may feel strange at first. Tracking like this has a way of opening up a channel between people. You may see things you don't understand. Memories that aren't yours, sensations—"

"Are you telling me you'll be able to see inside my head?" Henry looked as if he were about to turn and walk right back out of the cave.

"Only for a moment. And you'll be in my head as much as I'm in yours." Henry didn't look reassured. Lydia cleared her throat, desperate to relieve the tension. "It may take me some time. I'll need to look around once I get there, to know where I am, and where we need to go to find the book. And, well . . ."

"What?"

Lydia hesitated. "I won't be alone. I expect the Nazis will be casting their own tracking spell at the same moment we are. That means when I project to the book, they'll be doing the same."

Henry shifted back on his heels. "That sounds dangerous."

"Neither of us will be in our bodies. If René is still there, no one will be able to harm him. I promise."

Henry didn't look convinced, but nodded. "Midnight."

Lydia reached out and took both of Henry's hands. His palms felt warm and smooth pressed against her own. Around them, the hum of the cave became more urgent. Lydia let her gaze go soft as she reached for Henry in her mind. He was there—reticent, suspicious, but present, just the same.

The first sensation she noticed was a smell—a sweet, green forest smell, like the woods around Château de Laurier, one that reminded her of dappled, dancing sunlight and fresh, cool water. Then, something else—a stale, dusty book smell that could only have been a library. Then tobacco smoke. Horses. Cooking smells, onions, citrus, peppers so hot they made her nose prickle. Then something almost like coffee that she couldn't quite put her finger on. *Chicory.* The word appeared in her mind like something rising from deep water, then receded again.

Sounds followed. She heard drums and singing, and felt a swell of something she could only describe as *joy.* She saw complex, looping symbols she didn't understand, but knew carried strong magic. She saw a glimpse of a beautiful, middle-aged woman dressed all in white, hair tied beneath a cloth, with sharp eyes and deep bronze skin. *Mama,* Henry's mind whispered, and Lydia felt a steady warmth blooming beneath her rib cage like jasmine blossoms.

The scene changed, and for one strange, disorienting moment she saw herself. She was standing on the hillside outside of Château de Laurier, but through the lens of Henry's memory she hardly recognized herself. She looked different in his mind, all dark, windswept hair and flashing gray eyes. Not prim or severe like she'd always imagined herself, but wild and mysterious, and achingly, searingly beautiful.

That image disappeared as quickly as it had appeared, and slowly, Lydia began to feel something like dread churning up from the riverbed of Henry's memories. She saw things she didn't understand—doors, dozens of them, standing open, with nothing on the other side but a black, yawning void. She saw eyes, all pearly white and glowing, set into faces that looked like death masks. She heard whispered voices making demands. She felt cold hands pawing at her, fingers scrabbling at her face, her eyes, her mouth. One of them worked its way into her throat, and Lydia gagged.

Reeling, she stumbled away from the dead eyes and the desperate, probing fingers, fighting toward the silent, lurking thing at the center of Henry's mind. It was a cold, empty space, far away from everything else, as if whatever lived there had driven every other memory into hiding. And there, surrounded by the droning of corpse flies, she saw it—an ancient book, with a cracked leather binding.

Lydia braced herself as the power in the cave awoke, as it began to thrash and howl. It was wilder than any magic she had ever encountered, and more powerful—nothing like the tame, orderly magic she had experienced in the ceremonial chamber of the academy. She felt her breath quicken as it coursed through her, lifting her up out of her body on a current, electric and intoxicating. She felt a stomach-churning tug as she was pulled through space and matter. For one terrifying moment it felt as if she would be torn apart and become one with the magic itself. She tried not to scream as she twisted and writhed within it. Then, abruptly, all was quiet.

She was in a farmhouse.

She let the frenzied magic of the cave leave her, feeling her pulse return to normal. She blinked to clear the spots from her vision and looked around.

The place was abandoned. A bitter wind blew through the open door, and the hearth was cold. Remnants of some long-ago meal sat forgotten at the kitchen table, the bread gone moldy. A chair lay overturned on the wood floor, surrounded by shards of blue and white crockery.

"*Hallo.*" A woman stood by the open window, moonlight turning her blond hair silver. Even though her image trembled like water, Lydia recognized her.

"*You.*"

The blond witch tilted her head and grinned. Lydia could make out faint shapes in the darkness behind her. Other women, standing shoulder to shoulder in some candlelit room, far, far away.

"You're not alone," Lydia said. *Isadora was right*, she realized with a rush of grief and pride. *They have a coven.*

"But you are." Her English was clipped, with a distinctly Germanic flavor. "Interesting. Has your high council abandoned you, then?" She chuckled softly. "Oh dear. That is unfortunate."

Lydia wanted to hurt her. She wanted to do it with her hands, no spells, no magic. She wanted her to die the way Kitty and Isadora had. Bleeding and afraid.

The witch seemed to know what she was thinking. "It's not personal, you know. We have no quarrel with you. We are not so different from one another, after all."

Lydia was filled with revulsion. "We have nothing in common."

"No?" The witch raised an eyebrow. "We are all followers of the old ways."

"You twist the old ways to support the cause of a madman. How could you do it?"

The witch shrugged, amused.

"Answer me!"

She looked around, considering her reply. "What will you do after the war? Will you go back into hiding? Continue to cast your little spells in secret while your country forgets you? While the witches of Britain fade into myth?"

Lydia did not respond.

"My mother lived her whole life in secret, you know. Ashamed of what she was, unable to control her powers. She thought she was losing her mind. And soon enough, she did." The witch's eyes glittered in the dark. "*That* is what comes from a life lived in secret. Suffering and death, nothing more. But the Führer remembers that once the witches of Germany were more than fairy stories. He knows that returning Germany to her true glory will require the power of the witch." She stepped closer, so close they could have touched. "The Führer will bring about a Thousand-Year Reich, and when he does, the witches of Germany will be by his side. We are done hiding in the shadows."

Lydia couldn't conceal her contempt. "Selling your soul to the most evil man in Europe in exchange for power and glory."

The witch laughed. "So self-righteous! But just wait. When Germany is victorious, you will see how much better life can be for people like us."

She's distracting you, Lydia thought. She forced herself to turn her back on the witch and focus on the task at hand. *Plaster walls, wood floor, humble furnishings.* She stole a glance at a book, sitting open on a tattered armchair. It was written in French.

The witch seemed uninterested in investigating the farmhouse, as if she had all the time in the world. Instead, she watched Lydia, chuckling to herself.

"So, you're a Projectionist," Lydia said. "A Projectionist, and a Glamourer, and a Traveler. That's rather rare, to be all three." The witch smiled. "What's your name?"

"Why, so you can use it to hex me?" The witch clicked her tongue. "I think not."

"Just exchanging pleasantries."

Lydia made her way to the window. Outside, scrubby hills lay bare under a clear night sky. *No mountains,* Lydia thought. *No cities, no church, no landmarks.* A giant oak tree stood in the distance, branches twisting in the wind. She strained her eyes against the darkness. There was something odd about the tree, something she couldn't quite make out. Something slumped against the massive trunk, framed in moonlight.

A body.

Lydia stared. It was the body of a man, but that was all she could make out in the dark. Behind her, the blond witch laughed softly to herself.

"You know, when we have the *Grimorium Bellum*, the witches of England will be wiped from the earth, along with the Juden, and the Homosexuelle, and the Zigeuner. A necessary evil, you understand. All who oppose the Führer must be exterminated." She grinned wide. "Unless, of course, you join us. What has Britain done for witches, after all? Hanged them and despised them and drove them into hiding." Her voice became serious. "Swear your allegiance to the Führer. Join the Witches of the Third Reich. And the *Grimorium Bellum* will spare you."

Lydia turned to face her. "You'll never find the *Grimorium Bellum*."

"On the contrary. I've already found it."

Lydia felt cold dread rising in her. "Nonsense."

"You should think about my offer. It would be a shame if any more of your friends died in vain."

Hate swelled in Lydia's chest. "You should know I'm going to kill you."

The witch grinned. "Perhaps. But not tonight."

Lydia did not respond.

"Auf Wiedersehen, Lydia Polk."

And she was gone.

Lydia stood in the silence as despair began to slowly close around her like water. The Nazis had discovered the location of the book. And they were coming for it.

"*Focus*, damn you," she hissed. There was still time.

Without the witch to distract her, Lydia could begin to feel the hideous call of dark magic that filled the house. She went and stood where the humming was loudest, and thought she could feel the book reaching up, clawing at her through the floorboards, wanting to be found.

She scoured the room, looking for letters, anything with an address. She scanned the horizon, searching again for signposts, buildings, mountains, anything to give her a hint to the location. She paced the room, taking an inventory of every detail: knitting left half-finished in a basket. A pair of glasses. An unusual silver ornament nailed to the doorframe. A child's drawing, with the name Jean-Luc scrawled in clumsy script at the bottom.

She considered the body in the yard. Perhaps it held some clue, some hint about the location of the house. The problem, of course, was the *Grimorium Bellum*—her projection was tied to it, and wandering very far from its location would be impossible. She stood in the open doorway and looked out at the slumped figure. Even here, she could feel the book drawing her back like gravity. She took one step forward, then another, but collapsed under the weight of its pull. She turned back, hysteria rising in her. She'd been projecting for too long. Her body was beginning to tire, and she was no closer to discovering the location of the house. She choked back a sob. She had seen everything the house had to offer her. And it wasn't enough.

She returned to her body with a gasp.

"*Jesus.*" Henry held her shoulders as she gulped air. "Your hands were so cold. And you were so still. For a minute I thought . . ."

"That happens. I'm all right."

To her surprise, he didn't let her go right away. He kept his hands on her, steadying her as she caught her breath. She could feel his eyes on her, watching as the color returned to her cheeks. He seemed to be catching his breath as well, like he'd been holding it, waiting for her to come back.

"Did you find it?" There, under his words, Lydia could hear the other silent question. *Did you find René?*

The cave seemed to swim around her. *How long was I gone?*, she wondered dimly.

"Lydia?"

"I could feel it. I was there, I could feel the book, but I don't know where I was."

"Okay, but you can try again, right?"

She felt as if she might burst into tears. "No. You don't understand. This was my one chance. I can't track the book again until the next full moon, and by then it will be too late."

Henry was quiet. "And the Germans?"

"They sent someone, but she left before I did." Lydia's voice shook. "It was the same woman, the one who killed Kitty and Isadora. She knows the location. I don't know how, but she does."

Henry's eyes went wide. "If René is still there . . ."

"He isn't."

Tell him, a voice inside her head commanded. *He deserves to know.*

"Henry, when I was at the house . . . I saw what I believe was the body of a man. I couldn't see his face, but . . ." She trailed off, unable to finish the thought. She watched him as the full meaning of her words sank in.

Henry slumped back against the cave wall. They sat in the yellow glow of the kerosene lamp, the only sound the dripping of water somewhere deeper in the cave. After a long moment, Henry ran a hand over his face and stared up at the painted menagerie of ancient deer and oxen, as if asking them for the answer to some question.

"Tell me what you saw at the house."

She shook her head. "Nothing useful. No street markers or letters, nothing with an address." She hung her head. "Besides, we're too late. It doesn't matter now."

"Of course it *matters*," Henry said sharply. "It matters to me."

Lydia looked at his face, all hard angles in the sputtering lamp-light.

Like a father. That's what Henry had said about René. René, who more than likely was out there even now, cold and alone under that oak tree.

"I didn't mean . . ." She stopped. "I'm sorry. I only meant that it's too late to find the book. The other witch, the one who was there with me at the house. She's a Traveler."

Henry's brow furrowed. "You've lost me. What's a Traveler?"

"A Traveler is a witch who can move from place to place at will. All she has to do is close her eyes and she can be anywhere. Which means she probably has the book even now."

"Did you see her take it?"

The room stopped spinning. She looked at Henry. "No."

"So maybe she didn't figure it out, after all. Maybe she was lying."

"Why would she do that?"

"I don't know. But you didn't see her take the book, so there's still hope. And if René is—" He stopped. There was a quick sound in his throat, a sort of choking spasm. Lydia knew it well. "Please. Tell me about the house."

"It was just an ordinary house. The books were in French, so maybe France, but it could just as easily be Belgium or Switzerland, or a hundred other places. It was abandoned, like everyone had been spirited away in the middle of dinner."

Henry closed his eyes, thinking.

"Any landmarks?"

"No."

"Rivers? Lakes? Bodies of water?"

"No. I looked everywhere. No address, no landmarks, no photographs."

"Artwork? The Louvre hid pieces in homes and castles all over France, maybe René went to one of them."

The cold, helpless feeling was rising in her again, ready to drown her. "No. The only art was a child's drawing. And some sort of silver ornament hanging by the door."

Henry tilted his head. "An ornament?"

"Yes. Long and narrow, the size of a finger. Nailed to the doorframe."

He closed his eyes. "A mezuzah."

"A what?"

"A mezuzah. Jewish families hang them on their doorposts as a sign of faith." His voice was low. Almost mournful.

Lydia remembered the overturned chair, the broken crockery. Food left on the table, as if the family had been dragged away mid-meal.

"What about the drawing?" He didn't look at her, but Lydia could feel something dark and heavy slip into the room with them. Something ugly.

"It was a cat. It was signed 'Jean-Luc.'"

Henry stood, rubbing the bridge of his nose as if he had a headache. He was silent for a long time.

"Jean-Luc is René's nephew."

The heaviness crawled inside Lydia's chest, coiling itself around her heart.

"How old is Jean-Luc?" She'd nearly said, *How old was Jean-Luc?*

"Nine."

Mother, protect him, she thought.

She looked at Henry. His posture was rigid, as if even the slightest movement would cause everything he was feeling to burst out of him. She wanted to tell him she was sorry. She wanted to tell him she understood what it was to lose someone, how it feels like you're the one who's dying, even when you keep on living, day after day.

"Maybe it isn't René." She almost reached out and took his hand, but something in the shape of his body let her know the gesture would not be welcome. "The body. Maybe it's someone else."

Henry didn't look at her. Instead he stared into the darkness in front of him, grappling with some monster only he could see. After a moment his eyes cleared. He looked at her, his face resigned.

"I know where the house is."

Fourteen

Rebecca's contact was late.

She had chosen her seat at this café for its view of the clock tower in the town square, which now indicated that it was ten past two. She should have left five minutes ago. It was one of her rules not to hang around if a contact was late, one of the many ways she'd stayed alive as long as she had. But André was notorious for never being where he was supposed to be when he was supposed to be there—and he was carrying an envelope full of intelligence for the SOE, which Rebecca was meant to hand off to David Harlowe at their next rendezvous.

Five more minutes, she told herself.

She sipped her wine. At another table, two men were discussing the excitement from the night before in hushed tones.

"Did you see the smoke?"

"Couldn't miss it. My nephew walked by there this morning on his way to work. Said there was a train on the tracks, got blown straight to hell. Looted, too, from the looks of it."

"What was it carrying?"

"Guns."

The other man whistled low. Rebecca raised her book to cover her smile.

The waitress approached Rebecca's table. She was a sweet-faced girl, strawberry blond and covered in freckles.

"Can I get you anything else, mademoiselle?"

Rebecca set down her book. "Another glass of the cabernet for me, and one for my tardy friend as well."

The waitress cleared her throat, then held Rebecca's gaze. "I'm afraid we are all out of the cabernet." Her eyes flicked toward the door. "Will there be anything else?" The girl's irises seemed to pulse.

Rebecca felt a stab of dread. She smiled. "Non. Merci beaucoup." She pulled a ration ticket from her purse to pay for her wine, then quietly removed an envelope full of banknotes and placed it on her seat for the waitress.

Waiters see everything, her friend Colette once told her. *Barmen too. Keep a few in your pocket, and you can learn all sorts of interesting things.*

She surveyed the room. Two men were seated by the window, clearly locals. One elderly woman, drunk and alone. Two young women with babes in arms. And the man at the table by the door, reading the newspaper without moving his eyes.

She placed her book inside her bag and walked calmly toward the door. She did not look back when she reached the street, but knew he was behind her just the same. She reached inside her bag and wrapped her hand around her pistol.

She didn't notice the young woman with the chestnut curls, walking toward her as if she were on her way into the café. They were just about to pass each other when the woman changed course, stepping swiftly into Rebecca's path and taking her by the lapel.

"*Behave.*" Her voice seemed to slip inside Rebecca's skull like a snake.

It wrapped itself around her mind, until Rebecca found she could not speak a word or take another step unless the woman told her to.

"Ether won't be necessary," the woman said. Rebecca turned to see the man from the café, with a rag in his hand. He looked disappointed. "You're going to *come with us*, aren't you?" The words seemed to penetrate deep into her brain, sharp and violating.

To her horror, Rebecca found herself walking placidly alongside the woman, as if they were old friends. Inside she screamed and fought, yet somehow, she could not bring her feet to disobey.

They came to a black car. "*Get in.*"

Rebecca did as she was told, climbing into the back seat even as panic swelled up inside her. She willed herself to run, but it was no use. She was no longer in control of her own body.

"We're just going to leave her sitting in the back seat like that?" said the man.

"Why not? She's not going anywhere."

"It's creepy," he grumbled.

"Well, if it makes you more comfortable . . ." The woman leaned down and placed her face close to Rebecca's. "*Sleep.*"

Rebecca felt a terror like electricity flow through her. She fought to stay awake, trying to focus her attention on anything she could—green flecks in the irises of the chestnut-haired woman, cracks in the stones outside the café, ivy creeping up the base of the clock tower, and—just before she closed her eyes—a bone-handled dagger, sheathed on the woman's hip, with a rune carved into the hilt.

SHE WOKE IN A COLD, gray room, wrists bound to her chair, with a blinding light in her face.

"Your friend betrayed you."

Rebecca blinked. The room was dark and windowless, with water stains running down the walls, and a single bulb hanging overhead. She smelled bleach, the stink of it searing her nostrils. The man from the café sat before her, smoking a cigarette. She strained at her ropes, finding to her relief that her body was hers to control once again.

"To his credit, he held out two, almost three hours before he started talking." The man exhaled a plume of smoke into her face.

André, you weak, stupid putz. She'd known André was a liability from the start. He was careless and arrogant, flouting the rules at every turn. He'd never been truly committed to the Resistance. Just a boy, running from the city to avoid compulsory service in some German work camp. And now he'd broken the most important rule of all—that on the day the bastards finally catch you, you keep your mouth shut. You keep your mouth shut for one full day, long enough for your friends to realize you've gone missing, and scatter. Only then do you give them what they want. Only then do you break.

The Gestapo flicked ash from his cigarette onto the cement floor. "He didn't know much. Just a small fish. But he assured us that you would be far more knowledgeable. Lucky for you, we are prepared to make you the same offer we made your friend. Give us the names and locations of all of your coconspirators, and you will be allowed to live."

"Please, monsieur, I don't know what you're talking about!" The fear in her voice was real. Letting it out was almost a relief—she imagined the terrified girl she'd always kept buried deep inside her, breathing free air, just this once. "Please, you have the wrong person."

He smiled. "No. I don't."

She strained at her bonds. "I'm not with the Resistance. I'm nothing. I'm just a woman. Please."

"You Frenchwomen. You are beautiful. But you lie like you breathe."

He reached out and grabbed her roughly by the jaw, turning her head to the side. He placed his lit cigarette close to the flesh of her throat. "You will not be so beautiful when you leave here."

Fear snatched the breath from her lungs. "Please—"

He ground the cigarette into her neck, and she screamed as the pain coursed through her like fire.

"Names." The man lit another cigarette.

"I don't know what you—"

He punched her, hard. She tasted blood.

"Names."

"Please—"

"*Names.*" He raised his fist.

"Okay, okay." She took a breath. "Claudette Colbert. Buster Keaton. Bette Davis, Humphrey Bogart, Claude Raines . . ."

"Bitch." He punched her again. Her vision slipped inside her skull.

"Shirley Temple, Jimmy Stewart—"

"Enough."

"You said you wanted names." Rebecca stared at him through her blurring vision.

The man let out a barking laugh and examined his knuckles. "You will get worse than a beating if you don't talk, you know." He raised his eyebrows, waiting for a reaction. "Not from me, of course. I am a gentleman. Some of the others here . . ." He shrugged. "Not so much." He leaned down so they were face to face. "I don't think you want to die." He reached out and stroked her cheek, and Rebecca felt all the fear inside of her congealing into a thick, black spite.

She spat, blood and spit swirling together on the man's face. He reared back in disgust. She laughed, then took a deep breath, and sang as loudly as she could:

"Allons enfants de la Patrie, le jour de gloire est arrivé! Contre nous de la tyrannie, l'étendard sanglant est levé! L'étendard sanglant est levé!"

"Have it your way." He opened the heavy metal door and left, wiping the blood and spit from his face.

She carried on singing until she was hoarse, and her vision stopped swimming. *Let the bastards hear me,* she thought. *If I die it will be with "La Marseillaise" on my tongue.* When her voice failed her, she found other ways to keep her mind occupied. She strained at her bonds until her wrists were raw. She took an inventory of the room. There was a telephone on a table in the corner—she imagined she could put the cord to good use should the opportunity arise. On the floor next to the wall sat a brick, the type one might have used to prop a door open—small enough to wield one-handed, but large enough to use as a bludgeon. She understood that she would probably die here—she could feel the truth of it deep in her guts, like a tumor. Still, it brought her comfort to pretend she might live.

In the murky far corner of the room, something caught her eye—movement, like something glimpsed under water. Was there someone else in here? No, she was certain she was alone. She closed her eyes. She counted to ten.

When she opened her eyes, the Englishwoman was there in the room with her.

"Rebecca? Great Mother, what's happened?"

She blinked at Lydia's trembling image. "*You.*"

Lydia cocked her head to one side. "Yes, me. What on earth—"

"Putain de sorcière démoniaque! C'est toi qui a fait ça n'est ce pas? J'aurais dû te tuer lorsque j'en avais l'opportunité—"

Lydia blanched. "Rebecca, what are you—"

"Do you think I'm stupid? Twenty-two years I've never met a witch. This week I've met *two.* Am I supposed to think that's a coincidence?"

"Another witch? Rebecca—"

"She was inside my head!" Rebecca's voice cracked. "She told me to get in the car, and I did it. She told me to *behave.* You expect me to believe that had nothing to do with you?" The violation seemed to hit her all at once—the loss of her autonomy for those few horrible moments. She had been helpless, and that enraged her.

"Rebecca, I promise, whatever happened to you, I had nothing to do with it."

Rebecca felt blood gathering in her mouth. She spat it out on the floor. "Go to hell."

Lydia watched silently for a moment, her image wavering in the dim light. She seemed somehow less solid than she ought to be. Eventually, Rebecca's curiosity got the better of her.

"Why do you look like that?"

Lydia sighed. "What you're seeing is my projection. I'm not really here. My body is at Château de Laurier. Rebecca, *where are you?*"

Rebecca stared at the floor in front of her and did not answer.

"Goddamn it, Rebecca, I'm trying to help you!"

"I don't know where I am. I was unconscious when they brought me here."

"They who? Who took you?"

"A man and a woman. He's Gestapo. The woman, she's . . ." Rebecca felt a shudder run through her. She could still see the woman's smiling face, with something cruel lurking just behind the eyes. "When she spoke to me, I couldn't disobey. Anything she told me to do, I had to do it. And she had a knife. Bone handle, with a rune."

Rebecca watched as the color drained from Lydia's face.

"I'm going to get you out of there."

"That would be good. What are you doing here, anyway, *sorcière?*" She felt her rage beginning to ebb, replaced by a feeble whiff of hope.

"I need to get to Auvergne. I was going to talk to you about your car, although I can see now that will have to wait."

The sound of footsteps made them both fall silent.

Lydia spoke quickly. "They can't see or hear me. You're the only one who knows I'm here. Do you understand?"

Rebecca blinked at her. "I don't understand any of this."

The door opened. The woman with the chestnut curls entered the room and gave a sympathetic pout as she regarded Rebecca's battered face. Then she closed the door firmly behind her. Rebecca heard the lock click into place with a horrible finality and felt her heart skitter against her rib cage.

The chestnut-haired woman removed her jacket and draped it carefully over the back of her chair. It was crimson red, the color of fresh blood. She clucked over Rebecca like a mother hen as she took her seat.

"Oh dear, he really let you have it, didn't he?" She spoke French with only a wisp of an accent, subtle enough that a casual listener might not notice it at all. "So unnecessary. And pointless. You strike me as a woman who can withstand a beating."

Rebecca did not reply.

The woman leaned in conspiratorially. "The secret, of course, is that they're not interested in extracting information at all. Only in causing pain." She rolled her eyes. "*Men.*"

"But not you," Rebecca said. "You want to be my friend, yes?"

"Your friend? Goodness, no. I want what I came for. I want the names and locations of every member of your organization. And you're going to give them to me."

"I don't know—"

"*The next lie you tell, you will bite off your own tongue.*" The woman smiled sweetly.

Rebecca fell silent, terror spiking in her, knowing with her whole body that she would do exactly as she'd been commanded.

The woman's smile widened. "*Names.* Names of your fellow Resistance members, and your SOE counterparts. Locations of any safe houses and supply caches. And . . ." She slowly ran her thumb across the knife on her hip. "I want you to tell me about the Englishwoman you transported to Dordogne."

Rebecca's eyes flicked to Lydia, then back to the chestnut-haired woman.

"Don't look so shocked." The woman laughed. "Did she tell you what she really is? She's not your *friend*, either, you know, even if you believe you're on the same side. She put you in danger the moment she met you. It was wrong of her to put you in such a position." The woman leaned forward. "Tell me now. What did she say to you on that long drive to Dordogne?"

The lie was so small. *Nothing. She told me nothing.* But even as Rebecca's mind formed the words, she felt her jaw tighten and her teeth clench around her tongue, ready to bite down. She whimpered. After a moment the tension released.

"She's a Force," Lydia whispered. "I've never met one before." If the chestnut-haired woman sensed Lydia in the room with them, she gave no indication of it.

"Here's what we are going to do," the woman said. "I'm going to cut your bonds. And you are going to *sit right there, and not give me any trouble*. Isn't that right?" She waited for a response.

"Yes." Rebecca's voice came out as a hoarse whisper.

The woman took the knife from her belt and cut the ropes from Rebecca's wrists. "Here." She turned the dagger so the handle faced Rebecca. "Go on. *Take it*. But no funny business."

Rebecca didn't want to take it, not for anything in the world, but found herself reaching for the dagger, nonetheless. A single tear fell onto her bloodied blouse. She wanted her mother. She wanted to go back in time, back to when she was a child. *Did you have a nightmare, little dove?* Yes, a nightmare. Her mother always wore the same perfume, Vol de Nuit, and whenever Rebecca had a bad dream, her mother would spray a little bit onto her pillow, to keep the monsters away. She looked down at the knife in her hand, breathing fast, but smelled only sweat, and bleach, and fear. *Wake up, wake up, wake up.*

"Now, here's *my* secret," the woman said in her singsong voice. "I can make you do aaaaanything I want. Anything at all. But your mind is another matter. I can't do anything about the thoughts in your head, which means I can't force you to say anything you don't want to say. Understand?"

Rebecca nodded. She could feel her pulse in her throat.

"So, we're going to play a game. I want you to tell me everything you know. All about the Englishwoman. The names of all your coconspirators. The locations of your safe houses. Details of any planned attacks against the Reich. Everything."

The dagger shook in Rebecca's hand, the tendons pressing through the skin. *You will not break,* she told herself. *No matter what she does to you.*

"You can of course choose to remain silent. But for every second you're not telling me what I want to know, you're going to *cut yourself with that dagger.*"

Rebecca looked up at Lydia, eyes wide.

"Ready?" the woman said.

"Wait, wait, wait—" Rebecca screamed.

"Begin."

Without hesitation, Rebecca took the dagger and dragged it across the skin of her forearm. She shrieked in pain but continued to carve in slow, deft strokes.

"Not too deep. We don't want the game to end too soon."

The pain was not the point, she realized with growing panic as she sliced away at her own flesh. It was the terror, the knowledge that she would cut herself to ribbons if she did not speak. She would chop off her own fingers, peel off her own face, and nothing would be able to stop her, nothing except a word from the chestnut-haired woman.

"*Rebecca!*" Lydia came closer, kneeling at her side. "Rebecca, listen to me, listen very carefully."

Rebecca carried on slicing her own skin. The chestnut-haired woman watched on, smiling.

Lydia spoke slowly and clearly to be heard over the screams. "I want you to draw an X with the knife."

Rebecca continued to cut into her own flesh, weeping, but did as Lydia instructed. Tears sluiced their way down her face, leaving streaks in the blood and the dust.

"Now draw another X, right above the first, so the top of the first X touches the bottom of the second."

Rebecca did as she was told. The woman with the chestnut hair leaned forward.

"What are you doodling there?"

"Now draw a vertical line, right down the middle," Lydia commanded.

The woman squinted. "Why, that looks like—"

She never finished the sentence. Rebecca drove the blade through the woman's throat, straight up to the hilt, and watched as her lovely face opened up in a gasp of surprise and outrage. A hideous gurgle escaped her lips, before her eyes rolled back and she fell to the floor with a thud.

Rebecca sat, silent and shaking, as Lydia stood over the dead witch. Slowly, Rebecca staggered to the far end of the room, leaned into the corner, and retched.

Lydia went to the door and listened. "We need to get you out of here. Someone will be coming soon."

Rebecca felt very far away from herself. She understood what was happening, but she was dazed and numb.

"Rebecca, it's time to go."

She looked up. "Go where? I'll be shot the moment I walk out that door."

"Well, you can't stay here."

Rebecca sat back down in the chair. She imagined the look on the Gestapo's face when he returned and saw what she had done. It brought her some small amount of satisfaction. Lydia watched her, thinking. "Wait here."

"Where else would I go?" But Lydia had already slipped through the closed metal door. She returned a moment later.

"Outside this door is a long hallway. It's not guarded. There's another door at the other end."

"And beyond that door?"

Lydia's image trembled. "I don't know. My projection is tied to you. I can only go so far before I'm pulled back."

Rebecca nodded, still staring at the body of the dead woman on the floor.

"Rebecca," Lydia said firmly. "I know you've been through something horrible. I know you're scared. But you don't want to die in this place."

She was right, of course. The numbness ebbed away. Rebecca could feel herself inside her skin—bruised, bleeding, and frightened, but alive.

She stood. "If I survive, we can talk about you using my car."

"Fair enough." An uneasy look appeared on Lydia's face, like she had just been caught by a wave of dizziness.

"What's wrong with you?" Rebecca asked.

"I . . . can't stay."

"What?"

"I can only leave my body for a short time, and I was already spent long before I came here. I'll stay as long as I can, but in a moment, I'll be gone."

"*You can't leave me here!*" Rebecca hissed.

"I wouldn't if I had a choice." Lydia's image was becoming less stable by the moment, flickering and trembling. "Listen to me. You can do this. Meet me in Dordogne. Stay—"

Her image snuffed out like a candle flame.

"No. Non! Putain de sorcière!" Rebecca looked around in her growing panic. The dead woman lay on the floor, growing colder by the second. Any moment now the Gestapo would return, and she was in no condition to defend herself from an armed man twice her size. She tried the door, but found it locked, just as she knew she would. Blood dripped from her mangled arm onto the concrete floor. She was beginning to feel woozy.

"I don't want to die in this place," she whispered.

Rebecca crouched next to the dead woman and removed one of her shoes and the stocking underneath, then wrapped the stocking tightly around her bloodied right arm. The witch's red jacket lay where she had left it, draped across the back of the chair. Rebecca put it on. She considered taking the woman's skirt, as well, but it was soaked through with blood, and would only draw unwanted attention.

She looked down at her shaking hands. She couldn't possibly wield a knife in her condition. It would be taken from her in a second, and then she would be as dead as the witch on the floor. No, she needed a more forgiving weapon. She picked up the brick from its place by the door, tucked herself into the corner, and waited.

It wasn't long before she heard a man's footsteps echoing in the hallway. Rebecca stood next to the door with her body pushed flat against the wall, her heart hammering in her ears. She heard the lock disengage. The door swung open. Rebecca stood behind it and waited.

"Scheiße!" The Gestapo burst into the room and knelt by the dead witch, spewing expletives in German. Rebecca stepped out from her hiding place and lifted the brick high. The man turned, but before he could make a sound, she brought the brick down, hard and fast. He flinched, and the blow glanced, leaving a red gash behind his ear as he cried out in pain. She reared back and struck again, and this time the blow hit him in the temple, and he collapsed to the floor. She raised the brick one more time, ready to strike again, but the Gestapo lay motionless.

She could feel her pulse racing. Her vision swam. She nudged the man with her toe. He made a horrible sound, a low moan followed by a hiss of air. A pool of blood spread around his cratered skull. Rebecca knelt, searching his limp body until her fingers landed on the ring of keys stashed inside his right pocket. She gave them a quick glance, then kept searching, rifling through the man's jacket until she found it—the key to her own beloved Citroën. She breathed a sigh of relief. They had confiscated her car, which meant it must be somewhere close by.

She stood and walked quickly out the door, shutting it behind her.

She was in a long, unguarded hallway, just like Lydia had described. The air was cold and damp, and smelled of urine. Doors lined the empty hallway. Some were identical to the one she'd just come out of, while others looked more like washrooms or storage closets. A great metal door loomed at the end of the corridor.

She wanted to run screaming from this place. She wanted to throw open every door until she found the sunlight, then flee as fast and as far as she could and not look back. Male voices floated through the air, coming from the door at the far end of the hallway. She was not free yet by any measure.

Rebecca tried the handle of the first door she came to, but the knob wouldn't turn. She considered the mess of keys in her hand, but there were too many to try them all, and she abandoned the thought almost immediately. The second door swung open easily. It was a washroom with a cracked mirror hanging over a dirty sink. Two stinking urinals stood against the wall, along with a single stall. Rebecca opened the stall door to make certain she was alone, then stood in front of the dingy mirror. Dark brown blood had crusted on her bottom lip and under her nose, and there was a fat purple bruise forming on the left side of her face. She ran the water and dabbed away the blood as best she could, but there was nothing to be done about the bruising, or the cigarette burn on her neck. She hastily pulled the pins from her hair and rearranged it into a style similar to the one worn by the chestnut-haired woman, taking extra care to arrange her curls so they obscured the worst of the damage.

Rebecca took one last, shaking breath, then walked out of the washroom, striding toward the door at the end of the hallway. She could hear the men's voices growing louder as she approached the door.

Don't run, she told herself. *If you run, you die.* The door was unlocked. She straightened her spine and walked through.

Fifteen

Lydia sat at the battered kitchen table at Château de Laurier, watching the rising sun slice through the morning mist like a scalpel.

"Did you sleep?" Henry asked. Lydia hadn't heard him come in.

She shook her head. "You?"

"On and off." He sat. He looked puffy and tired. "Have you found a car?"

"I believe so," she said, although in truth, she wasn't so sure. She'd been too exhausted to project again after the previous night's efforts, and now she had no idea where Rebecca was, or whether she'd managed to escape. Lydia imagined Rebecca as she'd last seen her—dazed and bleeding in some Nazi interrogation room—and felt a quick pang of terror mixed with regret.

Henry grimaced at the morning light. He hadn't looked at her since they'd left the cave. She imagined it had something to do with the things she'd seen inside his head or, perhaps, something he'd seen in hers. Strangers weren't often afforded such a private glimpse into each other's minds, and the effect could be disconcerting, to say the least. She'd wanted to ask about what she'd seen—the dozens of lifeless eyes, the fear she'd felt, the sense of violation—but she didn't dare.

"I've decided I'd like to come with you. To Auvergne," he said.

She looked at him, surprised. "What about your art?"

He made a sound that was almost a chuckle, but not quite. "It won't miss me. It's just one day."

"You're very kind, but you don't need to do that."

Henry turned and looked at her then. His eyes were bloodshot, and Lydia realized that the heaviness she saw in his face wasn't sleeplessness at all, but grief.

"René is my family. If he's—" He stopped, took a breath. "If that's his body you saw, then I need to go. I need to see that he's taken care of."

"You don't know that it's him. Maybe it's someone else. Maybe he'd already moved on by the time—"

"I hope you're right. Either way, I need to go."

Lydia watched his face. The pain seemed to be caught there, like he was holding his breath to keep it from pouring out of him. She understood that pain and felt a stab of guilt for having caused it.

"All right. Of course. Yes."

Henry nodded, and the tension seemed to seep out of his shoulders, just a little. He looked up at the window and frowned.

"A car is coming."

Lydia jumped from her place at the table.

"Lydia, wait, what if it's—" But Lydia was already outside, walking swiftly to meet the approaching car, with Henry on her heels.

The Citroën came to a halt a few meters from where they stood. Slowly, painfully, Rebecca opened the door and got out. Her bruises had darkened. The left side of her mouth looked discolored and swollen, and her right arm was seeping blood.

"You made it," Lydia said.

Rebecca nodded with her eyes on the dirt at her feet.

"Rebecca?"

Rebecca didn't look up. Lydia approached slowly and tried to embrace her, but Rebecca backed away, and Lydia didn't push. She could hear Rebecca's shaking breath and saw the tremor that ran through her body.

"You made it, Rebecca. You're safe."

Rebecca shook her head. "My friends are dead. I went to the safe house. André betrayed them, just like he betrayed me. They tried to fight back, but they—" She fell silent, unable to continue.

"I'm so sorry." Even as they came out, the words felt hollow. Useless.

Rebecca looked up, and Lydia saw that her eyes were glassy. "So, where are we going?"

Henry looked from Rebecca to Lydia. "Auvergne. But—"

"But you should stay here and rest," Lydia said. "You're in no condition to travel."

Rebecca looked at Henry. "Who the hell is he?"

For a moment Henry looked like a schoolboy caught talking in class. "Henry Boudreaux," he said. It sounded like an apology.

"Well, Henry Boudreaux, where my car goes, I go."

Lydia shook her head. "Rebecca—"

"I have to do *something*." She held Lydia with her eyes, which were somehow too large, the irises swimming. When she spoke again, her voice was small and empty, almost too quiet to hear. "They killed all my friends."

Lydia looked at Henry, who lowered his eyes.

She took Rebecca by the hand; Rebecca let her. "Give me five minutes. Let me see what I can do about that arm."

. . .

THE CUTS WERE MANY, but shallow, and Lydia was able to heal Rebecca's arm with relative ease.

"That's a good skill to know," Rebecca admitted grudgingly, watching as Lydia ran her fingers along the wounds like rivers on a map.

"These are mostly superficial. Any deeper and—" She stopped short, wincing as a bloody vision streaked through her mind. *Isadora on the chamber floor, lifeblood pouring out of her as Lydia spoke the words of power, and watched the wound open under her fingers again and again.* She cleared her throat. "I'm not a healer. I'm useless with anything deeper than a scratch."

She carried on speaking the words of power until she came to the sigil she had commanded Rebecca to carve into her skin.

"What does it mean?" Rebecca asked. Her voice was flat, eyes cast down.

"It's for protection. A hex-breaking sigil."

Rebecca nodded. "Does it work forever? Or just once?"

Lydia hesitated. "I'm not sure. We don't normally go around carving things into our skin. I wasn't even sure it would work, what with you not being a witch. I think . . ." She faltered. "I think it was your need that gave it power." She looked down at the ugly, bloody wound, already beginning to scab over. "I can take it away, or . . ."

"Leave it," Rebecca said.

Lydia closed the wound but left the scar. "How did you escape?"

Rebecca stared at the floor in front of her, never looking at Lydia. "I put on the dead woman's jacket and walked out the front door." She sniffed. "It was a police station. One of the policemen stopped me on my way out. I was sure I'd been caught. But he thought I was *her*. Turns out he wanted to take the Nazi bitch to dinner." She made a disgusted sound. "*Men*. He didn't even notice the bruises. He was too busy trying to look down my shirt."

Lydia looked at Rebecca's face, the way it had been morphed by grief. "I'm sorry about your friends."

Rebecca said nothing.

"You were close?"

Rebecca nodded. "Like a family. The closest thing to a family some of us had left." She looked down at her bloody blouse. "This belonged to Colette. She loaned it to me the last time I saw her. It was her favorite. Ruined now." She rolled up her sleeve, revealing a long, curved scar on her right bicep. "Her boyfriend Alain stitched that himself. I have half a dozen just like it, all by him." She laughed—a wet, sobbing sound. "Colette used to say Alain was a better seamstress than she would ever be. Roland, he once said that—" She stopped, the muscles in her throat tremoring as she pressed one hand over her mouth.

"I'm glad you survived," Lydia said softly. "I'm . . ." She struggled for a moment, looking for the right words. "I'm grateful you're here."

"I'm not staying." Rebecca swiped at her eyes and kept her face turned away from Lydia when she spoke, as if looking at her would tear open something newly healed. "You saved my life, so you can use my car. Once you've found your book, I'm leaving. Understand?"

Lydia nodded. "Where will you go?"

Rebecca did not answer.

WHEN THEY RETURNED to the car, Henry was standing by the driver's side door.

"I'd like to drive," he said.

Rebecca's chin shot up. "Like hell. No one drives my car but me."

"I understand. It's just that if we're stopped, they might think I'm . . ." He drifted off.

"What?" Lydia searched his face, confused.

Henry let out a breath. "Fraternizing. With white women." Lydia and

Rebecca were silent as the implication sank in. "If you both sit in the back, you can tell them you hired me to drive." Henry held his head high, but there was a tension in him that was new, a strain through the neck and jaw.

"Your papers are in order?" Rebecca asked.

"They say I was born in Paris, and my accent will confirm it."

Rebecca raised an eyebrow at that.

"Je suis un excellent conducteur. Je serai très prudent." He extended his hand, waiting.

Rebecca looked at Lydia. "You could take a lesson from him."

"Yes, I know."

Rebecca handed the keys to Henry, then opened the passenger side door and tossed herself onto the back seat. "Allons-y!" she shouted.

Lydia lingered for a moment with Henry. "If we do get stopped, will they really believe you're only the driver?"

"I have no idea. Probably not." He peered out across the hillside, never looking at her directly.

"What's the punishment for you if they don't?"

Henry rocked on his heels, considering. "I suppose they'll sterilize me, if I'm lucky. Then again, they might just shoot me."

Lydia felt slightly ill. "You don't have to come. René would forgive you."

Henry nodded. "I know he would. But I wouldn't."

Lydia looked into his eyes and saw that there was no sense in trying to change his mind. "Right." She peered out anxiously at the miles of road ahead of them. "Back roads, then."

"Back roads," he replied.

LYDIA WATCHED OUT her window as hills rose and fell alongside them like slowly cresting waves. Clouds rolled in, turning the sky a velvety gray. All around them the remaining leaves shone in shades of copper and gold, looking otherworldly in the November fog. Next to her, Rebecca sagged against the car window, fast asleep.

Henry was, in fact, an exceptionally careful driver. Normally Lydia would have appreciated his prudence, but today it took every ounce of her self-control not to scream at him to drive faster. She imagined arriving at the farmhouse only to find the floorboards torn up, the book already long gone. She felt herself spiraling in the silence of the car, imagining all the horror that would come to pass if she failed; in that moment, it seemed inevitable.

"You all right?" She looked up to see Henry's eyes on her in the mirror. She wondered what she'd done to call his attention.

She cleared her throat. "May I ask you something personal?" The panicked howl inside her skull lowered to a moan. Next to her, Rebecca snored softly.

Henry shifted in his seat. "Sure."

"Why did you decide to stay in France? Going back to America would surely have been safer."

He shrugged. "Not necessarily. Sure, I might get killed by the Nazis because I stayed. But if I'd gone home, I probably would have been drafted. And then I would have ended up in some trench. Getting killed by Nazis."

"But that's not why you stayed."

His eyes flicked to hers in the mirror. "No. It's not."

"Then why?"

Henry was quiet for a moment. "Hitler covets art. It isn't the same as loving it. He takes the things he wants and destroys the rest. Anything that doesn't align with his worldview, anything that isn't *Aryan* enough for them, they have a name for it, they call it *Entartete Kunst*. Degenerate art." He was quiet for several seconds. "How can art be degenerate?"

Lydia couldn't think of anything to say, and so she said nothing.

"I had a responsibility. I couldn't just let them take whatever they wanted and pick and choose what to keep, what to destroy. And I couldn't leave, not when the people I'd worked alongside were risking everything. It would have been . . . cowardly."

"I understand." Lydia was beginning to think Henry was a bit like herself—principled to the point of self-destruction. They drove in silence for a few minutes, watching the fog blanketing the hillside. "Do you think you'll go back home someday? After the war?"

"No." Henry's hands flexed on the wheel. "*Maybe*. I don't know."

"You don't care for New Orleans?"

"I love New Orleans. Greatest city on earth. The food, the music . . ."

"You miss it."

A beat. "Yes."

"Then why?"

Henry frowned. "It's . . . complicated."

"I see." Lydia thought again about what she'd seen in Henry's mind—the doors, the pearl-white eyes, the terror. "But you wouldn't have to go back to New Orleans. America is a big country. You could go anywhere."

"I could." Lydia could hear from Henry's tone that she had missed something vital.

"But you won't," she said. "Why?"

Henry glanced at his mirror, then away again. "In America, when you're a Black man, you're a *boy*. It doesn't matter how old, or how educated. You're a boy until the day you die. 'Watch your mouth, boy. Don't get smart, boy.'" He shrugged. "In France I'm a man."

"The Nazis don't see you as a man."

"There are Nazis everywhere. They just go by different names."

They were quiet for a moment. Lydia waited until the panic began rising in her again before speaking.

"May I ask you something else?"

"Why not?" Lydia couldn't tell if he was amused or annoyed, but she pressed on.

"That first night . . ." She was suddenly terribly embarrassed. "That first night at the château, I'm afraid I went . . . *exploring*, and—"

"That was you." Lydia was surprised to hear him laugh. "I should have known."

"I'm sorry." She waited a moment. "Who were you talking to?"

Henry didn't answer right away. He waited so long that Lydia was sure he wouldn't answer at all. Then, finally, he spoke.

"My father. He died when I was just a baby. And sometimes I . . . talk to him. Ask his advice. I've done it ever since I was a kid."

It was a lie. Whoever or whatever Henry had been talking to that night, it wasn't advice he'd been asking for. Lydia remembered the desperation she'd heard in his voice. *Please. I can't do this right now. I know you think I can do something for you. And I'm sorry. I really am. But I am tired, and I just . . . can't.*

"Does it help?" She watched his face in the mirror, as if she would find the truth there.

Henry kept his eyes on the road. "Sometimes."

They drove in silence. Bare trees seemed to reach through the mist like skeletons, casting eerie shapes in the fog.

"Can I ask *you* a personal question?" Henry asked.

"Of course."

He didn't speak right away, as if he were reconsidering. "Why do you change your face?"

Lydia couldn't conceal her surprise. "*Oh*. How did you—"

"Back in the cave, when you were in my head. I could sort of . . . *see* these little pieces of you. Just flashes, but it was enough." He chuckled. "Your mother seems like an interesting woman."

Lydia couldn't think of anything to say. She felt exposed and immensely vulnerable.

"I saw you. The real you, I mean. At first, I didn't recognize you, but then . . ." His eyes flashed toward her in the mirror again, curious and intense. "You're working at it all the time, aren't you? In the back of your mind, a part of you is always keeping up the illusion."

She felt her heart flutter, an unnerving, confusing sensation she couldn't make sense of. "It's not as bad as all that," she said softly. "After a while it becomes second nature."

Henry nodded. "I'm not judging. It's very good. I never would have known you were doing it. But, it's funny. Now that I know, I can almost tell it's not real. It's like an optical illusion. Once you've seen it, you can't unsee it."

"I beg your pardon?"

"I don't mean any offense. I like your face." He sounded so serious as he said it. So sincere.

"*Oh?*" She laughed. "Which one?"

There they were again, his eyes, watching her. Lydia felt herself grow warm under his gaze.

"Both of them," he said.

THE FARMHOUSE APPEARED through the fog like a ghost ship. To Lydia, it felt as if someone had plucked it from a dream and set it before her, whole, but not quite real.

"Did we beat them?" Rebecca mumbled, stirring. "Is the book still here?"

"I believe it is." Lydia winced. There was a menacing hum in the air, like the house was full of wasps. She scanned the horizon warily, searching for any sign of the blond witch or her coven, but they were alone. It seemed impossible.

Where are you?

They pulled the Citroën around to the side of the house, where it wouldn't be seen from the road. The front door was open, just as she remembered. As she stepped from the car, the humming became louder, more urgent.

"It's here." She looked at Rebecca and Henry. "Do you feel that?"

Rebecca frowned. "Feel what?"

Lydia locked eyes with Henry. He looked sick, the skin on his face too tight. He gave an almost imperceptible nod.

Lydia was first inside, her heart racing as she crossed the threshold. Everything was the same as she remembered—the abandoned meal, the broken crockery scattered across the floor. She heard a sound behind her and turned. Rebecca was standing in the doorway, examining the silver ornament—the mezuzah, Henry had called it, with a look on her face that Lydia couldn't quite read—something that looked almost like grief.

As she walked the creaking floorboards, Lydia felt the ever-present hum grow into a wail, an insistent keening rising from the ground under her feet. She moved through the house until she found the place where it reached a crescendo, transforming into a bone-rattling howl. The book was crying out. It wanted to be found.

Almost there, she thought. *Great Mother, at last.*

Lydia took the poker from the fireplace and raised it high, bringing it down hard on the wooden floorboards. Again and again, she drove the iron point into the wood, working herself into a frenzy, until she'd created a splintered hole the size of her palm. Kneeling, she wedged the poker underneath the broken floorboard and, using all the force she could muster, pried up the wood with a hard crack. She thrust her arm inside the hole, blocking out any thoughts of what creatures might be found in a hole such as this one. Her fingers brushed against something rough and solid, and as they did, the wailing was accompanied by a chattering, like a thousand voices hissing and gibbering at once.

Lydia withdrew, and the chattering stopped.

She looked up. Rebecca was watching her from the doorway.

Steeling herself, Lydia reached in again, and pulled the book up and into the light.

It had been wrapped in canvas before being hidden away and was covered with dirt and wood splinters. As she unwrapped it, she found to her surprise that it was warm. *Like it's alive*, she thought with a sudden, nauseating thrill. The binding was leather, the cover cracked and brittle, though not nearly as damaged as Lydia had expected, given its age. Very carefully, she lifted the cover with the tips of her fingers.

"Lydia." Rebecca's voice cut the silence.

She looked up. She'd nearly forgotten Rebecca was there.

"Do you really think you should open that?"

The book was whispering to her.

"It's fine," she said.

The pages of the *Grimorium Bellum* were inked in a dense wall of illegible script. The characters were hard and linear, laid out in tight lines with no breaks or pictures. She let her fingers trace the letters, and felt the chattering change, settling into a single tune, a commanding chorus, rising to meet her from the pages of the book.

"I can read it."

Lydia felt a rush of euphoria as the realization swept over her, and the power of the book seemed to bloom inside her mind. It felt like she was breathing magic, like the book was infusing itself into her bloodstream. The characters remained as foreign to her as ever, and still, somehow, she knew every syllable. Each spell seemed to unravel before her like spools of ribbon: Spells for bringing plague. Spells for blighting crops and killing livestock. Spells to snuff out joy, and bring despair and madness. One particularly grisly spell that promised to unmake the spellcaster's enemies, consuming them from the inside out and leaving nothing but ash in its wake. Lydia knelt there on the farmhouse floor, listening to the song of the book, feeling its warmth under her hands, until something, a voice, pulled her back.

"*Lydia.*"

She looked up, and for a moment she couldn't see Rebecca's face. It was like she'd been veiled under a teeming mass of insects, pulsing and writhing around her. It was horrifying, as if Rebecca had been replaced by something inhuman. Lydia nearly screamed, but then her eyes cleared, and Rebecca was as she had always been. Lydia lifted her fingers from the page. The voices subsided.

"Look," Rebecca said softly.

Lydia went to the window where Rebecca stood. In the distance, she could just make out Henry, hunched under the old oak tree, a shovel in his hand.

Lydia walked out of the house and across the field, clutching the *Grimorium Bellum* to her chest. She stopped a short distance from where Henry stood.

"René?" she asked.

Henry nodded tightly.

"I'm so sorry." She cast her gaze toward the road. No one coming yet. "What happened?"

Henry took a piece of paper from his pocket. "He said I was right about the book. That it was talking to him. Telling him to . . . *do things*. To himself. And other people." He rubbed his thumb along the yellowed scrap of paper in a movement that seemed to be unconscious.

The book had spoken to René? Lydia's mind reeled with possibilities. Maybe there had been some witch blood in his family, buried so deep even René himself didn't know. It would explain why he hadn't felt the book's influence until he'd had it for some time, while Henry had felt it right away.

Or perhaps . . .

Or perhaps the book's influence was so strong that given enough time it could be felt by anyone, witch or no. Lydia looked down at the thing in her hands and shuddered.

"He rolled the truck into a ravine behind the barn." Henry glanced over his shoulder. "I think he was trying to make sure he couldn't leave. He wanted it to stop, so he . . ." His voice failed him as he gestured toward the place where René had spent his final moments. Lydia saw what looked like an amber pill bottle lying in the grass.

"His family?" Rebecca asked. Lydia hadn't heard her approach.

Henry looked at the piece of paper in his hand. "They were taken to Drancy before he arrived."

Rebecca lowered her head.

"What's in Drancy?" Lydia asked.

"A transit camp." Rebecca said the words without looking up. "Last stop before deportation."

Deportation. Lydia thought again of René's nephew, Jean-Luc. About the cat he'd drawn, his name printed so proudly below it.

The swell of despair she felt was too heavy to hold—she had to let go or drown. She glanced back toward the road, snaking like a river through the fog.

"Henry? We can't stay here. We have to go."

"I can't leave him." Henry went back to his work.

Lydia could have screamed, but she steadied herself and tried again. "The Germans are coming. It's a miracle they're not here already."

"I have to take care of him." He said it simply, no anger, just a fact. A task that must be done.

"Henry—"

"I'll help," Rebecca said. She strode toward the barn and returned a moment later with a shovel in her hand. Lydia stood back for a moment, the need to flee making her frantic. She watched as they dug side by side, and realized that neither would be moved. Not until the job was done.

She made her way to the barn, holding the *Grimorium Bellum* against her like an infant. It was dark inside, barely lit by the soft gray light pouring in from the open door. She smelled hay, and dirt, and animals, now long gone. It was very still inside, and quiet, as if the fog had built an impenetrable wall between herself and the rest of the world. Like she had disappeared.

There was a spade by the door. She returned to the tree and reluctantly set the *Grimorium Bellum* in the grass. Henry looked up briefly from his work and nodded. Lydia started digging.

It was growing dark by the time they finished the grave and maneuvered René's body into its final resting place. Henry had placed René onto a canvas tarp before covering him, which made things easier. Lydia never saw his face.

They stood by the grave in silence. Lydia looked at Henry.

"I feel like I'm supposed to say something, but I don't—" He made a low, strangled sound.

"It's all right," she said. "He knows."

The fog seemed to thicken, enveloping them. The silence deepened, draping itself over them like heavy blankets soaked with seawater. And there, rumbling low and sinister in the air around them, the *Grimorium Bellum* whispered in a thousand voices, like swarms of insects only Lydia could hear.

Just when Lydia thought she could no longer bear it—the silence, the sadness, the incessant, relentless chatter of the book—Rebecca took an audible breath. She looked like perhaps she wasn't sure what she'd wanted to say. Then she began to speak. The words were rhythmic like a poem, but Lydia couldn't understand their meaning. Rebecca closed her eyes and called out the words into the fog:

Yitgadal v'yitkadash sh'mei raba

b'alma di-v'ra chirutei, v'yamlich malchutei

b'chayeichon uvyomeichon uvchayei d'chol beit yisrael,

ba'agala uvizman kariv, v'im'ru. Amen . . .

Y'hei sh'mei raba m'varach l'alam ul'almei almaya.

Yitbarach v'yishtabach, v'yitpa'ar v'yitromam v'yitnaseh,

v'yithadar v'yit'aleh v'yit'halal

sh'mei d'kud'sha, b'rich hu,

l'eila min-kol-birchata v'shirata,

tushb'chata v'nechemata da'amiran b'alma

v'im'ru. Amen.

Y'hei shlama raba min-sh'maya v'chayim aleinu v'al-kol-yisrael,

v'im'ru. Amen.

Oseh shalom bimromav, hu ya'aseh shalom aleinu v'al kol-yisrael,

v'imru. Amen.

Rebecca carried on until the syllables seemed to run out, and then there was quiet once again. The book lay at Lydia's feet, silent as a stone.

"Amen," Henry said. His face was streaked with tears. Lydia looked at Rebecca and saw that she was crying as well.

They drove back without speaking.

IT WAS NIGHT by the time they reached the château. The morning's fog had dissipated, replaced by a sharp-toothed wind that bit into Lydia's skin through her thin coat. A delicate frost blanketed the ground, and moonlight illuminated the icy crystals, making the grass glitter in the dark.

Henry collected some pillows and blankets for Rebecca, then disappeared without a word.

Lydia studied Rebecca's face as she eased herself into a kitchen chair.

Her skin was streaked with dirt. Yellow bruises still mottled the skin around her eye and mouth, and there were black crescents of dirt under her nails. Two days ago, Lydia had thought of Rebecca as thin, perhaps a little too thin. Now she looked gaunt.

"You're leaving us?"

Rebecca nodded. "Tomorrow."

Lydia considered her bloody, blistered palms, but couldn't seem to gather the energy needed to heal them. The *Grimorium Bellum* sat heavy in her lap.

"Those words you spoke. At the grave. It was a prayer?"

Rebecca stared at the table. "The Mourner's Kaddish. It shouldn't have been me. There should have been a minyan, but . . ." She shook her head.

"You're Jewish." Lydia watched Rebecca's face for some reaction. "I didn't know."

"I didn't want you to."

She wondered why she'd never considered it before. "Is your family . . ." Lydia didn't know how to finish the question.

Rebecca exhaled. "My father was taken away by the police two years ago. Then, last July, they came back and took my mother, and my little sister, Noémie. They took them to the Vélodrome d'Hiver, along with everyone else they could round up. Then to Drancy. Then . . ." She didn't need to say it. Lydia knew. *Deportation. Poland.* Rebecca glanced at Lydia, then away again. "I wasn't home when it happened."

The pitch of the grimoire's incessant humming seemed to heighten. Lydia looked down and saw that her palms had left streaks of reddish-brown blood on the cracked leather of the book, and now it was practically vibrating. She wiped her palms on her skirt, trying to make it stop, but it only seemed to become more agitated.

"Have you decided what you're going to do with that?" Rebecca glanced at the grimoire.

Lydia looked down at the book in her hands. She shook her head.

"Not so sure about taking it back to your academy?"

The academy. She knew she should have been gone already. She should have called for her Traveler and been back in London the second she laid her hands on the *Grimorium Bellum.* It would be safe there, she told herself. It had to be.

But when she closed her eyes, she could still see the shredded doorway in the warding, just as clearly as she had on that Samhain night. She imagined a shadowy figure, blade in hand, standing before that tattered portal. Even though she could not see the figure's face, she was sure she knew who it was, just the same.

Vivian.

"I saw you, you know," Rebecca said. "At the farmhouse. I saw what that thing did to you."

Lydia looked into Rebecca's knowing face.

"I may not have magic, but I can see well enough." She nodded toward the book like it might turn around and bite at any moment. "A part of you disappeared when you opened that book. Your eyes, they were all wrong. Being in the room with that thing, it feels like being in a room with a corpse. It stinks of the grave."

Lydia held the book closer and felt it turn warm, like a kitten in her lap. *Funny,* she thought. To her, the book only smelled like clean earth.

Rebecca's eyes flicked to Lydia's hands, softly caressing the book. "If you hold on to that thing for too long, it will *eat you.* Do you understand what I'm telling you?"

Lydia looked down. The bloody streaks had disappeared, as if some hungry thing had lapped them up. She nodded.

"If you take it back to your academy, will it be safe?" Lydia did not reply. She didn't need to. Rebecca saw the answer in her eyes. "You should destroy it."

"What happened to using it against the Germans and ending the war?"

Rebecca stood with a grimace. "Is that what you think you should do? Now that you have it?"

For a moment, Lydia considered it—the glory and the power, the intoxicating violence, the triumph—and felt a wave of terrible shame wash over her. "No."

Rebecca looked at her, and Lydia was sure that she could see the ugly truth, lurking just beneath her skin. That she had considered using the book. And that it had excited her.

LATER, LYDIA SAT on the edge of her bed with the *Grimorium Bellum* balanced on her lap. She knew she should try to sleep, but something about the book held her captive.

The *Grimorium Bellum* was dangerous. She knew it the way you knew a particular dog was dangerous, or a man who walks too close behind you on the street. It wasn't so much about what it was doing, but what it *could* do. Lydia could feel the potential of it under her hands, like a spring wound too tight, begging to be released. But there was something alluring in it too. The book seemed to speak to her, to want her touch. She felt it curling around her ankles, rubbing against her skin. It *liked* her.

Think of all the things we could do, it seemed to whisper.

Lydia stood and walked quickly to the chest of drawers across the room, and shoved the book inside. She needed to get away from it, just for a few minutes.

She stepped into the hallway, ignoring the way the book seemed to clamor for her attention, even from a distance. She walked, passing room after room, until she stood in front of Henry's door.

She knew she should leave him be. He hadn't spoken a word since the farm, not even to say good night. She understood all too well what he was going through, and knew she shouldn't push her presence on him.

Still, she had thought she might offer him some words of comfort, but now she felt foolish. Henry didn't want to see her. He wanted to be alone. She was just about to return to her own room, when a voice drifted through the door.

"If you're going to come in, then come."

Henry was perched on the edge of the bed, just as he had been that first night when she'd stumbled into his room by accident. His head was bowed, but he looked up when she entered. He wasn't crying. Lydia expected he would, later, but now he was looking at her with a naked mixture of grief and exhaustion that felt intimately familiar to her. It had changed the shape of him, making him both very young and impossibly old at the same time.

For a moment they were silent. It felt wrong, being in his bedroom like this, even though she'd been here before. It felt different, now that she was inside her body.

"I'm sorry. I didn't mean to hover. I just . . . I wanted to see if you're all right."

He looked at her for a moment. Lydia thought he had never looked at her directly for quite that long before. Then the moment passed, and his gaze dropped to the floor again.

"I didn't want to believe it was him. Even after the cave. Even after you told me . . ." He stopped, and Lydia watched the muscles in his throat constrict. "I didn't want to believe he was dead."

"I'm so sorry," she said again. Henry gazed down at the blistered skin of his hands.

"Let me see that." She crossed the room and sat on the bed next to him, taking one of his hands in hers.

"What are you doing?"

"Healing these. It won't take me a minute." She laid her fingertips on his palm, and was about to speak the words, when Henry pulled away.

"Don't." He swallowed, then looked down at the bloodied skin of his palms. "I'm sorry. Just . . . thank you. But don't."

She could feel the warmth of him, sitting this close. She could see the muscles in his neck and jaw, straining to keep him from falling apart. She looked at his injured hands and at her own bloody palms. She reached out and touched the tips of Henry's fingers with her own, gently, so as not to cause him any more pain. She was sure he would pull away from her at any moment, but he never did. Instead, he expelled one long, unsteady breath, and reached back, caressing her fingertips. They sat quietly for a few minutes, neither of them looking at the other.

"What was he like?" she whispered.

Out of the corner of her eye, Lydia saw Henry's lips lift in a smile. "Funny. Smart, but never snobby. He always watched out for me. Took an interest, gave me a job when nobody else would, made sure nobody gave me a hard time. He was . . ." He took a stuttering breath, and Lydia saw his throat straining against the pain.

"What else?"

Henry took a moment to collect himself, weaving his fingers more tightly with hers.

"What else?" she asked again.

He talked for a long time, the words flowing faster and easier the longer he spoke. It seemed like a relief, like he'd been desperate to tell someone, anyone, about his friend. Sometimes he laughed, relating some tale of René's many eccentricities. Once or twice the grief seemed to sweep up all at once and overwhelm him, and when that happened, Lydia would wait, not speaking, until he regained his composure and continued.

When he finished, Lydia rested her head on his shoulder, their hands still intertwined as they sat together in silence.

"Thank you," Henry said softly.

"For what?"

"For being here."

She tilted her face up to look at him. He was beautiful. Square jaw and soft eyes, large hands with long fingers, the kind that seemed to belong more to a pianist than a scholar. He looked back at her, their faces so close that she could see the flecks of copper in the deep brown of his irises, and Lydia felt the air become charged.

Something shifted almost imperceptibly between them. Henry's hand drifted toward her cheek, his thumb making soft circles on her jaw. His eyes lingered on her mouth. She felt his heart beating in his fingertips, or maybe that was hers, she wasn't sure. His nose grazed hers, and she felt a rush of heat, low in her stomach. A warm, hungry need.

"*Lydia*," he whispered, and the sound of her name on his lips made her breath catch. "I—"

Suddenly, he took a sharp breath and stood, the change so abrupt it left her dizzy.

"Henry?" She rose, too, alarmed. His posture had gone rigid, and he was staring at something in the corner, his breath gone fast and shallow. She tried to put one hand to his cheek, but he flinched, and she stopped. Lydia turned to see what had startled him so, but when she followed his gaze, there was nothing. When she turned back, he was blinking at her, as if he'd just woken from a nightmare.

"I'm sorry," he said. "I'm sorry, I—" He took one step away from her, and then another. "Forgive me. That was . . ." He swallowed, then shook his head, trying to steady himself. "It's late. We should . . ." He glanced toward the door.

"Oh." Lydia felt a flood of embarrassment wash over her. She couldn't understand what had happened. Was it possible she could have misunderstood so completely? She looked down, smoothing the wrinkles from her skirt. "Yes. Of course." She went and stood by the door, looking back in the hopes that he would say more, but he wouldn't even look at her. She felt her stomach sink. She opened the door. "Well. Good night, Henry."

He opened his mouth, and for a moment, she was sure he was going to explain. Then she saw his jaw tense, and it was as if a wall had gone up around him.

"Good night, Lydia."

LYDIA MADE HER WAY QUIETLY back to her room, shame and desire and bewilderment all twisting endlessly inside her. She noticed the heat in her cheeks, the soft pulsing in her fingertips as she closed the door behind her, the way they tingled slightly where she and Henry had touched.

The *Grimorium Bellum* was there, waiting for her. It greeted her with a surge of excitement, humming and chattering in its own strange language. Lydia listened to it for a moment, to the way it seemed to respond to her. Its presence felt seductive, almost loving.

She hesitated, then pressed the bloodied skin of her palm to the cover.

She stayed that way, feeling the *Grimorium Bellum* grow warm and content under her touch. It made her feel powerful, important. She tuned herself to that sensation, observing as it bloomed into mania, making her head ache.

"*What do you want?*" she whispered as the mania turned to horror.

You, the book whispered back. *You you you you you you you.*

Sixteen

That night, Rebecca couldn't sleep. Her arm itched where Lydia had healed her wounds, and her head throbbed. Her muscles were heavy and sore from digging.

She hated the drafty old château. The blankets smelled of mildew, and every tiny sound sent her heart racing. She felt a hollow panic in her chest, growing deeper as the night ticked forward. In two years, she'd only ever told one person that she was a Jew. She'd shed the name Rebecca Gaiser like an old coat the day her mother and sister were taken, transforming herself into someone new—Rebecca Gagne, the fearless maquisarde. The lie had been her armor, and now that she'd abandoned it, she was consumed by bone-deep fear.

She wished she had kept her mouth shut and let them bury the old man in silence. She almost had, but then she'd thought about her father, gone now for more than two years. He'd been a scholar, too, like René. She could still see the crinkles beside his eyes, his little round spectacles pushed down on his nose as he devoured some book, sitting in the frayed old armchair in his study. *Come here, Rebecca, let me read you this passage. Come look at this drawing. Read this bit in English. Now this one in German. My clever girl, here's a piece of chocolate for you, don't tell your mother.*

Josef! Her mother's voice would call from the next room. *You'll spoil her dinner.*

My love! I would never. And then he would wink at Rebecca and slip her the chocolate anyway, before sending her off to play.

It was her father who'd taught her the Mourner's Kaddish. She'd heard the men reciting it as they sat shiva after her grandfather died when she was thirteen. Girls didn't recite the Kaddish, but she'd wanted to know it anyway, and her father, who loved learning, had never denied his children the answer to any question they could imagine, no matter how big or small. He sat with Rebecca every evening, patiently talking her through every syllable until she could recite the entire prayer by heart.

She remembered finding his glasses, crushed on the floor of their flat after the police had come and gone. She'd fretted for months about how he would see without them, before finally realizing that he was probably long dead. Still, she'd kept them with her always, as if someday he might come back and ask for them. And now the Gestapo had them, tossed aside in some little room in that stinking police station, next to her pistol and her fake papers. She would never see them again. Silent, bitter tears spilled from her eyes, rolling down her face and collecting on the pillow beneath her head. She sniffed and wiped them away.

Footsteps sounded in the hallway. Rebecca felt her heart turn over in her chest before realizing it was only Lydia, quietly making her way to the kitchen in the dark. Perhaps she couldn't sleep either. She considered joining her but thought better of it. She listened for a long time, waiting for Lydia to return, but she never did, and finally, sleep crept in, slithering unnoticed on its belly through the dark of her room, and carried her away.

SHE WOKE TO the sound of crying.

"*Noémie?*" she murmured. Then she realized that wasn't right. Noémie was gone. She sat up.

Dull gray light filled the room where she slept. Slowly, she dressed and made her way downstairs, cursing to herself. Her whole body ached, and her hands were raw from digging.

The crying grew louder.

She saw Henry first, crouching on the kitchen floor. She could hear Lydia's muffled sobs but couldn't make out the words. Only Henry, speaking softly and gently. Then he shifted, and Rebecca saw her—Lydia, head hung low, her dark, tangled hair veiling her face. Her hands were filthy, blackened with something that might have been soot. A carpet of embers glowed in the stone hearth.

Rebecca stepped into the kitchen. "What's happened?"

Henry shook his head, helpless. "I found her like this when I got up. I don't know what's wrong with her."

Lydia looked up then, and Rebecca saw something in her eyes that made her draw back—she looked half-crazed, like she'd seen something terrible. There was something different about her face, as well. It wasn't just that Lydia clearly hadn't slept. Her nose was more pronounced, her lips thinner, and there was a sharpness to her image that hadn't been there before. Rebecca wondered for a moment if she had cast some spell on herself to look as she did now, but if so, for what purpose? Then she realized the truth. The face she'd always thought of as Lydia's had never been real at all. *This* was her true face. Whatever illusion Lydia had been casting, she had lost either the ability or the inclination to conjure it.

"Rebecca." Lydia's voice sounded different, wrong, somehow. "I tried. I tried to destroy it, but I can't. I'm not strong enough." A sob ripped through her chest like broken glass. The book lay between them on the floor. The cover was smudged with soot but appeared otherwise intact.

Rebecca watched as Henry helped Lydia into a chair. She looked down at the book and felt a strange sense of calm wash over her.

She knelt and rebuilt the fire. She waited until there was a roaring blaze, then lifted the book from the floor.

Lydia looked up. "What are you doing?"

Rebecca considered the thing in her hand. She'd seen the power the book held over Lydia, like it was speaking in a voice only she could hear. Even Henry seemed unsettled whenever he was in the same room with it. Rebecca turned the book over in her hands and waited to feel something, anything.

"I'll do it," she said.

Lydia shook her head miserably. "You don't understand. It won't let you."

For so long, Rebecca had felt helpless. Helpless as her father and mother and sister were taken from their home and dragged away, never to be heard from again. Helpless, cutting away at her own flesh in that stinking prison cell. Helpless when she'd discovered the bodies of her friends—Roland, slumped against the bathroom sink. Colette and Alain, their limbs tangled together like they had been embracing. All of them, slaughtered by the Gestapo.

But *this*. This was something she could do. Something that mattered.

"You forget," she said. "There's no witch blood in me. To you, it's a thing of power. But to me? It's just a book."

She tossed the grimoire into the fire.

"Wait!" Lydia cried, but it was too late.

Rebecca was thrown violently to her knees, as if someone had come up from behind and tossed her to the ground with great force. She felt herself snatch the book back from the fire with no hesitation, no regard for the flames that licked at her skin. It was as if something else were driving her body, something unfeeling and inanimate. Blackness crept into her vision as mortal terror washed over her. Her body felt cold and rigid, like the constricting of her muscles would crush her bones to dust.

"She's not breathing!" Rebecca was vaguely aware of Henry dragging her away from the fire, the book still clutched to her chest, hands frozen in claws. She felt as if her lungs would burst, like she was thousands of meters underwater, with the incredible weight of the entire ocean stacked on top of her like bricks. And all the while, the book clung to her breast like a monstrous child.

"Rebecca. *Hey*. Look at me." Henry's voice was calm, but Rebecca could see the fear in his eyes. "Breathe," he commanded. "Breathe."

No air came, and her terror deepened as the seconds ticked by. She wanted to thrash, to fight for air, but she couldn't, and that was worse than anything. She felt like she was swimming toward the surface of the water, but it was impossibly far away. Henry took her by the shoulders and shook her, hard.

There was a shrouded figure standing in the corner, leering.

Rebecca blinked at the ceiling. The figure moved closer, hovering over Henry as he held her. It didn't move like a person, but more like a collection of creatures, all running over and around each other, pulsing and swarming. It was grotesque, horrifying, and Rebecca felt the urge to scream, but only a thin hiss of air escaped.

"Good," Henry said. "Now come on back. Come on. *Breathe*."

Air exploded into her lungs, icy and painful. The book released its grasp, and she tossed it into the corner, where it hit the wall and landed with a thud. She turned onto her side and gasped, never certain the next breath would come until it did.

She looked up. There was no shadow creature, only dust and cob-webs. Across the room, Lydia crouched on the stone floor, curled into a ball. They looked at each other, two people who had stared into the same terrible void.

"How many times?" Rebecca's voice sounded hoarse. "How many times did you throw that book into the fire?"

Lydia's face was smeared with soot and tears. "Six."

The feeling was back, as if it had never left. *Helplessness.* Thick as tar, suffocating her.

They sat in silence for a long time, while the fire burned back down to embers and the air grew cold. Lydia kept her face turned toward the book, as if listening to some secret it was murmuring, just for her. Finally, she got to her feet, swaying slightly.

"Lydia?" Henry stood.

She didn't look at him. "It's all right. I know what I have to do."

Rebecca watched her, waiting.

"The book can't be destroyed, and it can't stay here. The academy is the only place where it will be safe."

"*Safe?*" Rebecca stared at her in disbelief. "Those Nazi witches broke into your academy once already. Who's to say they can't do it again?"

"It's the only choice I have left."

Henry shook his head. "Lydia, Rebecca's right. If they—"

"*There's nowhere else to go!*" She held him with her wild-eyed gaze until he looked away.

Lydia took a rag from the table and used it to pick up the book, then disappeared up the stairs, avoiding Henry's pleading gaze as she passed. Rebecca heard a door close a moment later. Henry fell back against the wall, defeated.

She sat for a moment, exhausted and afraid, listening to the birds outside. It was a perfect morning. A beautiful morning.

Why do birds sing in the morning, little dove?

"What did you feel?" Henry asked quietly. "When you held it?"

Rebecca looked at him. "What did I *feel*?" She felt inexplicably violated by the question.

Henry nodded. "Did it . . . speak to you?"

Rebecca stood. "No. It didn't speak to me." He watched her, waiting, but she would have rather died than say another word about it.

"Are you leaving?"

"Yes." She walked stiffly toward the door.

"But—"

Rebecca turned on him, blood racing. "But *what*?"

Henry looked down and said nothing.

She limped slightly as she walked. She was sure she saw that monstrous figure again at the edge of her vision, but when she turned, it wasn't there.

"I'm sorry about your friend," she said.

She opened the door and stopped. Three black cars were coming up the hill toward the château. Her heart lurched in her chest. "Someone is here."

Henry sat up. "What?"

"Look."

In a second, he was next to her. "Shit."

Rebecca ran, taking the stairs two at a time until she reached Lydia's door, and pounded with her fist until it swung open. Lydia was still holding the book in her hands, so tightly that Rebecca could see the bones of her knuckles pressing through the skin.

"The grand mistress is sending a Traveler to bring me home," Lydia said. "She'll be here soon, and then I'll—"

Rebecca cut her off. "Someone is coming."

"*What?*"

Rebecca turned and ran back down the stairs without bothering to repeat herself. Lydia followed a moment later.

"I think they're Gestapo." Henry was standing at the window now. The door was shut and bolted.

Rebecca felt her blood stutter. She went and stood next to him. "How many?"

"Seven? No, nine."

"How did they find us?" Lydia asked. "If they followed us from the farmhouse we would have—" She stopped suddenly.

Rebecca turned and looked at her. "What is it?"

Lydia sat at the table, holding the book tight against her chest. "It's her."

"*Her*? Who is *her*?"

"I still don't know her name." Lydia's voice was nearly a whisper. "The witch from the academy. And from the farmhouse."

"The one who killed your friend?" Rebecca thought of that bone-handled dagger again and felt a sickening dread in her veins.

Lydia nodded.

"Is she tracking the book?" Henry asked. "I thought she could only do that during the full moon."

Lydia shook her head. Her right hand moved absently over the book, tracing the cracks in the leather. "Once you touch something, you can track it anytime you like. No full moon. No coven." She looked at Rebecca. "It's how I found you, when you were captured."

Slow, creeping realization dawned on Rebecca. "She touched *you*."

Lydia looked down at her hand as if there were a mark there that she could wipe away. "The night she attacked the academy." She looked at Henry. "I should have thought of it. I should have remembered that she touched me. I should have tried to track her, the way she tracked me, but I was only thinking of the book. I—" She stopped and shook her head in shame and disbelief. "You were right. She never knew the location of the farmhouse."

"She was tracking you," Henry said. Lydia hung her head.

"I don't understand," Rebecca said. "Why send the Gestapo? Why not come and take it herself?"

"I don't know."

"But why didn't she—"

"*I don't know!*"

Outside, voices called to each other in German. Rebecca went to the window. "They're surrounding the château. They'll block all the exits. We'll have no way out." She could feel it now, the amphetamine clarity that sometimes took hold of her in moments of crisis. She looked at Henry. "Do you have any weapons?"

"Just an old hunting rifle."

"Bring it to me."

Henry turned and moved quietly through the house, crouching to stay below the windows. Rebecca turned to Lydia.

"The spell you cast on me, on the road to Dordogne. Can you do it again?"

Lydia's eyes were wide. "I can only freeze one person at a time."

"One is better than none."

Henry returned with the hunting rifle and handed it to Rebecca. She felt better, holding that gun. Stronger. "It's loaded?"

"Yes. I hope you're a good shot. I'm lousy."

"I'm good."

There was a knock at the door, and the sound of it shot a metallic slug of fear through her chest. She crouched, and Henry and Lydia followed, moving together to the far side of the room. The knock came again, more insistent this time. A voice called to them through the door in broken French, telling them to open up.

She had an idea. It would work. But for a price.

"I think we should open the door," Rebecca said.

"What?" Henry hissed. "Are you crazy?"

"If we open this door, it might draw them away from all the others. You and Lydia can escape out the back while I hold them off."

"You can't hold them off, there are too many of them. It's suicide."

Yes. Perhaps. But she couldn't think about that now. She could see the shadow again, that phantom she somehow understood could only have come from within the book itself. She saw that squirming, writhing thing, and knew with her whole being that if the Nazis got ahold of the *Grimorium Bellum*, it wouldn't make one bit of difference if they survived the day. They would all be dead within a month.

"Get out of here," Rebecca said as the pounding grew more insistent. She kept her eyes on the door, and away from the thing in the corner. "Don't be stupid. Take the book and run."

"Rebecca—"

"My parents are Josef and Miriam Gaiser. My sister is Noémie. She would be sixteen now. Sixteen and a half." She swallowed to force the tremor from her voice. "They're probably gone. I know. *I know* they're probably gone. But if they're not . . . I would want them to know . . ."

Her voice failed her. She stared at Henry, and he stared back, helpless. Finally, he nodded.

"Thank you," she whispered. She stood and began to walk slowly toward the door.

"Wait," Lydia said. Rebecca ignored her. "Rebecca, stop. *Stop!*"

Lydia threw open the book, letting her fingers skim frantically over the pages as Rebecca watched. The characters looked alien, a wall of script so dense the pages were nearly black. Lydia didn't seem to be reading the words as much as absorbing them through her fingertips, shuddering as they entered her bloodstream.

"What are you doing?" Henry asked.

But Rebecca understood.

She nearly stopped her. She nearly said, *Don't. Please. It's not worth it.*

Leave me. Run. But then the will to survive rose up so strong in her, so stubborn and selfish—it refused to be denied. Even after everything she'd been through, everything she'd seen, she didn't want to die. Not like this. Not yet.

"Leave her," she said. She crouched beside Lydia, aimed her rifle at the door, and waited.

Lydia's eyes wandered in their sockets as her fingers traveled over the pages. Rebecca thought she felt an electric charge in the air, but told herself it was only fear that made the hairs on her arms stand on end. The knocking came again, harder now, a final warning.

Then Lydia spoke.

The voice that came from her throat did not sound like her own. She chanted in a tongue Rebecca had never heard before and hoped never to hear again. Sometimes the voice sounded like water in a hot pan, hissing and spitting, other times hard and cold, like striking flint. Sometimes it sounded like a guttural sob; sometimes the consonants seemed to run on forever, creating cascading rivers of plosives and clicks. Each syllable made Rebecca want to cover her ears, but she straightened her spine and kept her rifle trained on the door.

From the other side of the door, there came a low moan. It sounded inhuman, like the lowing of a cow. The moaning rose in pitch and volume, turning to wails of agony and then shrieks, but Lydia carried on as if she did not hear. Something about her voice made Rebecca feel ill. She smelled something horrible—a sticky, deathbed stink that clung to the inside of her nostrils. The screams crescendoed, reaching a fever pitch, until very suddenly, they stopped. Rebecca's hands shook as she held the rifle. She heard labored breathing on the other side of the door, and then a rattle, and then nothing. The final word escaped Lydia's mouth with a withering hiss, and then there was silence.

Rebecca forced herself to stand, gun still raised. She stepped quietly to the door and placed one hand on the knob.

"Rebecca, don't," Henry said. Rebecca ignored him and opened the door.

She smelled them before she saw them. A thick, evil smell, like an infected wound. Three dead bodies lay in a twisted heap in the doorway. Two were curled so their faces were hidden, but the third lay sprawled on his back, head tilted toward the door, mouth open. His face was a mass of boils, black and yellow and red, all oozing pus. Foam poured from his gaping mouth, his bloodshot eyes staring blindly at Rebecca, and for one horrible second, she thought she would be sick.

"Jesus," Henry murmured. Rebecca took a step back, covering her nose and mouth with her sleeve. In the distance, she could see more men running toward them, shouting to one another in frantic German. She raised the rifle.

"Close the door," Henry said.

She stared down her prey as their shouts became more urgent.

"*Rebecca.*"

She pulled the trigger, and the shouts were replaced by a sudden scream as one of the men fell, clutching at his heart with his hand. The others opened fire. Rebecca tucked herself against the wall but left the door open. She steeled her nerves, then stepped into the doorway and fired twice more, missing both times.

"Merde."

"The door!" Henry shouted.

Rebecca closed the door and bolted it. "There are five left. All on this side. They've left the back unguarded. You should go."

Henry shook his head. "We're not leaving you."

"It's okay," she said, and in that moment, somehow, it really was. She felt that stubborn shred of survival instinct let out one last, heaving sigh, and then go quiet as something else took its place. A cold, hard resignation.

Henry's mouth fell open as he searched for the words that would change her mind. He turned to Lydia for help, and then his face changed.

"Lydia?"

The color had left Lydia's face, and beads of sweat stood out on her forehead. Her lips were dry and cracked. She opened her mouth to speak, but only a hoarse croak came out.

"What's wrong with her?" Henry placed a hand to Lydia's cheek, and she moaned softly. Outside, the shouting grew louder. Rebecca watched in growing alarm as Lydia's eyes rolled back and she began to convulse. The veins in her throat bulged, and foam gathered at the corners of her lips.

Henry placed his hand under Lydia's head just before it hit the floor, cradling her as she shook. "Oh, God. No, please, no."

She's dying, Rebecca realized, watching helplessly as Henry held her, and Lydia's fingers curled into fists. What was it Lydia had said, as they drove to Château de Laurier?

Magic that powerful would burn through a lone witch like kindling.

And now, here they were, watching Lydia be consumed from the inside out.

Rebecca forced herself to keep the rifle trained on the door, blocking out the sound of Lydia's muffled gags and Henry's desperate prayers for help. She heard Lydia go silent. She heard Henry's pleas grow more frantic.

In the air all around them, something shifted, almost imperceptibly. She smelled ozone, and felt the air seem to condense, like the moment just before a storm.

She heard Henry gasp, and turned.

A smartly dressed woman stood over Henry and Lydia, an irritated look on her porcelain face. She was around Lydia's age, beautiful in a way that was almost unreal, with red lips and hair the color of dark honey. Her shoes and dress were both a rich shade of pink that enhanced the sapphire blue of her eyes. On her lapel she wore a silver rose, encircled with thorns. The woman looked down at Lydia and pursed her lips.

"Bloody hell, girl. What have you got yourself into?" She looked up at Rebecca expectantly. Then she narrowed her eyes at the gun and opened her mouth to speak.

"Wait! You're the Traveler, yes?" Rebecca stammered. "We're friends. Please help her. *Please*." She held her breath and hoped her words would be enough to keep the woman from casting whatever spell was waiting on her pretty lips.

A loud crack filled the room, turning her blood to ice. Rebecca spun and trained the rifle on the door. "They're breaking it down!"

She stole a glance over her shoulder. Lydia lay deathly still on the stone floor, her lips gone blue. Henry knelt on one side of her, his face ashen; the golden-haired woman knelt on the other. The woman squeezed Lydia's limp fingers in her hand.

"Come on, girl," she said. "Let's go home."

The *Grimorium Bellum*, tossed aside in the commotion, lay open on the floor, forgotten.

"*Wait*," Rebecca cried, but the ozone smell had returned, and before the word had finished forming, Lydia and the woman were gone, leaving the book behind. Henry looked at her as the terrible realization settled on them both.

The door cracked again, and then again. Rebecca could see the splinters forming in the wood. In a moment, the Gestapo would be inside.

She looked at Henry. "Was she breathing?"

"I don't know." He stared down at the place where Lydia had been just a moment ago. "I don't think so."

The pounding continued. Rebecca could see light through the cracks in the door. She saw the men on the other side. She felt her spine go hard as grim reality finally set in.

"We can't let them have the book," she said. "Take it. Run."

Henry looked up. "I'm not leaving you to die."

He was being stupid, and he knew it. Letting his gallantry get in the way of the only thing that mattered.

"Please," she said.

Henry shook his head. "No."

She knew what had to be done. She hoped that maybe someday he would forgive her.

Rebecca aimed the rifle at his heart. "Run, or I'll shoot you."

He cocked his head, confused. "You won't." The door cracked again.

She fired once, and Henry staggered back, covering his head as plaster exploded from the wall just to the left of him. Shock and hurt flashed across his face.

"You don't know me very well."

I'm sorry, she thought. *Forgive me.*

He opened his mouth to speak, but something in her eyes seemed to change his mind.

"Pick it up," she said.

He did.

"Now run."

He looked at her for a moment, pleading silently for her to reconsider. She stared back, gun steady.

Henry turned and ran.

She kept the gun on him until he was out of sight, then returned her attention to the door. The voices grew louder, and the wood began to give way.

She raised the rifle and waited.

THE
HERMIT

Seventeen

When he was very small, Henry had imaginary friends.

Some of Henry's friends spoke, and some were silent. Some were little kids and would play games with him when he was lonely. Some were grown-ups and watched over him when he slept. Most of them were friendly, but not all. He understood that other kids had imaginary friends, and that eventually they grew out of them.

His friends were different.

As he grew older, he found that he had more friends, not less. They began asking him for things—cigarettes, stolen from his mother's purse. Half his dinner, beer or rum. They told him to do things: *Leave your pocket money in the mailbox of that house. Go up to the lady in black and tell her Jim is sorry. Tell her now.* He would wake in the middle of the night and find his room crowded with them, standing shoulder to shoulder.

One night Henry's mother, Fabienne, came into his room and sat on the edge of his bed while he cowered under the covers, pretending to be asleep.

"Henry," she said sternly, "you haven't slept in three days, and you're not sleeping now. Stop playing."

Henry poked his head out from under the covers.

"Why aren't you sleeping?"

"I don't know." Over his mother's shoulder, one of his invisible friends glowered at him, demanding his attention.

"Henry, stop lying."

Henry knew better than to make his mother ask him the same question twice. He tried a half-truth.

"It's too loud."

Fabienne watched him, her eyes seeming to slice into his skin until she got to the truth underneath.

"Too loud, huh? You never thought it was too loud before."

Henry shrugged. The man standing behind his mother began to shout, screaming, *I want a fucking drink! A man needs a drink! You get me a drink right now or I swear to God—*

"You got some new friends, huh?" she said. The shouting man looked at Henry's mother for the first time, as if she had just appeared in the room. She never acknowledged him, but there was a change in the air, a subtle power shift that came from the straightness of her spine, the upward tilt of her chin. Grumbling, the man retreated to the window, where he sat on the sill, waiting.

Henry's mother stroked his hair. "You know, cheri, the thing about friends is that it goes both ways." Fabienne rarely called him anything other than his name, and the endearment made him relax just a little. "A real friend knows they can't just take; they have to give too. And a real friend won't try to get you in trouble, or keep you up all night because you're scared. Do you understand what I'm telling you?"

"Yes, Mama."

"You have some friends like that?"

Henry swallowed. "Yes."

"That's no kind of friend, Henry. And you don't have to give that kind of friend the time of day. You don't owe them nothing. You just tell them to go away. You understand?"

"Yes," Henry whispered.

"I want to hear you say it." She placed a hand on his shoulder, firm as a vise. "Say, 'You're no kind of friend. Go away.'"

Henry wasn't sure he could.

"Say it."

He looked at the man on his windowsill. "You're not my friend. Go away."

"Say, 'I'm going to sleep now.'"

"I'm going to sleep now."

The man on the windowsill sneered.

"Say, 'Goodbye.' Say it like you mean it."

"*Goodbye.*" He said it in the biggest, strongest voice he could manage. The man on the windowsill bared his teeth, the inside of his mouth rotted and stinking, but then he turned and climbed out the window, and did not return.

Henry's mother sat on the edge of the bed until the man was gone, then stood without a word. She went to the window and glanced out, then turned her back to it.

"You sleep now, you hear?"

Henry nodded. He lay awake in his bed for a long time after she left, waiting for the shouting man to return, but he never did.

HENRY LEFT CHÂTEAU DE LAURIER and ran like hell until nightfall, only stopping a handful of times to catch his breath and get his bearings. Once or twice, certain he'd been followed, he crouched in shadows, shivering in the cold until he was sure he was alone. The *Grimorium Bellum* hung from his shoulder in a canvas pack, chattering gleefully.

At sundown he stumbled out of the woods and found himself looking down from a hilltop onto a small stone farmhouse—a squat, drab little spot against the spectacular pink and crimson of the late-autumn sunset. It was the Boucher farm. He knew Richard Boucher only by reputation, but he'd heard enough—that the man sold milk to his neighbors on the black market, that he sheltered liberation fighters— so-called maquisards—on his property. Henry staggered toward the house, sweating through his clothes in the bitter cold, and knocked on the door. He heard voices inside. The family was eating their dinner.

Richard Boucher opened the door. He was an enormous man, bigger even than Henry, with sleepy eyes and a heavy, downturned mouth. Boucher took one long look at Henry, this half-mad stranger panting in his doorway, then glanced toward the tree line.

"Were you followed?"

Henry shook his head, too winded to speak.

Boucher gave him another stony look.

"Come with me."

He led the way across the field to a little gray barn. Henry was so exhausted he could barely keep up. He tripped over his own feet once and nearly toppled to the ground, but managed to right himself in time.

Boucher opened the barn door and directed Henry toward the hayloft, where he discovered several rough sleeping pallets, already made up with stacks of threadbare quilts.

So, it's true, he thought. He turned to thank Boucher, but the man was already gone.

HENRY TRIED TO REST, but his mind wouldn't allow it.

Lydia was gone, maybe dead. He saw her face every time he closed his eyes, lips blue, seizing on the floor of Château de Laurier as he cradled her in his arms. And now he'd abandoned Rebecca to the Gestapo, a fact that filled him with sickening shame. Yes, she had shoved a rifle in his face and ordered him to go, but still. He should have insisted. He should have stayed.

Pushed to the farthest corner of the hayloft, the *Grimorium Bellum* sat, buzzing like a hive. Carrying it had felt like clutching a bomb, one that would tear him to pieces come the next full moon, when the Nazis would conduct their tracking spell again, and then there would be nothing Henry could do. They would find him, kill him, and take the book. It was only a matter of time.

Henry hated the thing. It seemed to make demands in a language he couldn't understand, like an itch he could never quite scratch. Lydia had been able to decipher the incessant chattering, like there was a private conversation happening that Henry couldn't hear. And then it had poisoned her from the inside out.

He wished he could see her. Talk to her. To know that she was alive and safe, and also, selfishly, to know that he wasn't alone. He remembered what Lydia had said to him that first morning after they'd met—that he had witch blood in his veins, and that was why the book spoke to him. She'd seen it on him, the thing Henry had been running from for fifteen years. She'd named it like it had been written on his face.

He wondered what his mother would say. He imagined she would laugh.

His mother, Fabienne, had grown up in Haiti before coming to New Orleans when she was just sixteen. She fell in love with Henry's father—handsome, charming, doomed George Boudreaux, a grocer's son from Tremé. George died of Spanish flu before Henry ever learned to walk, leaving Fabienne to raise their son alone, immersed in the world of Vodou, the spirits as ever present to Henry as air. If he closed his eyes, he could almost imagine he was there again: in his mother's tiny shotgun house, crammed full of people all dressed in white, the drumming and dancing, his mother moving her body until it seemed as if her soul had departed and something else had come and taken her place. He'd found so much joy and wonder in his mother's traditions, a sense of pride and belonging that made his ribs ache from holding in all of that love.

From his mother, Henry learned about the Lwa—the Vodou spirits who became as familiar to him as family. There was Agwé, who watched over sailors and helped them find their way. There was raunchy Baron Samedi and his wife, Maman Brigitte, who felt to Henry like a beloved aunt and uncle, the kind who would sneak you rum under the table and tell you dirty jokes. And there was Papa Legba, with his pipe and his cane, who loved dogs, spoke every language, and would grant you permission to commune with the Lwa, and with the dead, but only if it pleased him. Henry loved Papa Legba best of all and would leave him gifts at the crossroads near his house every day. He would close his eyes at night and imagine he was conversing with his departed ancestors, just like his mother. He imagined his mind as a great room full of doors, each one an invitation for someone or something to step through.

Until one day, they did.

First one at a time, and then all at once, the dead flowed through Henry's open doors. At first, he didn't mind. Mostly they just left him alone. Some were even friendly. But then they began to want things from him. Some of them made strange demands and would punish Henry if he didn't comply. Some delivered confusing messages, advice that didn't make sense until months or even years later: *Stay away from the man in the white hat. Don't drive with John. Stay in France. Trust the girl.*

"How do they know things that haven't happened yet?" Henry would ask his mother.

"That's Papa Legba sending you a message," Fabienne would reply. "When the dead tell you things, best you listen."

Henry trusted his mother and tried to heed her advice. But it was hard, at seven, to know the difference between a spirit who was delivering an important message and one who only wanted to make trouble for him. For years he fought to keep some sort of boundary between himself and the dead, but it was no use. The more he tried, the more enraged they became. They laughed at his childish demands that they leave him be. They screamed obscenities in his face—at home, on the street, sometimes at school. For a while, he stopped talking altogether, thinking that maybe they would grow bored of his silence, but they only grew more insistent. Some would become violent, pawing at him, trying to get inside him, as if curling up against his warm, soft insides would make them feel alive again. One spirit would linger on the street near his home, leering and exposing himself, muttering things as Henry walked by that made him feel queasy.

Some were quieter than others. The spirits that lingered by the cemeteries were always strangely subdued, standing among the raised tombs in the summer heat, dazed and silent. The ones at Dryades Street Library pored over the books or sat hunched at the tables, mute and sullen.

"Quiet places make quiet spirits," Fabienne told him.

Fabienne's house was never quiet. It was teeming with life, and food, and music, and laughter. The dead were drawn to it like a magnet, and Fabienne welcomed them with open arms, inviting them inside her home, her body. But always, with Fabienne, they remembered who was really in charge.

"You can't let them walk all over you," she would say. "This is your house. You're the boss. Tell them."

Henry didn't want to tell them. He wanted them to leave him alone. He began escaping his mother's house as often as he could, eager to avoid the lively spirits that flocked to her like moths to a flame. He stopped going to the dances and ceremonies, even when missing them filled him with a sense of loss akin to amputating a limb. He stopped leaving gifts for Papa Legba.

By the time he was ten, Henry was spending endless hours in the library, making friends with the librarians and devouring books indiscriminately to pass the time. It was there that he fell in love with art and history, with language, with architecture. He dreamed of enveloping himself in the cavernous quiet of Notre-Dame, the Louvre, Mahabodhi Temple, the lost city of Petra, Angkor Wat, places where even the most riotous spirits would feel compelled to silence. Soon he was writing to his father's sister in Paris, begging her to intercede with Fabienne, to let him come and live with her.

"You think they don't have ghosts in France?" Fabienne asked, one hand on her hip. But then she saw the haunted look in her son's face, and her resolve softened.

She let him go.

They did have ghosts in France. Plenty of them, following him through the streets of Montmartre, leering at him in the markets and at the cafés—but relief was never more than a few steps away. Cathedrals abounded in Paris. Museums became a safe haven for him, the dead so docile they almost blended in among the tourists and the students. With space to breathe, Henry could finally put his mind to the work of building the boundaries Fabienne had told him about. He set about closing every door inside his mind and dedicated a sliver of himself to always stand guard, night and day, keeping them closed, and the dead at bay. Sometimes they still managed to slip through, but most days, the only dead Henry encountered were the faces of the paintings and statues he studied. Hundreds of them, staring out at him with flat eyes from across the centuries. Lifeless and silent.

LATER THAT EVENING, Madame Boucher appeared in the barn carrying a bowl of watery soup and a heel of crusty bread. She was a small woman, hard around the edges, with a severe mouth and a head of fair hair, gone prematurely gray.

"I can bring more blankets," she offered. "I know you must be cold."

"I'm fine," Henry said. "I can't thank you enough for your hospitality."

"We do what we can." There was a defiant jut of the chin as she said it, an unexpected spark behind the eyes.

But Henry knew that every second he stayed, he was putting this family in danger. "I won't overstay my welcome."

"Stay as long as you need," she said lightly. "Bonne soirée."

"Bonne soirée, madame."

There was a lantern in the barn, but Henry dared not light it, and so he ate his meal in the dark. Steam poured off the bowl, condensing in the frozen air, and the soup was stone cold by the time he finished. Still, he was grateful for the food, and the shelter, and most of all, for the danger the Bouchers were putting themselves in to hide him. If he survived, he would need to find a way to repay them.

He lay in the dark, terror and loneliness swirling inside him. René was dead, and the loss of him stuck like shrapnel in Henry's chest, so painful he could hardly breathe. Rebecca had almost certainly been killed or captured. And Lydia had been spirited away back to England, gray and lifeless.

Lydia.

He should have kissed her that night. He should have pulled her into his arms and held her there until sunrise, then sent her and the *Grimorium Bellum* home to London, where they would both be safe. He'd wanted to—*God*, he had wanted to. Not just because she was beautiful, although she was. It was that he had been inside her mind, and what he'd felt there had been so vibrant and intoxicating, so *intimate*, he'd barely been able to think of anything else since.

He'd seen the flat where she'd grown up, all tea leaves and tarot cards, a jumbled, upside-down version of his own childhood home. He'd felt her elation the first time she managed to project out of her own skin, the memory so clear he was sure for a moment it must have been his own. He felt the deep well of love inside of her, for Kitty, and Isadora, and Sybil, sweet and green as new spring leaves. The tangled, frustrating, complicated love she felt for her mother, like trying to unknot a mass of string that refuses to be anything other than a mess. He felt how desperately she wanted to be perfect, the impossible standards, the self-recriminations. He felt her stubbornness, her bravery, her unyielding, uncompromising nature, and he wanted more of it, in his lungs, in his bloodstream. He wanted her.

But sitting there in his bedroom, with his heart pulsing in his fingertips, their lips inches apart, Henry had felt something slip through his defenses. He had let his guard down, and the piece of himself that had always stood sentinel over those damned doors had stepped away from its post, wanting to be there too. Wanting to be with her. And one of those doors had opened, just a crack.

The spirit had been harmless. Just a confused old woman with skin like paper, wondering what they were doing in her house. But her appearance had unnerved Henry so completely that there had been no recovering. The moment had been lost. And now Lydia was gone.

Henry sat up, blinking in the dark. He remembered how Lydia had projected out of her body, that first night at the château. If he called to her, could she leave her body again, and come and find him? He didn't think it really worked that way, but he felt compelled to try.

"Lydia?" He listened and waited. Somewhere outside, something small was scooped up by a larger animal and carried off, screaming into the night.

Another thought occurred to him then. Maybe Lydia hadn't survived. Maybe she really had died that morning on the floor of Château de Laurier, and he was calling out to a ghost. The thought was almost too terrible to consider, and yet he couldn't let it go. He sat in silence for a long time, imagining the worst, until he couldn't stand it for another second.

Henry closed his eyes and pictured a single door inside his mind. He felt a rush of cold air as it opened, prickling his skin.

"*Lydia?*" he whispered. He waited, every nerve and cell in his body alive with dread. Waiting.

But behind the door was nothing but darkness and silence.

BY MORNING, Henry had made up his mind to return to Château de Laurier.

He'd stood before that open door all night long, calling Lydia's name and then Rebecca's into the void, and received no reply. It was possible he would never learn what had become of Lydia. But Rebecca had been alive when he'd left her, just a few short miles through those woods.

He needed to know.

Madame Boucher provided him with a winter coat that had once belonged to her oldest son, along with some water, and bread and cheese. In his pack, Henry carried the *Grimorium Bellum*, which gave off an electric hum like cicadas and made his teeth ache. The day was bright and crisp, and the hike became a sort of meditation.

He reached the château by late afternoon, just as the sky began to turn a shade of brilliant, saturated blue—the last, dazzling gasp of daytime before the sun began its descent into evening.

He approached the château carefully, in case the Nazis had left someone behind to guard it, but the place was abandoned. Tire tracks marked where the Gestapo vehicles had come and gone. Henry spied dark brown stains by the front door, and more by the kitchen window. He looked for Rebecca's car, but it was nowhere to be found.

Maybe she made it after all, he thought. It was a wild hope, too dangerous and fragile to believe.

The door to the kitchen lay in splinters on the floor. As he entered, Henry found even more blood pooling on the stones and splattered across the wall, along with what looked like brain and fragments of bone. There was a revolting smell in the room, like bad meat. He swallowed to keep from gagging.

No bodies. Whatever happened, there had been at least a few survivors to carry away the dead.

There was more blood in the stairwell. Henry followed the droplets scattered across the floor like breadcrumbs, leading up and into a lesser-used wing of the château. He reached a door he was certain had always been kept closed but that now stood wide open. Streaks of rust-colored blood stained the doorframe, and dark, sticky fingerprints congealed on the handle.

The room had been turned upside down. The wardrobe was thrown open, with coats and furs strewn across the floor. An old mattress had been torn from the bed and slashed open, spilling horsehair across the room, and the blankets were piled in a heap by the footboard. A carved wooden chest had been emptied and tossed aside, lying half-broken where it had landed. *A shame*, Henry thought. He'd always had a soft spot for beautiful old things.

He continued down the hall, following the trail of dark brown droplets as he went, leading to the library. More blood stained the floor in front of the open doorway, smeared as if someone had been dragged away. At the far end of the library, the narrow door leading to the chapel stood open, with a splintered hole where the handle had once been. Dust motes floated in the golden afternoon light, looking strangely peaceful against the blood and debris.

Whatever happened, she didn't make it easy for them, Henry thought.

There was an unexpected smell in the air—the bitter stink of old smoke. Henry noticed an enormous leatherbound book lying on the floor. The book's cover was charred as if it had been set on fire, and the musty old rug had blackened around it like a dark halo. The base of an oil lamp lay nearby.

"What happened here?" The sound of his own voice was jarring, a startling break in the deep silence of the empty château.

With a sick sense of dread in his stomach, Henry left the library the way he had entered and climbed the stone steps to the topmost floor, to the secret rooms where he and René had hidden some of the Louvre's most precious works of art. He felt queasy, imagining what he might find behind that door. He placed his hand on the cold iron knob, prepared himself for the worst, and pushed.

Everything was exactly as he had left it; every painting and sculpture in its proper place, safe and hidden. Relief washed over him. It seemed the Gestapo had missed the cache of treasures that had been right under their noses the entire time. He could have wept. *Three years of his life.* His sacrifice, René's sacrifice, had not been for nothing.

A figure passed through Henry's vision, there and then gone.

He staggered back, with his heart pounding inside his chest. He was certain there had been someone standing in the doorway, but now there was no one. He waited and listened.

"Hello?"

But the silence was complete. He was alone.

He descended the stairs warily, adrenaline still coursing through his veins. He returned to the library and sat at the mahogany writing desk. Inside the drawer he found a piece of stationery and a pen. He wrote:

Dear Monsieur Jaujard,

I regret to inform you that René Dreyfus has passed away unexpectedly. I am afraid that despite my commitment to our work together, I'm unable to remain at the château any longer. I humbly request that someone be sent to collect Monsieur Dreyfus's personal effects at the earliest convenience.

Sincerely,
H. Boudreaux

He sealed and addressed the letter. He felt fairly certain that his message wouldn't catch the attention of the government censors. With any luck, the Louvre's director would receive it and send someone to re-locate the art before the Nazis discovered it. His heart ached knowing that he wouldn't be able to accompany the artwork to its new home, but he had a more pressing duty now.

Henry turned away from the desk, then staggered as a wave of dizzi-ness caught him by surprise. The hairs on the back of his neck stood up. He tried to get his bearings, unsure what had brought on the sudden disorientation.

It was a smell, he realized. Not the bitter, burning smell he had no-ticed earlier, but something spicy and familiar. Cologne.

René's cologne.

He looked up.

There, framed in the open doorway, was the shape of a man.

Eighteen

R un, or I'll shoot you." Rebecca aimed the rifle at Henry's heart.

"You won't," Henry said. The door cracked again. Rebecca fired, plaster exploding around them.

"You don't know me very well."

She hated herself. She wondered if he hated her too. She hoped that years from now, he would understand.

"Pick it up."

He did.

"Now run."

She held the gun on him until he was out of sight, then turned her attention to the door. She held the rifle steady, watching as the wood split before her eyes, daylight streaming between the cracks.

Wait, she told herself.

The doorframe broke apart with a final snap, and the first Gestapo stepped through. Rebecca took a breath, held it, and pulled the trigger. Noise filled the room, and the man's face disappeared in a spray of red.

His body sank to the ground and landed in a heap. Blood pooled around what remained of his head and spread across the kitchen floor.

Four left.

There was a brief and frantic retreat. Angry shouts filled the air. Another face appeared in the doorway but pulled back before Rebecca could fire. She stood her ground, waiting for them to make another appearance. She caught movement out of the corner of her eye and turned her head, just in time to see one of the Gestapo standing at the window, gun drawn. Both fired, the deafening cracks following each other in rapid succession, and Rebecca fell back as a searing pain tore through her left shoulder. As she stumbled into the shelter of the stairwell, she saw the side of the man's neck, torn open and hemorrhaging, and he fell out of sight.

Three.

She looked down. Blood bubbled forth from the hole in her shoulder. She knew that whatever happened next, she needed to keep the remaining Gestapo occupied long enough for Henry to escape. She pressed one hand to the wound and felt a lightning bolt of pain explode through her body. She let out a low whimper but did not scream.

Her ears pricked to the unexpected sound of silence. The Gestapo were regrouping. Straining at the stillness, she heard an almost imperceptible click followed by a soft padding of feet. One of them had circled around and come in through a back door. They were trying to get behind her.

She climbed the stairs backward, keeping the rifle pointed toward the bottom step. Blood fell in fat droplets at her feet and left crimson streaks along the wall where she leaned for support. As she reached the landing, she glimpsed an approaching shadow as it crept across the floor.

She ran.

Doors lined the long corridor. She was running blind, her feet carrying her as fast as they could away from the approaching footsteps. She opened a door and saw that it was a bedroom, musty and unused. Thinking fast, she smeared her bloody hand across the doorknob and on the frame, leaving the door ajar. She heard voices behind her and kept running, coming to a stop in front of an open door at the far end of the corridor. It was a sunny room lined with books. A library. She stepped inside and closed the door behind her.

Angry shouts filled the air as the Gestapo searched the bedroom at the other end of the hall. She had perhaps a minute before they realized their mistake and came looking for her. There was another door at the far end of the library, and she ran to it, biting back the urge to cry out in pain as she pressed against it with all of her weight, but it was no use. It was locked.

"No, no, no, no. Merde!"

The voices in the corridor grew louder.

"*She's not in here*," one of them said in German.

"*Do you see the book anywhere?*"

"*No, it's not here.*"

On the writing desk by the window was an old oil lamp and a canister of matches. Rebecca turned to the shelf closest to her, grabbing the biggest book she could find—a beautiful leather-bound volume with gold lettering and illuminated pages. She thought of her father, the hours he would have spent poring over a book like this one, and felt a pang of guilt as she tossed it onto the floor.

"For the cause." She picked up the lamp. She heard heavy footsteps getting closer by the second. They were coming for her.

She tossed aside the glass chimney and poured the oil from the lamp onto the book. She heard voices outside as she struck a match. The door swung open, and the match fell, instantly engulfing the book in flames.

The Gestapo opened fire, but Rebecca was already on the move, ducking behind the tattered yellow sofa that stood in the center of the room. From where she crouched, she could see her only means of escape—the locked door, mocking her.

"You want the book?" she shouted. "There it is!"

She heard one of the Germans curse. *"She's burning the book!"*

"Put it out, you idiot!"

Rebecca popped her head above the edge of the sofa, aimed, and fired, hitting one of the Gestapo in the gut. She didn't wait for him to hit the ground. She ducked behind the sofa, aimed her rifle at the locked door, and fired again.

The lock disappeared in an explosion of splinters. She heard the two remaining Germans speaking frantically to each other, and to their gut-shot companion, now crying for his mother on the floor. The two men grabbed their injured friend by the shoulders and dragged him, screaming, into the safety of the hallway.

Rebecca wasted no time. She ran, exploding through the shattered door and down the stairs, running so fast it felt as if her feet could fly, skipping steps as she went. She'd had dreams like this, panic making her lighter and faster than she had ever known possible. The pain in her shoulder seemed like nothing now. Now there was only room for one thought—escape.

She heard shouts behind her.

"She's getting away!"

"Forget the girl, save the book!"

"Keep pressure on that!"

Rebecca found herself in a dusty room filled with old wooden pews. A chapel. There was a door, and she threw herself against it, crying out with relief when it swung open. She saw her car in the distance, knew that the keys were on the seat. Only when she'd reached the car did she look back. No one was coming. She tossed the rifle onto the back seat, and a laughing sob escaped from her chest as the Citroën sputtered to life. She drove as fast as she could and didn't look behind her again until she was miles away.

REBECCA DROVE. Sometimes she laughed all alone in her car, a high, triumphant laugh of disbelief. Sometimes she cried quietly, and sometimes she screamed. For a while she talked to herself, cursing the Nazis in French, English, German, and then in Yiddish, which felt best of all. Finally, when she was certain she had not been followed, she pulled to the side of the road and turned off the engine.

She inspected her injured shoulder. The bleeding had slowed but not stopped, and the left side of her blouse was soaked through with blood. There was no exit wound. The bullet was still inside her, and without attention, the wound would fester. She needed help, and soon, but the safe house was gone, and any hospital she stumbled into was sure to be overrun with Germans.

There was only one safe place she could think of. She sat in the silence of her car for a long time, wondering if dying might not be preferable.

Then she cursed out loud and began to drive once again.

SHE REACHED THE HOUSE by nightfall. She was hungry and parched, exhausted to the point of collapse, and yet, when she saw the shabby little farmhouse come into view, she nearly kept driving. Rebecca stopped the car and got out, a groan escaping her lips as the sudden movement caused an explosion of pain from her shoulder.

The house had fallen into an even worse state than she remembered. The front gate had come loose and hung limply from its hinges, and the azure blue paint on the front door peeled off in sheets. They would be watching her, of course. She imagined the commotion happening this very moment behind that closed door, the frantic whispers as she approached. She raised her hands in the air a moment before the door swung open.

"Hands up," a young man said. He was barely more than a boy, wearing a black wool beret and holding a machine gun he obviously had no idea how to handle.

"My hands are up." Rebecca tried to look past the boy. "Where's Claire?"

"Who the hell are you?"

"I'm one of you." She continued her slow approach toward the house, her hands still raised.

"Hey, stop." The boy's voice cracked as it rose. "Do you hear me, I said stop!"

"*Claire!*" Rebecca called. Two more men in berets appeared in the doorway, carrying more guns. Rebecca looked up and saw movement behind the curtains. She felt foggier than she had just a moment ago. She must have lost more blood than she'd realized.

"Go get Claire," she said. Her tongue felt thick.

One of the older men snorted, then turned to the boy.

"Shoot her."

Nineteen

hoot her." The man sounded almost casual as he gave the order.

One moment Rebecca was upright, then she was in the dirt, too weak to stand. She looked at her hands and saw that the left one was covered in blood. The boy grinned and pointed the machine gun at her skull.

No, she thought wildly, but no words came out. Only a pathetic whimper.

A woman's voice came from inside the house. "Who is it?"

"We've got it under control," the boy said.

"So it seems."

Rebecca looked up through the veil that shrouded her vision. Someone was walking toward her with long strides. They were backlit by the yellow light from the house, but Rebecca could make out the figure—slim and feminine, dressed in men's trousers and a button-down shirt, her blond hair forming a halo around her face. Even through the wall of pain, Rebecca felt a complicated rush of feelings as she took in that familiar silhouette.

"Christ. Rebecca." She didn't sound concerned so much as annoyed, and perhaps just a little impressed.

"Good to see you, Claire."

Claire turned and looked at the men behind her, still pointing their weapons. "Put those things away. Jesus."

The men did as they were told. Claire crouched in front of her.

"Were you followed?"

Rebecca shook her head.

"How can you be sure?"

Everything was out of focus. She was seeing auras. "I'm sure."

Claire waited, considering. Rebecca feared she would pass out before Claire made up her mind.

"I had nowhere else to go," she said softly.

Claire looked at her for a moment longer. Then she turned and addressed the men behind her. "Help her inside. Find her a bed. And get Lucas."

Two men came and scooped Rebecca up by the shoulders, and she cried out in pain.

"Gently!" Claire shouted. "Look at her. Gently. *Idiots.*"

Rebecca locked eyes with Claire just before she lost consciousness. "Thank you."

Then everything went black.

REBECCA WOKE TO a bespectacled man hovering over her with a look of intense concentration on his face. She felt an incredible pressure in her left shoulder and groaned.

"Sorry." A lock of dark hair fell over his forehead as he dug inside her shoulder with a pair of forceps.

Rebecca gritted her teeth. "Just get it out."

She was in a bed, one of several she could see from her prone position. The room had an odor that she recognized as the smell of too many young men in too small a space—a thick, sour stink of sweat and beer and cheese.

After a moment of digging, the man held up the bullet and dropped it into a cracked teacup on the bedside table. Rebecca gasped with relief, until he opened a bottle of clear liquid and smiled apologetically.

She braced herself. "Do it."

He poured the liquid onto the wound. A muffled moan escaped from between her teeth.

"You must be Lucas," she gasped as she caught her breath.

"I am." He had a kind face, with large brown eyes and a jaw he owed as much to hunger as he did to luck.

"Are you a doctor, Lucas?"

He set about stitching her wound. "Technically no, although I was heading in that direction before the war. As it stands, I'm the closest thing you've got."

A shadow fell across the door, and both Rebecca and Lucas looked up. Claire watched from a distance, holding a pitcher of water.

"Almost done." Lucas carried on stitching with practiced movements.

"Don't rush on her account," Rebecca said. He chuckled.

When he'd finished his work, Lucas cleaned and gathered his tools and gave Rebecca a reassuring smile. She watched as he and Claire huddled just outside the room, speaking in tones too low for her to hear. They stood close, and Lucas's fingers brushed Claire's as he walked away.

Oh.

Rebecca studied Claire's profile, the golden spirals falling out of her chignon and curling around her ears as she watched Lucas leave, and told herself that the ache she felt was just the pain in her shoulder, nothing more.

Claire sat at Rebecca's bedside, setting the pitcher on the table.

"So, he's the one," Rebecca said.

Claire rolled her eyes. "Don't start."

"No, he seems nice. Handsome."

Claire ignored her. "Does it hurt?"

"No."

"Rebecca . . ." She noticed that Claire wouldn't quite meet her eyes. "What the hell happened to you? André is dead. So is the rest of your group. I assumed you were dead too."

André is dead, Rebecca thought. *Good*. At least the traitor got what he deserved in the end.

"I was captured." Rebecca watched Claire's eyes go small and hard, and realized she'd made a terrible mistake. Claire had strict rules about maquisards who were captured and then released. The fear was that a fighter could be turned, either through torture or threat of violence against their family, and be made to betray their countrymen. "They didn't let me go," she said quickly. "I never broke. I escaped."

"Escaped? How?"

She wasn't sure what to say. Telling Claire she'd been saved by a witch would be ludicrous.

She settled on a version of the truth. "There was a woman there, a German. I killed her with her own knife, stole her jacket, and walked out."

Claire looked down and said nothing.

"There was a policeman there who tried to flirt with me. He thought I was her." Rebecca reached for Claire's hand. "I bet he was surprised when he found that bitch dead in my cell." She had hoped to make Claire smile, but her face remained stony, and a moment later, she pulled away.

"And that's when you were shot, when they captured you?"

All business, then. Fine.

"No, that happened later." She was getting tired and feared she might say too much. "I can tell you everything tomorrow if you like, but right now, I'm hungry, and thirsty, and I'm in a lot of pain."

"I thought you said it didn't hurt."

Rebecca sighed. Things had always been this way with her and Claire, even when they were lovers. Every word a weapon, every misstep an opportunity for rebuke. She would have liked to blame Claire for the way things had been, but in her heart, Rebecca knew she'd been just as responsible.

She remembered their last fight, the words that had become a constant refrain in their relationship.

You're so angry, Rebecca! Claire had shouted. Rebecca had lost her temper at dinner again, over something so insignificant, she couldn't even remember it now. *Why are you so angry all the time, with everyone?*

You keep saying that! You keep saying I'm angry, like there's something wrong with me, but aren't you angry too? She had felt consumed by it, like she was sitting atop a pyre, burning alive. She'd seen the look in Claire's eyes, the way she recoiled from her, but she couldn't stop. *I've lost everything, everyone I ever loved, my whole family, and you want me to not be angry?*

That's not what I'm saying—

Then what are you saying?

Claire had hesitated, like she knew that once she opened this door, there would be no closing it. She sat on the edge of the bed they'd shared, and hung her head.

How can you say you love me, when all you feel is this rage, every second of every day? How can there be room for anything else?

Rebecca had tried to dig inside herself for that messy, beating vessel of her love. She'd wanted to pull it out of her chest, hold it in her hands for Claire to see. *Here. Here it is. Here's my love for you.* But she couldn't seem to reach it.

It was Claire who finally put them both out of their misery.

"You've been recruiting." Rebecca hoped the change of topic would lighten the mood. "There are twice as many here as last time. All new faces." She didn't ask what had happened to the old ones.

Claire raked her fingers through her hair. "They just keep coming. These *boys*, useless and scared and running for their lives, just desperate not to get carted off to some German work camp. They want to feel like freedom fighters, and carry a gun, but they don't listen. They're undisciplined, and impossible to train."

"And Lucas?" She didn't want to know, but couldn't seem to help herself. Like picking a scab.

Claire's face turned hard. "He's here because he wants to be."

"Good," Rebecca said, but she had waded into unfriendly waters, and they both knew it.

Claire stood. "Try to sleep. We'll talk more tomorrow."

Rebecca didn't want her to leave. She almost reached out and grabbed her. She almost said, *Please, stay with me. Please don't leave me alone.* But then, Rebecca always had been a stubborn mule. She watched Claire go. And a moment later, exhaustion came and draped itself over her, and she fell into a fitful sleep.

WHEN SHE WOKE AGAIN it was midday, and all the beds were empty, save for hers. She sat up, wincing at the pain in her shoulder. A pair of trousers and a gray wool jumper lay folded on the table next to the water pitcher. Rebecca stripped off her ruined clothes and pulled on the trousers and jumper over her bloodstained undergarments.

A group was gathered around the massive kitchen table, sharing a midday meal. Claire was with them, along with one other woman, a mousy-haired girl with birdlike features and a puckish, turned-up mouth. The rest were men, about a half dozen in total, all sullen looking with bad skin and teeth. Lucas was nowhere to be seen.

Claire looked up as she entered. "You're awake. Come, eat something."

Rebecca's skin felt grimy as she sat at the table. She could smell the blood that still clung to her skin and her underclothes. She recognized the person next to her as the boy from the night before, the one who had held her at gunpoint. She gave him a nod, but he didn't nod back.

Claire passed her a mug of beer and a heel of stale bread. "Not much to go around." She shrugged.

Rebecca ate, all too aware of the many sets of eyes watching her. She looked up and met the gaze of the bird-faced girl, who offered a flat smile and looked away.

"Heard you were with one of the groups out in Lyon," the boy next to her said.

"That's right."

"Heard you know André." There was something about his tone that set Rebecca's teeth on edge.

"Knew him. Yes."

The boy kept his eyes on the table in front of him. Rebecca looked at Claire.

"André was Roger's cousin," Claire said evenly.

Roger took a swig from his mug. "André was a good man. Died for the cause." There were nods and murmurs of agreement around the table.

This was more than Rebecca could take. She sipped her beer. "André betrayed every man and woman he fought beside, and now they're all dead."

Silence fell over the room. Claire sighed and shook her head.

Roger stared at Rebecca, mouth open. She stared back, wondering if he was about to strike her, or spit in her face.

"Except you, right?"

"Excuse me?"

"They're all dead, except for you."

Rebecca held his gaze. "That's right."

Roger's face rearranged itself into an unpleasant smile. "That must be one hell of a story."

She looked at Claire, but found no help there.

"Tell us," he said.

Rebecca did not look at Roger. She looked only at Claire, and Claire looked back, waiting. She felt a pulse of danger.

"I was supposed to meet André at a café outside Lyon. But André never came. I decided to leave, and that's when I realized I was being followed. They captured me and took me to a room where I was interrogated. And then I escaped."

"Escaped how?" Roger's mouth was full as he spoke, and a speck of food flew from his mouth and landed on the table between them.

"I killed the guard."

"How?" Roger demanded.

Now Rebecca did look at him.

"How did you kill him?" Roger smiled around the food in his mouth.

"Her," Rebecca corrected. "The guard was a woman. I stabbed her through the throat with her own knife."

Roger's face twisted. "They didn't tie you up?"

Rebecca shifted her eyes to Claire, who raised her eyebrows expectantly. *Well?*

She took another sip of her beer. "I guess they thought they had beaten me enough that I no longer posed a threat. As it turns out, they were wrong."

The bird-faced girl grinned. A soft chuckle made its way around the table.

"Where did they beat you?" Roger was no longer smiling.

"What?"

He shrugged, and Rebecca could see the menace settling into his wiry frame. "You said they beat you. But I don't see a single bruise. Where did they beat you?"

Rebecca felt the mood at the table shift as the laughter died away. *Stupid*, she thought. She should have held on to her scars and her bruises. She should have worn them like a badge of honor instead of letting Lydia gather them up, tucking them out of sight with her magic words. Out of the corner of her eye, she saw Claire lean forward.

Rebecca inched toward Roger until they were uncomfortably close, as close as lovers. She could smell the sour hunger stink of his breath.

"I could show you the marks." She ran her fingers delicately along Roger's wrist, a dare. "But we would have to go someplace private." She winked. Someone whistled softly.

Roger was the first to break eye contact. He leaned back in his chair, and the room seemed to give a collective sigh of relief.

"Fuck the Huns," said the man to Rebecca's right, smiling.

"To the Maquis!" cried another, and the rest of the table raised their mugs.

"The Maquis!" they shouted happily. "Vive la France!"

The bird-faced girl refilled Rebecca's mug. Rebecca looked at Claire and saw that she was still watching her.

"I could use some fresh air," Rebecca said.

REBECCA SLIPPED OUT the back door and into the damp November air. Her breath plumed around her, but the bracing cold felt good after the heavy, wet laundry stink of the house. After a moment, Claire appeared beside her.

She noticed how careful Claire was to keep her distance. There had been a time when they were never more than a few inches apart, always drifting toward one another like magnets. Now it seemed like Claire was doing her best not to fall back into Rebecca's gravity.

"Not exactly a diplomat, are you?" Claire said.

"Was I ever?"

Claire sipped her beer. "Roger won't forget what you said about André. He'll make trouble for you."

"André was a coward and a traitor. I wasn't going to sit there and listen to them toast him like some fallen hero."

"He got caught and he cracked," Claire said reasonably. "Everyone cracks. You know that."

"I didn't."

Claire pursed her lips. "Right. Of course."

Rebecca didn't care for Claire's tone. "What?"

Claire looked at her with those blue-green eyes that seemed to see through every kind of lie. "You forget. Lucas cut that blouse off you last night so he could take the bullet out. There was blood everywhere, but I saw clearly enough. Other than that hole in your shoulder, there's not a scratch on you."

"As scratches go, it's a good one."

Claire frowned. "You lied. I don't know why, but you did."

Rebecca could feel the tension between them begin to simmer. "Is there something you want to ask me?"

Claire stared her down, her eyes steady and unblinking. "I'm saying you may have been captured two days ago, but you didn't take any beating."

"You're saying I collaborated with the Nazis in exchange for my freedom." Even hearing herself say the words made Rebecca feel sick.

"What would you say, if you were in my position?" Claire stepped closer, anger making her forget to keep her distance. "You would say that anyone who leaves a Nazi interrogation room with air in their lungs probably talked, and that anyone who talks should be shot and left on the side of the road as a warning to others."

Claire was right, of course. It didn't even matter that she hadn't turned on her coconspirators. Rebecca knew what it looked like. She stared into Claire's eyes and saw how hard they were, how cold. And for the very first time, she understood the gravity of her situation.

"I'm not a traitor."

Claire looked out over the rolling patchwork of gray and gold and said nothing.

"Fine, then. If you want, I'll go."

Claire looked at her and sighed. "You can't go."

Rebecca felt something cold drop into the pit of her stomach like a coin in a well.

"Why not?"

"Pierre and Lucas took your car."

"They what?" Rebecca's voice rose. "Where did they take it?"

"They had business in town. They should be back in a day or two."

She felt her face go hot. "Who said they could take my car?"

"Well, Pierre is a communist, so he feels that whatever belongs to one of us belongs to the Resistance."

Rebecca snorted.

"And more importantly," Claire said, "it's not your car. It's mine."

Rebecca stared at her. "Like hell it is. I bought that car."

"With my money."

"It was *our* . . . that's *my*—" Rebecca sputtered. Claire watched her, arms folded across her chest. "Do you want me to go, or not?"

"I want you to tell me the truth," Claire said.

"I told you the truth. I was captured. I escaped. There's nothing more to tell." Rebecca stepped forward and pressed her forehead against Claire's, taking her face in her hands, and Claire let her. Rebecca felt her heart ache like an old wound. "Mon cœur," she whispered, "I would never lie to you. Never."

Claire looked into her eyes, and Rebecca thought she saw something there she recognized. A softness, hidden behind all that armor. For one moment, Rebecca was sure that everything would be all right.

Then Claire shook her head, pushing Rebecca away, and the cold air rushed to fill the space between them.

"You have until Pierre and Lucas return to think about your story," she said. "I thought I owed you that much."

Rebecca stared at Claire's face, at the splotches that had crept into her neck and cheeks. "And if my story doesn't change?"

But she already knew the answer.

Mon cœur, she wanted to say, *you know me*. She wanted to hold her like she did whenever they'd have a fight, so tight and so close that Claire would have no choice but to relent, and love her again. She felt fear, yes, deep in her bone marrow, because she knew Claire and knew what she would do. But more than that, she felt a horrible sadness—not for herself, but for Claire, who would do this terrible, incomprehensible thing, without question. She would kill Rebecca, rip open her own chest for the Resistance, and never share that burden with another soul. And that broke Rebecca's heart.

"They'll be back in two days," Claire said. She opened the door to go inside, no longer looking at Rebecca. "You should tell me what really happened before then."

Claire walked through the door, and Rebecca was alone, watching her breath as it turned to vapor in the November air.

Twenty

Henry stared at the man-shaped thing in the doorway. It was looking at him.

"René?"

The figure stood perfectly still, its face hidden in the gathering darkness, but Henry knew René's shape as well as he knew his own. He was afraid to move, afraid of scaring away whatever part of René stood before him now.

"They didn't find it." He kept his eyes on the thing in the doorway. "The art. It's still here. It's safe."

The thing that looked like René did not move.

"I'm so sorry I wasn't there for you." Henry felt the grief rise in his throat, hot and bitter. He thought he saw the figure's head move just a little, but he wasn't sure. He didn't know how to talk to this thing that was not quite René. He tried to imagine what Fabienne would do.

"Is there something you need to tell me?" he asked.

He blinked, and the figure was gone.

He blinked again, and René was next to him, staring out the window. The air felt colder. Henry had to fight the urge to back away.

René looked like himself, and also nothing like himself at all. He looked solid, but Henry knew that he wouldn't be able to touch him. To his relief, René appeared to be whole, and not the unrecognizable husk that he had buried just days before, and yet something about him looked profoundly lifeless. Nothing like the robust, pink-cheeked man who had loved wine, and dirty jokes, and Gustav Klimt paintings. That man was gone. This was something else entirely.

"René," Henry said quietly. The figure blinked. "René, what do you need to tell me?"

The spirit stared at Henry. Later, Henry would recall that it didn't speak at all, or if it did, it did not use words. Images appeared in Henry's mind, fragmented, like pieces of a puzzle. They materialized there as if there were a film projector behind René's milky eyes, playing a strange, silent film just for him. He saw a road, one he recognized, leading into the distance. There was a dead tree lying in a field with its roots above the ground, and then a farmhouse with a blue door, and a broken gate hanging half off its hinges. And there was a feeling, a sense of danger and foreboding. *Go there. Do not stay.*

"Thank you." Henry was shaking.

The spirit stared into his eyes, unseeing and uncomprehending. It did not reply. "René, I need to know. Rebecca and Lydia. Are they—"

But René was gone, and Henry was alone.

THE NEXT DAY he set out in Richard Boucher's borrowed milk truck, traveling down the road he'd seen in his vision, with no idea what he was driving toward. The temperature had dropped overnight, and half-hearted snow flurries danced across the road as he drove. Overhead, the sky was a flat, gray void.

The first time he noticed someone staring, he didn't pay them much mind. He assumed it was because of the color of his skin. On the side of the road, a middle-aged woman in a brown housedress stood very still and watched him pass. The wind whipped her hair, half obscuring her face, but she didn't seem to notice, and she never looked away.

The second time it was an elderly man, stooped and staring, exactly like the woman he'd seen a few miles earlier. He tried to ignore the old man and focus on the road, but the dark stain on the front of the man's shirt made him look again. He told himself it could have been mud, or motor oil, but Henry had seen enough blood by now to know it when he saw it.

The next man was young, as young as Henry, with broad shoulders and a crop of straight blond hair like straw. The man turned to watch Henry as he passed, and he saw that the man was missing half of his face. Flesh hung in shreds from the exposed bone, and blood matted his blond hair against his skull. A horrible emptiness sat where the left side of the man's jaw should have been.

Henry waited until the man was out of sight, then pulled to the side of the road. He felt sick and lightheaded. He looked out across the field and saw more figures in the distance, standing still as posts in the howling wind.

He understood what was happening. He knew it in an awful, falling sort of way, like a thing you wish you could undo, but can't.

You opened a door, a small voice inside him said. *You don't get to decide who comes through.*

There in the stuffy cab of the truck, Henry felt the *Grimorium Bellum* sniffing at the air like an animal smelling blood.

HE'D TRAVELED ONLY a few more miles before he came to a fork in the road and had to stop. The hazy vision René had shared with him showed only the first part of the journey, but that familiar stretch of road was hours behind him, and now he didn't know which way to go. He looked around for some sign to guide him, but there was nothing— no fallen trees that he could see, no farmhouse with a blue door and a broken gate. Nothing but empty road, stretching for miles in each direction. Henry closed his eyes, rubbing the bridge of his nose to relieve the headache he felt coming on.

He opened his eyes, and there was a boy standing in the road.

He was certain there hadn't been anyone there just a second before. The boy had simply appeared—gaunt and sallow, and no more than twelve years old. He stood perfectly still, dressed in summer clothes despite the cold. Henry could practically hear his mother's voice inside his head.

When the dead tell you things, best you listen.

He let the engine idle as he stared at the boy, and the boy stared back.

"Goddamn it," he whispered.

Henry turned off the engine and got out of the truck. Very slowly, he approached the boy. As he got closer, he saw that the boy's eyes looked like two silver cataracts, just like René's had. He didn't fidget or look away, only stared as if he were a wax figure, but Henry was sure he saw something like recognition behind the boy's milky eyes. The hollows of his cheekbones were two empty craters. The wind tugged at the boy's threadbare shirt and trousers, but he didn't seem to notice.

"Hello?" Henry said.

The boy blinked but did not reply.

He tried again. "What's your name?"

The boy looked momentarily stricken, like he couldn't quite remember the answer, and it frightened him. Then the expression faded.

Henry swallowed, looking around. "I'm a little lost. Do you know a farmhouse with a blue door? Broken gate out front?"

Henry waited for a reply, but the boy only stared. He felt so helpless, watching the wind tear through the boy's thin summer clothes. He wished he could have wrapped his coat around him, taken him someplace warm, given him something to eat.

"That's okay," he said softly. "I think it's time for you to go home."

The boy made a small movement that might have been a nod, or might have been nothing at all. Henry began to back away, unsure if he had helped or only made things worse. Then the boy spoke.

"*North.*"

Henry stopped. "What?"

The boy's throat bobbed, like the words were crawling up toward his mouth from someplace deep inside. "The man said go north."

His voice was strange and thin, like many voices all sighing and murmuring together, coming not from his throat, but from someplace else very far away. It was the voice more than anything that made Henry want to turn and run.

"What man?" Henry whispered.

The boy stared at him, and after a moment, Henry understood that he was not going to receive an answer. Perhaps the boy didn't know himself.

"North. I will. Thank you. Go on home now, okay?"

He got back into the truck and started the engine. As he drove, he saw the boy in his mirror, still watching the truck as it puttered away. Henry kept looking back, hoping each time that the boy wouldn't be there, but the fragile figure remained until he was just a speck in the distance, only disappearing when the horizon swallowed him up.

HENRY DROVE NORTH, watching his speed, keeping his eye out for Germans, and for the dead. They were everywhere—old and young, some bloodied and broken, some looking as if they had just come from the market, their dazed expressions and unnatural stillness the only hint that there was anything unusual about them.

He could feel the book's interest like hot breath on his neck. Before, its presence had felt merely unsettling. Now it seemed to howl and cry, shaking the windows, screaming for his attention. Several times he was sure he saw a dark specter looming next to him, but when he turned his head, there was nothing there. Henry held the wheel so tightly his fingers went numb. He kept his eyes on the road, and away from the shade in the passenger seat.

It was nearly dark when the gas ran out and he felt the truck begin to sputter. He pulled to the side of the road, cursing as the engine died. The book seemed to sense his panic. It reached for him, whipping itself into a frenzy, but Henry refused to acknowledge the thing. Outside the sky had gone an ominous slate gray, the half-bare trees twisting in the wind.

He stepped out of the truck. The wind was bitter, but the sudden burst of cold helped to clear his head. If he stayed with the truck, it would only be a matter of time before he was spotted, and then there would be trouble. He thought about abandoning it and setting out on foot to find safe harbor for the night, but he was lost, and the temperature was falling fast, and so he wavered, rubbing his hands together for warmth as his breath plumed around him. The dread that had been growing inside him split open, blooming into full-blown fear as the sky grew darker every second. Henry looked up and down the empty road, and seeing no better options, took his pack from the truck, tucked the book inside, and set out on foot.

The sun had disappeared behind the horizon, and the moon was not yet up, and soon Henry was enveloped in a thick, impenetrable darkness. He had no hat and no gloves, and his cheeks and fingers burned with cold. Inside the pack, the *Grimorium Bellum* shrieked and jabbered, furious at being ignored.

Henry tried thinking of ways to distract himself. He sang songs, recited Shakespeare, Walt Whitman, Langston Hughes. He tried to recall a presentation he had given years ago on Caravaggio, speaking the parts he remembered out loud and making up the rest. He talked to himself until the cold made his tongue thick and he began to slur his words. He chattered to himself, and listened to his footsteps, and to the wind, until eventually he reached another crossroads and was forced to stop.

Henry shivered in the cold, peering down one path and then the other. There was no spirit to guide him here, no dead boy to tell him which way to go. He looked around for any sign of a house with a blue door and a broken gate, or a fallen tree, but there was nothing but icy fields.

Panic seized inside of him like a bird caught in a chimney. He was lost, exhausted and half-frozen, with no relief in sight. He thought again about turning around, taking shelter inside the truck, and hoping for the best. He turned to go back the way he had come, and stopped.

There was a dog in the road, just a stone's throw from where he stood. It regarded him silently, alert and watchful.

"*Shit*," Henry said.

It must have been following him, but for how long, he had no idea. The dog didn't look dangerous, but Henry had been wrong before. He considered the contents of his pack—only a half-empty canteen, a little bread and cheese, and the book.

"Good boy," he said. The dog cocked its head in reply. Slowly, Henry reached inside his pack and broke off a bite-sized piece of cheese. He held it up high, and the dog caught the scent, shuffling his feet eagerly.

"Here." He tossed the cheese, and the dog caught it midair. "*Good*. Nice dog." He held his empty hands in the air and backed away slowly. "All done now. No more."

The dog finished eating and watched Henry for another moment.

Clouds of frozen breath formed around its open mouth. For several long, horrible seconds, Henry wondered what he would do if the dog decided to attack.

Just then, a whistle rang out through the night. The dog perked up, then trotted past Henry without glancing back, disappearing down the road that curved off to the left.

There was someone else out there in the darkness, Henry realized with a chill; the dog had a master.

He considered what to do. Henry wasn't keen on meeting some small-minded farmer in the middle of the night, but he would freeze to death if he stayed out in the cold much longer. Wherever the dog and its owner were heading, Henry had to assume there would be shelter there: a barn or a garden shed, someplace where he could sleep a few hours in secret, and be gone by morning.

Steeling his nerves, he followed after the dog at a quick clip, making sure to keep a safe distance.

At first, he saw nothing but the black silhouettes of trees, and the road directly in front of him. Then, slowly, the moon appeared from behind the clouds, and Henry began to make out the shape of a man, walking with a cane about twenty yards ahead of him, and a dog trotting along at his side. It was hard to see much in the silvery darkness, but Henry could just make out the man's wide-brimmed hat, and note his halting gait. As the old man came into focus, the keening of the book seemed to rise on the night air, and for a moment, he thought he heard it speak a single word.

No.

Henry thought the night must be playing tricks on him, because no matter how fast he walked, the old man never seemed to get any closer. He wondered how it was possible that he couldn't catch up to an old man with a cane and a limp, and walked faster.

No, said the book. Henry was sure of it now, a maddening chorus of voices all saying, *No no no no no no no*. Henry picked up his pace.

A gust of wind blew through his clothes, slicing through to the bones, and he cursed under his breath at the cold. Henry thought there was a melodic quality to the wind's howling. It took him a moment to realize it wasn't the wind he was hearing at all, but the old man, out there ahead of him in the darkness, singing to himself. It was a jaunty song, upbeat and familiar—the man's voice was deep, but cheerful. Henry strained his ears, trying to make out the tune over the wind and the frantic protests of the book. He thought he could hear the stranger smiling. He wondered if the old man was mocking him.

He stumbled over a fallen branch, cursing, but quickly regained his balance. He was sure the old man must have heard him, but he never turned back or called out. He only sang. Henry listened hard, trying to place the familiar tune. That was when he heard the words, floating toward him on the biting wind. "Ti Zwazo kote ou prale," the man sang, "Mwenn prale kay fiyét Lalo." It was a Haitian children's song, one Henry had heard a thousand times growing up.

> *Little bird where are you going?*
> *I am going to Lalo's house*
> *Lalo eats little kids*
> *If you go she'll eat you too*

Impossible, Henry thought. He saw an orange spark bobbing through the night ahead of him—a pipe. The man was smoking a pipe. Henry was running now, running toward the spark, toward the familiar song, the Kreyòl words dancing through the night.

He looked to his right, and there, barely visible in the darkness, he could just make out the root structure of a massive tree, lying like a nest of snakes on the wrong side of the dirt, just like the one René had shown him.

Nononononononononono, the book droned. The words bled together and formed a wail. Henry could feel it like a child having a tantrum, pulling away from him, and from the old man in the dark.

"*Wait!*" Henry wanted to see the man's face, needed to see it. "Wait, please!"

He was sprinting, the air burning inside his lungs, and at last he saw that he was getting closer. The old man passed through a pool of silver moonlight, and Henry saw him in full—the dog, the cane, the pipe, the broad-brimmed hat, and yes, his face, just for a second, his skin darker even than Henry's, kind and mischievous and withered like an apple. He knew him then, knew him as well as he knew his own mother. Henry had left him gifts as a child—sweets and toys at the crossroads near his house. He nearly called the man by his name, but something, doubt or fear, held his tongue.

He ran so hard and fast he was sure his heart would burst. The book was begging now, shrieking for him to turn back, but he wouldn't. The song rang out as the stranger passed out of the light, all of him slipping into darkness except for the orange spark of his pipe, and now Henry was right behind him, close enough to reach out and touch, nearly on top of him, and then—

The orange spark blinked out. The song was swallowed up, like a needle lifted from a record.

"Wait." Henry doubled over, gasping. "Wait. Wait. Wait . . ." He felt his legs give out under him, and he sank to the frozen ground. He squinted into the darkness, searching, but the man was gone and Henry was alone.

Henry reached inside the pack and touched the book with his fingertips. He waited for a chorus of voices to rise up and greet him, but it was silent. He thought he could feel a dull, menacing pulse—the low rumble of an animal, frightened into submission by something larger and more powerful—but nothing more.

Henry dragged himself to his feet. He looked around one last time, as if expecting to see an orange spark, bobbing somewhere in the distance. But there was no spark—only trees, and fields, and there, far off in the distance, just barely visible against the dark hills and clouds, a squat black shape that might have been a house.

Twenty-One

Rebecca was pretending to sleep.

Downstairs in the kitchen, a heated conversation was going on. It was about her. She sat up and placed both feet on the floor. Around her, the dreaming sounds of the sleeping maquisards carried on uninterrupted. Rebecca stood, cautiously testing each floorboard as she made her way to the top of the stairs.

"Why is she still here?" Roger's voice floated toward her from the kitchen. "You know as well as I do she's been turned."

"Did I say that?" Claire asked, in that even tone that had always meant danger. "Did I say I *know* she's been turned?"

A pause, heavy with tension.

Roger continued. "You were the one who always said, if someone gets caught, that's it. It's too risky to let them come back."

"I told her she had until Lucas and Pierre returned. I wanted to give her time to tell me the truth about what happened."

"Well, they're back, so, I'd say her time is up."

Behind her, someone turned over on their mattress, making the springs scream in protest. Rebecca went very still, waiting to see if they would come and catch her out, but no one did.

"I'll deal with it in the morning."

"Deal with it *now*," Roger demanded.

Even from where she sat, Rebecca knew he'd made a fatal error. Claire was never one to take orders.

"You want to go up there and drag her out of bed right now, do you? Take her out back and shoot her in the head?"

"I'd do it. Absolutely."

"Because she talked about your cousin?" Rebecca heard the derisive sneer in Claire's voice.

"Because that's what we do to traitors," Roger hissed.

"I said I'd deal with it tomorrow."

"And if she feeds you more bullshit?"

Another pause. Then Claire's voice, low and calm. "I'll kill her myself. You can watch."

Even though Rebecca had known what Claire would say, she wasn't prepared for the pain of hearing it.

Oh, mon cœur, mon cœur, she thought. *I'm so sorry. I never should have come.*

She padded back into the bedroom and took her shoes from under the bed, slipping them on in the dark. A man's wool coat lay within reach, draped across the back of a chair; she put that on too. Whoever it belonged to might have needed it, but she would need it more. Claire had the keys to her car—Rebecca had seen them on the chain she wore around her neck, the one she never took off. There was a truck, but the bird-faced girl had taken it out earlier that day and hadn't returned. That meant Rebecca had only one option—she would be leaving on foot.

She was just about to duck into bed and wait for the house to go silent so she could slip out unseen under cover of darkness, when she heard shouting from downstairs.

"Someone's coming!"

She heard a chair scraping across the floor, then Claire's voice. "Where?"

Someone stirred in their bed. "What's going on?" they murmured.

Rebecca, sitting upright on the edge of the bed, fully dressed in someone else's coat, said nothing.

Soon, the whole room was awake and gathering at the windows, the air gone electric as the stranger approached the house. Rebecca quickly unbuttoned the coat, leaving it on the chair where she'd found it, and went to the window.

It took her eyes a moment to make out the figure in the darkness. It was a man, taller than average, and carrying something on a strap over his shoulder, but everything else was obscured by shadows. She heard cursing all around her as men scrambled to gather their weapons, but Rebecca stayed at the window, watching. When the stranger stepped into a patch of moonlight and looked up, she could just make out the contours of his face.

"*Henry.*"

She took the stairs two at a time, ignoring the footsteps and shouts behind her. Henry's eyes widened as she sprinted toward him, out the peeling blue door and through the broken gate. She laughed in disbelief as his lips formed her name.

"Hands up!" someone yelled. Henry obeyed.

"He's with me!" Rebecca barreled into him at full speed. She stumbled, then turned to see half a dozen men with guns drawn, pointed directly at them.

"Don't shoot, damn it, he's with me!"

Claire appeared in the doorway of the house.

"*Claire!*" Rebecca shouted. Claire watched in silence, leaning against the door frame, her face obscured in the dark. There was a long, terrible moment when Rebecca was sure she would order her men to shoot them both. Finally, Claire spoke.

"Relax. Rebecca says he's with her." She looked at Rebecca, each word falling heavy as a stone. The men lowered their weapons. Rebecca turned and hugged Henry tightly. They barely knew each other, but Henry never hesitated or pulled away.

"How did you find this place?" She could feel Henry's heart beating fast against her chest.

"It's complicated."

Rebecca pulled away. There was a strange look in his eyes. She'd seen that look before, in the faces of people who had seen too many terrible things. More than once she'd seen it in the mirror.

"Is the book safe?"

Henry nodded, and his hand went to the pack on his shoulder.

Rebecca felt a mixture of relief and revulsion forming a knot in her stomach as she instinctively recoiled from the thing, cradled like an infant inside the pack. She was sure she saw a shadowy figure out of the corner of her eye, writhing and pulsing like a mass of larvae, but a moment later it was gone.

Rebecca placed her lips next to Henry's ear. *"We can't stay here."*

"I know," he murmured back.

Claire appeared next to them a second later. She looked Henry up and down. "What's your name?"

Henry's hand tightened on the pack. "Henry Boudreaux."

Rebecca saw Claire's eyes flick to the bag, then back to Henry's face. "Nice to meet you, Henry Boudreaux. This is Roger. He'll find you someplace to sleep tonight."

Roger hovered just behind Claire's right shoulder, wearing a smirk that curdled Rebecca's stomach. She watched, helplessly, as Henry was led away. She did her best to appear calm as he turned and looked at her one last time and then disappeared from view.

"I think it's time we had that talk," Claire said softly. She walked away without waiting for a reply.

Rebecca followed her into the empty kitchen, past the long table to the pantry, where Claire stood waiting. A few cloudy jars of vegetables and sacks of turnips and potatoes were shoved to one side of the room. The other side was lined with tools, ammunition, spools of wire and cables in every size, and cans of petrol. A single naked bulb hung overhead.

"How did he find us?" Claire asked as the door swung closed behind them.

"I don't know."

"You didn't tell him to meet you here?"

"No."

Claire's face was an impenetrable barrier, all hints of their former closeness now evaporated.

"Should we be expecting any more of your friends?"

"No." Rebecca held Claire's gaze and waited, knowing what would come next. Her time was up.

"How did you really escape the Gestapo?" Claire asked quietly.

"I already told you."

"*Rebecca.*" Claire paused, and when she spoke again, her voice was almost tender. "You know what they'll do to you. What *I'll* have to do. Please. Tell me something. Anything."

Rebecca looked into Claire's eyes and felt a tidal wave of sadness. She wanted to trust her, more than anything.

"You won't believe me."

"If you tell me the truth," Claire said, "I'll believe you."

Rebecca was silent for a long time.

And then, she told her everything: About David Harlowe and the SOE. About the Englishwoman who could disappear, change her face, paralyze you with a word. She told her about the beautiful, sadistic woman with the voice that could strip you of your free will, how she'd made Rebecca carve into her own flesh, until Lydia had intervened. She showed Claire the symbol she had carved into herself, now nothing more than a raised, pink scar, told her how Lydia had healed her wounds, leaving only this. And she told her about the *Grimorium Bellum*—what it could do, what it had done to her when she'd tried to destroy it, and what would happen if it fell into the wrong hands. She almost told Claire that Henry had the book with him now, but didn't, and she hated herself for that. Something about the omission felt like a confirmation—that Claire was right not to trust her. When she finished, she watched Claire's face, waiting.

"Claire. Please say something."

Claire looked up, her expression unreadable. "What do you want me to say?"

"I want you to say you believe me."

Claire looked away. "I really missed you, you know. When you left. I really thought you would come back. And then you didn't—"

"You asked me to leave."

"I know I did."

The silence filled the tiny room, the space between them seeming to grow wider until it was an uncrossable canyon.

"Claire. Please look at me."

She did.

"Do you believe me?"

Claire took a breath. "Yes. I believe you."

And in that moment, Rebecca knew with complete certainty that Claire did not believe her. Not at all.

"Good." Rebecca was careful to keep her voice even. "Thank you."

"You should go back to bed," Claire said.

"You're right." Rebecca turned toward the door. Then, as casually as she could manage, she said, "What about my friend?"

Claire didn't look at her. "We'll take care of him."

There it was again, the buzzing amphetamine clarity that had been her survival for so long. She didn't feel afraid—not yet. Only a single-minded focus. *Get Henry. Get out.*

"Right. Well then, I should get some sleep."

Claire nodded.

Rebecca looked at Claire's face, the lines harder than she'd remembered from strain and hunger, and suddenly, more than anything, she wanted to touch her again. Even though she knew it wouldn't change anything. Rebecca closed the space between them and stood in front of her, so close she could feel the warmth from her body and smell the faint, familiar scent of her skin. She leaned in and grazed her lips against Claire's, and after a moment, Claire kissed her back—hesitantly at first, then easing into something softer, more tender. Time stretched, and the kiss deepened, turning to something sad and hungry. Something that felt like goodbye. Rebecca wanted to stay in that moment, drag her lips across every inch of Claire's skin, memorize her body so she could take it with her. Claire gasped against Rebecca's mouth, a sob caught just in the back of her throat. Then she pulled away, so fast it left Rebecca reeling, eyes down, her bruised lips hidden behind her fingertips.

"Good night, Rebecca."

Rebecca nodded, shaken and heartsick. Her mouth tasted like salt water. "Good night, Claire."

She walked out of the pantry and through the kitchen, passing the two maquisards smoking on the stairs, and returned to the empty bedroom. Now, finally, she felt it—fear, vibrating under her skin. She shook her head, trying to bring back that clarity that had saved her life so many times before.

Fear makes you stupid, she told herself. *Stupid people die.*

Rebecca picked up the coat from the chair where she had abandoned it a few minutes before. She put it on, every nerve in her body buzzing like a wire.

She stood by the window, peering out into the darkness. Behind the house, just beyond the frostbitten vegetable garden, was a shed, and inside the shed, she could see the yellow glow of a single lamp. Henry was nowhere to be seen, but Rebecca could make out Roger's stooped shape silhouetted in the doorway, smoking a cigarette in the cold.

There was a knife on one of the bedside tables, lying next to a half-eaten apple. She picked it up and slipped it into her coat pocket. After a moment, Roger disappeared back inside the shed.

Rebecca threw open the window as a rush of freezing air swept across her face like needles. Moving fast before she lost her nerve, she straddled the windowsill, one leg inside the room, the other dangling in the open air. To the left of the window was a thick, woody vine, now stripped bare of its leaves by the cold. Rebecca gave it a tug and found that it held firmly to the stone wall. She grabbed hold of the vine with her good arm and began to climb down.

Right away, she knew she'd made a terrible mistake. Fear had made her forget the pain in her shoulder, but now it erupted to the surface with a new urgency. She tried to fight through it, but she was still weak, and her stitches strained with every movement. She hung on for one final moment, gritting her teeth against the pain, then lost her purchase and fell. The air left her lungs all at once as she hit the ground, and she lay there for several agonizing seconds, willing herself to breathe.

She raised herself up carefully and took stock. Her wrist was tender, and she had torn her stitches, but she seemed otherwise unharmed. She got to her feet and made her way slowly to the shed, remembering to pull the leaves from her hair just before she stepped through the door.

Stay sharp, she told herself. *Stay alive.*

Henry was there, clutching his pack like a life raft. Roger looked up from his cigarette as she walked in.

"The hell do you want?"

She nodded toward Henry. "Claire wants to talk to him."

Roger chewed on something as he regarded her. "Why doesn't she come out here herself if she wants to talk to him so badly?"

Rebecca shrugged. "You'd have to ask her."

Roger spat on the ground and didn't reply.

"Look, I can tell her she needs to come out here herself, but then she'll be pissed off with both of us instead of just me. Your choice."

Roger sneered. A fleck of something dark clung to one of his teeth. "Fine." He looked at Henry. "Let's go."

"I'll take him," Rebecca said, too eagerly. "Lucas has something he wants to show you out front."

"Lucas, eh?" Roger squinted at her, and she knew that somehow, she had made a misstep. He spat again, and a strand of yellow spittle clung to his chin. He wiped it away with his sleeve, then cocked his head. "Come here."

Rebecca took one step forward. Inside her coat pocket, her fingers curled tightly around the wooden handle of the knife. She could feel her pulse in her fingertips, but whether it was fear or focus making her blood pump faster, she couldn't tell anymore.

"Whose coat is that?"

Merde.

"I don't know. I just threw it on."

"Mmph. You planning on going somewhere?" Before she could react, Roger reached out and snatched her by the coat, shaking her hard.

"Hey!" Henry shouted.

Rebecca pulled the knife from the coat and slashed wildly, catching Roger across the cheek. He cried out and released her, pressing his hand to his bleeding face.

"Bitch!"

"Run!" Rebecca commanded. She turned to flee, but found her exit blocked by an enormous man holding a gun. *Pierre*, Rebecca remembered. They called him Pierre.

"Ah, no." Pierre smiled apologetically. "So sorry, lovely girl. Nobody is leaving. Put that down." He looked at the knife in Rebecca's hand. Rebecca dropped it.

Pierre turned to Roger. "You all right?"

"She cut me! Cette putain!" Roger shouted, still holding his cheek.

Pierre said nothing, and Rebecca saw what might have been the hint of a smirk tug at the corners of his mouth, as if he found the whole thing amusing. He looked at Henry, and then at Rebecca, and finally back at Roger.

"Claire says it's time."

Twenty-Two

They were taken to the Citroën and forced into the back seat, with Pierre and Roger in the front. Pierre drove, while Roger sat in the passenger seat, one hand pressed to his face, the other holding Rebecca and Henry at gunpoint. Rebecca felt a surge of dread at every turn and bump in the road, watching Roger's clumsy finger as it fondled the trigger.

"So"—Roger licked his lips, the gun bouncing in his hand as they drove—"Claire won't do it herself after all, eh? No stomach for it?"

"Her stomach's fine." Pierre gestured toward Rebecca. "She and this one have history is all."

Roger's face twisted into a shape Rebecca had seen many times before, an unmistakable marriage of revulsion and arousal that had become all too familiar to her.

"I knew it." He curled his lip in disgust, even as his eyes wandered over her body.

She understood what came next. She and Henry would be executed, their corpses left with a note identifying them as collaborators, a warning to others. She should have been terrified, but as the car rattled through the darkness, black trees passing in and out of their headlights, all she could seem to feel was an incredible flush of rage.

She stared at Roger with a look of flat contempt. "He was a moron, you know. Your cousin."

Roger's smug smile turned to a frown. "You shut your mouth, whore."

"The Gestapo told me he didn't last three hours under questioning. Can you believe that? I bet even you would have lasted longer than that."

"Rebecca . . ." Henry said quietly, but she was beyond caring.

"You can call me a traitor all you want, but I know the truth. And the truth is that André was a coward who betrayed everyone he knew just to save his own skin, and still he managed to die like an idiot. Do you think they shot him? Or did he just drop dead of shame?"

Roger pressed the gun against Rebecca's forehead. She felt the cold metal grinding into her skin, making her guts lurch, but she did not flinch.

"The only reason he didn't betray you, too, is that deep down he knew you're not a real maquisard. Just a boy, hiding in the woods, playing with your guns and wearing that *stupid*-looking beret, pretending you're a big man while the rest of us fight and die for France. Hell, even André managed to die for his country, and he was an imbecile."

"Hey," Pierre said calmly. "*You*, shut up. Roger, put that thing away. If you shoot them inside the car, I'm going to make you clean up the brains by yourself."

Rebecca found herself fighting the urge to laugh—a joyless, reflexive impulse she had seen before in those about to die. Roger leaned in close, his breath hot and sour, and whispered, "I'm going to take my time killing you."

Pierre grunted. "You're not killing anybody. I'm killing them, you're staying with the car."

Roger's mouth fell open. "Why?"

"Because Claire doesn't trust you to do it right, and neither do I." Roger looked like he was about to argue, but Pierre cut him off. "We're here."

And then it finally hit her, choking off that bitter laugh like a weed. Rebecca looked out into that deep, black night, and there it was—in her veins, in her skin, in her teeth. *Terror.*

They stopped the car along a narrow dirt road, flanked on both sides by thick woods. Above them, the moon drifted from behind the silver clouds, sailing across the sky.

Rebecca looked at Henry and felt all that fear mixing with a terrible regret. Henry hadn't asked for any of this. He wasn't a soldier or a freedom fighter. Rebecca had always imagined she might die a violent death, but looking at Henry, she felt the urge to give him some kind of comfort, for whatever it might be worth. She waited for him to look at her, but he was staring out the window, his gaze on something far away.

"I'm sorry I got you into this," she said. Henry looked startled, as if he'd only just remembered she was there. There was something unsettling in his gaze that Rebecca couldn't quite name—his eyes kept drifting back toward the tree line, fixing themselves on some unseen thing in the dark. She was about to ask him what it was, when Pierre's jolly voice announced, "Everybody out!"

The doors opened, and Rebecca and Henry stepped from the car. Roger stood too close as she climbed out, placing his face inches from hers, smiling his rotten smile. He waved the gun mockingly, and Rebecca was just beginning to think about taking it from him when Pierre snatched it from his hand.

"Give me that."

Roger's smug smile evaporated, and he slunk away, leaving Rebecca where she stood. She was shaking and couldn't seem to stop.

Pierre looked at her, not unkindly. "Let's go." She noticed that he never spoke roughly or barked commands. He was a man who understood that his imposing size spoke for itself, and so he never bothered to raise his voice, a trait that Rebecca viewed with a grudging sort of respect, even under the circumstances.

"Why not do it right here?" Roger asked. "Why drag them all the way into the woods if we don't have to?"

Rebecca knew why. It was a gift from Claire. One final kindness. Traitors were always left in public places, left to rot in the open, with a note, and a warning—*collaborators beware*. Their bloated corpses would serve as an example to others, clucked over and spat upon. Reviled. But not Rebecca. Her death would be private, her body returning to the earth, surrounded by trees, and birds, and darkness. Her name would be clean. She would have found the notion strangely calming if it weren't for Henry, whose only crime was having had the bad luck of meeting her. She glanced at him and felt his fear mingling with her own dread and self-loathing, threatening to consume her if she let it.

"Stay with the car," Pierre said. "If someone comes this way, you leave. I can find my own way back." He handed Roger the keys, then turned to Rebecca. "Come on."

Rebecca and Henry walked side by side with Pierre behind them, holding the gun. There was no path through these woods, and the uneven ground was thick with rocks and shrubs. Rebecca stumbled as the moon dipped behind another cloud, and Henry caught her by the arm.

Pierre chatted as if they were all good friends. "I'm sorry about Roger. He's an idiot, but he's one of us. Don't worry about that 'kill you slowly' business either. This isn't my first time. You won't feel a thing."

"I appreciate it," Rebecca said, desperately clinging to the last of her bravado, even as her knees turned to jelly beneath her. "Would it make a difference if I told you we're not collaborators?"

Pierre chuckled. "I'm sure you'd tell me anything right now. So no, not really."

"I didn't think so. Still. I thought you should know."

Out of the corner of her eye, Rebecca saw Henry stop and then stumble as Pierre shoved him from behind to keep him moving forward. He fell, and Rebecca knelt to help him to his feet, but he wouldn't be moved. He stared wide eyed into the darkness in front of him, as if looking at something only he could see.

"Henry." She squeezed his arm, but he didn't seem to notice. "Henry, I know you're scared. I'm scared too. But you have to get up."

There was something disturbing about Henry's face, his glazed expression as he peered into the darkness. He nodded slowly, and Rebecca felt a cold, creeping realization that the nod was not meant for her.

"Well, I guess this is as good a place as any," Pierre said with a sigh. Rebecca felt her guts go icy. "Do you pray?"

"I do," Henry said, still staring into the darkness.

"Have at it, then."

Henry nodded again, his eyes still trained on the woods. Rebecca wondered if it was the book making him act this way, and the thought of it filled her with the kind of terror that caused animals to chew off their own limbs.

There was a moment of quiet, and then Henry spoke.

"I see you." He stared, unblinking, at a fixed point in the darkness. "What's your name?"

Pierre took a step forward. "What did he say?"

Rebecca stared between the trees, straining her eyes to see what Henry saw, but there was nothing. "I don't know."

Henry smiled, and the sight of it was so unnerving Rebecca found herself backing away from him. "Hannah. It's nice to meet you. I'm Henry." A pause. "Can you help us?"

"What the hell is this?" Pierre stepped closer. "Is he having a fit?"

Rebecca reached out and touched Henry's shoulder. "Henry?"

He nodded once. "That's fine. Thank you."

What came next happened very quickly. There was a shifting in the darkness, a flutter of movement in the moonlight. Rebecca felt something move past her, close enough to make her yelp and shrink from the unseen thing. And then she heard a sound, one she had heard before, too distinctive to be mistaken for anything other than what it was—a long, hissing expulsion of air, the kind you sometimes hear from the newly dead.

She looked at Pierre. He was on his feet, but his posture looked strange, twisted and unnatural. His mouth hung open, his face frozen in an empty mask. He'd gone pale, so pale he seemed to reflect the moonlight, and as Rebecca got to her feet, she saw that his eyes were all wrong—they had gone milky white, like two pearls. The gun lay forgotten at his feet.

Henry was standing now, too, watching Pierre. After a moment, the death rattle fell silent, and Pierre turned his clouded eyes on Henry. Rebecca thought she would scream looking into those blank, unseeing eyes.

"*Henry.*" Rebecca's voice was a strangled whisper. "Henry, we have to go. We have to go *now.*"

Henry cocked his head to one side. "It's okay. She won't hurt us."

He approached Pierre slowly, as if approaching an animal in the wild. Pierre's blind eyes followed him as he moved, making Rebecca's skin crawl.

"Thank you, Hannah," he whispered.

Pierre blinked.

"I'd like to do something for you in return. How can I help you?"

Pierre spoke, but the voice that came out of him didn't sound human. It sounded like radio static, howling wind, clattering stones, and death, death most of all.

"*My boy,*" Pierre said. And then nothing.

"Your son?" Henry took a step closer. "You had to leave him. You want to make sure he's okay."

Pierre nodded. Henry stepped closer still, so close that Rebecca wanted to shriek, to warn him to *stay away from that thing*, but he didn't seem afraid. Pierre opened his mouth, and the voice was there again, empty and terrifying, but if there were words, Rebecca couldn't make them out. She backed away, watching Henry and the thing that was no longer Pierre, her body quaking beyond her control. After a moment, Henry stepped away.

"I will," he said. "I promise."

Pierre stared and said nothing.

Henry knelt and picked up the gun. He looked at Rebecca.

"We should go."

Rebecca understood, but could not force her feet to move.

He held out his hand. "It's okay."

Slowly, Rebecca went to him, keeping her gaze away from the looming husk that had once been Pierre. Henry caught hold of her hand, and his touch was warm and reassuring. He turned back toward Pierre.

"Will you keep him here a little while longer? Just until we're gone."

Pierre nodded.

Henry hesitated. "Will he be all right? The man you're . . . occupying? After you leave?"

The thing inside Pierre said nothing, either because it did not care to, or simply did not know.

Henry looked as if he'd known that he wouldn't receive a reply. "I'll do what I said. I promise. You can go home, Hannah."

The thing watched them as they made their way out of the woods, the two pearly eyes the last thing to disappear into the darkness. Once they were alone, the tremor that had been coursing through Rebecca's body turned into a convulsion. Henry squeezed her hand tighter.

"Almost there."

The car was still parked where they'd left it when they reached the road. Roger leaned against the luggage compartment, smoking, his face turned away from them. Henry dropped Rebecca's hand and approached quickly, gun raised.

"Roger."

Roger turned to find the gun inches from his face. His cigarette fell to the ground.

"Move."

Roger stepped away from the car, hands raised, his face a sickly shade of white.

"Your friend is still in the woods. He'll be confused. You should go get him. Ten minutes south if you hurry. Go now."

Roger took off at a run, spewing curses as he went. Only when he was out of sight did Henry lower the gun.

"Time to go."

He opened the passenger side door for Rebecca and placed the bag with the *Grimorium Bellum* inside on her lap, careful not to slam the door after she was settled. Henry got in and drove, the moon above them peeking in and out of the treetops. He talked softly as they made their way through the darkness, more to himself than her, but there was something soothing about his tone that began to settle Rebecca's rattled nerves.

"I'm going to take you somewhere safe. I just have a few things I need to do first. There's a truck broken down a few miles back, I'll need to go get it in the morning, return it to its owner. I can visit Hannah's boy on the way. I'll need to come up with an excuse for the father. I'll think of something. . . ."

After a few minutes, Rebecca stopped shaking. She felt numb all the way through. She wondered if she was in shock.

"Henry?" She looked at him, staring straight ahead with his hands firmly on the steering wheel. "What happened back there?"

He kept his eyes on the road, and didn't answer.

She tried again. "Who is Hannah?"

Henry readjusted his hands on the wheel. "Hannah died last summer. Her son lives with his father on the other side of those woods. The father drinks." He cleared his throat. "That's what she told me, anyway."

Rebecca watched him. She felt her mind struggling to catch up with Henry's meaning. "You can speak with the dead?"

Henry hesitated. "Yes."

It might have been the shock, but Rebecca wasn't surprised by Henry's answer. She wondered if anything could surprise her anymore.

"So . . ." she said, "is everyone magic now except for me?"

Laughter burst out of Henry like a balloon, surprising them both. She laughed, too, the weight lifting from her shoulders as the air filled her lungs.

"I guess so," Henry said, the laughter still pouring out of him. "Sorry."

"No, it's okay. It seems horrible. You keep it."

They drove on, the headlights cutting a path through the darkness, the trees forming arches as they reached for each other with naked branches. Silence fell back over the car. Rebecca stared out the window as a question unfurled inside her chest. She looked at Henry as he gripped the wheel and stared straight ahead into the darkness, and thought he might have been pondering the same question.

"Do you think Lydia is alive?"

Twenty-Three

Lydia stared at the ceiling of her childhood bedroom, listening to the familiar sound of Evelyn puttering in the kitchen just outside her door. The bedroom was exactly as she had left it when she was eleven years old, before departing for the academy. Books sat atop the peeling white chest of drawers in haphazard stacks—*Swallows and Amazons*, *The Secret Garden*, a beautiful, secondhand copy of *Pride and Prejudice* that Lydia had begged for, only to get bored within the first few pages and never pick it up again. On the wall next to the bed, secured with tape, was a letter of acceptance addressed to Lydia from the academy, printed on creamy white stationery, now gone yellow around the edges. Beside the door, a 1935 wall calendar counted down the days to Lydia's departure, with the magical date circled in pen and decorated with hearts and stars.

Lydia sat up and immediately felt lightheaded. She breathed deeply, waiting for the feeling to pass, and planted both feet firmly on the ground. She chose a spot on the wall and allowed her eyes to relax. She pictured herself standing in the kitchen. She could conjure up the room in her mind's eye with no effort at all; every copper pot and faded tea-cup, the earthy, musty smell of Evelyn's jars of assorted herbs and po-tions. *Just on the other side of this wall*, she told herself. She waited for the familiar sensation, the feeling of sinking into the floor that always came just before she left her body. But the feeling never came.

She'd been back in London for three weeks. The first week she barely remembered, just a jumble of visions and voices—Fiona McGann's pretty face hovering over her: *Bloody hell, girl. What have you got yourself into?* Lying half-conscious in the infirmary while Helena worked her magic, fighting to keep her alive. Sybil, asleep by her bedside, a book open in her lap. Her mother, such an incongruous sight in the halls of the academy that Lydia was certain she must have dreamed it. And all the while, Lydia, half-dead and half-delirious, trying and failing to say the words: *The book. I left the book.* By the time she'd regained her senses, the terrible mistake had been realized, but it was too late. Fiona returned to the château to search for it, but the book was nowhere to be found. When she was able to speak, Lydia demanded to know if there had been any news of Rebecca or Henry. No sign of them at the châ-teau, Fiona reported. However, there had been quite a lot of blood.

After a week, Lydia was strong enough to leave the infirmary, albeit barely. Standing for even short periods of time left her dizzy. Her hands trembled, and she was terrifyingly thin. Worst of all, she found herself incapable of doing even the simplest magic.

"Worry about walking to the loo by yourself, then we can talk about spellwork," Evelyn chided her.

But Lydia felt caged. Rebecca and Henry were in danger, maybe dead, and it was her fault. The book was gone, and the next full moon was only one week away. In seven days, the Witches of the Third Reich would have all they needed to find the *Grimorium Bellum*, if they hadn't found it already. At full power Lydia could have tracked the book herself, with no need for full moons or ceremony now that she'd held the thing in her hands. As it stood, she barely had the strength to walk into the next room, let alone project there.

There was a knock at the bedroom door, and Evelyn's face appeared before Lydia had a chance to answer—a habit that had always driven her mad, even as a girl.

"Visitor for you, love. Sybil. Again."

Lydia ran her fingers through her hair in a feeble attempt to make herself presentable. She felt naked without her glamour, sallow and homely. The room seemed to swim, and Evelyn reached out to steady her.

"I'm fine," Lydia said, even as the room continued to sway.

Sybil looked altogether out of place in Evelyn's shabby sitting room. Her dress was aubergine silk, with shoes and a bag in matching suede. A silver crescent moon pendant hung around her neck, and her gold and silver hair was pinned up and away from her face.

"Grand Mistress," Lydia said as Evelyn helped her into her chair.

"Oh, darling, I told you before, none of that." Sybil smiled up at Evelyn. "I do apologize for dropping in uninvited again, Mrs. Polk."

"Tea, Grand Mistress?" Evelyn's mouth twisted into a tight scowl.

Lydia sighed. Evelyn had been simmering for weeks. She suspected her mother blamed Sybil for her misadventures in France, even though Lydia had acted alone.

"That would be lovely." Sybil looked at Lydia. "Coffee for you, darling?"

Evelyn frowned. "I'm afraid not. She's finished the bag you brought last time."

"Tea is fine," Lydia said.

Evelyn made a small clicking sound, then disappeared into the kitchen.

Sybil smiled apologetically. "I don't think she cares for me."

"You're in good company," Lydia said. "She didn't care for Isadora either."

Sybil's smile faltered, as if the mere mention of Isadora's name was too painful for her, then soldiered on. "How are you feeling?"

"How do I look?"

"Honestly? Ghastly. Are you eating?"

"When I can."

"And your powers?"

At that moment, Evelyn returned. They sat in silence as she laid out tea and biscuits, carefully avoiding Sybil's gaze.

"Thank you," Sybil murmured, and Evelyn excused herself. She looked at Lydia, who stared into her teacup and said nothing.

"Give it time," said Sybil.

Lydia sipped her tea. The cup shook in her hand. "We don't have time," she whispered.

Sybil leaned closer and took the teacup from Lydia, setting it on the table. "Darling, you've done so much. You've given everything you have to this cause. Please, let me take this burden from you so you can focus on getting well."

Lydia felt as if there were a clock hanging above her head, ticking down to catastrophe. *Seven days.*

"You have to find it." Lydia's voice was thin and brittle. "Please, promise me you'll find it."

Sybil nodded, but then her face fell just a little. She fussed with her jewelry, spinning one of her rings on her finger.

"What is it?"

Sybil huffed. "It's Vivian. She's vehemently opposed to any further efforts to retrieve the *Grimorium Bellum*. She claims that you were operating under my orders in France, and that I should be removed as Grand Mistress as punishment. Of course, she's after *your* head as well.

But don't you worry about that. I have it all in hand. It will take a stronger witch than Vivian Osborne to stop me."

Vivian. Everywhere Lydia looked, there she was, standing in their way, moving the *Grimorium Bellum* even farther out of reach, with no one to stop her, and no one the wiser.

Lydia felt like the world was turning sideways around her. "Sybil, I'm so sorry for everything. . . ."

"None of that! I'll not have you apologizing for doing what's right. Not after you were the only one of us with the courage to do it. We'll find the book. That's all that matters now."

Lydia took a stuttering breath. She ducked her head to hide the tears that gathered in her eyes, but it was no use.

"Lydia? What's wrong?" Sybil clucked over her, taking her by the hand. "Are you worried about your companions from the château? Is that it?"

Lydia could feel her pulse ticking ever upward, an unnerving sensation that had plagued her ever since she'd returned home, brought on by even the most minor excitement.

"I . . . yes. They were holding off the Gestapo when I lost consciousness. I don't know what happened to them after that."

Sybil tsked sympathetically and refilled Lydia's teacup. "It must be very difficult for you, not being able to reach them. But, darling, your friends would want you to recover from your ordeal. I know how you are when you set your mind to a thing, but you're only doing yourself more harm by not allowing yourself to rest."

"But if I could just project, I would know where to find the *Grimorium Bellum*. . . ." Her voice was rising, her heart beating too fast.

"There are other ways."

Lydia couldn't seem to get enough air. Her pulse raced, irregular and stumbling over itself. "I can't just give up, I can't. . . ."

Sybil came off the couch and knelt by her side, holding her hand firmly. "You mustn't overexcite yourself, darling." She brushed the damp hair from Lydia's forehead and smoothed her curls with her fingers. Lydia felt panicky and feverish. She knew Sybil was right, that she was only prolonging her recovery by pushing herself too hard, but she couldn't bear the thought of simply handing over responsibility for the *Grimorium Bellum* to someone else. She couldn't explain the things she imagined every time she closed her eyes, what she knew would come to pass if she failed. Millions dead—of disease, madness, starvation, consumed alive by magic and turned to ash. The book had shown her. She had seen it.

"Drink your tea." Sybil examined her with motherly care. Lydia looked up and saw Evelyn standing in the doorway, watching.

"Her heart's been weakened, Grand Mistress. Too much excitement isn't good for her."

"Of course." Sybil stood. "I should be going, then."

"But you've only just arrived!" Lydia protested.

"And I've upset you terribly, so now I'm off again. I'll come by soon. I promise. Here." She took a brown paper package from inside her purse and handed it to Lydia. The dark, earthy smell of coffee rose to meet Lydia's nostrils as she crinkled the paper.

"Oh, bless you, Sybil." She clutched the precious cargo to her chest and inhaled deeply.

Sybil winked. "Can't have you running out again."

Evelyn retrieved Sybil's coat and offered a stiff curtsy. To Lydia's great surprise, Sybil took Evelyn by both shoulders and embraced her warmly, planting a kiss on each of her cheeks. Evelyn allowed it but did not return the gesture.

"Grand Mistress."

Evelyn waited until the sound of Sybil's footsteps in the stairwell faded, then turned her attention back to her daughter.

"Come on, love. Back to bed with you."

Lydia stood and braced herself against the wall, resisting her mother's outstretched hand. "Is she at least more tolerable to you than Isadora?"

Evelyn frowned. "I had no quarrel with Isadora."

"Oh, Mother, don't lie."

Evelyn made a face, and Lydia knew she was doing it again—biting her tongue. Minding her mouth.

"I won't fight with you, Lydia. It's not good for your heart." She took Lydia by the arm and escorted her back to her bed. Even the short trip left Lydia gasping, her pulse skittering in her throat.

"Broth for supper, I think." Evelyn tucked her into bed, wrapping the blankets around her tightly, just like she had when Lydia was a little girl. "Do you think you can stomach it?"

Lydia nodded, too winded to speak.

"Right, then. Can I bring you anything for now, love?"

Lydia shook her head. Evelyn got up to leave, but just as she reached the door, Lydia spoke.

"Mum."

"Yes, pet?"

Lydia thought that Evelyn looked smaller than she'd remembered. Older.

"I liked that tea you fixed me yesterday. With the chamomile. Do you think I could have that again?"

Evelyn looked genuinely surprised. "Of course, pet. Won't take but a moment."

She closed the door, and Lydia felt her pulse slow. She listened to the sounds of Evelyn opening jars and putting on the kettle, and fixed her eyes on a single point on the ceiling. She focused all of her attention, this time not on a place, but a person. She reached out with her mind, searching, imagining green woods, and old books, and joyful, singing voices.

Henry, she thought.

Henry, Henry, Henry.

LYDIA WOKE WITH A START. It was dark in her bedroom, the furniture nothing more than spectral shapes in a deep gray void. A cup of chamomile tea sat on the bedside table, stone cold and untouched.

She couldn't catch her breath. This had happened every so often since she'd returned. She would wake in the night gasping, with her heart racing in her chest. She would wait for her pulse to slow, but instead it would only quicken, faster and faster, until she was sure she would die. Now she sat up in bed with one hand on her chest, waiting and praying for the frantic rhythm to calm.

Her eyes began to adjust to the dark, flicking over the dim shapes: the chest of drawers, the writing desk, her coat tossed across a chair, conspiring to look just enough like a person in the darkness. And there, in the corner, something that didn't belong. A hazy outline, tall and slim.

She stared at the shape in the shadows, her heart humming like a motor, no hope of slowing it down now. She blinked, willing her eyes to bring the thing into focus, but it remained maddeningly intangible, the edges blurring into the surrounding darkness.

She had played this trick on herself as a girl, inventing monsters and evil men from shadows and imagination. She knew how this would end. She would stare into the darkness for several minutes, an hour, maybe. Then the light would change, and she would realize that there had never been anything there at all, and she would go back to sleep feeling childish and stupid. She knew because she had done it a hundred times.

Still.

"I see you." She expected to feel foolish as soon as the words left her mouth, but hearing herself speak into the darkness, she didn't feel foolish at all. She felt frightened. She strained her eyes, but the figure did not take form. The humming in her heart crept ever upward, threatening to explode.

"You won't find it," she said. "I won't let you."

There was a sound, she was sure of it, too faint to name. A low, soft whisper.

Laughter.

Twenty-Four

"It's midday, love. Come on now. Up with you."

Lydia was racked with aches and chills, and her bedsheets had an unsavory, lived-in feeling. She'd spent the better part of the night searching the shadows, waiting for whoever or whatever was in her room to reveal itself. Then, slowly, the sun had emerged, flooding her room with weak morning light, and Lydia had realized that she was alone. She'd fallen back into a troubled sleep and woken later that morning, long enough to wash and have a coffee, before returning to her bed, where she'd spent the remainder of the day.

"I don't understand why I'm not getting stronger," Lydia gasped as she pushed herself upright.

"Perhaps it's because every time I leave you alone for more than a minute, you're trying to leave your body and fly off to France." Lydia looked at her mother in surprise. "Oh please. You think you're such a mystery?"

Lydia reached for her dressing gown. Her legs quivered as she stood. "What are we doing?"

"Reading cards."

"Mother, *no*."

Evelyn rummaged through the chest of drawers. "Where is that deck I gave you? I was sure it was in here. Ah! There we are." She produced a small bundle, wrapped in an old green silk scarf. There was a sprig of something tucked into the knot of the fabric, now dried beyond recognition.

"I think I should lie down." Lydia tried to return to her bed, but Evelyn intercepted her with a firm hand on the arm.

"Lie down long enough, you'll never get back up. Come on, the tea's ready."

She settled Lydia in a kitchen chair with a pillow behind her back. Evelyn's own tarot deck was already on the table, set atop a swatch of black silk. Grudgingly, Lydia unwrapped the bundle in front of her, setting the tiny dried flower off to one side. The deck had been a gift from her mother for her tenth birthday, a perfect copy of the one Evelyn used. She turned the deck over in her hands and noted how the cards were still crisp and new looking, barely touched all these years later. Meanwhile, Evelyn's deck was worn at the edges from decades of use.

"I'm not sure I remember how to read them."

Evelyn clucked her tongue. "There you go again, always so concerned about the meanings. Relax. Go with your instincts."

"Easy for you to say."

Evelyn poured the tea, then handed her own faded deck to Lydia. "I'll read first, give you a moment to get reacquainted. Go on, then. Think of a question and give them a shuffle."

Lydia began to shuffle the cards in her hands. They gave off a familiar odor—oakmoss, vanilla, tea, dust.

"What's your question?"

Lydia hadn't told Evelyn anything about what had happened in France. She'd become so accustomed to keeping her mother in the dark about her work within the academy, she'd hardly known where to begin.

"My friends," she said after a moment. "Are they alive?"

Evelyn frowned, but nodded. "Cut." Lydia cut the deck, as she had a hundred times when she was a child.

Evelyn began laying out cards, drawing two to start—the knight of swords and the Hermit. She laid these at the top of the black silk, then drew five more. The images didn't speak to Lydia the same way they did Evelyn, but they still stirred strange feelings in her—like a story being told in a language she only vaguely understood. Evelyn arranged the cards in a straight line: five of cups, five of swords, six of swords, eight of swords. Too many swords always made Lydia anxious. When Evelyn laid down the final card, Lydia took in a quick breath: *Death*.

"What have I told you about the Death card?" Evelyn said calmly. "It represents changes, transformations."

"Is it ever interpreted literally?" Lydia tried to hide the tremor in her voice.

"Sometimes. But not today." Evelyn placed her fingers on the two cards at the top of the spread, the knight and the Hermit. "They're alive."

Lydia exhaled. She and Evelyn had their differences, but Lydia knew one thing for certain—her mother's cards always spoke the truth.

Evelyn laid her fingertips on the five of cups, with its solemn figure standing morosely over his spilled chalices.

"They're worried about you. They don't know if you're alive or dead. They fear the worst."

She moved on to the five of swords. A smirking figure stood in the foreground, with his two vanquished foes behind him. Their swords lay abandoned at his feet.

"They were captured."

Lydia's heart stumbled in her chest. "By the Gestapo?"

"No. Friends. Hers, if I'm not mistaken. A betrayal. Now they've escaped." Evelyn's hand rested on the six of swords, showing two passengers huddled inside a boat. She reached for the next card, the eight of swords, but hesitated. On the card, a dark-haired woman stood bound and blindfolded, surrounded by swords. A castle loomed in the background. Lydia knew without having to ask that the woman was her. Evelyn's hand hovered briefly over the bound woman, then moved on, picking up the final card, Death.

"Something's happened. One of them is going through a great change. Him, I think." She picked up the Hermit and held it next to Death. "He's transforming. Getting stronger, embracing his true nature." She set down the two cards. "I think he has a little magic in him, your Henry."

Lydia frowned. "I never told you his name. Did the cards tell you that?"

Evelyn paused, the hint of a smirk curling her mouth. "The walls are thin, and you talk in your sleep."

"Ah. Well. Thank you." Lydia wished she weren't so inclined toward blushing. She reached for her own deck, but Evelyn stopped her.

"You get a second question. Remember?"

She remembered. This had been their arrangement, years ago when Evelyn had first started teaching her to read the cards. Evelyn's way of teaching was to have them take turns reading for each other, but Lydia always felt exposed when it was her mother's turn to read. She saw too clearly, knew too much. It was just like the tea leaves, but so much worse—Lydia's whole inner life, laid out in full color on the kitchen table. Evelyn had been the one to suggest a solution. Each time Evelyn read for Lydia, Lydia would get to ask a second question—no cards this time, just the truth. She could ask anything she liked, and Evelyn would have to answer. This way, they were always on even footing. This was how Lydia had learned about the birds and the bees, and about her father, run off when Evelyn was six months pregnant, too much of a scoundrel to be any kind of husband, let alone a parent.

Lydia looked her mother in the eye. "Why did you hate Isadora?"

Evelyn knit her brow. "I didn't hate Isadora."

"No lies, that's the rule. I want to know why."

Evelyn gathered up the cards from the table and shuffled them back into the deck. "That's the truth. I never hated Isadora. She was a strong woman. A leader, principled, intelligent. She cared for you like her own, challenged you."

Lydia was bewildered. "Then why—"

"Do you remember the first time you came home from that school? You'd been there, oh, a few months I guess, and they sent you home for winter break. And it was like you were a different child. Everything I did filled you with disdain, everything I did embarrassed you. You weren't interested in herbs, or cards, you called them *low magic*. You were only interested in *high magic*, academy magic. We had a terrible row that week, and do you remember what you called me? 'Dirty old hedge witch.' I don't know where you even heard such a thing. I barely recognized you." Evelyn didn't look at Lydia as she refilled her teacup. "I didn't hate Isadora. I hated the academy."

"But every time I said her name . . ."

"You *worshipped* her, love. I was jealous. I wanted my daughter back. But I didn't hate her. Not at all."

Lydia felt ashamed. For years she had taken for granted that Evelyn had loathed Isadora. Now she realized that it was Lydia herself that her mother had resented. Not the girl who left for the academy all those years ago, but the person she had become.

"And Sybil?" Lydia asked.

"That's another question, love. No extras." Evelyn held out her hand, waiting.

Lydia handed Evelyn her own deck of cards. Evelyn gave them an expert shuffle and a cut. "Will business pick back up after the war?"

It was a meaningless question, and one Evelyn could have answered just as easily as Lydia, but that wasn't the point. It was the ritual, drawing Lydia back into their familiar routine. Lydia opted for a simple spread, unable to remember any of the more complex arrangements Evelyn had taught her as a girl. She pulled a single card for Evelyn and smiled.

The Empress.

It was a card that had a way of appearing in most of Evelyn's readings. She stood for motherhood, fertility, bounty. Evelyn smiled, too, like seeing an old friend.

Lydia pulled three more cards. The eight of pentacles appeared first, then more pentacles, the seven this time, followed by the Wheel of Fortune, but the final two cards had landed upside down.

"Well?" Evelyn looked at her expectantly.

Lydia hesitated. "I told you, I barely remember how to read them anymore."

"Nonsense. You know as well as I do what they say. The cards don't lie. Don't you start lying for them."

It was one of Evelyn's favorite sayings. As a child, Lydia was always trying to soften the truth, make the readings more favorable than they were. Evelyn had always insisted on brutal honesty.

"No. Business does not improve after the war."

Evelyn appeared utterly unbothered. "Well then, that wasn't so hard, was it?"

Lydia was beginning to feel queasy. "Mother, I'm tired, I think I should go back to bed."

"One more while you finish your tea," Evelyn insisted.

"Mother—"

Evelyn handed her deck to Lydia. "Go on, then. Give them a shuffle."

Lydia knew there was no sense in arguing. She shuffled thoroughly and cut the deck, placing both stacks on the table.

"Will I regain my powers, before it's too late?"

She expected Evelyn to ask, *Too late for what?* Instead, she picked up the cards with a nod and set about her work.

She laid the cards out in a complicated spread of her own design, one she reserved for questions of grave importance. The High Priestess sat in the center of the spread, watching the story unfold around her. Placed sideways across her, the five of pentacles showed a man and a woman, sick and suffering in the snow. The Moon hung at the bottom of the spread, flanked on one side by Strength, golden haired, taming a lion with her bare hands, but the card had landed upside down. On the other side of the Moon sat the Tower, harbinger of catastrophe. Lydia felt her blood run cold at the sight of the burning pillar, the bodies flung to their deaths on the rocks below. And there, sitting above them all, filling Lydia with a familiar sense of unease, was the Devil—horned and leering, with a naked couple chained at his feet. *Violence,* thought Lydia. *Manipulation. Obsession. Evil.*

Evelyn gazed at the cards for a long time before she spoke. Then she looked up suddenly, as if she smelled something burning. She stood and walked swiftly to her bedroom.

"Mother?"

Lydia could hear her shuffling around in the other room, moving boxes and opening drawers. A moment later she reappeared, holding a smooth black stone on the end of a silver chain.

"I just remembered. This once belonged to your grandmother. She wanted you to have it."

Lydia didn't understand. "Mum, Gran's been dead for fifteen years."

"I know. Silly me." She stood behind Lydia and draped the chain around her neck. The stone was ridiculously large and felt cold and heavy against her chest. It gave off a subtle hum of magic, vibrating faintly against her skin. Once it was secured, Evelyn returned to her place at the table.

"Mum?" There was something about the look on Evelyn's face that frightened her.

"Your gran made that herself, you know. She was a Projectionist. Like you."

Evelyn wasn't making any sense. "I thought Gran was an herbalist. All the Polk women are herbalists."

"She was both. Polk women have a talent for every kind of magic, the high and the *low*, as you call it. Your gran could fix any sort of potion, knew a thousand herbs by sight alone. And she could send her mind anywhere she pleased, just like you." Evelyn turned her teacup in her hands as she spoke, swirling the leaves in the bottom.

"During the Great War, before you were born, women would come to your gran with some object belonging to their sons or husbands, and they'd ask your gran if their men were alive or dead. Gran would leave her body and go find them on the battlefields in France, then come back and tell the women if they were all right."

She pointed to the heavy pendant hanging around Lydia's neck.

"That is a shield stone. Your grandmother made it as protection against other witches like her, witches who could use their power of projection to follow her, spy on her. I always thought she was just getting paranoid in her old age, but now I see she had her reasons. Who knows, maybe she made it for you. You won't be able to project as long as you're wearing it, and it won't protect you against *all* magic, but it will keep you safe from wandering eyes. No witch will be able to use projection to follow your comings and goings."

Lydia looked down at the cards spread out on the table, then back up at her mother. A chilly sense of foreboding crept over her, making the hairs on her arms stand up. "I'm being watched."

Evelyn nodded.

Lydia thought of the figure in her room, the unshakable sense that she wasn't alone, and shuddered. She felt violated, imagining such a thing could happen in her childhood home. Her *mother's* home.

"There's more." Evelyn lifted two cards from the table: the five of pentacles, with the sickly pair in the snow, and the inverted Strength card. Lydia looked at those cards and felt a sense of dread in the pit of her stomach, like a premonition. "Your magic's been bound. That's why you're not getting better."

Twenty-Five

Lydia felt as if she'd been defiled. As if the deepest, most essential part of her had been excised. She languished in bed for one day, and then another, surviving on warm broth and healing potions, wearing her grandmother's shield stone, all the while knowing that none of it would make a bit of difference until they discovered how she'd been bound, and by whom. She felt helpless and panic-stricken, and as she lay there, too weak to stand, a constant chorus seemed to drone inside her mind.

Five days until the full moon.

Four.

Three.

Visitors came and were dismissed without Lydia ever seeing them. Helena came to the flat, her arms stuffed with potions from the infirmary. Evelyn thanked her for coming, then poured every drop down the sink. Vivian appeared later that same day, with some paper-thin well-wishes and a dusty old copy of *The True Sight: Accessing Wisdom through Dreams and Visions.*

"To keep the mind busy during her convalescence."

Lydia listened as Evelyn greeted her and thanked her for the gift. Evelyn waited until Vivian was gone, then carried the book down three flights of stairs to the street, where she deposited it in the bin.

"Never too safe," she said.

By the third day, Lydia couldn't spend another second in bed, and so she asked Evelyn to set her up by the kitchen window, where she could breathe the fresh air. It was an unseasonably mild day. On the street, people walked briskly, occasionally greeting one another as they went about their business, but otherwise keeping to themselves. Lydia found herself observing them from the window as they passed. There was an old man in a flat cap, his nose and cheeks a deep, ruddy pink. He tipped his hat to an auburn-haired woman on the corner, waiting for the bus in her sky-blue coat and matching hat, and she nodded back. A young mother and a little boy emerged from the building across the street. The woman looked frazzled. Lydia imagined that the boy must have been a handful, and even as she thought it, he took off running and tripped and fell on the pavement. Just at that moment the bus came, blocking her view, and then left again, to reveal the boy back on his feet, sprinting down the street as if nothing had happened. His mother said something as she passed the woman in blue, and the woman laughed.

Lydia leaned forward, watching the woman at the bus stop more closely. The bus had come and gone, and still she waited. There was something about her appearance, as well; her clothing was too fine for the neighborhood, gold buttons flashing, the bright blue of her coat an anomaly among the sea of gray and brown.

"Mother . . ."

"I saw her." Evelyn placed a warm cup of tea into Lydia's hands. The steam smelled of baking spices. "Academy girl?"

"No. I've never seen her before."

"Do you think she's a Nazi?"

"That was my first thought, yes." She looked for a knife on the girl's hip, but if it was there, it was well hidden under her coat.

"It makes sense. I'm sure they've realized by now that they can't use magic to spy on you anymore, so they've resorted to doing things the old-fashioned way."

"Or else she's the one who was sent to bind me," Lydia said.

As they spoke, the young woman glanced up at the window, then away again, peering up the street as if looking for the next bus.

Evelyn sniffed. "Not very subtle, if you ask me."

"What do you think she's waiting for?" Lydia asked.

Evelyn set about making toast. "Maybe they think you're going to go after the book again, and they're hoping you'll lead them to it. Or they might be wondering if you're dead, since you've become untraceable."

Lydia was about to say something funny, something about being only half-dead, but even as she thought the words, a wave of dizziness washed over her.

Evelyn looked at her knowingly. "Rest, love. Nothing to be done about it before breakfast."

LYDIA STAYED BY THE WINDOW for hours, watching the woman in the blue coat as a dozen bright red buses came and went. She didn't realize she'd fallen asleep until she woke much later, bleary and confused, to find Evelyn busily working in her kitchen. Jars of various shapes and sizes sat open on the table, filled with all manner of herbs and powders. Evelyn stood over a massive stone mortar, grinding away at some new concoction with a pestle the size of a club.

"What are you making?" Lydia's tongue was thick from sleep.

"A surprise." Evelyn ground away with the pestle without pausing. "How are you feeling?"

"Dreadful."

Evelyn went to Lydia's side and smoothed her hair, clucking over her as she peered out through the lace curtains. The young woman was still there, conspicuous as a peacock in her bright blue coat.

"She's barely trying anymore," Lydia remarked.

She turned to find Evelyn scooping the powder from the mortar into a leather pouch. The powder was a light pink color and gave off a smell that prickled Lydia's nose and made her eyes water.

"What is that?"

Evelyn continued filling her pouch. "I think it's high time we have a conversation with that little bird outside."

Lydia shook her head. "I've dealt with these witches before. They're dangerous. Best to avoid direct confrontation if we can."

"Nonsense. She knows things. I'd like to know what they are, wouldn't you?"

"Yes, but—"

"Stay here," Evelyn said brightly.

Lydia placed a hand on her arm. "Mother, don't—"

"*Stay.*" There was something about the way she said the word that left no room for argument. On the contrary, Lydia found that even as she tried to get up and follow Evelyn, she was unable to do so. She felt a growing alarm rise in her as she realized that she had been pinned to her chair, immobile as a butterfly under glass.

She watched in horror from the window as Evelyn appeared on the street below, walking straight toward the woman in the blue coat. Evelyn halted several yards from the bus stop and said something Lydia couldn't hear. The woman looked up. A moment later, Evelyn was walking back toward the flat with the woman behind her.

Evelyn came back through the door not a minute later, followed by a very red-faced girl. She was younger than Lydia had originally thought, no older than sixteen, with spots on her chin she'd done her best to hide with powder, and a crimson flush mottling her milky complexion. Evelyn turned to the girl.

"*Sit.*" She spoke in a voice devoid of all friendliness. The girl did as she was told. Evelyn turned to Lydia. "My apologies, love. You're free to do as you please." Lydia felt some invisible thing lift from her shoulders, a weight she hadn't known was there. The girl in blue scowled, the veins in her neck bulging with effort, but she did not move from her chair.

"Mother?" Lydia looked from Evelyn to the girl, bewildered.

"Yes, love?" Evelyn looked extremely pleased with herself.

"Should I get anything for our guest? A *rope*, perhaps?"

Evelyn smiled. "I don't see why that should be necessary."

The realization struck her like a blow.

"Mother, could I have a word?"

"Certainly." Evelyn turned to the girl. "*Don't move.*"

Lydia stood, slowly and with great effort, and walked to the sitting room with Evelyn behind her.

"You're a *Force?*" she asked in a hoarse whisper. Even speaking the words felt ludicrous. Forces were rare and dangerous. Evelyn was . . . well, Evelyn.

"I told you, dear, Polk women are gifted in many forms of magic, both high and low."

Lydia gaped at her mother. "You've never mentioned it. Why?"

Evelyn shrugged. "It never seemed important. I always had a talent for it, but it's herbs and cards that have my heart."

"I don't . . . do you have any idea how rare . . . how special? How have I never seen you do this before now?"

Evelyn seemed confused by the question. "It's a wretched thing to do to a person. Who would I have forced before now, hmm? The butcher, to give me free lamb chops? Why, I never even forced *you* before today, and you were a hellion at two and three, let me tell you."

Lydia suddenly remembered every time she'd ever sensed that Evelyn was holding something back. *Minding her mouth*. What must it have been like to hold all that power and never wield it? Lydia imagined it must have felt like trying to hold lightning in a jelly jar.

She craned her neck to see the girl sitting obediently in her wooden chair. "Can she cast spells?"

"Well, I can't force her tongue, so I suppose she can say whatever she likes. But she's already been warned there would be consequences."

Lydia decided not to ask what Evelyn meant by *consequences*.

"Come on, love," Evelyn said merrily. "We're being rude to our guest."

They returned to the kitchen, with Evelyn in the lead and Lydia trailing behind.

"What's your name?" Evelyn asked.

The girl spit on the floor. "Go to hell." Her voice carried the barest hint of an accent.

Slowly, Evelyn took a rag from the sink and handed it to the girl. *"Clean that up."*

The girl glowered but fell to her knees and wiped up the spittle from the floorboards.

"*Sit*," Evelyn said.

The girl did.

"Do not spit on my floor again."

Lydia had never heard this tone from Evelyn before. The voice itself was the same, but there was a steeliness to it that Lydia didn't recognize.

"What's your name?" Evelyn asked again.

"You can't make me betray my coven, and you can't have my name, hedge witch," the girl snarled. "I'll cut my own throat first."

Lydia flinched, hearing her own ugly words in this witch's mouth.

She looked at Evelyn, but Evelyn did not return the glance. Instead, she lifted the leather pouch from the table and held it lightly in her hand.

"Absolutely right. Clever girl. I can't force your mind, which means I can't force your tongue. But I can do this."

In one swift movement, she pulled a fistful of powder from the leather pouch, leaned down, and blew the dust into the girl's face. The reaction was immediate—the girl began hacking violently, tears streaming down her face, shrieks of outrage and vile language pouring from her mouth in English and in German. Lydia recoiled as the pungent aroma of the powder reached her nostrils.

"Open that window, love," Evelyn said calmly.

Lydia did, then sat, winded from the effort. "What was that?"

"Hedge magic."

"*Bitch,*" the girl spat, "what did you do to me?"

"*Language,*" Evelyn said in her steely voice.

"I'm blind!" the girl shrieked.

"That will wear off." Evelyn stood in front of the girl and waited for the hacking to stop, watching patiently as the tears and snot fell onto her beautiful blue coat in rivers.

"Now, let's try again." Evelyn leaned in close. "What's your name?"

"Gerda Horn." The girl looked up in alarm, as if the words had been spoken by someone else.

"And tell us, Gerda, what's your special power?"

"I'm a Traveler. What did you *do* to me?" she gasped.

Lydia turned to Evelyn. "A truth spell? How long will it last?"

"Hard to say. That's why I made so much. If she stops talking, I can always give her more. She won't like it. My understanding is that the burning sensation only gets stronger over time."

"You'll pay," Gerda hissed, but her indignation was shot through with fear. "You'll regret sullying a witch of the Third Reich with your dirt magic, *hag.*"

"If I wanted to," Evelyn said coolly, "I could order you to get up from that chair and walk straight into the Thames."

Gerda's eyes bulged as she awaited Evelyn's next words.

"The Witches of the Third Reich. How many are you?"

Gerda remained silent for a long time, fighting the words as they crawled up her throat. Evelyn picked up the pouch from the table and blew another dose of powder into her face, then stood back as Gerda screamed in pain.

"How many?"

"*Eleven!*" Gerda howled as the tears streamed down her face, turning the pink powder to mud.

"Including you?" Lydia asked. Gerda nodded.

Evelyn stepped closer as the powder dissipated. "Why so few?"

Gerda panted, enraged. "Deutschland is home to hundreds of witches. Twelve swore themselves to the service of the Führer. More will come."

Evelyn tilted her head at that. "Twelve swore themselves to the service of the Führer. So why are you now one short of a coven?"

"I know why," Lydia said. "It's because one of your own was killed. Stabbed through the throat with her own knife. Isn't that right, Gerda?"

Gerda stared at Lydia with a look of pure hatred. "Murdered by some filthy little Jüdin."

Lydia tsked. "I believe I share some of the credit for that. How do you think that Jüdin broke free of your friend's magic?" She watched as the realization washed over Gerda. "What was her name?"

Gerda's face darkened. "Margot."

"Margot. You should know that Margot died badly. She deserved worse."

"You'll pay," Gerda whispered.

Lydia ignored her. She was beginning to enjoy herself, even in her weakened state, and Evelyn did not stop her. "The witch who broke into the Royal Academy. The one who murdered the grand mistress. What is her name?"

"Ursula." Gerda smiled, a disconcerting sight under the circumstances. "Ursula Wolfe."

Lydia stopped. "Why are you smiling?"

"Because Ursula will kill you when she finds out you murdered Margot."

"I'd have thought she wanted to kill me before. Why hasn't she?"

"She wants to. But she was ordered to let you live."

She glanced at Evelyn, then back at Gerda. "I'm confused. I've been well informed that I can be a stubborn, meddlesome cow when I want to be. Killing me would have been the smart thing. Lord knows it would have been easy. Why let me live?"

Gerda sneered. "I can't imagine." Lydia took the leather pouch from Evelyn's outstretched hand, and Gerda flinched. "I don't *know* why! No one told me!"

Something was wriggling at the edge of Lydia's consciousness. Something she couldn't quite bear to look at. She felt her heart pick up speed.

"Was it Ursula who bound my magic?"

"No."

"Was it you?"

"No."

She felt herself breaking out into a sweat, cold dread bubbling in her guts. She thought her heart would burst.

"Was it Vivian Osborne?"

Gerda scowled. "*Who?*"

Lydia looked at her mother, suddenly gone very still in the cramped kitchen. She'd plucked something from her cupboard and was holding it in her hands, staring at it like she was just seeing it for the first time. A brown paper package. She met Lydia's gaze, and some unspoken thing seemed to pass between them, turning to sludge in the pit of Lydia's stomach.

"Who gave the order to keep me alive?" she asked very quietly.

Gerda was resisting the power of Evelyn's spell. The tendons in her neck strained through the skin, and a small whimper escaped from her tightly pressed lips.

"Shall we give you another dose?" Lydia stood, her head swimming. Before Gerda could answer, Lydia blew the powder into her face, and Gerda let loose another shriek of pain and rage.

"The grand mistress gave the order!"

Lydia gripped the table for support. *"Gerda."* She waited for the girl to stop her howling and look at her. "Who is your grand mistress?"

Oh, but you know, Lydia thought as she looked at Evelyn, gripping that brown paper package in her hands as if it were a bomb. As the thing in her stomach turned solid and alive. *Stupid, naive girl. You already know.*

Gerda lifted her chin and looked Lydia in the eye, defiant.

"My grand mistress is Sybil Winter."

Twenty-Six

Lydia walked out of the room without a word. Evelyn followed a moment later.

"She's lying." The room seemed to spin around her.

"She can't lie."

"Maybe she can. Maybe we should give her another dose."

"Love—"

"Don't do that. Please, don't do that." Lydia gripped Evelyn's shoulders for support. She felt her knees go weak.

"Do what?"

"That thing you do, that thing where you're so calm, and reasonable, and *right*." She couldn't breathe. "Please."

Evelyn said nothing. Lydia sank to the ground, all her strength gone. "I don't understand what's happening."

Evelyn knelt next to her. "Neither do I."

They stayed that way in silence as Lydia waited for the room to go still again. She felt like a piece of dust that could blow away at any second.

Sybil. It was as if she'd sustained a mortal injury. Like she was bleeding to death and nothing in the world could save her.

Finally, when she was sure she would not in fact die of heartbreak, she spoke.

"What are we going to do with the girl?"

Evelyn looked toward the kitchen, thinking. "If we cut her loose, she'll run right back to her coven."

Lydia looked at Evelyn. "You're not suggesting . . ."

"Heavens, no. This may be a war, but I'm no soldier. I won't murder her." There was a moment of silence. "I understand if you have to."

Lydia glanced toward the kitchen. *This is a war,* a voice whispered inside her mind. *People die in war.*

She had never killed before. She'd never needed to, although she suspected she knew girls who had. She imagined she could, if need be. If her life were on the line, or the outcome of the war itself.

She looked at the girl in her mother's kitchen, spots on her chin and nails bitten to the quick, wearing her grown-up clothes like they belonged to someone else.

"I am a soldier, in a manner of speaking," Lydia said. "But that girl is a child. An evil, foulmouthed child, but a child nonetheless. I don't want to kill her either."

"Well then." Evelyn stood. "Neither of us is going to kill her. So what now?"

WHEN THEY RETURNED to the kitchen, Gerda was wearing a brave face, but the pink of her cheeks had faded, and her pulse ticked visibly under the freckled skin of her throat.

She held her chin high. "What's it to be? Are you going to kill me now?"

Lydia eased herself into a chair. "We really ought to. But no."

"So, what then?" Gerda's eyes darted from Lydia to Evelyn and back again.

Neither woman answered. Instead, Evelyn busied herself at the stove. She put on the kettle and pulled the coffee grinder down from the shelf.

"Do you know, I never did care for coffee. Nasty, smelly, bitter stuff. I'm more of a tea girl myself." Evelyn reached for the brown paper package of coffee beans. She opened it and gave it a sniff. "*Bindweed*. Foxglove, too, if I'm not mistaken. I'd have noticed it right away, if it weren't for that smell. Clever." She dumped the contents of the bag into the grinder, letting the beans clatter across the counter and onto the floor. Gerda flinched. From where she sat, Lydia could see the tiny flecks of green among the black.

Bless you, Sybil. That was what Lydia had said when she received that brown paper package. *Bless you*. The grief and humiliation caught in her throat. She turned her face away so her mother wouldn't see it.

Evelyn worked quickly, turning away at the crank of the grinder, occasionally pausing to empty the grounds into an enormous gherkin jar. Gerda watched, her eyes growing wider as the minutes ticked by. By the time the kettle began to whistle, the jar was half-filled with coarsely ground coffee. Evelyn hummed to herself as she poured the boiling water into the jar. She wrapped the jar in a rag and handed it to Gerda.

"*Drink that*. All of it."

Gerda scowled but did as she was commanded. By the time she'd finished, she was close to retching, her teeth blackened with grit.

"Don't you dare vomit," Evelyn cautioned.

Gerda set down the jar, sweating and belching. Lydia waited for her to catch her breath, then took a small piece of paper from her pocket. On one side was an address: 64 Baker Street. On the other side was a note. She handed it to Gerda.

"Read that."

Gerda read. "Attention: David Harlowe. This woman is a German spy. Extremely dangerous. Treat with caution. Regards, L. Polk." She looked up at Lydia with a look of pure disdain.

"*Go to that address,*" Evelyn said. "When you arrive, you are to *present that note.*"

Gerda scoffed. "I'll escape."

"I'm certain you will, a distinguished Traveler such as yourself. But not until my influence over you wears off, which will take several hours, not to mention that binding potion you just ingested, which will take considerably longer."

"You're going to die, *hedge witch.*" Gerda folded the piece of paper and placed it inside her coat pocket before standing to leave.

"Wait," Evelyn said. Gerda stopped. "To make you suitably forthcoming when you arrive." She blew another puff of pink powder into Gerda's face, bringing on a fresh bout of coughs and shrieks of outrage.

"Now *run.*"

Lydia waited until the girl was out of sight, her shoes drumming on the stairs as she ran from the building and onto the street. Then she took a breath, and covered her face with her hands, and wept.

LATER, WHEN THE SUN had disappeared and Lydia's tears had finally run dry, Evelyn came into Lydia's room carrying a small brown bottle in one hand and a teacup in the other.

"What's this?" Lydia sat up in bed, wiping at her puffy face.

Evelyn placed the bottle on the bedside table. "This one is snakeroot, with angelica and black pepper, as well as a few other things you won't like, and I won't name. It will make you sick as hell, but by morning the poison will have left you." She set the teacup down next to the bottle. "This one is for healing broken hearts."

Lydia felt as if she would shatter into a thousand pieces. Her head and her heart ached from crying.

"I feel so stupid."

"Oh, my brave girl." Evelyn wrapped her arms around her. "You've been many things in your time on this earth, but stupid was never one of them. You think you're the first Polk woman to misplace her trust?"

Lydia buried her face in her mother's shoulder. "I was so sure it was Vivian, I never even considered . . ." Lydia stopped, breathless. "You knew about her. I thought you were just jealous, like with Isadora, but you sensed it, didn't you?"

Evelyn stroked her hair. "If I had known the truth, I would have beaten her silly before I let her anywhere near you. But I knew I didn't trust her."

"I trusted her," Lydia whispered.

Evelyn rubbed her daughter's back with one hand and, with the other, retrieved the teacup from the bedside table.

"Here. Tea first."

Lydia sipped her tea. It tasted of roses and cinnamon, and a dozen other familiar things she couldn't quite name. It was lovely.

Her grandmother's shield stone still hung around her neck. Lydia held it, turning it over in her hands.

"When I'm well again," she said softly, "I'll be going back to France first thing." She felt the panic rushing in her veins, as surely as if she'd been injected with it. "I have to go back, because if I don't . . . if I don't . . ."

Evelyn brushed Lydia's hair from her forehead. "What, my darling?"

Lydia was so tired. Tired of keeping secrets, of lying by omission. So she did something she'd never imagined she would: She told Evelyn everything. Everything that had happened since the night Kitty and Isadora were murdered, and every horrible thing that would come to pass should she fail to find the *Grimorium Bellum* before the Nazis did. She told her about the things she had felt, holding that book—all the dark, secret things it had whispered to her. Things she would carry with her until the day she died. She understood the book now. She knew what it wanted, how it worked. She told Evelyn how it could be harnessed, all the ways to negotiate with it, to make it do your bidding.

And then she told her about her plan.

Twenty-Seven

The Nazis cannot be allowed to have the book. They would exterminate half the world if it meant winning the war, and with the *Grimorium Bellum*, they could do it in an instant." Lydia felt sick, remembering the hunger she had felt that night at Château de Laurier. "It can't go to the academy, that much is clear. It's possible Sybil was working alone, but there may be others on the high council, as well." Her mind drifted back to Vivian, Helena, Jacqueline—all those useless, grandstanding biddies who hadn't lifted a finger when Isadora died. She couldn't imagine Sybil working with any of them, but then, she never could have imagined Sybil doing what she had done. "That leaves only one option—it has to be destroyed."

"Destroyed how?"

Lydia took a breath. "There's a spell called The Unmaking. It's the most powerful in the book. I read it, that first night after I found it. It unleashes a creature to consume the caster's enemies from the inside out, it can be used against one person or a thousand, it makes no difference, but the way it's written, it's a bit like a 'fill-in-the-blank' story. You can name anyone or anything you like, and it will be turned to ash. Not just armies. Cities. Objects. Anything at all."

Lydia watched Evelyn's eyes as the realization struck. "You're going to turn the book's own magic against itself."

"Exactly."

Evelyn opened her mouth to speak, then stopped. She composed herself and tried again.

"You nearly died, last time," she said softly. "If you do this, if you try to use it again? I'm afraid it will kill you."

Yes, Lydia had no doubt that the book would defend itself.

Because it was a living thing, wasn't it? That was what she hadn't understood, what the Nazis still didn't understand. The book wasn't simply a weapon, an inanimate thing to be pointed in any direction one liked. It had desires. *Appetites.* It had spoken to Lydia inside her head, and what she had heard was infinite, all-consuming hunger. If allowed to run free, it would turn the whole world to ash in order to satiate itself. *Yes*, she thought. *It will kill me, if it can. It will eat me alive.*

"There has to be another way." Lydia could hear the raw emotion in Evelyn's voice.

"There isn't. With a full coven, maybe I would have the strength to use the book and survive, but—"

Evelyn held up a hand. "Stop. What do you mean by that?"

Lydia sighed. "The spell isn't meant to be done by a single witch. The power of the book would destroy anyone who attempted to wield it alone. It can only be completed during the last few moments of daylight on the winter solstice, and with a full coven, but that's out of the question now that Sybil . . ." She paused. Sybil's betrayal was still so raw. "I can't trust Sybil. Which means I can't trust the high council. I have to do it alone."

Evelyn frowned, thinking. "Is that what the book said? That you need a coven?"

"Well . . . not exactly. It's in an ancient language, the translation is . . . fluid."

"What exactly did it say?"

Lydia thought about that, rolling the strange syllables around in her mind. "It's difficult to translate. It's meant for a group, but doesn't actually say how many." She paused. "The closest translation I suppose would be . . . 'sisterhood.'"

Evelyn wrapped her up in her arms. "My darling girl, as clever as you are, sometimes I fear that school has made you a little dull. Your book doesn't say anything about gathering twelve initiated elder witches to stand in a circle under the solstice moon. Do you honestly believe that the people who created this book had covens like we have today? Sisterhood means your people. Your *family*."

Lydia blinked, understanding at last. "I suppose so."

She finished her tea. Curls of leaves and rose petals formed tiny shapes in the bottom of her teacup. She wondered what they meant.

"How are you feeling?" Evelyn asked.

Lydia thought for a moment. "Angry."

Evelyn nodded. "Angry is better than heartbroken. Angry gets things done."

Lydia picked up the brown bottle from the bedside table, considering the cloudy liquid inside.

"Are you ready?" her mother asked.

Lydia turned the bottle over in her hands and nodded.

"Good. I'll get a bucket."

It was a blustery day in Hyde Park, and a biting wind whipped the leaves in circles, making them dance along the tree-lined path. Gentlemen clutched their hats to their heads as they rushed past the chestnut trees and scrubby vegetable allotments, and ladies cried out in frustration as the wind tugged at their hair, but Fiona McGann was the picture of well-groomed perfection. She walked alone, wrapped in a scarlet overcoat with glinting brass buttons, her golden hair neat and shiny, her cheeks glamoured a lovely, windswept pink.

Lydia Polk, standing in the shadow of a nearby tree, couldn't be bothered. She was saving her energy.

She observed the subtle labyrinth of spellwork that lay across the park like a hedge maze. It had been placed there by the academy as a special favor from Isadora to Churchill—a layer of confounding magic, meant to keep clandestine meetings within the park hidden from prying eyes. It's why she'd chosen this place, as public as it was. Lydia took comfort in the gentle hum of the spell at work as it buzzed across her skin, knowing that anyone who'd attempted to follow her would find themselves suddenly and inexplicably wandering in some far-flung corner of the park, their true purpose long forgotten.

"Look at you!" Fiona cried when she saw her. "To hear Sybil tell it you were half-dead and not taking visitors, but here you are, alive and well."

Lydia joined Fiona on the path as they walked side by side. "You didn't tell her you were meeting me, did you?"

"You told me not to. Besides, I love a secret. Whatever is all the cloak and dagger for, anyway?"

Fiona and Lydia were not close. They might have been—they were both accomplished in their fields, both well liked and respected, both active in the war effort. The trouble, as far as Lydia could tell, had always been Kitty. From the first day of school, Kitty and Fiona had taken an intense dislike to each other. Kitty thought Fiona was vain, spoiled, and moralistic, while Fiona maintained that Kitty was a disreputable hell-raiser. Lydia had never had any particular issue with Fiona herself, admired her skill in point of fact, but with Kitty always by her side, any chance they had of real friendship was dashed. Still, the two of them had always maintained a certain polite friendliness.

"I need a favor," Lydia said.

Fiona raised her perfectly arched eyebrows and waited.

"I need you to take me back to France, and I need you to tell no one. Including Sybil."

Fiona tilted her head. "Sybil is grand mistress now, Lydia."

"I know."

"You want me to *lie* to the grand mistress? Why?"

"I can't tell you."

Fiona paused. "Well, I'm afraid that's a bit of a nonstarter." She looked Lydia up and down appraisingly. "I'm so glad to see you're on the mend, Lydia. Really, I am. But I'm afraid I can't help you." She turned and began to walk back in the direction of the academy.

Lydia followed her. "Fiona, stop, listen—"

Fiona did neither. "No. You want me to take you to France, a place where you almost *died*, mind you, lie to the grand mistress about it, and you won't even tell me why? Lydia, I love a bit of trouble when I can get it, but this might be too rich even for my blood."

Lydia placed a hand on her arm. "Fiona, please."

Fiona eyed Lydia's hand coolly until she let go of her arm. Then she sighed dramatically and waited, smoothing an imaginary wrinkle from her sleeve as she did.

"I want to trust you," Lydia said.

"Then *do*."

"This isn't a game, Fiona. What I'm involved in is extremely serious."

Fiona looked at her in mock surprise, blue eyes flashing. "Goodness, I had no idea it was *serious*. Why, you'd think I would have put that much together while I was scraping you off the floor of that dirty château in Dordogne. How silly of me."

The silence stretched taut as bowstrings between them. Lydia imagined what Kitty would have said if she could see her now—probably that Fiona was a haughty, uptight prig, and not to be trusted. Fiona stared at Lydia, her face a beautiful, impenetrable wall.

"Perhaps this was a mistake after all." Lydia felt a wave of resignation. "I'm sorry I wasted your time."

She began to walk away, her mind already beginning to spiral. The full moon was in two days. Without a Traveler she would need to return to France by more traditional means, which would be slow and dangerous. She had wanted to confide in Fiona—for all her infamous frostiness, Fiona had always struck Lydia as someone who operated from a deep well of integrity. She'd never bullied the other girls when they were younger, never lorded her privilege or beauty over anyone. She'd never suffered fools, never hung around with silly girls, never spread ugly rumors. Once, in private, Isadora had hinted that if Lydia hadn't been selected to serve as her apprentice, it would have been Fiona McGann in her shoes. And if Isadora had thought Fiona virtuous enough to stand by her side . . .

But Lydia could see now that she had misjudged. Fiona had always been a solitary animal—respected, admired even, but infamously aloof. She kept everyone at arm's length. That had always been her way.

Lydia had walked only a few yards, pulling her coat tighter around her, when she heard Fiona's voice call out.

"She didn't tell me about the book, you know."

Lydia turned. "What?"

"Sybil. She came to me that day in an absolute panic. She said you were in France on some secret mission and needed to be extracted right away. She told me you were in trouble. But she never said anything about any book."

Lydia swallowed. "I see."

"Seems a rather important thing to overlook." Fiona looked at Lydia pointedly. "A few days later she remembered. She insisted that she had told me about the book from the start. Of course, I blamed myself. I let her convince me that the mistake had been mine. I returned to France. I looked for it everywhere. But I've gone over it in my head a hundred times since, and I'm absolutely certain: Sybil simply never told me to retrieve it."

Lydia watched Fiona's face. Fiona had always worn a sort of mask, separate from the intricate glamour that gilded her features, but no less cunning. It was a face that invited you in, but not too close, a mask of flashing eyes and coy downward glances and wry, pretty smirks. Utterly intoxicating and false as false could be, like beautiful armor. For the first time, Lydia saw the mask slip.

Lydia returned to Fiona's side. "Why didn't you say anything before?"

"It was only a feeling. If I was wrong, I would never regain the trust of the council, let alone the grand mistress." Fiona stared down the empty, tree-lined path. "Tell me, Lydia. You know Sybil better than anyone. Do *you* think it was just an honest mistake?"

Lydia didn't answer. They walked in silence, watching the people in the park, men and women all going about their days in the fading afternoon light.

"I have a proposal," Fiona said. "I'll go first. I'll tell you my suspicions, based on what I've observed. Once you hear me out, you can decide whether to tell me what you know. If you decide not to trust me after all, well, that's fine. I hope you'll refrain from telling the high council about my wild and unsubstantiated theories, and in return, I won't tell the grand mistress that you asked me to ferry you back to France. Do we have a deal?"

"That sounds fair," Lydia said.

Fiona peered out across the windswept park. "Sybil is no fool. If she'd wanted the book brought to London, she would have told me. I think she knew that there would be Gestapo waiting outside that château when I arrived, and she preferred them to have it over us. A thing like that would be nearly impossible to remove from the academy once the council had their hands on it, after all. I think the only reason she mentioned it at all was because by then she'd discovered that the book had *not* in fact been recovered by the Gestapo, but had gone missing, along with your two friends, and she needed it found." Fiona looked at Lydia then, her perfect glamour marred by worry. "I think Sybil has been compromised."

The air had become colder, the sunlight dimming to a burnished bronze. As Lydia watched, Fiona rearranged her face. The clever, pretty mask reappeared before her eyes.

"Well, how did I do?"

As good as Fiona was at managing her face, it was her voice that gave her away. She was harboring a terrible suspicion, and she had no one she could trust—and she was scared. Lydia made up her mind.

"I have reason to believe that Sybil is not only working with the Witches of the Third Reich, she's leading them. I have no idea which members of the high council might have been compromised, or whom we can trust. Meanwhile my only allies in France are in danger, the book is missing, and I need to find it before the Nazis do. And I can't do it without you."

Fiona stood for a moment, staring into the distance. She pulled a silver cigarette case from her pocket and offered it to Lydia. Lydia shook her head. Fiona lit her cigarette and exhaled a plume of smoke.

"I was sorry about Kitty, you know," she said.

Lydia looked at her, surprised.

"Oh, there was no love lost between us, to be sure. But she didn't deserve to die like that. She was one of us."

Lydia's eyes stung, and she blinked to keep the tears from falling.

"Do you think we'll run into her? The witch who killed Kitty?"

A chill ran through Lydia's blood. "Yes. I believe we will."

Fiona took a thoughtful drag. Lydia noticed that her cherry-red lips left no mark on the cigarette. "I should like to meet her. I have a few things I'd like to express in person."

"I daresay you'll get the chance," Lydia said. "There's just one thing we need to do first."

THEY ARRIVED AT THE FLAT separately so no one would note their arrival. First Lydia, slipping unnoticed up the back stairwell she'd used to sneak out earlier that day; then Fiona a few minutes later, appearing from thin air in Evelyn's kitchen on a gust of wind that smelled of fresh rain.

"You must be Fiona!" Evelyn stood to greet her guest. "I'm Lydia's mum."

"Delighted to meet you, Mrs. Polk." Fiona smiled warmly as she took Evelyn's hand.

"Please, call me Evelyn. I've got the kettle on. I can fix us all a cuppa before we get on our way, if there's time."

Fiona glanced at Lydia but said nothing.

"Milk?" Evelyn asked. "I'm afraid I'm all out of sugar."

"Milk is fine." Fiona turned her gaze on Lydia. "Might I speak with you for a moment? Please excuse us, Evelyn."

"Go on, dear." Evelyn retreated to the kitchen while Lydia led Fiona to the sitting room.

Fiona's smile dissolved the moment Evelyn was out of sight. "You said we were going to pick up a few things."

"Yes, well, strictly speaking—"

"You didn't think to mention one of those things would be *your mother?*"

"As well as some other assorted provisions."

Lydia glanced over her shoulder into the kitchen. Evelyn was seated at her table, the kettle already hissing away, with one of Lydia's plain wool skirts in her lap. She was stitching something into the hem—a half dozen tiny, waxed paper packets, each one containing a different spell from Evelyn's own cupboard. Spells for healing, for hexing, for protection against dark magic. Lydia had tried to assure her that everything would go to plan, but Evelyn would not be dissuaded.

"Do you think I'm a bloody ferryman?" Fiona hissed. "You do know I can only travel with one person at a time, don't you?"

"I did realize that, yes."

"It will take time," Fiona went on. "I'll need at least a few minutes before I can travel again after the first trip. It's not easy, you know, dragging a whole extra person hundreds of miles in the blink of an eye."

"I understand." Lydia looked again toward the kitchen. "I wouldn't ask if I didn't think it was important. I need her."

Sisterhood means your people, Evelyn had said. *Your family.* Well, Evelyn was Lydia's only family. A family of two. She hoped they would be enough.

Fiona fumed, darting a look toward the kitchen as Evelyn hummed away. After a moment, her face softened.

"Is she up for this? What you're going to do, you don't need me to tell you it's bloody dangerous. Is she strong enough?"

"She's strong enough," Lydia said, but even as she spoke the words, a hard, metallic fear wedged itself inside of her.

"For her sake, I hope you're right."

Evelyn appeared in the doorway, wiping her hands on a worn, pink tea towel. Fiona quickly arranged her face, the bright smile reappearing in an instant.

"Tea's ready." Evelyn smiled as Fiona walked past her into the kitchen, but when she looked at Lydia, the smile faltered, and all of her anxiety seemed to be laid bare, just for a second. She did her best to hide it, but it was too late. Lydia had already seen.

"Come on, love." She held out her hand. "Tea first."

. . .

LYDIA SAT AT THE KITCHEN TABLE with her gran's shield stone hanging like an anchor around her neck. The plain wool skirt she wore felt strangely heavy, the hem weighed down with her mother's concoctions.

"Remember, you need to work quickly," Evelyn said. "The moment you take off the shield stone, they'll be able to track you. They might not notice right away, but I wager you'll only have a few minutes before they realize you're back on the board."

"I know." Lydia felt the magic in her blood pulsing at full strength against the weight of the stone.

"Are you ready?" Fiona asked. Her tea sat in front of her, untouched.

Lydia nodded and lifted the shield stone from around her neck, feeling the magic surge in her veins as she placed it on the table. She took a moment to center herself, then set her focus, letting her limbs grow heavy as Evelyn's kitchen seemed to grow dimmer around her. She felt the sudden sensation of falling, felt herself sink into the floor, and then—

Twenty-Eight

enry. Henry's face, his dark skin reflecting the sunset in shades of copper and pink. His jaw was darkened with stubble, and he was thinner than the last time she'd seen him. He came into focus, and Lydia saw his eyes lock onto hers as his mouth fell open. She wanted to ask if he was all right, if he was safe, but she was having trouble finding her voice. In the end, it was Rebecca who spoke first.

"Putain de merde. Lydia."

They were in a hayloft, dying light streaming in as the sun dipped low to touch the horizon. Rebecca was standing, dressed in trousers and a man's olive-green coat. Henry sat with his back against the wall, a canvas pack clutched to his chest. Lydia thought they both looked hungry and cold.

Henry didn't look happy to see her. On the contrary, he looked horrified, grief-stricken. Lydia couldn't understand why he was looking at her that way. She wanted to ask, but then Rebecca knelt by his side and placed a hand on his shoulder.

"It's all right, Henry. I see her too. She's not dead. She's all right."

It was like watching a spell lift. Henry's gaze cleared, and a broken smile found his lips, although the haunted quality in his eyes remained.

"Are you safe?" he asked.

She hesitated before answering, unsure what to make of the anguish she'd seen flash across Henry's face. "I'm fine. I'm coming to you. Do you have the book?"

"We have it," Rebecca said.

They told her they were hiding on a dairy farm a day's walk south from the château. They'd been sleeping in the hayloft, staying out of sight. They were cold and scared, but safe.

"I'm coming," Lydia said. Rebecca grinned in response, while Henry hung his head in relief.

She closed her eyes. One moment she could smell snow, and hay, and animals. The next she smelled tea, and beeswax, and then she was home.

"I found them." She repeated the location to Fiona, then turned to her mother. "Mum—"

"I'll be right behind you. Go."

Fiona took Lydia firmly by the hand. The rest happened in an instant. Lydia felt dizzy and smelled something electric, like the air after a thunderstorm. The room dropped away, and she felt the nauseating sensation of being flung through space.

She gasped, and the air that filled her lungs was icy.

"Come on. Up you get," she heard Fiona say.

She was on her hands and knees in a field. Frost covered the ground, and spiky bits of plant matter stuck up through the frozen earth, stabbing into her flesh. The sky was overcast, the sun falling below the horizon, drowning in a final splashy show of pink and gold. Off in the distance stood an old gray barn.

Lydia staggered to her feet, the cold air bracing in her lungs. She forced herself to walk, wobbling like a new calf over the uneven ground. She'd never been much for traveling. Before she'd gone a few yards, she saw a narrow figure emerge from the barn, ropes of dark hair whipping in the wind.

Rebecca.

"We thought you were dead." She wore a crooked smile, and Lydia thought that Rebecca looked almost pleased to see her.

"I know. I'm sorry."

Hiding had made Rebecca even harder around the edges, sharp as flint from too much fear and not enough food. But there was something else, too—something in the way she kept glancing back toward the barn.

"It's Henry, isn't it?" Lydia asked.

Rebecca nodded.

"What's happened? When I saw him, he looked so . . . different."

Rebecca seemed unsure how to answer. "I should probably let him explain."

When they stepped inside the barn, Henry was there waiting. He looked abnormally still to Lydia, standing with his hands in his pockets, face vigilant. They stood like that for a moment, taking each other in. Neither looked the way they had when they'd last seen each other.

Lydia was the first to move. She approached slowly, taking in every detail of him, the rigid posture and watchful eyes. He appeared less substantial than he had before, like something more than his size had been taken from him. She reached out and touched his face, letting her thumb caress the hard line of his jaw. His gaze dropped from hers, his chin trembling as he leaned his cheek into her hand. Then something seemed to break loose inside him. He stepped forward and wrapped his arms around her, squeezing her so tightly she could scarcely breathe, and Lydia held him back, breathless and shaking.

"Are you all right?" he whispered in her ear.

She pressed her cheek against his neck. "Better now. You?"

"Better now."

He let go, but she noticed the way he held on to just the tips of her fingers before releasing her, how her skin seemed to tingle where they'd touched. She wanted to stay that way, just for a moment, but—

"There's no time," she said, and Henry nodded. "You have it?"

He produced the book from the pack slung over his shoulder. It felt heavier than Lydia remembered, warmer. It seemed to respond to her touch, the tremor of dark magic rising off the pages like swarming flies. Lydia thought she felt a rush of something—heat, excitement, *glee*— rise from the book as it passed from Henry's hand to hers.

She called to Fiona. "How much longer?"

"Just a few minutes more."

"Right. I'm going to begin. As soon as you're able, go back for Evelyn. Don't wait for me."

Rebecca stepped into the barn. "Begin what?"

Lydia held the book against her chest and imagined it embracing her back, wrapping itself around her like dark tentacles. "I'm going to bind the book to myself."

Rebecca took another step forward. "Say that again?"

"It's a spell witches normally use to protect our own personal grimoires. We bind the book to ourselves, and no other witch can touch it. Not ever. The binding is meant to protect a witch's own book of spellwork, but in theory, it can be used on any book at all."

"You can't bind yourself to that thing," Rebecca protested. "The last time you used it, it nearly killed you."

"Rebecca's right," Henry said.

"I am not asking your permission." Lydia said it more forcefully than she'd meant to. Henry and Rebecca stared at her. Fiona looked at the floor. Lydia took a breath, and when she spoke again, her voice was low and steady. "I'm going to destroy it. Now. Tonight. But I can't do it alone, and it will take some time. I need to make sure that if the Witches of the Third Reich find us before I can finish the spell, they cannot use the book."

"And if they kill you?" Rebecca asked.

"If I die, the book will turn to ash."

Silence filled the barn. The rosy sunset was gone, replaced by a dull gray haze. It was Fiona who broke the silence.

"There's no time for this." She looked at Lydia. "Do what you need to do."

Lydia nodded gratefully. She turned to Henry. "Henry, listen to me—"

"I know what you're going to say."

"No, you don't."

Henry smiled sadly, and the sight of it made Lydia's heart feel like it was straining at the seams. "Yes, I do. I've been inside your head, remember?" He took her hand in his. "I'm not leaving."

She looked into Henry's eyes, and Rebecca's, and in that moment, she wished more than anything that she could be like Evelyn, sending them away with a single word. She wished she could force them to save themselves.

"Go. Do your spell." He let go of her hand.

Swallowing her fear, she walked to the far back corner of the barn, far away from the others. She knelt on the ground and placed the book in front of her. Cold radiated through the earth into her bones, and bits of hay and dirt stuck to her stockings. She closed her eyes and reached for the book with her mind. Sure enough, she felt it reaching back, feral and starving. She began the work of binding the book to herself, taking each tendril of dark magic, peeling it back, and weaving it into a piece of herself. It was delicate work, done not with words or potions but with pure energy. She was folding it into her and, in turn, placing essential pieces of herself inside the book, so that slowly they became one.

The energy of the *Grimorium Bellum* was thick and suffocating. It filled Lydia's throat with a taste like vomit. She tried to breathe deeply as she welcomed it to become a part of her, and the book did so greedily, with no hesitation, only hunger.

She had been working only a few minutes when she sensed something else with her, there in the shadows. A familiar presence, but not a friendly one. Even as she negotiated with the power of the book, braiding it into herself with steely determination, she couldn't help but smile.

"Is that you, Ursula?" She became aware of something pulling itself together in the darkness, congealing until it became whole. And then, crouching before her, she saw the blond hair and cruel mouth, the eyes shining in the darkness. The projection alone was enough to fill her with loathing.

"So," Ursula whispered, "not dead after all?"

"Not yet." Lydia closed her eyes, drawing more of the book into herself, pouring more of herself into the book.

"What are you doing there, I wonder?"

"You'll find out soon enough."

Out of the corner of her eye, she saw Fiona look her way, her attention drawn by the sound of Lydia's voice.

Ursula stood, circling Lydia as she spoke, her ghostly image wavering as she moved through the barn. "Where are you, Lydia Polk?" she sang. Lydia ignored her.

"Do we have company, then?" Fiona called. "Is it her?"

"I'm afraid so." Her blood felt sluggish in her veins.

Fiona raised her chin and addressed the air. "I'm looking forward to finally making your acquaintance!" She shouted gaily. "Though I promise, you won't find the meeting nearly so enjoyable."

Ursula chuckled as she worked her way around the perimeter of the barn, peering outside, searching for the one clue that would tell her where to retrieve her prize. She walked close to Rebecca, and to Henry, neither one aware of her presence as she passed by. Finally, she crossed to the far wall and stopped to examine a long metal object—a cattle brand, bearing the mark of the Boucher farm. She grinned.

"Tell your friend I'm on my way."

And then she was gone.

"Lydia?" Rebecca said.

She was almost finished. Just a few more moments and the *Grimorium Bellum* would be bound to her forever.

"She's coming." Lydia did not pause in her work. "Almost there." There was a sour taste in the back of her throat. Her skin itched and her cheeks felt hot. Suddenly, a smell like rain filled the barn.

Fiona looked up, sniffing the air. "They're here."

It was as if the book was eating her alive. Lydia's muscles twitched, and heat washed over her like a fever.

Fiona looked at Rebecca and Henry. "Get away from the door," she commanded. But it was too late.

Light flooded the barn as the door exploded into a thousand pieces, raining down like shrapnel, and the thunderstorm smell was replaced by the acrid stink of smoke. Six witches appeared, each one carrying an electric torch, and at the center of their ranks stood Ursula Wolfe— taller than the rest, silver hair haloed by torchlight, a smile on her face.

Rebecca and Henry were thrown to the earth by the blast. Rebecca's head struck the ground hard, and she rolled onto her side, dazed. Henry scrambled to her. Lydia watched, powerless, unable to tear herself from her spell. She needed more time. Fiona ran to where Henry and Rebecca lay, placing herself between them and the invading forces. Ursula drew a pistol and aimed.

"*Fyora bryn!*" Fiona called out, and the gun began to glow red in Ursula's hand. She dropped it, holding her singed fingers and cursing in German. Fiona looked at Rebecca and Henry. "Hide."

Henry tugged Rebecca to her feet, pulling her to the back of the barn. Fiona turned her attention back to Ursula. The remaining witches hung back, shifting on their feet, awaiting her command.

"You should run as well. We have no quarrel with you," Ursula said.

Fiona faced her. "Ah, but you see, I do have a quarrel with you. You killed two of our own. I'm afraid I can't let that stand."

Ursula shrugged. "As you wish."

Fiona made the first move. One moment she was standing in the center of the barn; the next she was gone, leaving nothing but the smell of rain in her wake. She reappeared a second later, standing behind a golden-haired witch at the rear of the formation. Fiona spoke a word in her ear, and then the earth seemed to reach up and grab the girl by both legs, dragging her to the dirt, which swallowed her up to the chest as she struggled. The witch screamed and reached for Fiona with both hands, but she was too fast and flicked away again.

A second later Fiona was back, standing inches from Ursula with a spade in her hand. Fiona raised the spade to deliver her blow, but Ursula pivoted, smoothly, like a dancer, and screamed. The scream seemed to contain not one voice, but many, an ear-shattering bellow that threw Fiona flat onto her back, the spade clattering uselessly against the wall. Ursula placed one boot on Fiona's chest, released the knife from her hip, and raised it high.

Lydia felt the *Grimorium Bellum* latch on to her with a sickening finality. She stood, holding the book in her hands, feeling the energy cycling between them, a pulsing circuit of magic, feeding them both like blood in an artery. She turned her head and was sure she saw an oily creature, clinging to her back like a parasite. She watched as Fiona was flung to the ground like a doll, as Ursula raised her knife, as if seeing it all unfold in slow motion. She felt the book surge in her hands, took a deep breath, and her projection left her body like a bullet.

It was as if someone had detonated a bomb. Ursula was thrown into the air, witches tossed in every direction by the force of the attack. Fiona curled into a ball as debris fell around her. Lydia returned to her body with a violent jolt, the power of the *Grimorium Bellum* raging through her veins like molten metal. It *burned*, and for a moment she was helpless, writhing in agony.

Fiona groaned and raised herself to her hands and knees. Ursula's discarded pistol lay in the dirt, just out of arm's reach. Her eyes widened and she scrambled toward the gun. Across the room, one of Ursula's soldiers raised herself to her feet and spoke a word in a strange tongue. As Fiona reached for the pistol, it flew away from her straining fingers, into the hand of the German witch. The witch aimed and fired.

The bullet tore through Fiona's shoulder, the impact sending her reeling backward into the dirt. The second bullet hit her in the side, and blood exploded through her white silk blouse. She screamed in rage and pain as the witch stepped closer and aimed a third time, leveling the pistol at her head.

No, Lydia thought as the *Grimorium Bellum* burned through her, helpless to do anything but watch. *No, please, no.*

The smell of ozone filled the air. The witch fired twice, hitting dirt both times. Fiona had disappeared into the ether, leaving nothing behind her but a bloody stain.

"Scheiße!" the witch screamed.

The searing pain ebbed away, and Lydia felt the *Grimorium Bellum* settling in her blood, acclimating her to its power. It didn't want to hurt her, she realized with a hideous thrill. They were one now.

Lydia's eyes cleared. She looked at the pool of blood, turning black as it seeped into the dirt. She looked at the witch, and at the gun. The witch raised the pistol and aimed.

"*Slaepna fae*," Lydia said, and the witch's eyes rolled back in her head as she fell to the ground, unconscious.

The thunderstorm smell dissipated. Lydia looked at the dark stain where Fiona had lain just a moment before. There was so much blood. She wondered where Fiona had escaped to. She hoped she'd gone back to Evelyn's flat. Evelyn would know what to do.

"Enough of this," Ursula said. The mocking smile had disappeared from her face, leaving only a hard red line. Three witches stood by her side. She raised her hand and made a sign in the air, calling out a word of power Lydia had never heard before. The three soldier-witches echoed her call. Lydia opened her mouth to counter, but too late.

The air left her lungs in a rush, and she was thrown to the ground. She could feel her hands grasping the book, but they felt as if they belonged to someone else. Darkness crept at her vision. The power of the *Grimorium Bellum* thrashed in her veins, enraged at being constrained.

She watched as Ursula retrieved her gun.

"Bring me the others." She said it in English, as if for Lydia's benefit.

Lydia struggled with every ounce of her power against the spell that held her. She drew from the book, pulling its magic deeper into herself, but it was no use—even with the power of the *Grimorium Bellum*, she was no match for four witches working a single spell in tandem. Not if she wanted to survive the effort.

Somewhere in the dark recesses of the barn, she heard a struggle—a grunt from Henry, Rebecca's garbled shout, then angry curses in German, before Lydia recognized the sizzle of hex words on the air. A moment later, Rebecca and Henry were thrown to the dirt beside her. Lydia noticed blood on one witch's face, and more under Rebecca's fingernails.

Ursula crouched before her. The smile had returned.

"You should have considered my offer. You could have saved yourself. And your friends." Ursula's fingers hovered over the *Grimorium Bellum*, still clutched tightly in Lydia's grip. "Now you're going to watch them die. And for what? Nothing."

She reached for the book. It slipped from Lydia's hands easily, and Ursula stood, holding the book high, triumphant. Lydia watched as Ursula took one step, then another. She felt the cord between herself and the book grow taut. Ursula tilted her head as if hearing some distant sound.

"Was ist das—" Then her words were cut short. She began to choke. Ursula's free hand went to her throat, clawing wildly, her fingernails leaving red welts on her skin. Her mouth hung open in terror, eyes wide, as one side of her face began to go slack.

"Ursula?" One of the witches took a step forward, but Ursula stumbled away from her. Her skin began to go purple, livid bruises appearing at her temples and around her eyes. She retched and gagged, clawing with both hands now, finally dropping the book, which landed in the dirt with a thud.

"Don't touch it!" she gasped. The color returned to her face, the bruises faded, but the raised, red claw marks on her neck remained. She looked at Lydia, pure rage contorting her features. "What did you do?" She crossed the distance between them in an instant, grabbing Lydia and shaking her hard. The spell broke, and air rushed into Lydia's lungs. "*What did you do?*"

Lydia's vision began to clear. She looked to Henry and Rebecca on either side of her. They were both dazed, battered and bruised, but the sight of them gave her strength.

"It's a grimoire," she said, once she'd regained her voice. "Now it's *my* grimoire."

She saw that Ursula understood. Slowly, Ursula got to her feet.

"I'll kill you," she whispered.

"By all means," Lydia said. "But you'll only destroy the book in the process."

Ursula shrieked in outrage, a high-pitched animal scream that made even the other members of her own coven recoil. Lydia tried to steady herself, working to summon the power for some spell that might save her, save her friends, but the lingering effects of the battle hex had left her weakened. Ursula turned her attention to Rebecca and Henry, eyes wild.

"Ingrid."

A witch stepped forward. She was older than Ursula, mean looking and famine thin. She smiled down on the three huddled figures kneeling in the dirt before her.

Ursula's face curled in contempt. "Leave the witch. I want her to watch. The other two you may do with as you please."

Ingrid's smile widened into a grin. She crouched before them, whispering something Lydia couldn't quite make out, the stream of words sizzling on the air.

Rebecca was the first to scream. The sound tore out of her, increasing in pitch and intensity until it transformed into a frantic shriek. Henry held out longer, the veins in his neck bulging as he struggled to stay silent, but he broke a moment later, and a river of tears flowed from his face as he howled in agony.

Lydia shouted to be heard over the screams. "What are you doing to them?"

Ursula did not reply, and Ingrid continued. It was as if her words were red-hot, searing Henry and Rebecca with every syllable, every unintelligible word like barbed wire. Their screams were deafening, filling the barn, sucking up every drop of oxygen.

"Stop it." Lydia's voice sounded childish in her own ears.

"Reverse the spell," Ursula replied.

"You know I can't!"

"Then your friends will die screaming." She stood behind Ingrid, staring down with satisfaction as Rebecca and Henry howled and wept. Lydia began to scream as well, helpless and enraged.

Just out of reach, the *Grimorium Bellum* lay discarded in the dirt, humming insistently, as if all of Lydia's pain and anguish was feeding it, calling the book to her aid. She could feel the invisible cord that bound them together tightening.

She closed her eyes, and when she opened them, there was a roiling shadow crouching over the book like a toad. No, not over it. It *was* the book. The shadow and the book occupied the same space, and Lydia's vision seemed to strobe as she saw one, then the other, then both. It morphed and twisted, looking for one instant like many creatures all slithering in and around each other, then the next, unnervingly human— a feminine figure, black hair floating all around it as if suspended in water, the face featureless in the dark of the barn, but somehow familiar.

In that moment it seemed as if the creature reached out a hand to Lydia, its image pulsing like a great, black vein. *A gift*, a voice whispered inside her head.

A word seemed to form on Lydia's lips. She could taste it, like honey in her mouth. It was no word of power she had ever spoken, but somehow, she knew the sound, and knew what would happen when she spoke it.

She blocked out the rising tide of screams all around her and focused only on that one word. She felt it become whole, a solid thing on her tongue. Her head throbbed, heat rushing up through the core of her as veins of night-black ink raced up her arms, her neck, into her eyes, filling her mouth like blood. She breathed it in, felt the power rise in her, and—

A voice called out from the misty darkness beyond the barn, speaking in a language Lydia didn't understand. It was a voice Lydia knew almost as well as her own.

Sybil's voice.

Lydia opened her mouth to speak, but no sound came out. Sybil had bound her tongue. The word of power withered in her mouth. The creature let loose a frustrated snarl, then slithered back inside the book and disappeared.

"*Enough.*"

Ingrid and Ursula looked up. The screaming stopped. Henry and Rebecca slumped to the ground.

"Grand Mistress." Ursula bowed.

Sybil did not look at Ursula. She looked only at Lydia, and Lydia stared back in silence. The betrayal stuck in her throat like bile. Until this moment, she hadn't truly believed.

Sybil approached and knelt before her, smiling sadly.

"Oh, my darling. I should have known you would never stop."

"Grand Mistress." Ursula's eyes were downcast. "She's . . . she's bound herself to the *Grimorium Bellum.*"

Sybil breathed a heavy sigh. "Of course she did. It's exactly what I would have done." She turned to Ursula. "Are you aware she nearly just killed you all?"

Ursula paled. Sybil turned back to Lydia, her eyes lingering over the black veins that wormed their way across her flesh and then disappeared a second later, like some ocean creature slipping beneath the water. "I'm right, aren't I? You were going to slaughter them all with a word. At great cost to yourself, I imagine."

Lydia stared back, defiant. Sybil leaned in closer, lowering her voice so only Lydia could hear. "Whatever you might think of me right now, please know that I have always thought of you as a daughter."

On any other day, Lydia would have wept. Now, with all her tears already spent, her tongue useless, she bared her teeth in a silent scream. Sybil stood and returned her attention to the *Grimorium Bellum,* nudging the book with her toe.

"One of you, get a sack."

Henry was starting to come around. He rolled onto his side and groaned, hay and dirt sticking to his sweat-slicked face.

Ursula stepped forward. "Would you like me to dispose of these two, Mistress?"

Sybil looked down at the two prone bodies, considering them dispassionately. "No. We'll bring them with us."

Ursula frowned. "Grand Mistress, with respect—" Sybil turned her cold, blue stare on Ursula, the ice in her gaze so alien that, for a moment, Lydia hardly recognized her. Ursula lowered her eyes. "Yes, Grand Mistress."

Rebecca and Henry were dragged to their feet. Rebecca's head still hung limply from her shoulders, but Henry was awake now, staring at Lydia with panic in his eyes. He looked like he was about to speak, but then the metallic smell filled the barn once again, and Rebecca and Henry flickered out of sight, along with the witches who held them.

Ursula and Ingrid set about tending to their fallen sisters, leaving Sybil and Lydia alone together. Lydia studied Sybil's face, searching for some clue, some sign that the woman she had known for so many years had been a fabrication, but the warmth had returned to Sybil's eyes, and she stared back with the same motherly affection Lydia had always known. Somehow, that only made the betrayal more painful.

"Lydia, darling," Sybil said after a moment. "Please listen to me. This doesn't need to be horrible. Are you going to give me trouble?"

Lydia, still deprived of the use of her tongue, held Sybil squarely in her gaze and nodded.

Sybil pressed two fingers to the bridge of her nose. "Very well." She stepped close to Lydia and, very gently, reached out and smoothed her dark curls with her fingertips.

"*Slaepna fae.*"

Lydia tried to stay awake, but the darkness took her just the same.

Twenty-Nine

ydia woke to the smell of snow.

Early morning sunlight streamed through the windows, clean and sharp and bright. The bed where she lay was heavy with blankets. The room was cavernous, the walls lined with gleaming carved wood panels that reflected the light.

She sat up and went to the window. Mountains loomed all around her, their white caps reflecting the morning light so brightly it was almost painful. A carpet of mist stretched across the landscape like an ocean, soft peaks undulating like waves in the distance. Frost etched intricate patterns on the windowpane like lace. When she looked to the right, she saw pristine stone walls and towering spires. She was in a gleaming white castle, like a kidnapped princess in a fairy tale.

Her hair was damp, and her clothing had been removed and replaced with a long satin nightgown the color of cream. She shuddered at the knowledge that one of these women had bathed and dressed her while she'd slept. Her own clothes lay neatly folded on a chair against the wall. In the wardrobe, a dozen dresses hung side by side, creating a lush rainbow of saturated jewel tones in cotton, silk, and cashmere. Lydia didn't need to try them on to know that each one had been made to her exact measurements. She selected the most subdued of her options—a simple, long-sleeved dress in a deep plum hue—and got dressed.

The silence in the room was so complete it became its own kind of sound. Lydia could hear her breathing, the shifting of fabric across her skin. At times she was sure she could hear her own pulse. It was that silence that first made her suspect all was not quite as it seemed.

She closed her eyes and thought of Evelyn. She would be worrying herself sick by now. Lydia could summon her face without difficulty, her rough hands, her warm, cluttered kitchen. She wanted to go to her, but try as she might, she could not seem to leave her body. She tried again, this time picturing Henry's face in her mind's eye, then Rebecca, then Fiona. Nothing happened. The magic felt dull inside her body, the silence growing like a moat all around her.

She stood and walked the perimeter of the room, tracing the carvings on the walls with her fingertips. The amber-colored wood seemed to vibrate under her hand. Finally, it dawned on her—the carvings were not decorative at all. The walls had been etched with one enormous sigil, encircling the room like a snake. It was a binding, designed to keep anyone inside from performing magic. The realization made her feel claustrophobic, and the unnatural silence picked up a sinister tone. The only break in the quiet was the ever-present hum of the *Grimorium Bellum*, which sat on a marble-topped table in a corner of the room. Lydia placed her hand on the book, and the energy seemed to rise up to meet her, like a cat wanting to be stroked. Even the book seemed tamer beneath the weight of the sigil, but no less seductive. She forced herself to back away.

A sound broke through the quiet, making her jump. A door opened, one she hadn't seen before, the serpentine carvings blending perfectly into the surrounding panels. Sybil appeared in the doorway, and the panel closed softly behind her a moment later. She looked so ordinary to Lydia, so out of place surrounded by all this opulence.

"You're angry." Sybil pursed her lips, and Lydia hated her for it, the condescension. "You can speak now, you know. If you want to."

"What could I possibly have to say to you?"

"I'm sure you have questions." Sybil smiled sweetly. It made Lydia want to slap her.

"Why?" said Lydia.

"Why what, darling?"

A single bark of disbelief erupted from Lydia's chest. "*Why?* Why have you betrayed your coven? Your country?"

"I promise you, I've done no such thing." She took a step forward. Lydia stepped back. Sybil gave a bemused chuckle. "Darling—"

"Never call me that again," Lydia said sharply. Sybil looked genuinely hurt.

"Lydia—"

Lydia cut her off. "Did you have Isadora killed?"

There was a long silence. Sybil's chin trembled. She nodded.

"And Kitty?"

A single tear fell onto Sybil's cheek, and as it did, a fresh fury rose up inside of Lydia. She lunged forward, forcing Sybil back.

"*Don't.* Don't you dare weep for them. Don't you ever let me see you do that, you *filthy* hypocrite, I will kill you myself, do you understand? I'll kill you with my bare hands."

"Lydia—"

"*Why?*" Now Lydia was the one weeping, hot tears streaming down her face as she raged. "Why did you do it? So you could take her place? So you could be grand mistress?"

"No! Not me. Of course not me. *You.*" Sybil looked astonished. "I nominated you myself, you silly thing. I never wanted to be grand mistress of the academy. It was always supposed to be you."

"They named you—"

"You *left*. You ran off, traipsing all over France in search of that damned book. They were going to elect Vivian, Mother help us all. You left me no choice but to step in. But it was always supposed to be you."

"I didn't want it!" Lydia shouted. "I never asked for it!"

"Which is exactly why you were meant for it. Isadora was a powerful woman, but she was calculating. Ambitious. Her ambition drove the academy into a war, something we had never done in our history, and for what? To be forced back into the shadows once we were no longer needed?"

"To defeat Hitler. To prevent him from murdering millions of innocent people. You've aligned yourself with a monster, Sybil."

Sybil looked as if she were disappointed, as if Lydia's reasoning were simple, childlike. "Darling—" Lydia took a warning step forward, and Sybil flinched. "*Lydia*. Can we sit? Please?"

Lydia wanted to draw on the power of the *Grimorium Bellum* and cast a pestilence down on Sybil's head. She wanted to fill her lying mouth with boils and sores before silencing her forever, but she knew it was futile. Lydia could cast no magic here. She took a seat. Sybil followed, letting the silence grow between them before Lydia finally spoke.

"Where are we?"

"Bavaria." A ray of sunlight fell on Sybil's face.

"And my friends?"

"They're here. They're safe."

"Bring me to them."

"No. Not until we understand one another."

"I don't see what there is to understand. You're a Nazi and a traitor."

Sybil's face colored. "I am your grand mistress."

"Isadora was my grand mistress."

The warmth in Sybil's blue eyes chilled. *Now*, Lydia thought. Now she could see it. The mask Sybil wore, and the face underneath it. Not a glamour. Something far more insidious.

Sybil looked out the window, fidgeting with one of her rings.

"My grandmother was from here, you know," she said. "Well, strictly speaking she was from the Black Forest. Beautiful country. My mother was born there as well, although you wouldn't know it from meeting her. She came to England as a child, no trace of an accent. Extraordinary witches, they were. Projectionists, both of them. Like me, I suppose, but they were more than that as well. Natural talent, nothing like what they teach at the academy. I used to think there wasn't anything they couldn't do. My grandmother could heal any wound, cure madness, call down the rain. When my mother was a girl, a local boy violated her behind his father's butcher shop. My grandmother turned the boy into a goat, then took him to his own father to be slaughtered and sold for stew. She was a *true* witch, like in the stories. My mother had a portion of her talent, not nearly as strong, and me, even less so.

"I always wondered why I wasn't more like my grandmother. Where had all the true witches gone? My grandmother assured me that her homeland had been full of powerful witches, just like her. But when I came and saw for myself, I found that the witches of Germany were no different than the witches of England. Their magic was small. *Tame.* And just like the witches of England, they'd all gone into hiding—in plain sight, that is. They'd made themselves ordinary in exchange for their safety."

Sybil reached out and pressed her fingers to the frozen windowpane and watched as the frost melted under her fingertips.

"My grandmother was never ordinary a day in her life. Everyone knew what she was. She could be strange, terrifying even, but oh, she was *powerful.* I began to wonder, Was it our secrecy that made our magic small? Magic is about actualization, after all, about changing what *isn't* into what *is*, using only the power of your will. How much power could a person really wield, pretending to be something she's not?"

"But that's exactly what you did. *You lied.* To me, and everyone else." Lydia felt sick at her own stupidity.

Sybil frowned. "I didn't. I withheld things, but I never lied. Not to you."

"You poisoned me."

A shadow crossed Sybil's face as the sun ducked behind a passing cloud. "I did that for your protection." Lydia scoffed. "You nearly *died.* I was only trying to keep you from doing yourself even greater harm."

"You wanted me out of the way." Lydia cast her a withering look. "Does the council know, by the way? What you really are?"

Sybil held her gaze. "No."

Foolish, naive child. She'd been so happy to believe that Vivian was the traitor inside the academy. Now she realized it was because she simply didn't like the woman. But *Sybil.* She had loved Sybil with all her heart.

Lydia forced her gaze away from her. After a moment, Sybil continued.

"When Hitler rose to power, we began to hear whispers. His obsession with the occult, with witchcraft. I found myself wondering, What might be possible if the witches of Europe no longer had to hide? What if, instead of living in fear of the persecution of men, we built an alliance with them? Stood alongside the right army, raised up the right man in order to take our rightful place, not as scapegoats to be singled out and despised, but as leaders? Powerful figures, to be feared and respected as we once were?"

Lydia stared, still not quite believing this could be Sybil's logic. "You talk as if he's meant to be our savior. He's a lunatic, Sybil."

Sybil looked insulted. "You think I don't know what he is? You think I enjoy watching his hateful rhetoric, those poor families torn apart? I know what he *is*, Lydia. But he is our one chance to live in the open again. I am doing this for the good of all of us, all witches."

"*All?* Don't you mean *Aryan* witches?" Sybil huffed, annoyed. "Or perhaps, you mean European witches, so long as they're fair skinned and blue eyed? Clearly you don't mean to include the brujas, or the vedmy, or the ćovaxană. What about—"

Sybil scowled. "Don't be cheeky. You know very well what I meant."

Lydia didn't, not at all, but she carried on. "If you find him so distasteful, why help him at all? Why not simply take power for yourself? Or has that been your plan all along? Ride Hitler's coattails into a position of power, only to take his place when the war is over?"

Sybil laughed, as if Lydia had made a joke. "I meant what I said before. I've never had the stomach for politics. I've always preferred a place behind the curtain. Besides, in my experience, people are much more inclined to follow the leadership of a man than a woman. And the coven, they believe in him. So many of them were raised for it, you know, and who am I to dissuade them? This way is best."

Lydia was stunned to silence, the dissonance between the madness of Sybil's words and the serenity of her demeanor almost too much to bear.

Sybil smiled, smugly oblivious. "Meeting the man was easier than you might think. Germany has always been rich with fairy stories, tales of the witch in the woods. Hitler jumped at the chance to meet the genuine article. I made my case for an alliance, gained his confidence. After that, it was simply a matter of recruitment. Germany is home to some of the most ancient witch bloodlines, after all. Ursula was the first to join, then Margot. They were like sisters, inseparable, both of them on fire for the cause and so eager to learn. A little fanatical, perhaps, although I admit, I encouraged it. A little youthful fanaticism can be a powerful motivator." Sybil made a face. "I believe it was your friend downstairs who murdered Margot. The Jewish girl."

Lydia said nothing.

"Ursula was nearly destroyed by Margot's death. A terrible tragedy. Margot had such talent, such potential."

"Margot was a sadist."

"Oh, don't think for a second I've forgotten *your* part in that ugly business. I know you helped the girl. Ursula knows it as well. The only reason you're still breathing is because I forbade her to kill you."

Lydia felt a quick, sinking sensation in her stomach. "That's why Ursula didn't come to collect the book herself, back at the château," she said, understanding at last. "You knew she wanted me dead, and I her. So, you forbade her, and sent the Gestapo instead." Sybil smiled, as if she thought herself very clever indeed. "They might have killed me just as easily as Ursula, you know."

"They had very strict orders not to."

Lydia stared. "And my friends?" Sybil's smile faded. Lydia couldn't imagine how she had never before realized what Sybil was. It seemed so plain now. "My God. You're all the same. You, Ursula, Margot. You're all monsters."

Sybil tsked. "You still don't understand. You think Margot was cruel without reason, but she had a very difficult life. Poor child killed her own family when she was seven years old because she didn't understand her magic, and they were too frightened of her power to teach her. A fate all too common among Forces, I'm afraid. I *saved* her from herself. Trained her, gave her a purpose. I was like a mother to her. To all of them."

Lydia felt the room go cold. She thought of Evelyn, and her gran, raising a child not so very different from Margot. *Seven years old.*

"What did she do to them?" she asked softly.

Sybil stared at her for a long moment. "She commanded them to drink lye."

Lydia shuddered and said nothing.

"You met young Gerda, I believe. She was sent to keep an eye on you and never returned. I expect you had something to do with that too. Is she safe?"

"Last I saw her."

Sybil frowned but didn't pursue it further. "The girl is a gifted Traveler, particularly for one so young. Until three years ago she was living in squalor, in one of the more Dickensian orphanages I've ever had the misfortune to see with my own eyes. When she was six years old, Gerda's father murdered her mother in cold blood, and then himself. In his suicide note he accused the girl's mother of being a witch."

"Sybil, none of this—"

"Ingrid was raised by religious zealots. Her mother suppressed her own powers, and beat Ingrid savagely for using hers. She's blind in her right eye as a result. Ursula's mother tried suppressing her powers as well. She went mad before Ursula was five years old. Nearly starved the poor girl to death, then threw herself and her daughter into a river with their pockets full of stones. Ursula only survived because her powers awakened while she was pinned to the bottom of that riverbed."

Lydia recalled Ursula's memories from that night they'd battled at the academy—cold water all around her. Her lungs on fire, screaming for air. The terror she had felt.

"And would you like to know what became of my grandmother? What they *did to her*, these civilized Britons you fight for with such passion?" There was a quiet venom in Sybil's voice that Lydia had never heard before. "When I was about your age, a local boy nailed the door to her house shut, and burned it to the ground while she was asleep in her bed. She was an old woman by then. Her power had faded. There was nothing she could do to save herself."

Sybil looked into Lydia's eyes. Lydia waited until she couldn't bear it for one more second, and looked away.

"You see, Lydia. Secrecy is a death sentence for witches. It breeds madness, and makes us weak. It turns us into nothing more than children's stories, and emboldens the littlest of men, so that even the best of us aren't safe in our own homes. Each and every witch in this sisterhood understands firsthand the tragedy that follows a life lived in the shadows. I understand it too. And I will do everything in my power to restore us to our former glory, if doing so means that not one more witch need suffer that fate ever again."

"But aligning yourself with that monster? Sacrificing millions of innocent lives? British lives, your own people—"

"*Witches* are my people. I will do what is best for them. Always."

Lydia leveled her gaze at Sybil. "What about Isadora? Did you do this for her?"

Sybil looked taken aback. "I *grieved* for Isadora." Her voice shook. "You have no idea how difficult—"

"Don't," Lydia warned.

"It was necessary. For the good of—"

"You allowed an enemy witch inside the academy. You stood by and watched as she cut Isadora's throat—"

"It's very difficult to talk to you when you're hysterical like this," Sybil snapped. "I did what I did for the academy. For *you*. So you could take your rightful place as grand mistress. Isadora would have ruined us all, she had no vision, no sense of what was possible, but *you*, Lydia, with the right guidance, the right mentorship . . ."

All at once Lydia understood. "You thought you could control me."

Sybil's mouth fell open. "No."

"You did. You thought you could manipulate me. You knew you could never turn Isadora, but *me* . . ." Lydia stood, lifted to her feet by a rush of anger and disbelief. "Did you honestly believe I would abandon everything Isadora had worked for? To join you in this . . . this crusade? Why would I?"

Sybil stood now as well. "Lydia, think. With you leading the academy, and me growing our numbers within the Reich . . ."

"My God, you did. You thought I would just blindly follow you as you united the witches of Europe behind Adolf *bloody* Hitler. Why would I do that? Because I *liked* you? Because you were kind to me?"

"Great Mother, this fixation with Hitler." Sybil's tone was calm, infuriatingly so, as if she were trying to soothe an infant. "He doesn't matter. He's just a man. A means to an end."

"But what he's *done*—"

"It doesn't matter," Sybil said. And she smiled.

Lydia felt she would go mad if she listened to any more. The room seemed to spin around her, the bright sunlight setting her teeth on edge, making her see auras.

"What do you want from me?"

"Isn't it obvious?" Sybil gazed at her tenderly. "I want you to join us."

Lydia stared, stunned at the sheer audacity of Sybil's words. "You can't be serious."

"You don't need to decide now." Sybil moved toward the door, her purple frock swishing in the unnatural silence. "Take your time. Think about what I said. I believe once you've calmed down, you will begin to understand." She pressed her palm to the carved panel, and the door opened. She stepped through, then seemed to remember something and reappeared. She looked at Lydia, eyes glinting like a woman with a delicious surprise.

"Oh, darling, I almost forgot to tell you! Your mother is here."

Thirty

Lydia felt a rush of horrified disbelief.

"What did you say?"

Sybil's face was all warmth and good humor. "Your mother is here. She's perfectly safe, you needn't worry." She winked. "You never told me she was a *Force*."

Lydia thought about beating her with her fists, gouging her eyes out, tearing at her flesh with her fingernails. But she never moved, and Sybil carried on, smugly oblivious.

"You can imagine my surprise. It took six of my girls to subdue her, and even that was a bit of a trial, from what I understand. Two of them required urgent medical care. She has a rather darkly creative mind, your mother."

Six witches. Lydia had heard of Forces who could command two, perhaps three at a time. She wondered how long Evelyn had held them off before they finally took her.

"Why?" Lydia's voice was strained. "Why did you do this?"

"Simply tying up loose ends, darling. If she'd gone running to the academy after you were taken, it would have made a terrible mess." Something in Lydia's face must have changed, because Sybil laughed, high and bright. "Oh dear, I would never *hurt* her."

"Of course you would. You murdered Isadora in cold blood. And Kitty. You don't even like Evelyn."

Sybil huffed. "Honestly, darling, I thought you knew me better than that. She may be a meddlesome thorn in my side, but she's still your *mother*."

It was a lie, of course. Sybil must have at least considered killing her. Evelyn, a powerful Force with no formal training, working from pure instinct. Backed into a corner, she would be unpredictable, lethal. There was only one reason Sybil would have kept her alive—because by killing Evelyn, she would lose all hope of ever winning Lydia to her side.

Lydia forced herself to speak calmly. "Take me to her."

"No."

"*Sybil!*" Lydia lurched forward, fists clenched, but stopped short. "Please," she whispered. "Please."

Sybil looked at her pityingly. "I meant what I said. I want you by my side." She reached out to brush a lock of hair from Lydia's face, and Lydia recoiled. "Please think about it." She turned and walked back toward the door.

"Sybil—"

The door opened, and Sybil stepped through.

"Sybil!"

But Lydia was alone.

SHE SPENT THE REMAINDER of the day in a frenzy, like an animal caught in a trap. The room had only one door, and it didn't take long for her to realize the hidden panel would open quite easily for anyone except herself. People came and went throughout the day, bringing food, or tea, but no one spoke to Lydia, and she did not attempt to engage them. The *Grimorium Bellum* beckoned to her with a constant, droning call, but she left it where it lay.

She imagined Evelyn, imprisoned somewhere in this very castle, frightened and alone. She wanted to murder the next person who walked through that door, slit their throat and fight her way to her mother, but she knew it would never work. They would kill her, and then they would kill Henry, and Rebecca, and Evelyn. No. That wasn't the way. She would need to be clever.

By the end of the first evening, she'd formulated her plan, but she knew that it was best not to rush. Deception had never been her forte, and so she waited as long as she could bear. A day passed in silence. Then a second. Then a third.

On the fourth day, she addressed the girl who brought her breakfast. "Tell Sybil I'd like to see her."

The girl scowled, then shuffled out.

SYBIL CAME THAT AFTERNOON, bringing tea for herself and coffee for Lydia.

"You'll be interested to know that Gerda has made her way back to us. She tells me it was your mother who was responsible for that little stunt."

Lydia sipped her coffee. "That took less time than I thought it would. Did she share anything interesting with our friends at the SOE while she was in their care?"

"Nothing they would believe." Sybil's irritation was barely masked. "Funny, I always thought of your mother as an eccentric, backward little hedge witch. Now I fear I've underestimated her."

Lydia suddenly remembered where she had picked up that horrible phrase, all those years ago. It had been Sybil. Some joke she'd made to the girls on their first day of class; Lydia didn't remember the particulars. She did remember that she'd laughed.

"Eva says you asked to see me," Sybil said carefully. "Would you like to discuss things calmly, now that you've had some time to think?"

Lydia directed her gaze downward. "The story you told me. About your grandmother turning that boy into a goat. Was that true?"

Sybil nodded. "My grandmother could do a great many things the average witch could only dream of."

Lydia kept her eyes on her cup. "I've read about transmutation in stories. I always wanted to learn it. I used to sit in my room by myself, staring at a sixpence, trying to make it turn into a crown. All I ever managed to do was give myself a headache."

Sybil chuckled. "I used to do that as well."

"They don't teach transmutation at the academy. I asked about it once, my first year. Mistress Jacqueline said that was only in fairy stories."

"Jacqueline has a small mind."

Lydia set down her cup. "It made me wonder what else might be possible. What other things could be achieved that I was told were only in fairy stories."

Sybil smiled. She'd never been one to pass up an opportunity to share her wisdom.

Sybil talked at length. She spoke of her grandmother, how she could make barren women fertile, cure disease, hex whole families. She repeated the stories her grandmother had told her as a girl, about witches who could fly under the full moon, transform into animals, wreck ships, or save them, depending on their mood. And she told stories that were older still—about the days before the Roman Empire, when the warrior kings of Europe bowed before the power of the witch, and knew their tribes would rise to greatness or fall into ruin at their pleasure. Lydia listened, and when Sybil finished, she sat quietly, her coffee growing cold.

"I never considered what it might be like to live openly. I always thought there was no way for us to live except in secret."

Sybil nodded sympathetically. Lydia looked up from her cup and held Sybil's gaze for the first time since they'd sat down.

"You hurt me terribly, you know. You broke my heart."

Sybil's face appeared to crumple before Lydia's eyes. "I know."

The tears that gathered in Lydia's throat were real, and she made no attempt to hide the tremor in her voice as she spoke. "I've always trusted you. You've been like a mother to me. But this . . ."

Sybil reached across the table and took Lydia's hand in hers. Lydia let her.

"It's in the past. I promise you, from now on, we will have no secrets from each other." Sybil's hand felt like a vise. Lydia slipped from her grasp.

"But if I give you access to the *Grimorium Bellum*, people will die."

"Darling," Sybil said, and this time Lydia did not reproach her, "people are already dying. They're dying on the battlefield every day. And they will continue to die until we put a stop to this war. We can do that with the power of the *Grimorium Bellum*."

It sounded so logical, so reasonable. It sounded like peace, if peace meant the destruction of anyone who would dare stand against you.

"What are you planning to do?"

Sybil drummed her fingers on the arm of her chair. "Some accounts of the *Grimorium Bellum* refer to a spell which calls forth a creature from inside the book itself. A silent assassin, which feeds on the souls of the caster's enemies, reducing them to ash. Do you know the spell I mean?"

Lydia's mouth felt dry. "The Unmaking."

Sybil nodded. "I think it's preferable to this messy famine and plague business, don't you? It will be clean. Simple. Painless." For a moment, Sybil looked almost saddened by the thought of so much death. But Lydia knew by now that it was all a show.

"And who will be the target? I expect Hitler would . . ." Lydia found she couldn't quite finish the thought, and Sybil spared her from having to voice it.

"You expect Hitler would use the book to wipe out the Jews?"

Lydia swallowed the acid that burned in her throat. Even though she knew it was all a farce, she couldn't help but feel a deep and terrible shame.

Sybil laughed, a sound that made Lydia's skin crawl. "Oh no, darling. There will be plenty of time for that sort of thing later." Lydia felt a sickening chill course through her. "Hitler has requested that the Witches of the Third Reich take on a more . . . *strategic* target for now. Stalingrad, for instance."

Something turned over inside Lydia's chest. "You plan to wipe out all of Stalingrad? Why?"

Sybil's tone was conspiratorial, as if she were discussing the caprices of a particularly moody teenager. "The Führer is still licking his wounds from his defeat there, and wants to make a statement. It makes sense, in a way. Once it was clear that the Reich could annihilate the population of an entire city without firing a single bullet, I expect the war would be over in fairly short order."

"I see," Lydia said. Sybil seemed to notice her discomfort.

"Darling, I know it sounds terrible. But it's for the best, believe me. When the war is won, you'll see."

Lydia feared she wouldn't be able to maintain her composure for much longer. She stood and looked out the window, turning her face away from Sybil's gaze.

"How do you know you can trust him? How do you know he won't turn on you when the war is over?"

Sybil sipped her tea. "I fully expect he will. And I expect he will regret it."

She's a fool, Lydia thought. An arrogant fool, drunk on her own fairy tales.

"And how do I know I can trust *you?*" Lydia turned to face Sybil once again. "The solstice is in eight days. You are one witch short of a full coven, and I alone control the *Grimorium Bellum*. You need me. How can I be sure you won't turn on *me*, once the spell is complete? Your coven doesn't trust me, and to be fair, I've given them good reason not to. You would do just as well to replace me at the earliest convenience with another girl from one of your ancient Germanic families. How do I know you won't?"

Sybil stood. "Because I love you like my own child. I will never betray you. Never."

It was exactly what Lydia had hoped she would say. Sybil had always been sentimental. Lydia might have felt guilty, under different circumstances. Now she felt only revulsion.

"I'm afraid Ursula will not be so easily won over."

Sybil gave her a wry look. "Ursula will do as she's told. I know you two have had your differences, but she's been with me since the beginning, and she is the most capable witch in this coven. I hope someday you two may be like sisters."

The notion was so ludicrous that Lydia had to turn her face away in order to hide her expression. When she turned back, Sybil was watching her expectantly.

"I'd like some time," Lydia said. "Just until tomorrow. Just to consider everything you've said. Can you give me that?"

Sybil's eyes were wide and hopeful. "Of course." And then, before Lydia could react, she closed the distance between them and embraced her, kissing her on the cheek. Lydia could smell Sybil's rose perfume, the tea and incense smell that clung to her hair. A terrible sorrow seized at her heart then, a full recognition of everything she had lost. Not just Isadora and Kitty, but Sybil too.

Lydia pulled away, breaking their embrace. "Come see me again tomorrow. You'll have your answer."

Sybil nodded. She looked for a moment like she was debating something. "Your mother has been asking for you. She's been quite insistent. Would you like me to give her a message?"

Lydia's heart leapt, but she kept her face implacable. *Tell her I'm safe,* she wanted to say. *Tell her I love her. Tell her I'm coming. Tell her this will all be over soon.*

"No," she said. "Thank you, Sybil."

Lydia saw a flicker of a smile flash across Sybil's lips. Then she left, and Lydia was alone once again. She was beginning to get used to the silence, the way every sound fell dead at her feet. She wished she could see Fiona, to know whether she'd survived her injuries, and to apologize for getting her into this mess. She wanted to see Rebecca, to hear whatever creative profanity she would have reserved for Sybil. She wanted Henry, his arms around her, the warm, steady comfort of him.

Most of all, she wanted Evelyn. She wanted her mother.

Patience, she thought.

Lydia went to the chair where her clothes from home had been neatly folded. She set aside the blouse and jumper and held up the gray wool skirt, running her fingers along the hem. She held the fabric to her nose, and smelled something faintly herbal, and for just a moment, she was back in her mother's kitchen. She folded the skirt and placed it back on the chair, exactly as she'd found it.

WHEN SYBIL ARRIVED the next morning, Lydia was ready for her. She did not wait for them to exchange pleasantries.

"I've made my decision." She stood in a shaft of morning sunshine, with Sybil standing opposite her, eyes intent on Lydia. "I don't relish the idea of causing more suffering. But if a little more will put a stop to this war once and for all . . . then I believe it will have been worth it. And I . . ." Lydia hesitated. "I want to know what it's like. To live without secrets. I want to know a world where witches may live openly."

A hopeful smile spread across Sybil's face. "Does that mean you will join us?"

Lydia had said the words in front of the mirror. She had practiced them in bed, had fallen asleep with them on her lips, worried that when the moment came, they might ring false. She had said them again and again, all night and all morning, until the falsehood fell away, and the words transformed, and became true.

"Yes. Yes, I will join you."

Thirty-One

Henry was dreaming about his mother. In the dream, Fabienne wore all white, her hair wrapped in a scarf. She was standing in their old house in Tremé, where Henry had grown up, but the house looked different than he remembered. Dust clung to the plants that lined the windowsill, growing wild out of chipped teacups, jelly jars, rusty coffee cans, all half-dead, yellow leaves clinging on for dear life. Spent candles melted onto the surfaces, leaving frozen pools and rivers of wax in shades of red, green, yellow, black, and white. The front door stood open, and leaves and refuse covered the floor, years of it, decaying in heaps, stinking of wet earth, as enormous swaths of black mold ate through the paint and stained the ceiling.

Henry's mother stood in the midst of it all, hands on her hips in a gesture that was so familiar, it was synonymous with Fabienne herself. She looked like she was trying to tell him something, but though her lips were moving, no sound came out.

Mama, I can't hear you, Henry said. *Mama, hang on, back up—*

A sound came out of his mother's mouth like a needle scratching on a record, and then he heard her voice.

. . . the door. It sounded like she was in the middle of a scolding.

What? Mama, I don't—

Don't just stand there, Henry. There's people waiting. Open the door.

People? Mama, we can't have people over. The place is a mess.

The place doesn't matter. They're waiting. Open the door.

When he woke, Rebecca was watching him.

"Bad dream?"

Henry pushed himself up to sitting. His skin itched. "Strange dream."

"Stranger than all this?"

He frowned. Already his mother's words were slipping away from him. He was so sure they'd been important.

They were being held in an underground cave, with arched walls made of rough stone like they had been excised from the side of a mountain. Elaborate ironwork gates blocked them in from both sides, and from each gate hung an enormous iron padlock. A string of bare yellow bulbs hung overhead.

They had lost track of the days. It had happened so quickly, with no sun to mark the time. At first Henry had kept track by counting the visits from the woman who brought them food. She would come twice a day with bread or broth, and Henry could tell when one day had turned into another by the change in her clothes. But the last few visits she had brought only water, and he was almost certain they had missed a day, if not more.

Rebecca was pacing. "We need to get out of here."

"No kidding."

"No. I mean right now. Today."

Henry looked up. "Why?"

Rebecca looked agitated. "They've stopped feeding us. They're bringing water, yes, but no food. I don't think they're planning on keeping us around much longer. A day. Maybe two."

They fell silent as the grim reality set in. The sound of water dripping somewhere deeper in the tunnel seemed to grow louder.

Henry had been looking for ghosts. He thought if he could make contact that they might be able to help, but they had been here for days, and no one had appeared. It seemed impossible that a place like this wouldn't have one or two spirits lurking around. Maybe it had once been full of them, but they'd since finished their business and moved on. Maybe they didn't like it underground. Maybe he'd lost the gift, his punishment for so many years spent running from it.

Open the door. That was what his mother had said to him, he remembered now. She'd said it simply, like a whole host of people were standing on the front porch, waiting to come in. And there was something else. Something about the house, or . . .

"The place doesn't matter," Henry said out loud.

Rebecca looked up. "What?"

"I don't . . . I don't know." But even as he said the words, he felt something slip inside his mind, like tumblers in a lock, clicking into place.

The place doesn't matter. They're waiting. Open the door.

He closed his eyes.

As a child, Henry had always assumed that the spirits he met were tied to whatever place he was in at that moment—stuck there, like flies in amber. He had never imagined bringing a spirit to him from somewhere else—not until that night in the Bouchers' barn, when he had called out to Lydia through the void. But even then, he had imagined his mind as a static place—a room full of doors for the dead to walk through.

Now, for the first time, he tried to imagine this space inside of himself as something else. Not a room, but a vehicle, a means of transit. A train that could carry the dead to him over any distance. He imagined calling into the darkness, calling for someone, anyone, to come join him.

All aboard, Henry thought.

When he opened his eyes, there was a woman there with them, standing very still. She was in her late forties, tall and dark haired, prim but stylish in her gray dress and practical heels. Her cheeks and eyes were sunken, her clothing too loose. She stood with her back to the wall, inches from where Rebecca sat.

"Hello," Henry said.

Rebecca saw the look in his eyes and knew what it meant. She inhaled sharply. Henry held up a hand.

"I'm Henry." He kept his voice steady. The spirit did not look at him. She was looking at Rebecca. "What's your name?"

Now the woman did look up, and in her eyes, Henry saw something he hadn't seen in any of his previous conversations with the dead: the woman looked deeply sad. Not just sad, but grief-stricken, her milky eyes shadowed with something more than just hunger. The woman looked away from him again, returning her gaze to Rebecca. She reached out and stroked Rebecca's tangled hair, crouching so their faces were inches apart. And then, as Henry watched, the woman's lips parted and formed a silent phrase.

Ma petite colombe, she said. *My little dove.*

And then he saw. The likeness was undeniable: long neck, dark brows, a certain squarish set to the jaw, like someone always ready for a fight. As the woman reached out to wipe a smudge of dirt from Rebecca's face, Henry saw a tear spill like quicksilver onto her sunken cheek.

"*Rebecca*," Henry whispered, but then the spirit turned and looked at him, pressing one finger to her mouth, her eyes pleading. *Don't tell her.*

Rebecca looked at him questioningly.

Henry shook his head. "It's okay."

He looked into the still, unseeing eyes of Rebecca's mother.

"*It's okay,*" he told her. She nodded gratefully. "We're in trouble. Can you help us?"

The woman nodded again. She lingered for just a moment longer, taking in Rebecca's face, and then she dissolved into the shadows.

THEY MIGHT HAVE waited for five minutes, or ten. In the cavernous underground silence, it was impossible to tell. Just as Henry began to wonder if the woman was coming back, they heard footsteps, and a plain-faced girl appeared around the corner. She reached through the bars and placed a pewter water pitcher on the floor of the cell.

Rebecca lunged with shocking speed, reaching for the girl and missing her by mere inches. The girl fell back, wide eyed, and Rebecca cackled.

"I'll have to be faster next time." She reached down and retrieved the pitcher, holding the girl in her stare the entire time.

The girl rearranged her face into a sour glare. "Don't play with me, *Jew*—"

"Or what?" Rebecca drew herself up to her full height and stepped close to the bars. She was at least four inches taller than the girl, and even with the iron bars between them, Henry could see that the witch was rattled. "Will you come in here and teach me a lesson? Hmm?"

Behind the girl, Henry watched as the gray woman materialized once again from the shadows, statue still and watching with lifeless white eyes.

"Your friend has betrayed you," the girl hissed, her cheeks flushed. "Tonight, she will swear herself to the Führer, and then you will be of no more use to us. Most likely you'll be dead before morning. Then again, maybe we'll ship you off to Poland with the other Jews. Let you sort rags for a few months before they dump you in a hole in the ground."

The gray woman stepped closer.

"Nazi bitch—" Rebecca snapped, but her words were cut short.

One moment the spirit hovered just behind the witch, so close they nearly touched. The next, the dead woman seemed to step into her, slipping into the witch's skin the way one might slip into a robe. The witch gasped, a spasm running through her, and then she blinked her milky eyes and was still.

Rebecca jumped back from the bars. Henry caught her by the shoulders.

"It's okay," he whispered. "It's okay. She's here to help."

The dead woman, now wearing the young witch like a suit, moved her hand slowly to her hip, where it came to rest on a brass key ring. She lifted the keys in front of her face and selected one, releasing the key from the ring and holding it delicately between her fingers before letting it fall to the ground.

The witch blinked again, and her clouded eyes cleared. "What did you say?"

Rebecca's mouth hung open. Henry cleared his throat, prompting her to speak.

"*Nothing,*" she said feebly. "I said nothing." Henry gave her shoulder a reassuring squeeze.

The witch looked confused. She placed the brass ring back on her hip without looking at it.

Henry was careful not to glance at the iron key that lay on the floor between them, just within reach. The witch gave her head a shake, as if dispelling an unpleasant dream, then turned and walked back the way she had come.

The gray woman stood, still and silent, and watched her go.

Thirty-Two

The afternoon of the solstice, Sybil requested Lydia's company for an early dinner. Lydia selected a dress from the wardrobe: a black, floor-length gown with long sleeves and a heart-shaped neckline, fashioned from silk that fell over her skin like water. She curled and pinned her hair, and fixed her makeup, rouging her cheeks and painting her lips a deep claret red. Funny, she thought. Already she'd become accustomed to the look of her face without the benefit of a glamour. In a way, she almost preferred it.

Just before leaving, Lydia took the ivory letter opener from the writing desk. Working quickly, she slipped it inside the hem of her gray wool skirt, tearing the stitches to reveal a tidy row of waxed paper packets, each stuffed with a thimbleful of herbs. She searched, holding them up to the light one by one, until she found what she was looking for. Lydia took the packet and slipped it inside her brassiere.

It was the first time she had been outside of her room since arriving in Bavaria, and the sensation as the binding magic lifted from her shoulders made her head swim. Lydia followed the girl called Eva as she silently led the way to Sybil's chambers.

Sybil embraced her when she arrived. "Wine?"

"Yes, please."

The room was much like Lydia's own, with tall windows and paneled wood walls, although she noticed that these walls were carved with an ordinary vine-work pattern, rather than the intricate binding sigil from her own bedroom. A table and chairs sat in the center of the room, with china and crystal for two. The furniture was richly uphol-stered in shades of mauve, just like Sybil's study at the academy. Sybil poured two glasses of wine, leaving the decanter on the table between them.

"You look lovely." Sybil sipped her wine. "I told you this gown was prettier than the other one. Wasn't I right?"

Lydia smiled. "As always. The other was far too severe."

Sybil had visited daily since Lydia's change of heart, drinking tea and expounding on everything from her own idyllic childhood in Surrey, to which frock Lydia should wear for her initiation. Lydia had spent every second of those visits biting her tongue until she tasted blood, and pray-ing to the Mother that her deception would hold.

"How are you feeling?" Sybil asked.

Terrified, Lydia thought.

"I feel well. I'm ready." She gazed at her wine. "Only . . ."

Sybil reached across the table. "What is it, darling?"

Lydia sighed. "It's my own fault. I'm still afraid the rest of the coven won't ever trust me, even after I've been initiated. It makes sense, really—"

"Nonsense. In a few hours, you will be one of us. After that, you will lead us all in the Unmaking ritual, and win the war for Germany. You will be a sister to them. You'll see."

Lydia gave Sybil's hand a squeeze, then pulled back, grazing Sybil's glass with her fingers. The glass toppled, spilling its contents and smashing on the floor.

"Oh, damn," Lydia said. "Did I spill any on your dress? I'm sorry, I guess I'm more nervous than I thought."

"No apologies! It's just a glass. We have others." Sybil stood. "Wait here."

Sybil walked to the door and said a few words to Eva, standing guard in the hallway. As she did, Lydia reached inside her dress and produced the waxed paper packet. She opened it with trembling hands, then hastily emptied the packet into the decanter, swirling it once before placing it back on the table. The powder dissolved to nothing.

Sybil returned with a fresh glass. "They'll clean up the rest once we've finished our meal."

Lydia refilled Sybil's glass. Sybil took a sip and smiled.

Dinner was stuffed pheasant served with wild mushrooms, and glazed pears for dessert. Lydia ate little and said nothing when Sybil poured them each a second glass of wine.

Just as they were finishing the meal, a knock came at the door. It was Ursula, already dressed for the evening's ritual in a black silk blouse and wide satin trousers, which gave the illusion of a voluminous skirt.

"Grand Mistress." Ursula's gaze landed on Lydia, then flicked away.

Lydia forced a smile. "Ursula, you look very nice."

Ursula did not return the compliment. "My apologies, Grand Mistress. I didn't realize you had company." She turned to leave.

"Stay!" cried Sybil. "We still have time before the initiation. Sit. Have a drink with us." She called for another chair, as well as a glass. Ursula scowled, but sat when the chair and the glass arrived. "Lydia and I were just discussing arrangements for this evening."

Lydia looked on in dismay as Ursula reached for the decanter and filled her glass with wine. She held the liquid to her nose and inhaled. Then she brought the glass to her lips and frowned. A small, wine-soaked fleck of dust clung to the edge of the glass. She looked at Lydia over the rim, holding her in her icy blue stare.

Sybil glanced at Ursula. "Everything all right, dear?"

Lydia felt herself flush under Ursula's gaze. With as much ease as she could muster, she reached for the decanter, refilled her own glass, and drank. She smiled at Ursula.

"Fine, Grand Mistress." Ursula drank her wine and said nothing.

Sybil cleared her throat. "As I was saying, after her initiation, Lydia will lead the coven in the Unmaking ritual. A fine beginning, don't you think?"

Ursula paused. "I was under the impression you would be the one to lead us, Grand Mistress."

"I'm afraid there is no other option," Lydia said. "Since the *Grimorium Bellum* is bound to me, no one else can touch it, let alone read it."

Ursula looked at her, the disdain barely hidden on her face. *She knows*, Lydia thought. *I can fool Sybil, but not her.*

Just then, Eva entered the room without knocking. She looked pale and skittish as she walked to Sybil's side and whispered something in her ear. Sybil's face grew serious.

"Thank you, Eva," she said quietly. The girl saw herself out, closing the door behind her.

Sybil looked at Ursula. "I'm afraid we've lost track of two of our guests."

It took Lydia a moment to realize what she meant. "Henry and Rebecca?"

Sybil nodded. "Johanna went to check on them earlier this evening. It seems they've gone missing."

Lydia could feel Ursula's eyes on her. "Where could they have gone?"

"Nowhere far. My worry is that they may create some disruption during the ceremony."

Ursula stood. "I'll find them."

Sybil frowned. "You'll miss Lydia's initiation."

"A small price to pay."

Sybil sipped her wine. "Agreed. Be back by sunset. You must be present for the Unmaking ritual."

"I wouldn't miss it. As you said, they couldn't have gone far." She gave Lydia one last withering glance and took her leave. Lydia tried to appear relaxed, even as a tangled panic snarled inside her breast.

Run, she thought. *Both of you, run as fast as you can, and don't stop.*

Thirty-Three

ydia walked through the labyrinth of corridors, with Sybil just ahead of her, leading the way. Their footsteps echoed through the halls of the magnificent castle, and many sets of eyes seemed to watch, peering down from paintings and tapestries. Sybil stopped before a door, ornately carved from amber-gold wood, much like the door to Lydia's own room, and Lydia felt her heart quicken.

"Are you certain this is what you want?" Sybil asked. "If you upset yourself before the ceremony—"

"I'll be fine." Lydia looked into her eyes. "She's my mother. I need to at least try to make her understand."

Sybil squeezed her arm. "I'll be with you the entire time."

She pressed her hand against the door, and as she did, a flicker of light ran through her moonstone ring. Lydia had seen the other girls wearing a similar piece of jewelry, and hadn't thought anything of it. Now she understood. It wasn't just a ring.

It was a *key*.

The door opened, and they stepped inside.

Evelyn was there, looking small and disheveled, standing in the center of the room. The walls bore the same binding sigil Lydia recognized from her own chamber, and although this room was smaller than her own, it was no less opulent. Tall windows allowed in the afternoon light, and the bed was piled high with blankets embroidered in creams and peaches. Evelyn looked furious, but her face softened when she laid eyes on Lydia.

"Oh, Lydia!" She threw herself at her daughter, holding her tightly. Lydia wanted to embrace her, to weep on her shoulder, but she forced herself to remain stoic.

"Hello, Mother."

"Have they hurt you? Are you all right?" Evelyn pawed at her, examining her for signs of rough handling.

"I'm fine, really." Lydia glanced at Sybil, who gave her a supportive nod. "Mother, please sit."

Evelyn looked confused, but did as she was asked, never letting go of Lydia's hands. They sat across from one another at a small table, with an overstuffed chair on each side.

"Fiona?" Lydia spoke softly, although she knew Sybil could hear every word.

Evelyn clucked. "Touch and go. She was a bloody mess when she came back. I did what I could, but then this lot showed up, and—" She tossed a sour look at Sybil. "She wasn't strong enough to travel with both of us, you understand. I told her to leave me behind."

Oh, Evelyn. Lydia couldn't imagine how she had never seen her clearly before now. How selfless she was. How brave.

"Mother, I . . ." She remembered herself then and let go of Evelyn's hands. "I need to tell you something important. Something I hope you'll understand, someday."

Evelyn glanced at Sybil, then back at Lydia.

"I'm going to help Sybil. I'm going to help her end the war."

Evelyn blinked at her. Her mouth fell open. "*Win* the war, you mean. For Germany." Her spine straightened. "My love, you cannot be serious."

Lydia sighed. "Just once, I wish you would listen before—"

"Are *you* listening to yourself?" Evelyn's voice rose. "Win the war for the bloody Nazis—"

"People are *dying*," Lydia said. "Good people. People like Kitty, and Isadora. We can put an end to it—"

"I can't believe you," Evelyn hissed. "Kitty and Isadora died fighting people like *her*—" Evelyn's finger sliced through the air, pointing at Sybil. She stood, and Sybil flinched. "Traitorous *bitch*. When I get out of this room, I'm going to make you stick your head right up your own—"

"Mother, enough." Lydia stood, placing herself between Evelyn and Sybil. "Sit down," she said quietly. Evelyn looked horribly wounded, and Lydia hated herself for that, but she forced herself to remain cool and remote. "I should have known you wouldn't understand."

"I don't. I never will." Evelyn's voice shook. "Isadora would die of shame."

"You don't know the first thing about Isadora!" Lydia snapped. She felt Sybil's attention sharpen, but dared not look at her. "Isadora was the most powerful witch in all of Britain. And what did she do with that power? Did she use it to bring us out of the shadows, to make the world a safer place for witches? *No*. Isadora offered us up like cannon fodder to fight a war on behalf of Britain, a country that for centuries has despised us, murdered us, and driven us into hiding. Throwing witches into harm's way with no promise of safety or recognition after the war was over. And for what? For her own stubborn pride."

"You don't mean that." Evelyn's mouth hung open, aghast.

"I do, actually." Shame twisted in Lydia's stomach, but she would not show it.

"So now you've aligned yourself with *her*?" Evelyn's chin jutted toward Sybil. "This evil, conniving—"

"Sybil is my grand mistress." Lydia's voice was a warning.

"She *murdered* your grand mistress," Evelyn spat. "And if you go through with this, she'll make a murderer of you too." She looked unbearably sad. Broken. "If you do this . . ." A tear fell onto Evelyn's cheek, but she wiped it away. Lydia watched her face go hard. "Lydia Polk, you'll be no daughter of mine."

Does she know? Lydia wondered. They hadn't planned this. It had been a last-minute improvisation, a necessary evil in order for Lydia to learn Evelyn's location. She watched the naked anguish on her mother's face, hoping and praying that she knew the truth. Hoping that she understood.

"I haven't been your daughter for a very long time," Lydia said quietly. She watched the pain ripple across Evelyn's face as she spoke the words. "How could I be? I'm nothing like you. I am a graduate of the Royal Academy of Witches. I am a Projectionist and a soldier, trained by the greatest witches in all of Britain. I have been the right hand to *two* grand mistresses, and someday, very soon, I will be selected to reign as grand mistress myself. And you will never be anything more than what you are right now—a dirty old *hedge witch*."

The silence was excruciating. Lydia watched Evelyn's face, waiting for some glimmer of understanding. She saw something harden behind Evelyn's eyes, but whether it was hurt or comprehension, Lydia did not know.

"I believe someday you will look back on this moment, and see that I had my reasons," she said softly.

She turned her back and walked away, following Sybil into the hallway. She waited until they were outside, then fell, sobbing, into Sybil's arms. Sybil shushed her gently and stroked her hair.

"Oh, my darling," she whispered. "I'm so proud of you."

Thirty-Four

The tunnels under the castle grew colder as Henry and Rebecca ran, as if they were descending deeper and deeper into the earth. The air was damp, and in the pitch black Henry saw nothing except the occasional glimpse of the gray woman drifting through the tunnel ahead of them, slipping in and out of view.

When they finally emerged, the light felt so bright it burned Henry's eyes, even though the sky was overcast, the sun hanging low. The air smelled crisp and green, like Christmas trees, and the freezing cold bite of it was dizzying after so long spent underground. He squinted and caught a glimpse of gray silhouette, lingering just at the edge of a thick forest.

"This way." His legs felt heavy from hunger and lack of use, but he forced himself forward.

"What about Lydia?"

Henry looked back at the looming castle, stark white against the dusky sky. He knew Lydia was inside. He wanted to go to her, a need as strong as hunger, deep in his belly. Then he turned and locked eyes with the gray woman. She was reaching out to him, beckoning to him with an urgency so palpable, he could almost hear her voice inside his head.

You can't save her if you're dead.

"They'll be looking for us. We'll go back for her, but right now we need to hide. Come on."

They ran for the tree line, letting the forest swallow them up until they could no longer see the castle through the spruce trees.

"Where is she? Your ghost?" Rebecca was doubled over, holding a stitch in her side.

"I don't know."

The gray woman had been ahead of them the whole time, guiding them out of the tunnels, beckoning them into the forest, but now, as Henry strained his eyes, she was nowhere to be seen.

Rebecca settled against the trunk of a tree. Her skin and clothes were dirty, her lips pale, and there were hollows in her cheeks where there hadn't been any before.

"Do you believe what she said?" Rebecca asked. "The witch?"

"About Lydia joining them, you mean?"

Rebecca nodded.

Henry didn't even have to wonder. He'd been inside Lydia's head. He'd felt her passion, her unbreakable will. He knew she would sooner die. "No."

Rebecca exhaled slowly. She hung her head. "What if they decide to—"

"*They won't.*" Henry shook his head, banishing the thought. "They need her. They can't hurt her."

Rebecca covered her face with her hands, her chest rising and falling as she caught her breath. Her shoulders began to shake, and for a moment, Henry thought she must be crying. But then a hysterical sort of wheezing began to emanate from her chest.

"Rebecca?"

She laughed and laughed, but even from where he stood, Henry could see there was no mirth in it. Tears gathered in her eyes and streamed down her cheeks, and still she laughed.

"*I'm always running,*" she said, gasping. She looked at him and wiped the tears away with her palm. The laughter stopped in her throat like it had been shot dead. "I'm a fucking coward."

Henry nearly reached out and touched her shoulder, but the look in her eyes stopped him. "Are you kidding? You're fearless. You gunned down half a dozen Gestapo like it was nothing. You killed a *witch*. Rebecca, you're still here because—"

"I'm here because I ran."

Birds sang to each other overhead. A gentle breeze glided through the spruce trees, making the needles fall around them like rain.

"What are you talking about?"

Rebecca's eyes fixed themselves on something far away. "When the police came for my father, I was there. I tried to fight them, to make them stop, but one of the policemen, he punched me, and I blacked out." She touched the side of her face, remembering. "That day, they were only taking men. They left the rest of us behind." She took a rattling breath, and a tear fell onto her cheek. "The next time, I wasn't at home. I was across the street, skulking around after spending all night in a car with some stupid boy I didn't even like." She laughed, quick and angry. "I was walking home when I saw the police outside my house. They were taking my mother and sister away."

She stared up at Henry. She looked as if at any moment she would crack into pieces, shattering into dust and mixing with the spruce needles scattered across the forest floor.

"My mother saw me. They were dragging them away, Noémie was crying, and I was frozen, I didn't know what to do. But my mother looked up, she looked right at me, and she mouthed something to me. *Run.* She said, 'Run.' And so, I did."

"You were right to do it," Henry said. "They would have taken you away too."

Rebecca hung her head. "We would have been together."

Henry looked around again, hoping for one last appearance from the gray woman, but she was nowhere to be seen.

"That morning after we got back from Auvergne," Rebecca said, "I was going to run then too. Even after I touched the book, even though I knew—" she stopped, her eyes gone glassy. "Even though I knew what it was. I was going to run as far and as fast as I possibly could. I didn't care what happened after that."

"But you didn't," Henry said. "You stayed."

Rebecca shook her head. She took a labored breath.

"I don't want to go back in there. I don't want to go back, but Lydia is in there with *them*, and with that *thing*, whatever is inside that evil fucking book, and I can't just . . . I can't . . ." Something snapped into place behind her eyes. "We can't leave her."

Henry looked into Rebecca's face and saw a liquid intensity there that might easily have been mistaken for madness.

"I know."

Rebecca looked as if she were about to say something else, but then her expression changed. "Do you smell that?"

Henry sniffed. One second the air was perfumed with the scent of spruce trees, and dirt, and snow. The next, he was struck with the familiar, metallic smell of ozone.

"*Run*," he said.

LYDIA'S FOOTSTEPS ECHOED off the marble floor and cavernous ceilings as she entered the ceremonial chamber. Tall, arched glass windows faced west, glowing with dying sunlight. An enormous fireplace burned at one end of the chamber, the mantel intricately carved with wolves and eagles. Lydia looked up and saw that the domed ceiling had been painted a deep royal blue, smattered with constellations in gold leaf. All around her, black-clad witches stood in the half-light, waiting. The *Grimorium Bellum* gave off a heat like a feverish child in her arms.

Lydia felt faint. Her initiation had always been part of the plan, an unavoidable evil, but now that it was here, she wanted nothing more than to run from this place as fast as she could. A witch's commitment to her coven was sacred, a lifelong vow of sisterhood, unbreakable. The thought of vowing herself to the Reich, even if only for show, made her want to scrub her skin with lye.

She looked up and saw Sybil watching her. She took a steadying breath, and on that breath formed a silent prayer.

Great Mother, forgive me for what I am about to do.

THEY CRASHED THROUGH the undergrowth, golden light strobing through the trees as they ran. Rebecca could feel Henry beside her, hear his labored breathing as they sprinted blindly through the trees hand in hand. Her heart felt like a balloon in her chest, ready to burst. Off to her left Rebecca saw a flash of silver-blond hair. She could hear stony laughter, first behind her, then to her left, then her right.

Henry pulled up short, dragging her down with him behind a rotten log. Rebecca could see the whites of his eyes in the dim light, the drops of sweat standing on his brow. He held a shaking finger to his lips. Rebecca pressed both hands over her mouth. Her heart thumped wildly in her chest, so loud she was certain the witch would hear.

From out of the darkness, Rebecca heard Ursula sigh.

"Hiding won't save you, Liebchen." Her voice seemed to move through the darkness, circling them, her shape appearing and disappearing through the trees. "You must know this already."

Rebecca stared at Henry. She wanted to run, but he held her tight.

"You have taken something precious from me, girl." The witch's voice seemed to be moving ever closer to their hiding place. "You murdered my Margot. My *sister*. I will make you suffer for that."

Henry tugged on Rebecca's sleeve and pointed over his shoulder toward a steep, rocky drop-off where a wide mountain stream gurgled below. They stayed low as they scrambled down the hill, hanging on to roots and stones as they went.

"You will die last," Ursula called, and Rebecca knew the words were meant for her. "The Negro I'll kill first. Then the witch. I will flay them alive, and you can listen to their screams as they beg for the release of death. And then I will save the very worst for you."

LYDIA STARED OUT at the faces of the Witches of the Third Reich. She could feel their suspicion, their resentment. She saw Ingrid and Eva, heads bent together. She saw Gerda, standing in shadow, lips pursed.

Sybil placed a hand on Lydia's arm. "Are you ready, my darling?"

"Yes, Grand Mistress."

Sybil made a subtle gesture, and the witches stepped into the light, encircling Lydia and Sybil in the center of the chamber. Yellow candlelight flickered around them, making their faces shape-shift, expressions morphing from benign to sinister and back again in an instant. Sybil turned away from Lydia and addressed the coven.

"Hail, sisters."

"Hail, Grand Mistress," came the reply.

"We gather today, on this, the winter solstice, to welcome our sister Lydia into our coven. Our sisterhood is a sacred thing, an unbreakable, lifelong bond. Support must be unanimous. If anyone here objects to this initiate, speak now."

Lydia scanned the gathered faces, trying to guess who would object first, but no one spoke. These witches did not trust her, but they would not defy their mistress. Sybil allowed the silence to linger a moment longer, then smiled, satisfied.

"Eva."

Eva stepped forward, a cup of wine in one hand, a blade in the other. Sybil took them both and turned to Lydia. The cup was silver and bore a five-pointed star. The knife was identical to the one Ursula carried, with a polished bone handle, inscribed with a rune—*Othala. Homeland.* Sybil rested the tip of the blade on Lydia's breast, just above her heart.

"Lydia Polk, daughter of Evelyn. Why do you come here today?"

Lydia had studied the words and knew her part from memory.

"I come to join with my sisters in devotion to the Great Mother, and in service of the fatherland." As she spoke, Lydia imagined a wall around her heart made of thorns and twisted metal. She imagined an impregnable barrier, one that her words could not penetrate. She lifted up a silent prayer for the Great Mother to look inside her heart and see the truth.

"How do you come before this coven?"

"With a true and willing heart."

There were curses for witches who betrayed their covens. *May her body burn to ashes. May she go unmourned. May the Great Mother forget her name.*

"Whom do you serve?"

"I serve the Great Mother, and the Führer, may he live forever." She tasted bile in the back of her throat.

For a moment, there was silence. She felt the blade, its tip resting above her heart, and for one second, she was certain that Sybil would realize her betrayal and plunge the knife deep into her chest. Instead, Sybil held out her hand, and Lydia offered her palm. Sybil lifted the blade and pressed it to the skin of Lydia's hand. It was sharp, and the flesh parted easily. Bright red blood sprang to the surface, but Lydia did not flinch. She held her hand over the silver chalice, letting her blood spill into the cup. Sybil then held the knife against her own palm, and let her blood fall into the wine, mixing with Lydia's.

"A vow made in blood cannot be broken. Do you make this vow of your own free will?"

"I do." The room seemed to darken, although the candle flames remained steady.

"Lydia Polk"—Sybil's voice rose, echoing throughout the chamber— "do you dedicate your life to the service of the Great Mother?"

"I do."

"Do you bind yourself with a willing heart to this coven, as a true sister for the rest of your days?"

"I do."

"Do you dedicate your life to the fatherland, and the glory of the Führer?"

"I do."

Sybil's face glowed in the firelight. She pressed the handle of the knife into Lydia's palm so that Lydia stood with the chalice in one hand and the dagger in the other. "Drink, child." Lydia drank. Blood dripped from her palm and collected on the marble floor.

Sybil addressed her coven, now standing shoulder to shoulder around them. "Hail to the Great Mother!" Sybil shouted.

"Heil, Great Mother!"

"Hail to the Führer!"

"Heil Hitler!"

"Hail to Lydia, daughter of Evelyn, our beloved sister!"

"*Heil Lydia!*" they cried back. "*Heil Lydia! Heil Lydia!*"

The Witches of the Third Reich shouted her name again and again, welcoming their newest sister with voices high, as Sybil beamed, radiant with pride. And there in their midst, Lydia threw open her arms, and embraced them, and smiled, as the dread and shame churned inside her like a serpent, threatening to eat her alive.

Thirty-Five

The sun began its slow descent behind the mountains, plunging Henry and Rebecca into a dull almost night. They ran alongside the stream, praying the rushing water might mask their footfalls, but Ursula was always close by, flitting through the trees, the smell of ozone burning inside their nostrils. Henry wondered why she didn't just kill them already. She was a powerful witch, able to move through space at will. They were weak and starving, with no way of defending themselves. Then he realized the truth—she was allowing herself the pleasure of the chase. She could end it whenever she liked.

As they ran, Henry spied a figure just ahead of them, half-hidden among the trees. At first, he thought it was the witch, but no—it was the gray woman, watching them, her milky eyes glowing. He kept moving forward, following as she faded out of sight and then reappeared again farther downstream. The witch's voice broke from the trees.

"I'm afraid we will need to bring this game to an end." Ursula appeared to their right, and Rebecca jerked away from the sound, causing them both to stumble. Henry regained his footing and tugged her forward, keeping his eyes on the gray woman. "It's been so much fun, but sadly I've somewhere to be." Ursula blinked out of sight, reappearing again on a flat rock in the middle of the stream. Henry ran faster, holding tightly to Rebecca.

They were approaching a waterfall. Not very tall, just a jagged point where the water tumbled a few meters down to the foam-covered rocks below. The rocks were slippery, and the climb down would be treacherous. They reached the edge of the fall and stopped. The gray woman was there waiting for them.

Time seemed to slow for Henry. The witch watched from a distance, laughing softly. The gray woman stared at Henry, her expression blank. She seemed to be asking him something, something she couldn't quite put to words. Her head tilted as she looked at him, her hand hovering in the air between them.

"*Henry.*" Rebecca stared wide eyed at the witch, who stared back, grinning.

"What is it?" Henry said, not to Rebecca, but to the gray woman.

The gray woman reached out, taking Henry's hand in hers. They didn't meet the way two hands should, warm and firm, woven together but still separate. Instead, the woman's hand seemed to reach *into* Henry's, making his flesh feel cold and numb and dead all the way through. Henry looked into her eyes and understood. She was asking for his consent.

"Yes," he said.

Rebecca looked at him. "What?"

Henry kept his eyes on the dead woman. "Yes. I understand. Yes."

The woman stepped inside Henry in one swift movement, forcing the air from his lungs. It felt as if he had been sent to the passenger seat of his own mind—he could feel his body, how everything warm and alive had been driven out of him, replaced with something hollow and icy cold. His body moved, but he was not the one moving it. He should have been afraid, but there was something almost comforting about the surrender, about letting go. He could feel the dead woman there alongside him, and in her presence, he felt a strange solace.

Miriam, a voice inside him said. Her name.

Together they turned and looked at Rebecca. She recoiled, horrified by the sudden change in him, and Henry could feel Miriam's grief as she looked at her daughter through his eyes. He felt her thoughts as clearly as if they were his own—how desperately she wanted to reach out to Rebecca, to hold her, the profound sense of helplessness. Henry wanted to tell Rebecca that it was all right, but he couldn't seem to form the words.

The smell of ozone filled the air, like a penny under the tongue.

Rebecca smelled it, too, and turned to run, but too late. Ursula appeared before them, and now she wasted no time. She turned her gaze on Rebecca and uttered a strange word, and Rebecca slumped to the ground. The witch bent over her and took her chin in her hand.

"This is not where you die, Liebchen," she cooed. Rebecca gasped like a fish, fighting against the spell that had dragged her down. The sound of water crashing onto the rocks below nearly drowned out the witch's words. "Oh, no no no. You will *beg* me for death before I am finished with you."

Henry watched as the gray woman crouched inside his skin. As she picked up a rock with his hand. Ursula looked up and sneered, unconcerned. She opened her mouth and spoke the word of power again.

Nothing happened. Henry waited for his body to weaken, to be overcome with pain or delirium. Then he understood.

Spells were meant for the living.

Now, thought Henry.

They raised the rock.

"Nein—" The smell of ozone filled the air, but too late.

The rock came down. A red gash split across Ursula's forehead, and her eyes bulged. The gray woman howled, and as she did, Henry felt all the rage and grief inside of her, the unthinkable loss, the unfairness. He looked down at Rebecca and saw her as Miriam saw her, as a child. Just a child, in need of a comb, and a bath, and a cry. Someone precious. Someone worth killing for.

Ursula was on all fours, dazed. She moaned, examining the blood on her fingers. Together, Henry and Miriam reached down and lifted Ursula to her feet. She kicked and fought, but she was no match for Henry's strength and size, nor Miriam's deep, maternal fury. She spat spells and shrieked curses, but each one fell flat. Miriam shook Ursula hard, howling in her face, and Henry stepped away, surrendering control.

And then, when the last drop of air in her lungs ran out and the howling ceased, Miriam fell silent and quietly, easily, tossed Ursula onto the rocks below.

LYDIA WAS PERSPIRING in her gown despite the cold draft that cut through the ceremonial chamber. Her hand had been bandaged, and the ceremonial cup replaced with a glass of champagne. The bone-handled knife sat heavy on her hip. All around her, witches spoke in low tones, darting occasional glances at the west-facing windows and the swiftly setting sun.

"Ursula should be back by now," said Sybil. "What on earth could be keeping her?"

"Ursula is very capable. I'm sure she's fine." For a moment, Lydia allowed her imagination to run wild—perhaps Rebecca and Henry had escaped after all, leading Ursula on a wild chase and causing her to lose track of the time. Perhaps she'd been disarmed somehow, or even killed.

Or perhaps she had successfully hunted down her prey, and was even at this very moment exacting her terrible revenge for the death of her friend. This last thought came with a flood of gruesome visions that felt to Lydia like a waking nightmare.

"Without her we don't have a full coven for the ritual," Sybil said, almost to herself. She looked to Lydia, her brow furrowed. "We may need to postpone."

Lydia nearly shouted *No!* but managed to stop herself. "Whatever you think is best, Grand Mistress. It's only . . ." Sybil looked at her expectantly. Lydia sighed. "Everything has been so fraught. This is my chance to earn the coven's trust." She took Sybil's hand in hers. "Please, let me try."

Lydia could see that Sybil was pleased, more certain than ever of Lydia's loyalty and devotion. Her cheeks flushed pink as she squeezed Lydia's uninjured hand.

"All right," she said.

Lydia squeezed back. "All right."

HENRY FELT A RUSH of blood and heat as Miriam left his body, and he fell to the ground, gasping. Rebecca reached out to him, her hand warm and solid in his. She felt like a rope, he thought dimly, pulling him back to shore. They lay there at the edge of the falls, both catching their breath, the crashing of water below them the only sound. Finally, Rebecca released her hold, crawled toward the edge of the falls, and peered over.

"Is she dead?" Henry asked.

"I can't tell."

Henry turned onto his side and looked around for Miriam, but saw only trees. Slowly, he sat up and looked over the edge of the falls, to where Ursula lay sprawled on the rocks below, one leg dangling in the churning water. She was on her back, blond hair obscuring her face, blood seeping through the silver strands where the gray woman had struck her with the rock. Sickly green foam bubbled at the base of the waterfall and gathered at the edge of her black trousers. Henry watched her, trying to see the rise and fall of her chest, but his vision was swimming, and the light was fading fast. Rebecca stood.

"What now?" She reached out a hand, and he took it, both of them groaning as she pulled him to his feet. Henry looked up and saw the castle, just visible through a break in the trees, silhouetted against the purple sky. He thought he saw the flicker of firelight somewhere inside. The Witches of the Third Reich would be gathering for their spell by now. No one else would be hunting them tonight.

"Now, we go back for Lydia."

LYDIA STOOD IN THE PERFECT silence of the ceremonial chamber. Through the window she could see the shimmering pink of the winter sky fading into shades of purple and indigo as the sun slipped behind the snowcapped mountains. In her hands, the *Grimorium Bellum* felt like a coiled snake, quiet for now but primed to rain down chaos at the slightest provocation. All around her, the coven stood in silent anticipation, awaiting her instruction.

She had never led a formal ceremony before. She closed her eyes and tried to remember the way Isadora could capture a room. Her straightforward intensity, her grace.

"Sisters." Her voice felt like a thunderclap in the stillness of the chamber. "Tonight, we gather to bring about the beginning of the end of this war. By the power of the *Grimorium Bellum*, let us purge the world of the darkness that has plagued it for too long. Let us raise up our voices as one coven to exterminate a great enemy." Lydia felt her voice rising, filling the chamber. "Let us usher in the golden age of the witch!" Across from her, Sybil beamed. "In the name of the Great Mother, blessed be."

"Blessed be," they replied.

The silence fell back into place like a curtain. Lydia stood for a moment, feeling her heart beating inside of her. Taking one last moment for herself.

She knelt on the cold floor and placed the *Grimorium Bellum* before her. The book seemed to thrill under her touch. She wondered if, in its own way, it knew what was about to happen.

She opened the book and placed her fingers on the final page.

The words began to flow immediately. Humming, moaning, sounds like insects swarming, like things being born, like things dying. The words sucked the air from her lungs, and from the vacuum emerged still more words, flowing through her so fast she was sure she would go insane. She could feel the book crawling inside of her, exactly the way it had felt at the château—a hot, evil sludge inside her veins.

Panic struck her heart like a mallet. The last casting had nearly killed her, but this—The Unmaking—was a spell so enormous, so evil, it threatened to tear her apart from the inside out, even as the words spilled from her mouth like poison. She felt the air leaving her, her lungs empty and burning, and still, somehow, she spoke. She was suffocating, choking to death, and still the words poured forth like vomit. She was sure she would fall dead at any moment, and that when she did, the words would continue to flow, long after her body had grown cold. She was a vessel now, nothing more. She was a sacrifice.

But then, cutting through the madness, a second voice called out, echoing Lydia's own. At first, she thought the voice came from her. Only after a third and then a fourth voice joined the chorus did she begin to understand. The Witches of the Third Reich were joining her in the ritual. The book was ensnaring them, taking hold of their tongues, and as it did, the burden on Lydia seemed to grow lighter, the words rolling from her lips in time with her breath. The magic took hold of Ingrid, and Eva, and then Sybil, until the full coven was caught in the grip of the same dark magic, and the air was filled with the feral chattering of the *Grimorium Bellum*.

Lydia felt her head clear as the weight of the spell lifted from her. There was a blank space left at the very end of the spell, a pause in the chanting where the spellcaster could give name to their enemy, and the spell would be complete.

Lydia knew the language of the book now, knew it as surely as she knew the King's English. All she would need to do to complete the ritual was speak the name of her target in the book's own language. The coven would speak the word back to her, and just like that, The Unmaking would be unleashed.

Lydia was barreling toward the spell's finale on a string of words that crackled like fire. The speed and intensity of the spell was overwhelming, terrifying—there would be no room for mistakes. In the ancient language of the *Grimorium Bellum*, she sang out to the coven, telling the story of the unmaking of a great enemy, and the coven sang the words back to her. She told them of an extinction, a silent death sweeping over the land, claiming its victims, not with violence, but with a perfect, bloodless efficiency. There would be no battle on this day, the book promised. The battle was already won.

At the edge of her vision, Lydia saw a churning mass of shadows, lurking between Eva and Johanna as they chanted in feverish unison. It looked almost entirely like a woman now—young and slim, wearing a black, floor-length gown, with long sleeves and a heart-shaped neckline. A thirteenth coven member, with swirling black hair and glowing gray eyes, her shape as familiar to Lydia as her own reflection.

Don't look at it, Lydia commanded herself.

With the small sliver of conscious thought she had remaining, Lydia searched the language of the book for the right word, the name of the evil she would wipe from the earth. She found it, the sound forming effortlessly inside her mind.

Are you sure? She heard a voice inside her mind, soft and familiar. The voice of a friend, but with an edge of something insidious lurking beneath. A clever mimic, speaking through a mouth filled with razor-sharp teeth.

Lydia glanced up and saw that the shadow had drawn closer.

Yes, Lydia thought. *Yes. I'm sure.*

The moment came, the spell falling away under her feet like a broken bridge, and when it did, Lydia didn't hesitate. She spoke the word that had formed inside her mind just a moment before, pronouncing each syllable clearly and carefully.

Lydia spoke the name of the Witches of the Third Reich.

Time seemed to slow. Lydia saw the shadow grin as it relinquished its woman's shape, morphing into something terrifying and primeval. A sound filled the air, a shriek like a train whistle, as the shadow expanded, growing tendrils and tentacles, all exploding outward at once with unnatural speed, enfolding each witch in its inky embrace with a single, violent motion. Then, just as quickly, the thing drew back in and disappeared, blinking out of existence like a dying star.

The stillness that followed felt like an explosion, sudden and perfect and deafening. Lydia blinked, shaking off the dark magic that still clung to her like raindrops. All around her, the Witches of the Third Reich stood, arms outstretched, faces turned toward the sky, transfixed. Lydia took them all in, and for one terrible moment, she was certain she had failed.

And then, Ingrid crumpled to the ground.

She didn't fall the way a person falls. She seemed to collapse inward on herself, her body suddenly nothing more than ash. The ash landed in a heap, with one side of Ingrid's face still intact, frozen in a mask of death.

The rest followed. One by one, gravity took hold, pulling the figures down in a cascade of ash. Some fell all at once, some more slowly, dropping pieces of themselves before they lost their form entirely, replaced by lifeless piles of dust.

All except one.

Sybil watched, gray faced, as all around her, her coven turned to ash. When the last body fell, Sybil screamed a full-throated shriek of grief and horror. She held herself tightly, as if expecting that she, too, would fall to pieces at any moment.

"What is *happening?*" Her eyes seemed to move without seeing. "Lydia! Great Mother, what is happening? Lydia, goddamn it, girl, *say something!*"

"*Faeste wyrde,*" Lydia said flatly, binding Sybil's tongue.

Sybil choked on her own words and fell silent. She looked bewildered. Her lips continued moving, but no sound emerged. Finally, her face darkened as the truth settled onto her like a storm.

Good, Lydia thought. They understood each other now.

Lydia rose to her feet. "You should know that I was going to let you die with the others."

Sybil tried to speak, but all that came out was a frustrated moan.

"I thought about it a great deal. Watching you turn to ash along with the rest of your wretched coven. Lord knows you deserve worse. You murdered Isadora, after all. And Kitty. You betrayed your country and your coven. Poisoned me. And you kidnapped *my mother.*" She stepped closer and watched Sybil's blue eyes pulse with fear. "I was going to let you die, but then I remembered what Evelyn said to me, the night I learned what you truly are. We had quite a bit of time to talk about it, while I was purging your poison from my body." She paused. "I was so *angry* with you. And with myself, for believing your lies. I wanted to turn you to a column of ash and forget you'd ever existed. But Evelyn convinced me that you should answer for your crimes before the high council so they would know what happened here. So they would continue to *fight*. And so that for the rest of time, your name would be synonymous with your betrayal." Lydia smiled. "It was her magic that saved your life, you know."

Sybil's eyes narrowed.

"The wine. Even I don't know everything she put in it. It's a very clever potion, actually. It protects against dark magic, like the kind in the *Grimorium Bellum*, but I'm afraid it's useless against something as mundane as a simple tongue binding."

Sybil held Lydia's gaze, fury and hatred spilling out of her. A flash of movement caught Lydia's eye as Sybil's hand moved to the bone-handled dagger on her hip.

"*Astyffn ban*," Lydia said, and Sybil froze where she stood.

Lydia crossed the space between them, gray ash collecting on her shoes and the hem of her skirt as she walked. She leaned in close, close enough that she could smell Sybil's rose-scented perfume, and the metallic scent of sweat and fear that wafted from her skin. She reached out and took Sybil's hand, and for a moment, she thought she saw something like hope spark behind those still blue eyes. Then she slipped the moonstone ring from Sybil's finger and watched as it was snuffed out.

"I want you to remember," Lydia said, "for the rest of your days, however few they may be, that you only survived tonight because of the love I hold for my mother. Her. Not you."

Sybil stood immobile, but Lydia thought she saw a glimmer of something new behind her eyes. Resignation? No. Rage.

Lydia felt strangely hollow, as if some essential part of herself had been scooped out. She had survived the ritual with the help of the coven, but she felt the price of it in her bones. She returned to where the *Grimorium Bellum* lay open on the floor, a film of gray ash now collecting on its pages. She felt stronger as she bent to touch it, but she knew the feeling wouldn't last. She still had a few moments left before the last rays of sunlight were gone, and she intended to use them well.

Thirty-Six

The temperature was falling quickly now as the sun sank below the mountains, and the fast-running stream was cast into shadow. The forest fell quiet, the sounds of small creatures in the undergrowth replaced by the mournful sound of the wind, whistling as it whipped between the spruce trees. A red deer appeared at the water's edge—a young female, dappled on her haunches. She sniffed the air cautiously, then bent her head to drink.

At the top of the falls, two figures stumbled to their feet—a man and a woman, exhausted beyond measure. Below them, a black-clad figure lay sprawled across the rocks, her body limp.

There in the deepening twilight, the gray woman watched it all—the stream, the deer, the man and woman, brushing themselves off as they staggered forward. Already she was starting to fade, going fuzzy at the edges. Already she was forgetting. She was sure just moments ago she'd been warm and solid, but now that felt like a distant memory. Now she felt like a curl of cold mist, just before it's blown away. She didn't mind.

This place was nice. Pretty. She'd have liked to stay a little longer, but she was sure there was somewhere else she was meant to be. She could feel herself being pulled there, little by little.

Just a little longer, please.

She watched the young woman's face as she made her way back up the mountain, and felt a sharp slice of something familiar that stuck in her chest; a deep, aching feeling like a bruise on her heart. It reminded her of something someone had once told her, or maybe it was something she had once said to someone else—something about birds. She wished she could remember.

Just then, a rabbit came darting out of the underbrush, startling the deer. The young woman heard it, too, and turned, almost as if someone had called her name. For a moment, she and the deer looked the same— still, silent, and alert. Both so young, and yet already so accustomed to danger.

The young woman stood and stared for a long time at the space where the gray woman was disappearing into the trees, but did not see her.

Why do birds sing in the morning, little dove?

That was it, she remembered now, even as she began to feel more and more of herself slip from this place to that one, even as she blew away like mist. She couldn't see the trees anymore, or the deer, didn't see the black-clad figure on the rocks begin to stir, the chest rising and falling in steady rhythm. She felt herself slowly seeping out of the world until there was nothing left but shadows, but in that moment of perfect peace, Miriam remembered. She remembered everything.

To let each other know they've made it safely through the night.

Thirty-Seven

ydia ran through the corridor, the setting sun strobing in the windows as she flew past. Her feet drummed against the marble floor, Sybil's moonstone ring burning in her hand.

She stopped before the amber-gold door, her heart racing. She put on the ring and pressed her hand against the wood, watching as a flicker of light passed through the stone. The door opened, and Lydia flung herself through it.

"Mum!"

Evelyn was sitting by the window, watching as the sun crept toward the horizon. When she saw Lydia, she grinned.

"Well?" She stood and smoothed the front of her housedress with her hands. "Did she believe it? I thought I was rather good, actually! I even cried."

Lydia closed the distance between them and held her tight. "Oh, Mum, I'm so sorry. The things I said, I—"

"Now, now, love." Evelyn patted her back. "You think I don't know when my own daughter is having me on?" She leaned back and wiped a tear from Lydia's cheek. "Don't go getting weepy on me now. The job's only half-done." She took Lydia firmly by both shoulders. "Come on. Let's finish it."

EVELYN WAS WHEEZING by the time they reached the ceremonial chamber.

"Why couldn't we have destroyed the damned thing in the east wing, instead of running all the way back here?" she asked.

Sybil stood where Lydia had left her, quivering as she bucked against the spell that held her. In the middle of the room, the *Grimorium Bellum* gave off an ominous drone.

"This ceremonial chamber is just like the one at the academy. It's been charmed to amplify any magic cast inside. This is the best place if we want the ritual to succeed."

Evelyn looked around the opulent chamber. "Our ancestors used to walk into the woods and talk to the trees. Simple." She turned her eye on Sybil. "This is all a bit much, don't you think?"

Lydia took her mother by the hand, pulling her attention back to the task before them. She looked toward the setting sun, turning to liquid bronze where it met the mountains. Her heart was racing, a rush of terror taking hold of her pulse. She felt breathless, weightless, and she was suddenly certain that they were doomed to failure, and the *Grimorium Bellum* would consume them both, crushing them to atoms. She felt Evelyn's hands tighten around her own.

"Breathe, my love."

Lydia did. The panic in her heart subsided.

She was about to speak, when she felt a strange sensation come over her—not the breathless terror she'd felt just a moment before, but a high-frequency whine, like a ringing in her ears. She shook her head, trying to clear it, but the ringing remained. Evelyn's brow furrowed.

"Love?"

Lydia turned, her eyes darting around the chamber, every cell in her body tuned to the unseen threat. It was the book, she realized. It was calling to her, alerting her to danger, but what, she couldn't see. The whining became more forceful, shaking her bones, aching in her teeth. She let go of Evelyn's hands and went to stand over the book, peering all around the room, but saw nothing. She felt the ringing building like a migraine, higher and higher, the crushing intensity becoming unbearable, and then, and then—

Silence. The ringing stopped.

She smelled rain.

The knife was in her hand before she understood why.

Ursula appeared like a wraith in the ceremonial chamber, wet clothes and hair clinging to her porcelain skin, mere feet from where Lydia stood. Her hair was soaked through on one side with blood, and the promise of violence rose off her like steam, curdling in the air.

And then the horrifying realization struck Lydia like a skipped heartbeat. *The wine. Ursula drank the wine.*

Ursula took in the scene in an instant—the ash that covered everything. The ruin that had come to her coven. Her grand mistress, bound and struggling. Lydia watched as Ursula's eyes narrowed, and she lunged for Lydia, knife drawn.

Lydia sidestepped, but too late, and felt the blade arc across her rib cage, so sharp the pain felt almost like ice. Ursula snarled a word of power, and Lydia felt her body still, the magic in her veins going deathly quiet. She tried to fight back, but The Unmaking had sapped her strength. Ursula grinned, closing the distance between them with long, swift strides, while Lydia stood as still as a statue, her blade gripped uselessly in her hand.

"Lydia, *move!*" Evelyn shouted.

Evelyn's command slid inside Lydia's skin, driving Ursula's spell out with a force that made her bones shake. Ursula raised her blade, aiming for her heart, and Lydia did not allow herself to think. She took Ursula by the back of the neck, driving the knife up and under her ribs until she felt the hilt meet flesh.

Ursula gasped, an empty, rattling sound, her mouth already filling with blood. Lydia held her tight as she struggled, her eyes so blue they looked inhuman. Ursula was shockingly strong, but Lydia held on, gripping her in a close embrace as the life seeped out of her. Her lips moved, shaping the same desperate syllables over and over again as she tried to summon one last spell, but the words of power shriveled and died on her lips. Her eyes began to swim, losing their focus.

"Ursula. Look at me," Lydia said.

Ursula did, the lucidity snapping back for one brief moment. She bared her bloodred teeth, defiant.

Lydia bent closer. "I told you."

She freed the knife from Ursula's body and slit her throat. Blood poured from the wound, a sea of red engulfing her ivory neck. Lydia stepped back, and Ursula collapsed to the marble and was still.

"*Nooooooo!*"

Lydia looked up and saw Sybil, mouth open in a howl, screaming in horror at the death of her protégé as her blood spread across the marble floor.

And then the whole world lurched to a halt.

Sybil was holding Evelyn.

"What have you done?" Sybil screamed. Ash covered her dress and her face. It clung to her hair, making her look wild and unnatural. She was gripping Evelyn tight against her with one arm, Evelyn's back pressed against Sybil's chest like a shield. Evelyn's face looked all wrong—her eyes were dazed, her lips pressed tight in a pained grimace. "You've betrayed your own coven! You murdered them all!"

Lydia understood then with awful certainty, fear seizing her in a viselike hold: Ursula's spell had paralyzed more than Lydia's body. It had stilled her magic, freeing Sybil from its grasp.

And now Sybil had her mother.

"*Agonna ban!*" Lydia called, but Sybil was ready, countering the spell with a word of power that sounded like a serpent's hiss. "*Astyffn ban!*" Lydia tried again, but Sybil batted that away as well.

"Evil, ungrateful bitch!" Sybil shrieked. "After everything I've done for you! Do you know the punishment for witches who betray their covens?"

They burn them, Lydia thought. It had been more than a hundred years since such a thing had happened. But she knew. Everyone did.

She felt the air crackle around them as Sybil readied her next word of power, and panic scrabbled at her heart as she realized which spell Sibyl intended to call down. Lydia had never uttered the words, they were forbidden, only to be called upon in the most dire of cases, but she knew them well. She'd learned them in her history lessons. They all had.

Fyora Grymm.

Burn the witch.

Lydia looked helplessly into her mother's eyes as the smell of smoke reached her nose, making her eyes water. Heat rose from the tiles beneath her feet, scorching the hem of her gown. She watched as Evelyn's eyes cleared, looking at her daughter, then turned grim and determined.

Evelyn leaned back and spoke a word in Sybil's ear, too low for Lydia to hear, and Sybil immediately let go, going as dull and docile as a lamb. Evelyn staggered away, landing on the floor a safe distance from where Sybil stood.

But something was wrong. Evelyn's face was hideously white against the sea of black marble, and a pained gasp erupted from her lips as her slick hands slid across the tile, looking for purchase. A crimson stain bloomed on the back of her blouse, making the fabric stick to her skin.

Lydia reached her mother just before she collapsed. She lowered Evelyn to the ground, her heart seizing as a pool of blood began to spread around them.

"Mum?" Lydia's voice shook, panic taking hold of her as the pool of red expanded and became an ocean.

Evelyn made a pained sound in the back of her throat. "The Nazi bitch got me." She laughed, dry and tight.

"Mum!" Lydia turned her and saw the slit in the back of Evelyn's blouse, the flesh underneath bleeding so profusely Lydia couldn't hope to hold it back with her hands. Lydia looked up at Sybil, with her cold, vacant eyes. She looked at the knife, still held tight in Sybil's grip, and felt a surge of rage and terror boiling inside her heart.

It was covered in blood.

She laid her mother on her back. The blood was everywhere now, covering them both. Evelyn's lips were white as death, and Lydia felt a horrible sense of déjà vu.

First Isadora. Now Evelyn.

"No!" Lydia took Evelyn's hands in hers and began to speak. "*Siowan-ban, hela-ban, siowan-lif, hela-lif!*"

She was no healer, not really. Nicks and scratches she could mend, but a wound like this one was beyond her power, and she knew it. Still, she spoke the words, feeling the life as it flowed out of Evelyn and onto the cold stone floor.

"Stop, my love," Evelyn whispered.

"No, I can do this! *Siowan-ban, hela-ban, siowan-lif, hela-lif!*" Lydia spoke, on and on, even though she knew she was failing.

She glanced to her right. The shadow was there. Her own spectral twin, looking like a dead thing left too long underwater. It was beckoning to her.

Yes. That was it. With the power of the book, she could save her mother. She could feel it, through the cord that bound them. It was making her an offering. Evelyn's life, in exchange for its own.

"Lydia, *stop*." Evelyn's command ripped the words of power out of Lydia's mouth, as surely as if she'd never learned them at all, and the book retreated from her, taking its offer with it.

Lydia began to cry as the sea of red crept ever outward. "Mum, I can do this, just let me. You have to let me . . ."

"No." Evelyn smiled. Her eyes looked dim. "You save your strength. You're going to need it."

"Mum, please!" She drew on all the power inside her, willing herself to defy her mother and speak the words that could save her life. She gritted her teeth, desperately trying to form the syllables, but it was no use. Even as Evelyn lay dying, Lydia was no match for her strength.

Evelyn's hands were tangled up with Lydia's. They felt cold.

"It's all right, my love," Evelyn said softly. She smiled again, and then Lydia watched as her face went slack, and her eyes went still.

The silence in the chamber was complete. Lydia looked down at her own bloody hands. She felt the words of power flowing back into her mouth once again on a river of despair, but she did not speak them. There was no longer any need. She looked down at her mother, cold and pale in her arms. She felt as if she would die right there, the grief and shock were so great, smothering her to death.

The clatter of footsteps broke the silence. Lydia looked up, and through her tears, saw Sybil running for the door.

"*Agonna ban*," Lydia hissed.

Sybil fell to the floor, flailing in agony.

Lydia picked up her knife and stood, crossing the room with quick strides. She would kill Sybil, just like she'd killed Ursula. Sybil, who had caused so much pain and suffering. Who had nearly brought about the deaths of thousands. Who had killed her mother. Lydia would slit her throat and leave her body to rot beside the ashes of her coven. She felt no hesitation, no remorse. Only an icy determination.

But then she heard it—a voice, like an echo in her mind.

Will they keep fighting, do you think?

Evelyn's voice, the night they learned the true depth of Sybil's betrayal.

If you tell the academy everything, will they continue to fight the good fight against the Nazis? Or will they sweep the whole ugly business under the rug and go back to how things were before?

Lydia had known the answer. They both did.

Make her tell them, Evelyn said. *Drag her before the high council and force her to confess her crimes. Make them see that the fate of witches and the fate of the world are one and the same.*

Lydia stood before Sybil's writhing body, knife in hand, shaking with rage and grief at the death of her mother.

"*Enough,*" she said.

Sybil carried on screaming.

"*Slaepna fae!*" she shouted.

Sybil fell silent and collapsed to the tile.

The knife felt slippery in Lydia's hand. She was covered to the elbow in blood. It was everywhere, seeping across the floor, running through the cracks in the tiles. It pooled beneath Ursula's twisted body. It pooled around Evelyn, and around the *Grimorium Bellum.*

Something shifted in the air, a low, sinister rumble.

"*What*—" The word was snatched from Lydia's mouth. The strange sensation grew, making her feel detached from herself. Her pulse trilled in her throat, so fast the beats ran together like a drumroll. She wanted to scream, if only to feel the release of it, but she couldn't. Something had caught hold of her, something she couldn't control.

She looked at the *Grimorium Bellum.* Where once there was only a book, now there was a hideous void, writhing like a mass of insects.

She looked at the pool of blood, slowly seeping into the pages of the book. She saw the creature, feeding on it like a leech. A roar like an oncoming train filled her skull, consuming her.

"*No—*"

Lydia fell to her knees, and the world went black.

Thirty-Eight

Rebecca's legs seemed to move without conscious thought, dragging her exhausted body up the mountain. Something heavy settled into the silence between herself and Henry as they walked, something deeper than exhaustion. She was sure it had to do with Henry's ghost, but he didn't offer any explanation, and she didn't ask.

When they reached the top, Henry stopped, listening to something only he could hear.

"More ghosts?" Rebecca was surprised to find she wasn't frightened anymore. Only tired.

Henry shook his head. "Something's happened. Come on."

The castle stood silent and empty. Rebecca braced herself, expecting to be assaulted by a phalanx of witches the moment they set foot inside, but all that greeted them was the echo of their own footsteps. Henry seemed to be guided by some invisible thing, and she followed closely, staying alert as they navigated the cavernous halls.

They stopped before an enormous ebony door, intricately carved and polished to a high gleam. The carving depicted a golden tree, branches splayed to the heavens, roots reaching deep into the earth, and all around the edges, an endless series of runes, carved into the shape of a great black serpent.

"Here." Henry looked like he was in pain. "The book is in here."

Which meant that Lydia would be here, as well. She was the only one who could touch the book, after all. The only one who could use it.

"Are we going to just *walk in?*" Rebecca hissed. "There could be a whole coven of witches in there."

They listened through the door for another moment and heard only silence.

"Awfully quiet for a whole coven of witches," Henry whispered.

Rebecca stayed very still, pressing her ear against the crack in the doors.

You're always running, a voice inside her head murmured. She straightened her spine and looked Henry in the eye, hoping she looked braver than she felt. "Let's go get her."

The air was still as they stepped inside the opulent chamber—tall windows overlooking the setting sun, gold stars sprayed across the ceiling, and so cold they could see their breath, though a blazing fire burned in the fireplace. Rebecca saw what she thought must be snow. It floated through the air, landing on her hair and clothes, and collecting on the floor in dunes. In the center of the room, something dark and hunched shifted from side to side.

At first glance it looked like two lovers caught in an embrace. Two women, nearly identical to one another in every detail, except that one was made of flesh, while the other seemed to be composed of nothing but ink and smoke—long black hair eddying like seaweed caught in a current, sharp features obscured beneath layers of shadows. Rebecca stepped closer, and the embrace became something sinister, like a vampire feeding on its prey.

And then Rebecca blinked, and the shadow disappeared, as if it had never been there at all. Lydia was standing alone in the center of the room.

"Lydia?" Henry called softly. She seemed not to hear. He took a step closer, but Rebecca stopped him, holding on firmly to his arm.

"*Lydia*," Rebecca said, louder now. This time, Lydia looked up. She was dressed in a black evening gown, face damp with sweat, an ugly wound in her side, and a bright red spray of blood arcing across her collarbone. Her arms and hands were slippery with it. In one hand she held a bone-handled knife. In the other she held the book.

"You're alive." Lydia smiled a broken smile. There was something wrong with her voice, Rebecca thought, although Henry didn't seem to hear it. He went to Lydia, crossing the room in long strides, but stopped short before reaching her. Rebecca followed, peering around to get a look at what had halted him in his tracks. Then she saw.

The blond witch Ursula lay sprawled at Lydia's feet. Her throat had been slashed, and blood covered her neck and chest, flecks of it already beginning to dry on her white cheek. Her eyes were open, staring blindly at the starry ceiling.

"Oh, God. Oh, Lydia." Henry took a step toward her, but Lydia stepped back.

"The blood," she said in her strange new voice. Rebecca could hear it now, the thing making her skin crawl. It wasn't one voice that came from Lydia's mouth. There were two.

Henry glanced at Rebecca, then back at Lydia. "What about the blood?"

"There was so much of it." Lydia stroked the book as she spoke, leaving rusty streaks with her fingertips. "The blood soaked into the book, and now it's . . . it's . . ." She trailed off, and her fingers went still.

"Lydia?" Rebecca said.

Lydia locked eyes with her, and Rebecca was sure she saw something in the dark void of those eyes—something black and alive, squirming behind her pupils.

"*Excited*," Lydia said.

Run, the voice in Rebecca's head commanded. *Run, run, run, save yourself, for God's sake, stupid girl, run!* But she stayed planted where she was. She watched as Henry reached out a hand to Lydia. She saw him tremble.

"Lydia," he said softly. "Lydia, look at me." She did, and Rebecca saw him flinch. "You can put it down."

Something curled across Lydia's face, a snarl of contempt. It slithered across her features, disappearing as quickly as it had appeared.

"You don't understand."

Henry took another step closer, but Rebecca was frozen in place, as if her feet had been nailed to the floor. She felt like prey, and the thing inside Lydia, speaking with its two voices, was the predator.

"Understand what?" Henry's voice was steady, his hand outstretched.

Lydia's face split into a beatific smile. "I'm going to end the war."

Henry faltered. His hand retreated.

"I didn't understand before. I do now. I can end the war today. No more death. No more needless, bloody death. Isn't it wonderful?"

Rebecca looked around with fresh eyes. Gray-white dust covered everything. No, not dust. *Ash*. It floated in the air and spread across the floor like a carpet. Heaps of it lay in a great circle, with Lydia at the center. Rebecca looked more closely at one of the piles of ash and saw what she was certain must have been a face.

"What happened here?" Rebecca asked.

Lydia's gaze slid toward hers. "They had to be stopped."

Rebecca tasted ash on her tongue and fought the urge to gag.

"They did. They needed to be stopped. And you stopped them. And now it's time to do what you came to do. It's time to destroy the book."

Lydia frowned, and Rebecca had to force herself not to recoil.

"I thought you of all people would understand," Lydia said, her two voices growing in number, now three, now four. "You were the one who spoke so passionately about the starving children of France. About Jewish families rounded up and carted away. *Your family.* I can make all that stop."

"How?" asked Henry.

But Rebecca knew. "She's going to use the book."

Henry looked from Rebecca to Lydia, disbelieving. "On who? The Nazis?"

"*All of them,*" Lydia whispered.

"All of who? Lydia—"

But then he stopped, and Rebecca saw that he finally understood. The book didn't want the Nazis.

It wanted everyone.

Lydia swayed where she stood as the silence filled the room.

Henry reached for her. "Lydia—"

"*I can end the war!*" Lydia screamed, her voices now a legion.

"Not like this." Rebecca kept her voice low, reasonable. "Not like this."

It was pointless, Rebecca knew. It wasn't Lydia she was fighting now. It was the book. And the book demanded to fulfill its purpose.

A rictus grin spread across Lydia's face, painful to look at. Her damp skin glowed in the firelight. Rebecca watched a shudder run through Henry as he realized that the thing he was looking at wasn't Lydia, not anymore. She was just a shell for the evil thing coiled inside.

Rebecca was stronger than Lydia. On any other day, she could have wrestled her to the ground in seconds, taken what she wanted and been off and running, but this wasn't any normal day. Rebecca was weak and hungry, and every cell in Lydia's body pulsed with black magic. Rebecca knew, she could feel it; Lydia could kill Rebecca with a word.

Lydia stood motionless in the circle of ash, muscles and tendons taut, teeth bared, but Rebecca looked only at Henry. She stared at him until he felt her eyes and turned. She looked into his eyes for a long moment, then very slowly, she turned and looked into the fire. When she turned back, she saw that Henry understood. He nodded once, a gesture so small she nearly missed it.

Rebecca looked at Lydia. "What will it be like?"

Lydia cocked her head. The grimace eased, just a little.

"When you've completed the ritual and the world is cleansed. What will it be like?" She took a step forward. Lydia did not retreat.

"Quiet." Lydia's smile was transcendent. "Peaceful."

Henry stepped closer, too, his gaze steady.

"An end to the war." Rebecca took another step. "I didn't understand before. Now I think I do."

Tears welled in Lydia's eyes and rolled down her cheeks. "I knew you would."

"An end to *all* war, yes?" Rebecca stepped over Ursula's body. Standing this close, she could see the blacks of Lydia's eyes, how the pupils seemed to pulse like a beating heart.

"Yes!" Lydia whispered, elated. "Yes, exactly."

Rebecca watched as Henry placed himself just behind Lydia, so close they nearly touched.

"Yes. Yes, I understand now."

Henry looked into her eyes and nodded.

Rebecca grabbed the book with both hands and yanked as hard as she could, just as Henry wrapped both arms around Lydia from behind, holding her tight. Lydia's mouth fell open in a silent howl as the book was wrenched free. The knife clattered to the ground.

"Cover her mouth!"

Henry did, stifling the spell that was forming on her tongue.

Rebecca ran as hard as she could, bracing for the pain she knew would come. It struck her like a locomotive, a crushing, suffocating agony that drove spikes through her brain and collapsed her lungs. This pain felt personal—sentient, and vindictive. She could feel the book clamoring for Lydia, the spell that bound them together commanding Rebecca to let go, but still she ran. She could see the flames through the veil of pain and sprinted as Lydia screamed wordlessly into Henry's hand. She reached the roaring fire and fell to her knees.

She was weaker than she'd been the first time she tried to burn the book. The weeks had not been kind to her. But the urgency was so much greater now, and she felt herself being driven forward by something more than her own power. She closed her eyes and imagined Noémie kneeling before her, reaching out to her. She imagined her father, heard him say, *My clever girl*. She saw her mother, could almost hear her whisper, *Ma petite colombe. My little dove.*

The pain was all-consuming now, a mountain of it sitting on her shoulders. The book seemed to know what she was planning, and doubled, then tripled its attack, pinning her to the floor. She pulled herself upright with great effort and, with both hands, thrust the book into the fire.

All at once, the book became a funnel of fury and power, with only one goal—saving itself. Rebecca looked back and watched through the fog of pain as the darkness leached itself from Lydia, who shuddered and slumped to the floor, then turned its predator's gaze on *her*. Rebecca tried with all her might to drop the book into the flames, but her hands weren't her own anymore. They gripped the book with a strength that wasn't hers, her nails driving themselves into the leather so hard they split. She could feel a shadow on her back, clawing at her neck, taking possession of her limbs. The flames licked at her sleeves, held just above the fire. There was no air left in her lungs to scream. She thought she heard Henry's voice, but she couldn't make out the words.

She thought she heard Lydia say, "I'm all right. Help her. Go."

There was a sound in her ears like airplane engines, but louder, so loud it was as if she were being erased. She felt someone dragging her away from the fire, the book still clutched in her hands. She saw Henry, and behind him, a deep-blue dome, filled with stars. The air flowed back into her lungs. A sob ripped from her chest, and then she was falling, floating in a sea of blackness, as all around her the stars winked out and went dark.

Thirty-Nine

I s she alive?" The words caught in Lydia's throat as Henry knelt over Rebecca's unconscious body, pressing his fingers to the side of her neck. Her skin looked waxy in the firelight. "Henry. Henry, please, *is she alive?*"

He looked up, just for a second. "She's alive."

Lydia let out a gasp of relief. She quivered with exhaustion as she watched Henry give Rebecca's shoulder a gentle squeeze, trying to rouse her. "How did you know it would work?"

Henry took Rebecca's hand gingerly in his. "We didn't."

Rebecca whimpered, but she didn't wake. Lydia wanted to go to her, but the book sat just inches from where she lay, and she didn't trust herself.

"I'm so sorry." Lydia hung her head in her hands. Evelyn's blood still clung to her skin. "Great Mother, forgive me, I'm so sorry, I'm sorry . . ."

"*Hey.*"

Lydia looked up. It took her a moment to realize Henry wasn't speaking to her at all, but Rebecca.

Rebecca grimaced at some internal pain as she rolled onto her side.

"Go slow." Henry whispered something else to her, something that sounded like *didn't learn your lesson the first time?* Rebecca laughed weakly in reply.

Lydia felt the shame like an ulcer in her stomach. "Rebecca . . . oh God, I'm sorry. I didn't—"

Rebecca shook her head. "No time for that." She nodded toward the *Grimorium Bellum.* "Finish it."

Something fluttered inside Lydia's chest, alive and afraid. She looked at the place where Evelyn had died, just moments before. The dust was covering her now, making her look like a statue on a tomb. The grief felt like water in her lungs. If she let it take hold of her, she wouldn't be able to complete the ritual, and everything she'd lost would have been for nothing.

She looked at Henry, and at Rebecca. "You should go."

Henry's head snapped to attention. "We're not leaving without you."

"Henry, listen to me—"

He crossed the room and knelt in front of her. "We're not leaving you. We're all getting out of here together, right after you—"

"I won't survive the ritual." Lydia's voice didn't feel like hers. It didn't convey any of the terror she felt.

"What are you talking about? You did it once already, just a few minutes ago. You can do it again."

"I wasn't alone before. I had the coven."

Rebecca pushed herself up to sitting. Lydia saw her eyes roam around the chamber, taking in the dunes of ash that covered the floor. "Why did you do this? Why didn't you let them help you destroy the book? You could have survived it."

Lydia shook her head. "They would have killed me as soon as they realized what I'd done. And then they'd just find something else. Some new monster for them to unleash. They would have never stopped." She swallowed. "My mother was going to help me finish it after they were gone, but she—" She gestured toward the place where Evelyn lay. Henry and Rebecca followed her gaze.

Henry spoke first. "Lydia, I'm so sorry."

Something about the tenderness in Henry's voice brought it all back to the surface again. Hot tears burned in her throat. She could hardly breathe.

"Maybe we can help you. Maybe if we—"

Lydia shook her head. "You can't help me with this—"

"You don't know that," he said. "Maybe we can."

"Henry—"

"We're not leaving!" he barked, more harshly than Lydia had ever heard him speak before. She glanced at the window, at the hazy whisper of light on the horizon.

"Henry," Lydia said softly, and now her voice did break, and she hated herself for it. She wanted to seem strong, just for this one moment. She wanted him to remember her as brave. "It's okay."

"You can take the book to London," Henry said, desperation seeping into his voice. "Find a coven. You don't have to do this alone. There will be other solstices. You can wait."

"No, she can't," Rebecca said.

Lydia looked at Rebecca, and Rebecca stared back with a grim certainty that Lydia found strangely comforting.

"She's bound the book to herself. It's a part of her now. If she leaves here with it, eventually it will consume her. And when that happens, no one will be safe." She spoke slowly, rationally, looking directly at Lydia as she did.

"This is insane." Henry's voice wavered. "Lydia, please—"

"Are you strong enough?" Rebecca looked at Lydia. "If we leave you here, can you destroy that thing, or will it take control of you again?"

"I'm strong enough." *Great Mother, please let me be strong enough,* she prayed, and when she did, it was her own mother's face that she saw.

Rebecca looked into her eyes, searching for something, for confirmation. After a moment, she nodded.

Henry stayed where he was, his head hung low.

"I'll stay with you," he whispered.

"Henry." She took his face in her hands. His cheeks were wet with tears, glowing in the firelight. "Henry, please. It's too dangerous. You have to go now. You have to. Please."

And then she kissed him. Because she wanted to. Because she would never get the chance again. He kissed her back, cradling her face in his hands. He cupped the nape of her neck, holding her close. She whispered her goodbyes against his skin. She told him that everything would be all right, and pressed the words into his lips with hers.

HENRY TRIED WITH EVERY CELL in his body to stop time. He felt Lydia, warm and solid in his arms. He could smell her skin, its sweet floral perfume, and sweat, and blood. He told himself that if he could inventory every part of this moment, every sensation down to the most minute detail, that he could make it last forever, and the terrible future they were racing toward would never come.

And then she pulled away from him.

"Go."

The candles had gone out. The sun was nothing but a splinter of light at the bottom of a swiftly darkening sky.

"Henry, please, *go!*"

The frozen air seemed to vibrate, like a bell being struck. Henry looked up.

There, standing on the other side of the chamber, was a woman.

She was instantly different from the other spirits Henry had encountered. Warmer, more alive. Perhaps it was the magic that still pulsed around her, humming like a battery, rising off her like heat waves. He knew her, he realized. He'd seen her in Lydia's memories—fixing her breakfast, braiding her hair. He knew her name. She looked up, and to his astonishment, she smiled.

"You must be Henry," she said.

One moment, they were surrounded by black marble tile, and candles, and ash, and the next it was midday, and they were in the sitting room of the house where he grew up. All the furniture had been stripped away, the potted plants, and candles, and family photographs, all gone. A gentle breeze blew through the old shotgun house, tickling his skin. As Henry looked around, he saw that where there should have been the cracked plaster walls of his childhood, now there were dozens upon dozens of *doors*. Some were ordinary, like the front door of a house, the type you'd walk past without ever really noticing. Some looked impossibly old, the brittle wood barely holding together. Some were painted vibrant colors—red, yellow, cobalt blue, emerald green. Some had heavy iron knockers or shining brass knobs. And each and every door was closed.

Henry looked at the woman in front of him. She looked so much like Lydia, and yet nothing like her at all. She was softer, rounder in the face and in her body, and yet something in the shape of her was unmistakable.

"You're Lydia's mother."

She smiled again. Henry had never seen a spirit smile. "Evelyn. I'd shake your hand, only . . ."

"No, that's all right." He shook his head in astonishment. "You're so different from the other . . . other—"

"Dead people?" Evelyn laughed. "I'm a witch, love. Witches live their whole lives on the edge of the veil, even if we don't always realize it. Crossing over must be very jarring for some." She winked. "Less so for people like us."

That word, *us*, bloomed in Henry's chest, warm and sweet as honey.

He looked around, almost expecting to see the black marble of the ceremonial chamber again, but seeing only the familiar, sunny sitting room. "What about the others? All those witches who were turned to ash?"

Evelyn made a face. "Ah, yes. I believe whatever's inside that book devoured them, body *and* soul. I don't expect we'll be seeing any more of them. I'd say I'm sorry about it, but . . ." She shrugged. Evelyn looked into Henry's eyes then, her irises gone soft and pewter, and for a moment, she looked almost alive. "She needs your help, you know. Lydia."

"She won't let me. She needs you. She—" Henry stopped. "Use *me*. My body. Maybe if you step inside me, together we can—"

Evelyn shook her head, a little sadly. "It won't be enough. She's weakened. Heartbroken. And I'm . . ." She tsked. "At full strength, we might have been enough, but now . . ." She stepped closer, looking into his eyes. "She won't survive it. Not alone. She needs her family, Henry."

All at once he understood. He looked at the rows of closed doors that surrounded them. Some of them had been painted shut. Some were bolted fast, padlocked, chained. Henry looked at each one, fear making his heart beat faster. Not the fear of what he was about to do, but the fear of what would happen if he failed.

He looked at Evelyn. He wished he could have known her while she was still alive.

"I've never called up so many at once. What if I . . ." He trailed off. Evelyn waited. "What if they don't come?"

Evelyn chuckled, a strange sound that seemed to be piped in from some other place. "Oh, my darling. Don't you know? They're already here. They're waiting."

First, Lydia smelled tea.

Not just tea. Bergamot. Lavender. Sage. She smelled dust, and old books, and beeswax, and peppermint, and mugwort, and castile soap, and the thousand other things that together could only be one impossible thing.

Evelyn. Her mother.

HENRY OPENED HIS EYES, and then he saw them.

Old, and young, some beautiful, some withered. Many of them with faces Henry almost recognized—fair skinned and dark haired, strange and hawkish and lovely, each of them radiating magic like a light bulb under the skin. He looked out at the sea of faces, features repeating like notes in a song. He saw a dozen women—this one with Lydia's eyes, that one her nose, her mouth, her smile. He saw a young woman he recognized, with red hair and a green dress, smiling like a girl with a secret. She stood shoulder to shoulder with another woman, older, but glamorous in a way Henry associated with opera singers and movie stars. And he saw Evelyn, standing over her daughter, tears glowing in her eyes.

"Mum," Lydia breathed.

Henry reached out and touched her hand. "Can you see them?"

"No, but I . . . I don't understand. What's happening?"

He wished he could explain. He wished he could describe in minute detail the face of every woman standing in this chamber so that when she closed her eyes, she would see them, too, and know that they were there for her. He wanted her to know that she wasn't alone, to know it the way he knew it, but the sky was growing dark, and the sun was nearly gone, and so he simply said, "It's okay. It's time."

LYDIA KNELT BEFORE THE *Grimorium Bellum*, placed her fingers on the page, and the spell began.

The words flowed from her tongue just as quickly as they had the first time. The air was ripped from her lungs, and then she was suffocating, the words tumbling out of her but no air coming back in. She'd known it was coming, and that this time there would be no coven to help ease the burden, but the fear came anyway, cold and mean.

Please, let me live long enough to finish it, she thought.

Just across from her, Lydia's spectral twin crouched on the chamber floor, seething and churning like black fire. It was strangely quiet in that space occupied by only the two of them, like sitting in the eye of a storm. The creature stared into Lydia's eyes, and for a moment it looked almost mournful, like a friend, begging her to save herself. To save them both.

It doesn't have to be this way, it seemed to whisper. *You can stop this.* She felt everything the book did, all its hope and fear, as clearly as if it were her own. *Think of all the things we could do together.*

Lydia tried not to listen, but it was no use. They were bound together. They were one.

You won't survive this, the creature whispered. It sounded deeply sad. Lydia saw her own gray eyes staring back at her, set into a face made of nothing but shadow.

Neither will you.

The creature twitched, inky hair twisting around its face. The air around the thing seemed to boil, and as it did, a deep, visceral loathing flooded through Lydia's skull.

So be it.

There was a rushing sensation, and Lydia felt something like electricity rising up through her spine, a column of pure power and rage burning through her, more than her body could possibly hold. She felt as if her blood had turned molten, like her lungs and skin and bones would turn to ash.

They will, the creature promised.

She could still smell the distinct aroma that could only be *Evelyn*, as familiar as her voice, or her smile, and for an instant, in spite of everything, she felt safe. She wondered if that meant she was dying. It seemed right, somehow. She closed her eyes and tried to conjure her mother's face—soft, and kind, and proud. She squeezed her eyes tight and felt as if she could almost see her.

She opened her eyes, and Evelyn was standing before her.

Air flooded her lungs, the crushing weight lifted from her shoulders. Evelyn, pale and lifeless but still somehow *Evelyn*, stood over Lydia and spoke the words in time with her, and a current of grief and joy rose up within her.

For a moment, Lydia was sure she must be dead already and that her mother had come to take her home. It was the only thing that made sense, the only way this could be real. Then she saw the shadow, kneeling across from her on the chamber floor, this dark sister. She saw it stare up with fear and loathing at Evelyn's ghostly form, and she understood.

You see her, Lydia thought, her voice carrying through the cord that bound her to the *Grimorium Bellum*. She had invited it inside her, this instrument of death. She had buried a shard of something evil deep inside her and made them one.

You see her, she thought. *And now, so do I.*

Lydia watched as more figures came into focus, their voices weaving into hers, as the creature recoiled in horror and confusion. Most of the women were strangers to her. They stood shoulder to shoulder, dark hair and milky eyes, speaking as one. Then she began to see—a stocky matron with hands like her mother's. A familiar profile, so much like her own. A young woman she knew only from photographs, her mother's favorite aunt, who had died in childbirth long before Lydia was born. Her gran, solid and upright, one hand held over her heart as she looked into Lydia's eyes, and chanted, and smiled. She saw Isadora, tall and regal as a queen. She saw Kitty, chin up and defiant, fists clenched, and Lydia heard the spell wrench out of her own chest on a ragged sob.

There was fear now, a deep, black terror, but Lydia knew that it did not come from her. The *Grimorium Bellum*, sensing the direction of the tide, had begun to pull in on itself, trying to drag itself from her veins, desperate to stop the ritual at all costs, but the struggle was futile. It was not in its nature to stop a thing once it had begun.

Their chanting lifted higher now, all of them together in one voice. The book writhed and protested, howling against the current of magic that pulled them all ever closer to the end. Lydia could hear it, making threats, whispering promises. It threatened destruction, not just of her body, but her soul, and of the souls of everyone she had ever loved. It promised her perfect peace, eternal life, and power, power above all else, if only she would stop, *Oh please, please stop.* Lydia heard it all and let it pass through her. Evelyn was kneeling before her now, looking into her eyes as they chanted together. Lydia could see the end laid out before her, a space in the text the length of a single breath. She ran toward it and leapt.

She spoke the name of the *Grimorium Bellum*.

This time, the silence came like snowfall.

Forty

The chorus of spirits faded and disappeared. Lydia could hear her own heart beating in the crystalline stillness. The book lay open on the floor, unchanged.

Slowly, she reached out and brushed the weathered page with her fingertips. The brittle paper parted easily at her touch, collapsing into a shapeless pile of ash.

"Putain de merde," Rebecca gasped. She sat on the floor and covered her face with her hands.

It didn't seem real. Lydia sat, staring for several long seconds at the space that the *Grimorium Bellum* had once inhabited.

"Lydia?" Henry whispered.

She looked into Henry's eyes and realized he was holding back from her, waiting to see if she, too, would crumble and turn to ash. She felt as if she could. There seemed to be an empty space deep inside of her that hadn't been there before. Something had been taken from her as the *Grimorium Bellum* had disappeared from the world—that piece of herself that she had given over when she'd bound them together. She could survive without it, she knew. But she would feel its loss forever.

Henry pulled Lydia into him, wrapping her in his arms and holding her as tightly as he could. She relaxed into his embrace, listening to his heart as they sat in the silence.

"Henry," she whispered after a moment. "I can't see them anymore. Are they still here?"

He looked around. "Some of them. They're starting to go."

She hesitated. "My mother. Is she . . ."

"She's here."

She paused, trying to feel her. There was so much she wanted to say, and she was suddenly choking on her grief, tears streaming down her cheeks. "I need to tell her—" She faltered, unable to form the words. "I love you," she said to the air. "And I'm sorry. I'm so sorry I couldn't save—" The words caught in her throat and lost their shape. Henry held her tighter.

"She's so proud of you," he whispered.

He looked up suddenly, almost as if he were listening to something. After a moment, he nodded.

"Do you trust me?" he asked.

HENRY HELD ON GENTLY to Lydia's hand as she closed her eyes, letting just the tips of their fingers brush against each other. She waited, unsure what was about to happen, feeling her skin prickle in the chilly room.

Then a rush of cold swept over her. It spread through her bones and her flesh, and suddenly she felt as if she were not fully alone inside her own skin. Her body felt strange to her. Alien, but also familiar. She could feel emotions that were not hers, a deep, primal love.

She saw things inside her mind, as clearly as if she were watching a film. She saw herself as Evelyn had once seen her—a squalling infant with thick black hair and startling gray eyes. The serious child, all knees and elbows, who seemed to see everything, and miss nothing. The woman—that beautiful, brilliant perfectionist, so hard on herself that it broke her mother's heart. Evelyn had adored them all with a savage, sharp-edged love.

And she saw Evelyn too. Not just as she'd died, but as she'd once been—a young woman, fierce and vibrant, running wild through the streets of London, bursting with magic so strong her skin could barely contain it. An expectant mother, barely older than Lydia, carrying her child inside of her, singing lullabies to her daughter in those last quiet days before she greeted the world.

We shared a body once before, she heard her mother say. *I loved you then, long before we'd even met. I will always love you.*

She sounded so far away, Lydia thought, and even as she thought it, she began to feel Evelyn fade. The memories were slipping away from her, like waking from a dream.

I think I'm going, love.

"No, Mum, stay." Her hands felt warm, when just a moment ago she'd been so cold. Something was seeping out of her, slowly but surely. Henry twined his fingers more tightly with hers. "She's leaving," she sobbed.

"I know."

She had never felt so alone.

"Mum?"

Silence. Terrible, heartbreaking silence. Lydia held her breath, and there, underneath her own thoughts, and her heartbeat, she thought she could hear her mother's voice. She was humming a song. A lullaby.

And then she was gone.

Forty-One

Lydia stood alone under a carpet of glittering stars. The air was icy, and mountains loomed around her, casting shadows over the white castle. Overhead, the crescent moon hung like a pendant in the sky.

Rebecca appeared beside her. They stood in silence for a moment.

"I'm sorry," Rebecca said. "About your mother."

Lydia couldn't seem to speak, the grief snatching the words from her mouth. She felt a deep ache in her rib cage, as if someone had cut a hole where her heart should be.

Rebecca glanced at her. "What are you going to do about . . ." She nodded toward the castle. Sybil was inside, locked away in one of her own binding sigils.

Lydia took an unsteady breath. "I'll project home and ask for a Traveler to transport her back to the academy. Sybil will answer for her crimes before the high council."

"What will they do with her, do you think?"

Lydia looked straight ahead. "Tradition dictates that a witch who betrays her coven must burn."

"Is that what you want?" Rebecca asked.

"I don't know." She paused. "I think she should pay for what she's done." It wasn't quite an answer.

They stood in silence for a moment, listening to the night.

"Where will you go now?" Lydia asked. "You can go anywhere you'd like, you know. I can see to it. France is still so dangerous, and—"

"Thank you, but no. France is my home."

Lydia had expected as much.

"I'd like to check on you, from time to time," she said. "If you're ever in trouble, just say the word and I'll send a Traveler to collect you. Would that be all right?"

"Could I stop you if it wasn't?" Lydia could hear the smile in her voice.

"Not really, no."

Rebecca laughed softly at that.

The sound of footsteps made them both turn. Behind them, Henry stood alone in the shadow of the massive castle.

"And you?" Rebecca called out to him. "Where will you go now, Henri Boudreaux?"

Henry's eyes lingered on Lydia's, and she felt something grow warm inside her. She nearly said something clever, something about the weather in London this time of year, but stopped herself. In her heart, she knew his answer before he said the words.

"I think it's time for me to go home," he said, and Lydia felt something twist inside her chest.

Rebecca looked from Henry to Lydia. "Seems like you two have some things to discuss." She turned, walking back toward the castle. She gave Henry's shoulder a nudge. "Give her a proper goodbye at least, eh, Romeo?"

Henry smiled. "I intend to." He looked at Lydia again, and she felt that something inside her chest loosen. He cleared his throat. "But actually, I was coming to talk to you." He looked at Rebecca, and his face turned serious. "There's something I need to tell you."

Rebecca frowned but followed Henry as he stepped out into the night. Lydia felt him reach for her as he passed, the tips of his fingers intertwining with hers, and for a moment she felt that heat again, like hot coals inside her belly.

She stayed there, alone, listening to the sound of the wind, and night creatures moving among the trees. She could just hear Henry's voice out there in the dark, saying something to Rebecca she couldn't quite make out. She thought she heard him say *little dove*. Heard him say *mother* and *peace*. And then *I'm so sorry*.

After a moment she heard the low, soft sound of Rebecca crying. She watched as Henry wrapped his arms around her, holding her close.

She stepped away, letting the night swallow her up, until the muffled sound faded behind her, and it was quiet once again.

THERE, IN THE DARK and the quiet, Lydia held herself against the cold, and tried to envision a world without her mother in it.

The universe seemed more enormous in that moment than it ever had before. The sky above her looked like an endless sea of stars, and Lydia was a boat, suddenly unmoored for the very first time, in a vast and terrifying ocean.

She tried to remember what Evelyn had said to her, years and years ago, just after her gran had died.

We don't die, my love, Evelyn had told her, though Lydia remembered her mother's eyes were red and rimmed with tears. *Not really. We change, yes. We become other things—the grass and flowers, trees and wind and stars. We rejoin the Great Mother, and our souls disperse into the universe, and become a part of a hundred million other living things, forever and ever.*

Lydia hadn't understood then. She'd only known that she wanted her gran, and her mother was always sad, and nothing would ever be the same.

But now, Lydia lingered on that strange mountaintop and thought about Evelyn. She imagined her spirit as it rejoined the Great Mother— mingling with the night, joining with the plants and stones and frozen earth. There would be herbs, waiting there beneath the snow: mint and gentian, stinging nettle, wild garlic, alpine rose. Evelyn would have known a hundred uses for each of them, all of their names, both common and arcane.

Lydia closed her eyes and envisioned her mother, dispersing and diffusing into those tender roots. She would be sleeping now, Lydia thought, curled upon herself like a seedling, waiting for the thaw. Waiting to rise up, green and triumphant, and rejoin the world as something new.

THE
WORLD

LONDON, 8 MAY 1945

Lydia Polk passed through the glossy black door of 10 Downing Street, and into a new world.

The newspapers had predicted showers that day, but by midafternoon the air was unseasonably warm, without a drop of rain to be seen. Most blamed the discrepancy on chance, or at best good luck. Lydia knew better.

The streets were thick with people, all shouting happily and jostling one another. Children rode on shoulders, waving Union Jack flags, while some of the bolder men climbed the streetlights, shouting and waving to the pretty girls. Someone began to sing, and now great throngs of people were joining in, men and women forming chains in the streets, holding each other by the waist, and dancing, and laughing.

"How's the old man?" someone called out. Lydia turned to see Fiona McGann, standing alone at the corner of Whitehall and Downing Street.

"Fiona!" Lydia embraced her friend and kissed her on the cheek.

"He's well. Victory looks good on him, I daresay. Tired, of course, although he won't admit it. You know Churchill. No rest for the wicked."

"Wicked, indeed." Fiona looped her arm through Lydia's. "I've never met a more shameless flirt." The crowd seemed to part slightly as they walked arm in arm, making their way north toward Trafalgar Square.

Lydia glanced at Fiona. "I'm happy you're here. We haven't seen you around the academy since you returned from your last assignment."

Fiona tensed. "I know. I'm sorry. I just . . . I needed some time. The things I saw there . . ." She ducked her head, and Lydia pretended not to hear the pain in her voice. "I've never seen so many so sick. Typhus." She swiped her cheek. "The army burned the camp to the ground after everyone was evacuated to stop it spreading." A beat. "I helped."

They walked in silence for a moment, each of them caught in their own private memories. Lydia felt a sharp, cold ache deep inside her, the way she sometimes did when she lingered too long in her own thoughts. An absence of something that had once belonged to her.

"Well, I hope you'll find your next assignment to be . . . cathartic," Lydia said. "You'll be heading to Austria. Italy. Then Syria. Whenever you're ready, of course."

"Syria? What on earth would you have me do in Syria?"

"Hunting. It seems a number of high-ranking German officers have gone missing in all the excitement. We'd like them found. Judith will provide you with a list of names."

Fiona looked thoughtful. "I see. And what shall I do with these high-ranking officers once they're found?"

"Return them to stand trial, ideally." Lydia paused. "But I trust you to use your best judgment, of course."

A small smile reached Fiona's lips. "Very good. Thank you, Grand Mistress."

Lydia gave Fiona's arm a gentle swat. Even after nearly two years, the title of grand mistress still felt like an ill-fitting suit. She kept waiting to grow into it.

"Any word from Rebecca?" Fiona asked.

Lydia hesitated. She was never sure how much to say about Rebecca's activities. "She's alive. She's in Morocco now."

"Oh?"

Lydia nodded. "I believe she's gone hunting, as well."

"I see." Fiona pulled a cigarette from her case, lit it, and took a long, thoughtful drag. "Good for her."

They sidestepped a circle of men, all holding each other by the shoulders and singing. Fiona smiled.

"I believe you and I deserve a drink. How about tonight? Gin martinis, your treat?"

"I'm afraid not. I'm leaving London tonight. Not for long, only a week, maybe two."

"Going where?"

"New Orleans." Lydia did not look at Fiona, but she could feel her eyes and her knowing smirk, like sunshine on her cheek.

"New Orleans. I see. Lovely this time of year." She grinned. "I suppose you'll be needing transportation."

"Only if you don't mind." Lydia kept her gaze straight ahead, even as her lips curled into a secret smile.

To anyone else, they looked like two ordinary women, walking arm in arm on an unusually warm afternoon in May. They moved through the crowd of revelers in Trafalgar Square, enjoying the air, singing the songs when they knew the words, and cheering on the daring young women who hiked up their trousers and waded, laughing, into the fountain. Once in a while their songs and laughter gave way to sudden tears, as if some darker thought had snuck through the crowd to disturb their celebration. And when that happened, they didn't try to chase the sadness away. They simply allowed it, and carried on.

Nearby, a little girl sat on her father's shoulders and watched them, enchanted by their smiles and their brightly colored clothes. The girl thought she caught a whiff of rain and looked up, expecting to see storm clouds rolling in, but the sky remained clear. And when she looked back into the crowd, she found to her disappointment that the women had disappeared, almost as if by magic.

Acknowledgments

Writing is a little bit like witchcraft.

A lot of the work—most of it really—can be done alone. It's done at kitchen tables and in coffee shops, in backyards and bedrooms and on the living room floor. A shocking amount of it is done in the middle of the night. Tremendous, dazzling acts of magic can be made by a single person, with nothing more than some words, the will, and a little imagination.

But for the really big work, you need a coven. And this is mine.

My never-ending gratitude goes out to my agent, Jenny Bent, who championed this story with such love and ferocity, and in so doing, changed my life forever; and to my editor, Nidhi Pugalia, for believing in me and this story so wholeheartedly and for making the editing process such a pure joy. Thank you also to Brian Tart, Andrea Schulz, and

Kate Stark, to my UK agent, Zoe Plant, and to Simon Taylor for your faith in me, and for keeping me honest about matters of London history. Any errors are purely my own.

To my husband, Matt, who supported me through it all with brainstorming sessions, budget spreadsheets, and beverages; who always insisted that this work was worth doing, and who read this book eight (!!!) times: I will never be able to repay you for everything you've given me. But I will try.

To my sister, Leigh: Thank you for daring me to write this story. I don't know where I would be if you hadn't demanded those first twenty pages from me, but I know I would not be here. I am so incredibly proud of you. Let's be writers.

To my parents, who showed up to every choir concert and school play, who let me major in theater without complaint or reservation, and who always told me that a real job is fine, but *please* don't forget about your writing. I love you.

Thank you to Kristin, Eli, Sonia, Lauren, John, and Benjamin for your incredibly thoughtful feedback, and to every beautiful soul who read this book when it was just a messy little book-baby and helped it to grow big and strong. Thank you also to Kathleen for her translation assistance, without which I would have undoubtedly embarrassed myself many, many times over.

To my Book Coven, who followed me through this crazy journey and lifted me up with cups of coffee and glasses of wine, with tarot cards, and astrology charts, and birthday books, and late-night gossip sessions, and who burned candles for me, screamed with me, popped champagne with me, let me vent when I needed to and hyped me up every single day. I adore you all.

And finally . . .

This is a story about mothers. I was unbelievably lucky to be raised by a mother who taught me from the beginning that words have power, and who modeled what it meant to live a creative life. Whatever magic I have, I got it from you.

About the Author

Morgan Ryan is the author of stories born from a lifelong love of magic, a fixation on historical minutiae that borders on obsessive, and a tendency to fall down rabbit holes. She was raised in a family of writers in upstate New York and received her degree in theatre performance from Northeastern University. She now lives in Chicago with her husband. *A Resistance of Witches* is her first novel.

To find out more:

X @moryanwrites

O @authormorganryan